with all my love

for Christmas & o...

Kate.

our friend sends love too!

X.

MY OWN TRUMPET

By the same Author

The Point of the Stick:
a Handbook on the Technique
of Conducting (1920, republished 1968)

Thoughts on Conducting (1963)

ADRIAN CEDRIC BOULT

MY
OWN
TRUMPET

HAMISH HAMILTON
LONDON

First published in Great Britain 1973
by Hamish Hamilton Ltd
90 Great Russell Street London W.C.1

Second Impression November 1973

SBN 241 02445 5

Copyright © Sir Adrian Boult 1973

Printed in Great Britain by
Western Printing Services Ltd, Bristol

TO MY FAMILY AND FRIENDS
WITH LOVE

CONTENTS

ILLUSTRATIONS

Chapter One

CHILDHOOD AND SCHOOL 1889–1908

FROM A dame school to Westminster; from schoolboy tweeds to Etons and a top hat; from a suburban home near Liverpool to a flat on Westminster Bridge; from a Unitarian chapel in Bootle to daily prayers in Westminster Abbey; from an occasional Liverpool Richter concert to Queen's Hall more than once a week.

Most people expect entry to a public school to be a major change in their lives, but it comes usually at thirteen or fourteen after some years at a preparatory school where they have already been boarding. I was twelve, and had hardly ever stayed away from home, so the wrench was considerable.

Perhaps someone will ask what kind of a creature I was before all these changes came about. There is nothing more tiresome than stories about other people's children, so we must try and keep this part of the narrative as short as possible. My mother patiently wrote down some of the stories, and here is a selection:

'From the time he was eight months old he noticed music—would stop fidgeting or murmuring to listen; but he was evidently pained by loud music altho' he did not mind a loud interlude. For instance, he took a Chopin Impromptu quite placidly, but frowned and grunted if I began the Polonaise in A.

'He was about sixteen months old when he first sat at the piano picking out tunes with one finger quite correctly. Next he used more fingers, then gradually played the same tune with both hands.

'At two years old he would sing anything he heard, and he loved to sit under the piano while I played. But we found it did not do to leave him very long, it racked his nerves too much and it was still worse to leave him to play by himself.

'At first we were delighted at having such a nice occupation for him for he was active-brained and restless and had to be constantly watched, without his knowing it, but it ended in frantic tempers, of which he was terribly ashamed even when he was three, so that we had to manoeuvre him away from the piano without actually telling him to come.

I

'He was a little over four when he realized, after much cogitation, that people did not play the same with both hands. For days we had storms at intervals; he kept going to the piano, playing a little and coming away in a tornado. Then one day he suddenly discovered how to make a reasonable bass, and all was peace. Of course it was very simple, but it was a true accompaniment.

'We went on the principle that whatever he asked should be told him, but he was never to be stimulated by being shown new things or taught in any way. He crammed things in much too fast as it was.

'With a picture alphabet book he taught himself to write. There were three sets of letters, prints, capitals and small letters. He mixed them all up at first and the result was comical, but we left him to sort them out by himself. He taught himself to read by the names on gateposts and shopfronts and then Marie, his nurse, did answer his questions.

'It was during 1893 when he was a little over four that an extraordinary thing happened. I am certain that no one had attempted to teach him his notes, but one day he found Reinecke's baby duets, which I meant to give him some day, lying on the piano. He sat up and began picking out the treble part. I went over and stood by him.

'"How do you know that is right, little son?"

'"Because it *is*, you silly"—in a sort of resigned tone.

'Then I found that, in some queer way, he measured up from the bottom of the piano, pitched on the right note, and of course after that it was plain sailing to his mathematical brain.

'After that I *did* tell him something he did not ask.

'He was playing new things while I worked at the other end of the room. He had no idea of sharps or flats, and what he was playing had some; the effect was excruciating. I called out "B flat, darling, B flat!"

'He stopped: "I don't know what you mean by B flat". So of course I had to go and explain both sharps and flats. But I never had to do it again. He grasped the idea of scales and semitones, and simply revelled in the new exercise. He could sing at sight any music he saw printed and had absolute pitch, so that it became a game to turn him out of the room and ask what notes we struck or chord we played.

'It was in November 1893 that he found it amusing to play his things in a major key and then turn them into minor or vice versa—his musical antics were most diverse. This was not his only development.

'Early in 1893 we thought of taking him to town, and his sister Olive said: "Baby, would you like to go in the train and see Papa in his office?"

'"Thank you, I will see what Miss Twint wants to do."

'We looked at each other in amazement. Who and what was Miss Twint? But I said casually: "Will it take long to ask her, because we wanted to go to-morrow?"

'"I will ask her to-day."

'Miss Twint was a blow. She was pure invention and seems to have lived among the sandhills, and when she was in residence we found her an everlasting nuisance, for she *would* go travelling with us and was always given the corner seat by the window (of course the one he liked best) and it was some time before I could make him see that she was not so voluminous that there was not room for him too. His father got into bad trouble by suggesting that she could ride in the luggage-rack, and I did also by saying she could quite well go on the box of the cab.

'Nothing but the best was good enough for Miss Twint, but she really was *de trop* in a hansom cab.

'Luckily she sometimes went to visit a certain Mrs Pompedo who lived in a star (Venus) so we were always thankful when Venus was clear.

'He had many strange speculations inside his big head, for one day he asked his father: "Do the days ever stop?"

'And he had a time of panic lest his father and I should die and leave him, but we managed to get that away without doing him harm.

'He was five when we took him to his first concert, a Recital by Mr Plunket Greene [a very well-known baritone at that time] and Mr Welsing (his Viennese godfather who lived in Liverpool), which delighted him. We also found that he needed boy companions, so got Mrs Lovegrove [who kept a school for small boys near our home] to let him go to her little school every afternoon as we knew there would not be much learning.

'At home he composed reams of music, but Mr Welsing said it had no coherence, was just what his memory had photographed of other people's. He always worked up in the playroom, never at the piano as we had always (without his knowing it) discouraged improvisation.

'It was just after his seventh birthday (May 1895) that he composed his first real original melody—a Romance for the Violin, as a present for his sister.

'He was quite good about his scales just at this time, although he hated them, and played either bass or treble of Sullivan's "Tempest" music quite charmingly. Bass or treble seemed equally easy to him. Occasionally we had strained relations as months went on, things came so easily to him that he resented having to practise a thing over and over again. And reading difficult music, much too big for his small hands, made him hold them very badly so that we feared he would never be a pianist.

'In October 1895 we made the great experiment of taking him to a Richter concert. It was a great success. He enjoyed every moment with scarlet cheeks and sparkling eyes. The Tchaikovsky Sixth was in the programme and he got a little *intrigué* at the 5 time movement, but soon got it clear and (quite unobtrusively) beat the whole thing quite correctly.

In the boxes at the Phil. there is no chance of worrying one's neighbours fortunately.

'Not long after this Mr Dawbarn, a near neighbour, brought him a beautiful little clarinet from London and the sounds he made were too terrible—only the dachshund enjoyed them and joined in. In March 1896 he went to his first operas—*Tannhäuser* and *The Flying Dutchman*—and he was also composing hard. The result was Boult's Concert Sonata in C major, but he understood enough to want each movement in a relative key.

'All this time it is important to remember that he was just a normal boy, happy with his school-fellows, joining in games though never very good at them, and quite ready to get into mischief as they did over a bottle of paraffin, which they tried to light with a match. But he always had exceptionally courtly manners, was most unselfish and thoughtful, and he possessed an extraordinary amount of tact.

'Miss Twint, in the pressure of school life and other interests, gradually disappeared, but she reigned for some years.' (I still remember my vision of Miss Twint: wasp-waisted, with a voluminous skirt which trailed on the ground, and an enormous hat.)

'Mr Dawbarn gave him a book of MS paper and he took to writing the most elaborate scores; he never gave any instrument work that it could not do, though how he knew—unless from watching and listening at concerts —we never discovered.

'In 1896 he composed a String Quartet, and we got some good-natured girls to come and play it with Olive. But, alas, he had copied it carelessly, leaving out rests and not marking blank bars, so, after long and patient struggling, it had to be abandoned. He thanked them very prettily and apologized; then went away.

'I knew there would be trouble so followed him and found him with his head rolled up in a big towel in the bathroom. The tears poured silently down, so I took him on my knee and let him finish. At last he gasped and said: "Oh, Mummie, it's very hard to do one's best and make such a mess of it". I explained that mistakes were what one learnt by, and suggested that we should go over it together and get things straight. But he would not hear of it.

'"It makes me perfectly sick. I shall burn it."

'And he did.

'Perhaps I ought to have insisted, but he was too nervous and strung up for a battle. I then found out a queer little idea—that a thing once written must not be touched or altered. It must be scrapped and re-written. We had one funny instance.

'A musician friend, whose breadth was nearly as great as his length, came to luncheon one day. Adrian showed him his latest composition and, in the most tactful manner, the friend showed him where he was wrong and what would improve his work, pencilling in a few notes here and there. Adrian stood by listening, then thanked him, took the music and went away to dress for a walk. Presently Olive, with a face that meant "Baby in a rage", came in and asked me to go to him.

'I went and found him sitting on the playroom divan, with a boot in each hand banging it on the cushions and saying savagely over and over again: "To think I have to go for a walk with a sausagy dumpling! A sausagy dumpling that alters one's things!!"'

'It took some time to soothe him, but finally he brightened up and all was peace. But his luckless composition was burnt.

'It was in 1898 that for some months his music fell off; he seemed to lose the power of reading; his scales were abominable; only theory seemed to come as easily as ever. We did not press him but just let things slide for my husband and I had agreed that if he were indeed musical the gift would withstand a public school and university education, and would be all the better for the sound scholarly foundation.

'If it were not a real gift it would be better left alone.

'He was taken abroad sometimes, once to Bonn and twice to France, and we found that he had a really beautiful boy's voice.

'At one time Mr Welsing was rather anxious that we should make him a "Wunderkind" performer. It would have been so easy for the falling off in his music only lasted a few months. But we knew he was far too nervous; it would have meant an unbalanced sort of genius, a misery to himself and a worry to everyone else. We preferred a normal, sane boy.'

*   *   *

London in 1901 was so different a place that it is difficult to remember what things were like in those days. Horses everywhere, no mechanical traction at all except the dignified steam-roller, then still preceded by a gentleman walking with a red flag, and occasionally an engine of the kind we sometimes see in the neighbourhood of Hampstead Heath before a Bank Holiday. The bus of that time, less than half the size, drawn by two horses, whose driver, perched high above them, enjoyed nothing more than a cheerful conversation with a passenger in the front seat 'on top', with an occasional cockney crack at a passing driver, or his own conductor, who would come round to exchange pleasantries while the horses had their two or three minutes' rest at every important stop. No uniform subservience to the London Passenger Transport Board in those days—there were buses of every colour, from the pink variety which shuttled for ½d. between St Thomas's Hospital and Charing Cross, up to the suburban expresses, sometimes with four horses, which would bring the top-hatted tycoon of that day to the City from his villa in Peckham or Sydenham. We must not forget that those two-minute stops were often filled by the conductor's cheerful recital of his destination and ports of call, and have given the 'Piccadilly' inspiration to the first subject of John Ireland's 'London' Overture. In the same way the jingle of the otherwise silent hansom cab has been quoted by Vaughan Williams in the slow movement of the London Symphony.

Other things arising from horse transport may well be almost forgotten by now. The laying of straw or peat moss litter to quieten the traffic past a house where someone was seriously ill was not uncommon, and I have been told that one of the last cases of this was when Arnold Bennett died in a flat near Baker Street.

And then there were the crossing-sweepers; poor men who tried to keep a passage clear from pavement to pavement; hard work it was with only a witch's besom to push the mud away as each passing vehicle splashed it back again. At one end of the crossing he usually laid his forlorn cap into which the more generous passers-by would drop a copper. I always dodged them and charged through the mud which could be removed later before school prayers. Red kneelers were provided, and they served admirably as boot polishers.

On the way to Queen's Hall I had often noticed a bus resting by a pub just off Great Portland Street. Its destination was shown to be 'Finchley'. On a half holiday I decided that I would take a trip on this bus with Miss Green, of whom more later. On climbing to the front seat we were soon horrified to hear someone booking a 10*d*. ticket. Our spree was not intended to cost a fortune, and anyhow a 10*d*. trip would probably last all day. After a whispered consultation we decided that we would offer the conductor 6*d*. and get off when he turned us out.

Sixpence took us as far as the Eyre Arms. It stood at the corner of Hoop Lane, a short stage beyond the present Golders Green Station. We got down and found the Eyre Arms standing in the open country, all by itself, miles from anywhere. So we just sat on a field gate until a returning bus picked us up and took us home to tea.

We didn't know then that the land on our right was soon to become the Hampstead Garden Suburb, the beginnings of which we were to hear about later from Canon and Mrs Barnett.

In those days everywhere soft coal was burned in grates. White collars were dirty before lunchtime; hands could be washed hourly with ample results (needless to say schoolboys didn't bother about that one!). Occasionally we had black fogs with two yards' visibility, and yellow ones quite often. It is difficult to remember it all, but it was very different.

Gradually as the century wore on the outer surface of London changed and new landmarks arose. The Piccadilly Hotel replaced the old St James's Hall, the finest hall in London until Queen's Hall was built; Adelphi Terrace was lost and with it much of the beauty of the view from the South Bank where the Festival Hall now stands. I cannot remember what formerly occupied the site of the War Office in Whitehall (built about 1903) or just how much the R.A.C. has changed the character of the old War Office in Pall Mall, on the site of which it stands, with the old Council Chamber intact. Many older people have forgotten that the Victoria Memorial in front of Buckingham Palace with the road round it, later became the first roundabout in London (a much-discussed experiment). The row of trees which ran down the centre of the Mall had made it hitherto an apology for a processional road with the processions slinking along on either side of the trees, and at night it was a dark, unsavoury and sometimes unsafe haunt. The re-fronting of Buckingham Palace now gives an impression of far greater height than before. At the other end of the Mall the Admiralty Arch now stands. I can actually remember a farmyard on its site, through the mud and manure of which foot-passengers could get to Trafalgar Square, buying, if they wished, a drink 'warm from the cow', milked specially for each customer for $\frac{1}{2}d$. Carriages coming from the West had to turn to the right and cross Horse Guards Parade, as there was no direct route to Trafalgar Square.

It was said that King Edward VII insisted that the old ladies who milked and presumably owned the cows and lived on the farm should be given another stand in St James's Park, but they and their cows disappeared altogether before long.

Westminster too was a very different place in those days. The School, which went daily to Vincent Square to play cricket and football, was not allowed to go directly through what was then a very slummy part of London. Our route was up Victoria Street to the Army and Navy Stores; we then doubled back along Artillery Row, past the Greycoat School by Greycoat Place to the gate of 'Fields'.

Although we weren't allowed to go through these streets, there was a pleasant friendliness between the School and our less fortunate contemporaries who lived in them. The School Mission had a popular Club near Vincent Square, and many old Westminsters spent time and money there. These boys had a great pride in the School, and in particular its achievements up-Fields. 'Pinks', and those who played regularly for the School, were all known by name, and on Saturdays at soccer matches the crowd outside the railings (often four and five deep) would roar with excitement and enthusiasm, while the decorous top-hatted audience on the touch line could only scrape up an occasional gentle pipe of 'Westminster'. W. B. Harris (Dick), captain of soccer, later to become a very popular preparatory schoolmaster, was very much loved by the 'scis' (pronounced skies) as we called those outside the railings. During our last three or four

years at school, he and I always walked together across Westminster
Bridge after 5 o'clock prayers, he to Waterloo and I to St Thomas's
Mansions. One day I must have gone on to Waterloo with him, or anyhow,
further than usual into the south side, when from behind a large grin,
literally in the gutter, came the cheerful call "Ello 'Erris', to which Dick,
as always, gave a friendly answer.

I was indeed lucky in my school friends for many of them, though we
meet seldom, are still just the same friends. As a new boy I fagged for two
monitors who were to distinguish themselves, W. T. S. Stallybrass, later
Vice-Chancellor of Oxford, whom I met again only a few weeks before his
untimely death, and J. Spedan Lewis, who has written a fascinating
account of his conversion of the business in Oxford Street which he
inherited from his father, into the remarkable 'John Lewis Partnership'
with its many ramifications. I used to see him and his younger brother
Oswald, arriving at school in an open 'Victoria', a comfortable conveyance
of that time; comfortable, that is, for the two people who sat on the back
seat. A rather scanty tip-up seat, back to back with the coachman, could
take two children, and here the younger brother would have to perch.
The two tall top-hatted boys would get out and leave the also top-hatted,
bearded figure of their father, the original John Lewis, to drive on to
Oxford Street.

Another boy of some seniority was Douglas Dickson, a superb violinist,
who befriended this new boy in many ways. He might well have greatly
adorned the musical profession, but his parents, who were among the
kindest hosts and hostesses in the world, thought otherwise, and after
school he went to live with his uncle (who later, as Lord Dickson, became
a Judge) in Edinburgh to study Scots law. I often quote him when I am
trying to console some youngster who has an urge toward the musical
profession and is meeting obstacles, parental or otherwise. Douglas might
have been, let us say, a Kreisler; a great player and a great teacher; instead
he became a most respected Writer to the Signet—head of a firm which
managed many of the great Scottish estates. He was also the father of four
children, one of whom, Hester, is, I am proud to say, my godchild, and
another, Joan, is one of the first 'cellists and teachers in this country. When
Douglas was alive the combined musical power of the family was such
that they could play any classical chamber music at a moment's notice,
exchanging instruments between movements, if they felt like it. They all,
including his wife, played at least two instruments.

Douglas was all his life a leader of Edinburgh music, closely supporting
Sir Donald Tovey as Chairman of the Reid Orchestra, and for a long time
conducting the Edinburgh Bach Society. He also had charge of the Nelson
Hall Concerts, a remarkable experiment in bringing chamber music to the
most humble audiences, originally founded by his friend, Mr Robert

Finnie McEwen, a great amateur, whose generosity to music and musicians both North of the Tweed and in London (where he was a member of the Council of the Royal College of Music) can never be fully estimated. I wonder if Douglas could have served the world better or have had more personal satisfaction as a wandering minstrel, however eminent.

A delightful story was told soon after Douglas went to Edinburgh. The telephone rang and his uncle answered it himself. 'May I speak to Mr Dickson, please?' 'This is Mr Dickson speaking.' (Hesitation) 'Is that the Mr Dickson who plays?' 'No, it is the Mr Dickson who wor-rks.'

It is, of course, with exact contemporaries that friendships are more likely to develop, and I think that the very first person I spoke to was Lawrence Tanner, my housemaster's son. Our friendship has passed its sixty-fifth year. At the age of twelve his knowledge of Westminster Abbey was exceeded by none and matched by few; he was, I believe, honoured with the Fellowship of the Society of Antiquaries at so young an age that his election was a record. After serving Westminster as a history master and, as it were, an unofficial historical consultant, for he knows the whole range of Westminster literature far more thoroughly than anyone living, he now, as Librarian (and, until recently, also as Keeper of the Muniments) of Westminster Abbey, graces a post for which no man could be more perfectly equipped and qualified.

In one respect besides my concert-going my musical development was greatly helped while at school by a young master named Piggott. He had joined the staff straight from Cambridge where Douglas Dickson's parents had known him and realized how intensely musical he was, though his main subject was physics. He did not stay long at Westminster but while he was there I had most valuable guidance from him, in a weekly 'private hour', in harmony, counterpoint and analysis, which opened the door for me into the whole idea of structure and formal balance. He showed me how to analyse scores we were about to hear at concerts; he made me write a violin sonata following, bar for bar, Beethoven's F major, and introduced me to Tovey's Meiningen programmes, the first annotations, I believe, that he ever wrote. Piggott went on to Dartmouth, where he ultimately became second master, and made the Navy musical. He must have been responsible for enormous sales of gramophones and records to Ward Rooms and individuals afloat.

The School was kindly tolerant of the curious nature of my home life. I was badly overgrown; a pretty weedy sort of individual in spite of careful feeding and the most strict discipline over things like bedtime, and it was generally felt that a boarding school could not reasonably be expected to keep me fit and healthy. My mother had always hoped for a pied-à-terre in London, with which she had very many ties, and so a little flat was found in St Thomas's Mansions, just behind the hospital, and also a devoted housekeeper, who was an excellent cook. So far so good, but neither school discipline nor common sense could quite stomach a boy of twelve living alone with a housekeeper who would presumably have to take all responsibility in case of illness.

For this reason, Mabel Green, a cousin of a very old friend of my mother's, agreed to come and live with me in term time, returning to her parents at Sydenham for the holidays, leaving Lizzie to hold the fort. The flat was often lent to friends when we weren't there. Miss Green entered marvellously into my life—she kept me firmly in order, but we always had the greatest fun. She married an uncle of mine just before I left school, but, precocious prig though I was in many ways, I don't think I can claim to have begun match-making at the age of seventeen. Uncle Alfred's office was in the City, but he sometimes visited a dentist in Victoria Street, after which tea at St Thomas's seemed a natural event.

Suddenly the visits to the dentist assumed a feverish frequency—I couldn't think why, but Miss Green let me into the secret as soon as he came to the point, and there followed many years of great happiness for them. I said she entered into my life thoroughly, coming with me to concerts, to church on Sunday (we attended the old Unitarian Chapel in Great Portland Street where my parents had been married), and also to school matches where she met many of my friends, and got on very well with them; Colin Davidson[1] called her Miss Daddy Boult, and the name was generally adopted.

I don't remember how the nickname Daddy (my first at school) originated—my second is perhaps just worth explaining. I had had two operations for adenoids. The first had not been completely successful as the wretched things had only just been discovered, and the operation was crude. This appears to be the reason why for several years my nose took on a colour that is usually associated with the bottle. One day at lunch I was (as often) being subjected to some jocular questioning on my musical activities, when someone mentioned Boosey, the famous music publisher; the spark caught, and for ten years I was seldom called anything else by school and Oxford contemporaries.

I was a dreamy sort of creature and concentration was often a bit erratic. One day I was brought up short in the middle of a lesson by hearing my form-master say 'Whatever's the matter with you, Boult? Have your thoughts gone off on a musical ride?'

I am afraid that my enormous height (six feet when I was fifteen) and all its attendant drawbacks fitted me ill for life as a conventional schoolboy. I tried to play the official games, but a wet day was always a godsend, as the games period (2 to 3) could then be spent with Lawrence Tanner

---

[1] The late Viscount Davidson.

in Abbey or an exciting hour spent listening to Questions in the Commons, an ancient School privilege.

There was, of course, little time for music; there were always 2½ hours of homework every day, and only on Sunday afternoons and occasional Saturdays could this passion be gratified. I was the proud possessor of a season ticket for the Sunday and Saturday concerts of Sir Henry Wood and rarely missed one. My collection of miniature scores (almost all bought with pocket money at that time) and the notes made in them all testify to a great admiration for Sir Henry and a sense of gratitude that time has not affected.

It is perhaps worth while recording the amazing prices of scores at that time, even if it cruelly arouses the envy of present students. Some very short overtures like *Figaro* cost sixpence, but a shilling would buy almost any overture or short tone-poem, running up to four shillings for Tchaikovsky symphonies. We thought five shillings, which Lengnicks charged for each of the Brahms symphonies, when they issued them somewhere about 1904, a very expensive proposition, and I remember my delight when I discovered that the Beethoven symphonies were listed in the full scores of the Peters Edition for three shillings, which meant that my student's discount brought them down to two and threepence. I still have most of those I bought at that time.

I always took the relevant scores to a concert and made notes in them, also entering the date and performers. It was rather a job to lug them round and I devised a very large pocket inside my overcoat where even full scores could be carried quite flat. They flapped a bit against my left knee, but it was better than carrying a music case, in the days when gloves and a stick or umbrella were essential parts of school uniform.

My mother came to London now and then and we indulged in the *Ring* cycles at Covent Garden for several years. Richter always conducted, and Ternina, Ernst Kraus and van Rooy were the greatest of our stars. Richter finally persuaded the management to announce, one winter, several cycles of the *Ring* in English. It was said at the time that it had been a long-cherished wish of his, which was curious when one remembers the many stories of his bad English, the best of which I always thought was his account of his poor wife's giddiness: 'When she does not lie she swindles'[1]. Richter took firm charge of the whole performance, and we got through very creditably. I was amused to note his grasp of every detail, when, in *Rheingold*, Alberich was embarking on his famous curse. He seemed to have started it on the wrong side of the stage because I saw Richter, with his imperturbable right arm driving us steadily forward, lift a threatening left index finger high in the air, and then bring it down to

[1] *Schwindeln* is, I should add, the German word meaning to be giddy.

point immediately at the far end of the footlights, whereat Alberich, albeit in mid-curse, scuttled across stage to obey the imperious behest.

I had a few other interests at school. I enjoyed a carpentry class once a week, and some of the products are still in existence. I was astonished that my parents, stern radical anti-conscriptionists, welcomed the formation of a cadet corps at school, so I felt I must join. I took little interest in it, and had no ambition for promotion until I suddenly realized one summer term that all the NCOs up-Grant's (as Mr Tanner's house was called) were leaving, and that I should be left as senior private in the autumn. I suppose it was a budding sense of responsibility that made me feel I *must* do something about it, so I immediately entered for the NCO examination and was made a Lance-Sergeant, with three stripes on my arm. Then I felt fit to take charge of the house contingent, but more was soon to come.

I was put in charge of the Armoury, which then consisted of a rack of rifles and tangled heaps of equipment of all kinds. It was fun, but a long job to get this tidied, listed and arranged so that each boy could draw and sign for his equipment when necessary. It took several large slices out of successive weekends, but it was a great privilege to be working alone in that magnificent Norman undercroft, the very spot where the wax effigies have now found their home, and great satisfaction finally to see the tidy rows of rifles and equipment. I thought no more of it, and once done it was easy to maintain, but it led to one of those fresh realizations from which adolescence gets such a kick.

My classics were never a strong point, in fact I doubt if my Greek could have kept me going on the classical side if it hadn't always been bolstered up by both French and mathematics, and so my report that term told the usual melancholy tale. Dr James Gow, the headmaster, had, however, for the very first time extended his usual contribution to the report. Instead of putting his soulless 'J.G.' at the bottom, he had also written 'Not a good classic, but a thoroughly good fellow whose music and whose work in the Cadet Corps is gaining him much influence; I can trust him to use that influence well'. Here was a revelation. I had always thought that influence meant little more than telling people how to do things. That I could be having a good influence unconsciously on others simply through doing a good job gave me a curious thrill.

Rifle shooting was the only way in which I could ever represent the School. I was tried and turned down in 1907, but managed to stick in the Eight in 1908, and Bisley was a very happy occasion.

The Corps had been originally constituted as a Cadet Branch of the Inns of Court Volunteers, who had what was said to be the best pavilion at Bisley. Here we were right royally entertained, messing in the pavilion with our hosts of the Temple, and sleeping in tents just outside, conveniently near a garden tap with a small length of hose fastened to it, with the help of which we saw to it that everyone was clean before he dressed. I always woke early, getting up at six in term time in order to do two hours' homework before breakfast, and into that Bisley tent the early sun streamed irresistibly. One morning I remember composing a complete setting of a two-verse lyric written for me by R. M. Barrington-Ward, with the poet asleep on the ground beside me.

It was a tragedy that his sterling work as editor of *The Times* should have been cut off so soon. He was a brilliant scholar already. I never could quite understand what he could see in the stupid, ugly musical boy, considerably older than himself, who had read so much less than he, who was no classic, and who had no political sense at all. But so it was. Several times I stayed at his home, a picturesque Cornish rectory, where his wonderfully hospitable parents always had a warm welcome for any friends of their nine children, many of whom were already making their mark in widely varied careers. Robin Barrington-Ward also asked me to travel with him, soon after 1918, round European capitals, where he went to re-establish contact with *Observer* correspondents, and later to Canada and the States, our first visit, packed with exciting experiences. Even near the end when Cabinet Ministers and Bishops were continually asking his advice, he always found time for a talk, and it is good that his family (one of them my godson) has settled where we can still have occasional contact.

The night after we came back from Bisley, having achieved something ghastly like 30th place, the Captain of the VIII, Chaplin Court Treatt (a fine singer, who also boxed for the School, and later was, I believe, the first person to drive a car from the Cape to Cairo) and I together buried our shame in the gallery at Covent Garden, from where we heard a fine performance of *Otello* with Melba, Zenatello and Scotti. It made a great impression on me, but I don't know why memory should have linked it with the match at Bisley.

Clifton and Maxwell Gordon were two other school friends; Maxwell was the younger and a casualty in the '14 war. Clifton, exactly my own age, was a very close friend, and his father was vicar of the parish of St John's, Waterloo Road, which stretched northward from Westminster Bridge, where our flat was, and included Waterloo Station and the Old Vic. The vicarage stood at our end of the parish, so we often overtook each other on the way to school. They were a delightful family; the Reverend Edward was one of those parsons who are almost actors—in fact he had been one of the founders of the Oxford University Dramatic Society, and this interest lasted through life; he was a Governor of the Old Vic whose redoubtable Dictator, Lilian Baylis, always called him 'Gordon M'Dear'.

The whole family went to every first night in London (homework seemed to be non-existent to those boys, though it often took me three hours). They could always tell you what play was on at any theatre, and what it was like, but this did not prevent them from making friends with their neighbours and parishioners—St John's was said to be one of the poorest parishes in London and the vicarage contained the only servants in the whole area. They also stimulated a very active parish life, and many were the concerts and 'penny readings' we used to take part in at the Parish Hall, York Road.

Mrs Gordon was an enormous figure who dressed most expensively, with very large hats, even when visiting in the parish, to the great delight of everyone. Her mother, Mrs Hornsby, lived in a large house in Queen's Gate, and entertained there on a most generous scale. Westminster boys and their friends would often go into the Park after school on a fine afternoon and be picked up by her in her stately Victoria, whence one could inspect the fashionable world driving round and round.

Young Maxwell took after his father in many ways, but Clifton, my friend, resembled his mother with rather less of her grace and dignity, but also with plenty of his father's talent for acting and reciting. He enjoyed laughing at himself and to appear 'négligé' was his constant aim. Once when we were both in camp with our respective Officers' Training Corps (he was at Cambridge) we had arranged to meet between the lines at a certain time. I went over to our boundary and in the distance I was delighted to see my friend in full sail in my direction. I have never known anyone else who could make a military greatcoat look so perfectly like a dressing-gown. He was an admirable clown; one day when he was staying with us for a dance we were playing some card game or other when someone accused him (I can't think why) of looking like a doughnut. 'Yes,' said one of the girls, 'one that is sad in the middle.' 'That I should ever have lived to be called sad in the middle' he mournfully answered, and with great dignity left the room.

I have said that he had a great acting talent. He once made himself up as a Cambridge bedmaker. Someone bet him that he would not succeed in walking out of his rooms, and out of one gate of Pembroke College, in at the other and back to his room without being spotted even by the porters. He won the bet.

He told me that when the first London taxis supplanted hansoms and growlers he happened to have a young cousin staying with him. Deciding that they must celebrate this great event in some suitable way, he hailed a taxi and told the cabby to drive to Eton. Then, after tea in a tuck shop, they drove back to London. He said that he nearly passed out when the eightpences (or was it sixpences?) began ticking up and went on even while they were having tea.

The Abbey authorities were (and are) always mindful of the School close to them. Besides the ancient privilege of representing the people of England at Coronations the boys are the first in the land to salute the new Sovereign (their acclaim being incorporated into Parry's great anthem 'I was glad'), they always watch the Queen go to open Parliament, and they are invited into Abbey on many other occasions.

During my time we attended the funerals of the Duke of Cambridge (Queen Victoria's cousin, who had been Commander-in-Chief of the British Army for many years) and of Sir Henry Irving, the great actor. One morning we were hastily called to greet the young Alfonso XIII, last King of Spain. It had been discovered that his predecessor, Philip II, had visited the Abbey, and on that occasion the School had lined the nave, and as he passed by, bowed in groups of five. This ritual was repeated, but before we began we could all note how the young man stopped on coming in through the Dean's doorway and gazed up as if he had never seen any building so high before.

At the funeral of the Duke of Cambridge in 1906 we were in the nave which was lined by the Guards in their bearskins. The command 'Reverse Arms' includes a drop of the head with eyes on the ground. A young Guardsman close to me lowered his head with such a jerk that the bearskin slipped right over his eyebrows and was in some danger of falling off. He just held it in position (his training of course prevented his raising a hand to put it back) and for the whole of the service he remained motionless. We cadets were full of admiration—I expect he must have had a stiff neck afterwards.

I suppose it is only a small proportion of Old Boys who revisit their old school at all often. It was, of course, an easier proposition for me with the school in the heart of London, and I was lucky enough to be asked back on occasions like the reopening of School after it was bombed (that is the great school hall) when I conducted a concert, and also was entertained by my friend and contemporary Colin Davidson to a dinner party in the Jerusalem Chamber. He was then Chairman of the Busby Trustees, a body of O.W.W. who meet twice a year to look after the administration of a trust founded by our great headmaster Richard Busby for the benefit of Midland clergy and their dependants. I always enjoyed these opportunities of seeing former colleagues as well as the pleasure of dispensing Dr Busby's largesse. The Headmaster also gives us an exciting account of the School year after dinner.

Douglas Dickson who, as I have said, was two or three years ahead of me, had written an account of how miserable the last few days at school can be, when the end of boyhood looms on top of us and we wonder if life is worth living. I was grateful to have had this warning as it prepared me and I was able to get, as it were, a good deal of misery off my chest beforehand,

and to enjoy the Election Sunday Service in Abbey, followed, by time-honoured custom, with a stroll on the Terrace of the Houses of Parliament with Lawrence Tanner, who was to stay on for another year, and other friends.

Chapter Two

GIANTS OF FORMER DAYS

DURING THE School years I had opportunities of hearing a number of those whose names are perhaps still known, but whose achievements are by now only legendary. Sir Henry Wood invited the world's chief artists and also many composers to appear at his symphony concerts. It may be worth while to tell of impressions that have survived, scanty though many of them are.

Much has been written about Ferrucio Busoni and E. J. Dent's book is a complete picture of the man. Dent, whose kindness to young musicians was proverbial, took me to meet Busoni at one of their dinner gatherings at the Monico in Piccadilly Circus. He was tired that night, and I have, I am afraid, no recollection of the talk. I heard him play a number of times. He often gave memorable sonata recitals with Ysaÿe, and I once heard him give a Chopin recital in Bechstein (Wigmore) Hall. His last performance of the 'Emperor' in Queen's Hall was at times startlingly unexpected; his reading began where others left off and some of his audience did not follow him all the way. But no one could deny the great power of his playing and the deep thought behind it.

Teresa Carreno was comparable with Busoni as a power among pianists; few women could come near her in her technique and command of tone. The Tchaikovsky B flat minor was an unhackneyed work in those days, and I remember a final (public) rehearsal at the 1913 Leeds Festival with Nikisch where they themselves seemed specially to enjoy the partnership. There was a charming exchange of gestures over the controversial fourth note of the flute solo in the slow movement. Nikisch turned to Carreno as much as to say 'Do you like this F or shall we play B flat?' Carreno's hand came up to indicate that she was happy either way, and I'm glad to say the F was left alone. I never can understand why the untidy Tchaikovsky should be forced to repeat his tunes identically every time.

Feodor Chaliapin happened to be engaged at Covent Garden in the season of 1926 when I was on the staff there. Eustace Blois (General Manager for Mrs Courtauld who inspired the Courtauld-Sargent concerts) asked me to go with him to the Savoy the night the great man arrived, and we had a cheerful half-hour with him and Fred Gaisberg, whose account of their friendship will be remembered by many readers.

His performance in Böito's *Mefistofele* was the high spot of his visit. The chorus was augmented for these performances and several well-known singers joined in order to study the great man. I was much amused to hear a 'Good morning, Sir' coming at me from a most repulsive-looking gnome, who, on close inspection, I could see to be John Goss the distinguished baritone. Chaliapin's suggestions to the chorus intrigued everybody with the exception of the Italian producer, who went off to his hotel in high dudgeon and Chaliapin was left to produce the opera, which he did with complete aplomb.

Chaliapin had made a sensational entry into London music by means of the Diaghilev Opera seasons at Drury Lane in 1913 and 1914. He played two parts in *Prince Igor*, then *Ivan the Terrible*, and, most famous of all, *Boris Godounoff*. I saw all three operas and even then my urge for balance made me feel somehow that Rimsky's handling of the Ivan story (*The Maid of Pskoff* is its real title) was a tidier business than the sprawling *Boris*, splendid though it was. The opera could go on all night if left alone, so a whole act was usually cut, and it didn't much matter which act you slashed.

I think I heard the Joseph Joachim Quartet two or three times. On one of their last visits they gave a Brahms series, which included the Sextets and Liebeslieder, at a Queen's Hall concert. Joachim, apparently, was a player whose tone became weaker in his last days, and it was an example of perfect loyalty to hear how the whole Quartet brought their tone down to balance that of their leader. I still remember the slow movement in Beethoven's Op. 18 No. 3 when Halir's second violin rose to the surface above the first violin for 4 bars and let us hear a beautiful cantabile which came from him at no other time.

One of Joachim's last performances in Queen's Hall was the Beethoven Violin Concerto. I missed it, but I remember how everyone admired the style of it, and people implied that it was the end of an era—certainly the next generation of players had an outlook that was different, but I don't think one need call it worse or better.

No one could fail to recognize Fritz Kreisler's greatness even at the age of fourteen, and we were lucky to have him often—he always seemed to enjoy playing with Sir Henry Wood. But it was not until 1910 that he linked himself closer still to our music by giving the first performance of the Elgar Violin Concerto. It was a great occasion. Elgar conducted, and both he and Kreisler came on to a large supper party which Frank Schuster gave in their honour. We sat at three separate tables, filling the big music room, and the menu at each table was headed with a theme from each of the three movements. I heard Elgar say to Claude Phillips, the great art critic, 'Well, Claude, did you think that was a work of art?'

Vladimir de Pachmann was a pianist of a most unusual type. An eccentric (in fact in later life he was said to be accompanied on his journeys by a powerful male nurse), he had a pianissimo touch which I still seem to remember as the loveliest I ever heard. I don't think he ever played with orchestra, and his recitals were always of the most intimate type; he made them so wherever he was. I once heard him in Oxford Town Hall, and can imagine that half the audience missed a great deal of the point for he talked a great deal, often during his playing, as an essential part of the recital. Once in Bechstein Hall he decided to play the Weber 'Invitation to the Waltz'. As he had strong views about the various editions of this work, he roped in his unfortunate manager, Mr Schulz-Curtius, to make a speech (freely punctuated by gestures and remarks from the recitalist) as to the impossibility of the Tausig edition, and the points in favour of the Henselt. This comedy went on for some time, and finally Mr Schulz-Curtius was allowed to melt away, and we were allowed to enjoy the music, though still with occasional verbal annotations.

In my childhood days I think Ignaz Jan Paderewski was the only musical name which was at all widely known outside the musical world. I have read somewhere how, when Liszt came to London, even the cab drivers were excited and wanted to catch a glimpse of the 'Habby Liszt' as he was mostly called. Paderewski's wonderful shock of flowing hair gave him also a special fame with the unmusical; he was the pattern of the great foreign performer.

A friend of mine who was in Paris at the time of the 1919 Peace Conference, and sometimes had to entertain distinguished people at her hotel, said that the hotel personnel took all her guests in their stride, with the exception of Paderewski. He was the man who excited them, and whom they tried to see, even if only with a glimpse round a corner.

In my school days I heard him give a recital at the Royal Albert Hall. It was a great sensation to see this remarkable man, then at the height of his powers when the world was still at peace, come in quite simply and sit down at the piano, but I shall never forget the sensation as the sound came up to us. In two bars we found ourselves face to face with Beethoven (it was the E flat Sonata Op. 27 No. 1). Everything else was forgotten, and concentration for us became easy, in fact compulsory, because it was so wonderfully strong in him.

I was lucky enough to have many friends who knew Sir Hubert Parry, including his daughter Lady Ponsonby, and his son-in-law Harry Plunket Greene, but my own meetings with him were few, though memorable. The first was when I was still at school; after the first English performance of Schönberg's Five Orchestral Pieces, at one of Sir Henry Wood's

Saturday Afternoon Symphony Concerts. I had a gangway seat and was astonished to feel a thump on my shoulder immediately the work was finished, and, looking up, saw a radiant smile from a total stranger and heard 'Bless my soul, that's funny stuff, don't you think so? I must say I rather like it when they do it loud, like Strauss, but when it's quiet all the time like this, it seems a bit obscene, doesn't it?'

It was Parry. He had just ceased to be Professor of Music when I went to Oxford in 1908, and Hugh Allen naturally arranged a Parry Concert as a farewell tribute, which included *Job* and 'The Glories of our Blood and State'. The profound impression they made on me is described in my chapter about Oxford.

Soon after the Parry concert we were at work rehearsing the choruses of Aristophanes' *The Frogs* which was to be given by the University Dramatic Society at the end of my second term. Singing on the stage as part of a very small chorus (whose leader was none other than Freddie Grisewood, later to be a B.B.C. friend and colleague whose singing voice had a very lovely mellow quality) was another new experience, and to this was added the task of conducting the first (frogs') chorus off-stage, peering through a hole in the scenery. Allen conducted most of the performances, and Parry a few. I found that unless I was beating a quaver ahead of the conductor of the music I could hear, I could see dirty looks coming up in my direction, and I realized that in the theatre it is essential that distant sounds should 'anticipate' to an extent which is really uncomfortable for the people concerned. This is why I always try to make any distant sub-conductor (as in 'The Planets', *Parsifal* and other works) set their own pace, and I feel that my job, placed as I am much nearer the audience, is to accompany him, and co-ordinate the balance. I shall never forget Parry's happy smile when I had got my frogs to sing well ahead of the accompaniment they could dimly hear.

Only a few months before his death he came to Queen's Hall to hear me rehearse the Variations, and here I had fallen into the easy trap of thinking that the theme runs a good deal faster than he wanted it. He had warned me that it should not go faster than 66 to the crotchet, but when I referred to him at the rehearsal he asked for it 'still slower', and as he vigorously sang the tune he made even the semiquavers sound strong and independent.

Several times when I was away at school or college he stayed with my parents at West Kirby for concerts there or in Liverpool. He was a delightful guest I know and I hated missing it all, but I still have a copy of his *Style in Musical Art* with this inscription:

The Family Boult from C. Hubert Parry in memory of
delightful experiences, 1909 and 1913.

A curious thing happened to that copy. During my B.B.C. time, my Chief, Sir John Reith, asked me whether I would go to St Andrews and talk to the Students' Musical Society one evening. His daughter was, I think, the Chairman, and of course I had a very happy day and was splendidly entertained. At one point Miss Reith produced a book and said 'I really feel I ought to send you this book when I have finished studying it for my degree—it is one of our "set" books and I got it in a secondhand bookshop in Harrow'. I looked and was amazed to see *Style in Musical Art* with Parry's inscription. I thought it was still on my shelf. It had, I suppose, been stolen by a servant who had a passion for autographs—a number of other things like treasured postcards from G.B.S. (Bernard Shaw) had disappeared at that time—and I was delighted to welcome it home again when she kindly sent it.

I can't help feeling that there will some day be a revival of Parry's music, and also the best of Stanford and other contemporaries. There is such great power and strength there, and Parry had a splendid literary sense to help him with all vocal works.

It was a startling surprise at a Queen's Hall Symphony Concert somewhere about 1905 when a very large benevolent-looking Frenchman with spectacles and a beard (so large, in fact, that someone suggested a concave keyboard for him) appeared with his music and someone to turn over and proceeded to play the Mozart A major Concerto (then quite unknown in London) with the utmost delicacy and beauty.

It was Raoul Pugno and he made a sensation that afternoon, and afterwards returned often, and introduced us to the D minor, to the 5th Brandenburg Concerto, to 'Les Djinns' of César Franck, as well as other better-known things. By this time Busoni's visits were less frequent, and so Ysaÿe used to partner him in recitals.

I was six when first allowed to go to an orchestral concert in Liverpool. Hans Richter was then conductor in charge of the Hallé Orchestra and he brought them to Liverpool once a month in winter. I have heard critics expressing doubts whether his performances would now be tolerated, but I am certain that his irresistible rhythm and splendid vision of the architecture of a work would still sound most impressive. It must not be forgotten either that Richter's ear had such deadly accuracy that he would sometimes tell one of his players to tune his A string. He was the last great exponent of the rule that the right hand beats time while the left adds the expression. Nowadays we expect our sticks to be expressive too.

Richter's influence on the whole course of British music was immense. He did a great deal for our composers (though in German-minded Manchester he had far less opportunity than Sir Henry Wood had at the Proms or Sir Dan Godfrey at Bournemouth) and his monumental performances of the *Ring* cycles and other great operas at Covent Garden set a notable standard. It was he who first welcomed the formation of the London Symphony Orchestra, conducted their first concert, and for several years most of their evening subscription concerts.

Richter as a young man jumped into respect and popularity with London orchestral players by suddenly asking a horn player, who was showing signs of conductor-resistance, to pass up his instrument. He then played the disputed passage superbly with the fingering he had advised, after which no one knew which instruments he could or could not play, and no one dared argue about anything.

Elgar's dedication of the First Symphony 'To Hans Richter, true artist and true friend' shows an unusual affection, and Richter commented on Elgar's scoring to the effect that he scored accurately for each instrument with the dynamic marks needed by the player, whereas most composers put their signs in from the point of view of the conductor. This difference is noted by Rimsky-Korsakov in his book on orchestration, when he says that if horns are contributing to a brass chord, there must either be two to each note in the chord (as against one each for trumpets and trombones) or the horns must be marked with a stronger dynamic than the others.

I suppose it is natural that the leading composer in a country should acquire a paternal function and be looked up to, not only in his own country. Camille Saint-Saëns was certainly widely respected and admired, though perhaps many readers will better remember his successor in this role, Gabriel Fauré. When I began going to concerts his symphonic poems, 'Le Rouet d'Omphale', 'Danse Macabre', 'Phaëton', and his concertos were often played in Queen's Hall, and my mother and I used to play several of his two-piano works at home with great pleasure, so it was a shock to me when one day I happened to mention him to Dr Ernest Walker at Oxford and he exploded with annoyance over everything he had written. Posterity agrees with Walker, but I can still enjoy the memory of some of Saint-Saëns' music, and his visits as conductor and pianist. He played the organ at the opening of the Aeolian Hall (now a B.B.C. studio, but for many years a most useful venue for recitals). I remember one of the critics saying that it was a pity that Dr Saint-Saëns had not taken the trouble to familiarize himself a little more closely with the beautiful little organ that had been installed. I wonder what went wrong.

Another memorable character of those days, Sir Charles Santley, was a tall figure—seen from the distance this usually meant just that he was thin—with a cheerful and friendly approach rolling out Handelian phrases with fine rhythm and flexibility. I only remember one appearance at a symphony concert and I think he sang 'O ruddier than the cherry' when he must have been over seventy.

From one performance only little remains in my mind of Pablo de Sarasate the great violinist except silky quality and impeccable technique

As a child with toy piano

As the Soothsayer in
Julius Caesar, O.U.D.S., 1911

The author stroking the Christ Church Second Boat, 1912

Hans Richter

Arthur Nikisch

Bruno Walter

Arturo Toscanini

Four famous conductors

coming from a venerable figure with white hair. His repertoire was in the lighter vein. I cannot remember that he ever played the great concertos. I suppose he must have done so, but Spanish pieces with light rhythmic accompaniments were his main field and here he was supreme.

Curiously enough on the day after I had heard Pachmann in Oxford in 1911 the Town Hall reverberated to a very different music. It was made by John Philip Sousa and his band, on their last visit to the United Kingdom. It was a glorious sound, if sometimes a bit overpowering, and we revelled in the irresistible swing of everything they played. Sousa's technique as a conductor was entirely adequate; he knew when to stop and drop both hands to his side, giving a slight swing to his stick down there, more as a sign of participation than of direction.

The programme was unusual. It began with the Liszt 'Les Préludes', then after a cornet solo and encore, came a 'Geographic Conceit', 'People who live in Glass Houses', by Sousa. I have no recollection of this piece, but it seems to have been an extended suite, as it occupied most of the programme though of course we had plenty of splendid marches dished out as encores, some of which, in orchestral dress, I have recently had the joy of recording.

From this distance of time it still seems that Eugène Ysaÿe commanded a breadth of tone as a violinist which remains unmatched. He was often in London in those days, when besides concerts with Sir Henry Wood, he partnered Busoni, and later Pugno, in sonata recitals.

My sister spent a year in Brussels working with a pupil of his, and she often heard Ysaÿe conduct, noting that somehow he seemed able to communicate his own richness of violin tone to the strings of his orchestra. I had heard that he had always wanted to conduct *Fidelio*, and in the winter of 1907 when a German company inhabited Covent Garden for a few weeks he realized his ambition (for a price, it was said). I went to a performance and I am afraid that stage and orchestra got unstuck occasionally but we had a fine Leonora No. III before the last scene.

Ysaÿe and Kreisler were great friends, and they were both staying in Liverpool over a wet weekend. Their host was Henry Rensburg, a great music-lover who was for many years Chairman of the Liverpool Philharmonic Society. To his delight they started playing concertos together on Sunday morning, alternately taking the solo and the accompaniment, and never needing a note of music. It was a joy to listen to them.

Chapter Three

OXFORD AND WAR—1908–1919

A STENTORIAN 'SIDDOWN' boomed round the open door and
a terrified freshman dropped like a stone: luckily a chair was ready
to catch him. After hearing some of the Bach Choir performances
in London under Dr H. P. Allen's direction I had decided that my first
action in Oxford must be to join the Oxford Bach Choir. This was all very
well, but I discovered that their first fixture was a performance of the
B minor Mass in Reading in the second week of term; no new members
would be accepted until after this date, as only those who had sung the
Mass in Oxford last term might sing at Reading.

This wouldn't do for me at all. I knew the Mass well though I had never
sung in it (or anything else for that matter), and I was determined to sing
at Reading. So I bearded the lion in his den, and without a test or question, he booked me in, out of pure kindness of heart, I suppose, as he *can't*
have known anything at all about me. I think there were two rehearsals,
so perhaps he thought he could spot an incompetent at one of them.
Words cannot describe the first experience of singing in a big choir in a
great Bach work: it is overwhelming. I remember nothing else that night,
except one moment (I think community feeding arrangements had been
made) when I first encountered the crowd and realized that I knew not a
soul, and was—'out of it'. I didn't mind that if I were only left alone to
sing. I felt if I met anyone's eye, we should have a Red Queen scene:
'Off with my head', and out I should go.

There was no question of being 'out of it' in Christ Church. There
were seven or eight other freshmen from Westminster, and we quickly
found other friends as well, and wasted our evenings just sitting about in
each other's rooms, drinking coffee till all hours. I soon realized it wouldn't
do: the conversation though most entertaining wasn't exactly inspiring,
and I had at school contracted the early rising habit which has made it
difficult for me ever to accomplish anything intelligent after 10 p.m.
However, on Mondays there was Bach Choir, on Tuesdays Musical Club,
and on Wednesdays orchestra, where Allen allowed me to go with a score

and beat out the parts of any missing instruments on the piano. There weren't many. It was amazing how few London professionals were needed for those concerts.

Soon the chorus for the Greek play began rehearsing too, and so the cheery evenings in Christ Church dropped out almost automatically. As for work, I had planned to do Pass Moderations, Honours History, and then a Music Degree. All went well for the first year and with Mods. comfortably behind me I started reading History. I attended regularly the few lectures laid down by my tutor, but when could I find time to read? There was always some urgent call to rehearse something or see somebody, and Authority was beginning to chaff me about 'half-terminal essays' (they should have been weekly). Finally Allen, who by this time had roped me in for many jobs, official and unofficial, suggested I should chuck History, and go for a pass degree—'anyhow go and talk to the Dean about it'. So I went to the Dean, that great man T. B. Strong, afterwards Bishop of Oxford. He listened readily and said that he had no contempt for the Pass Man: the crux was really whether the time thus saved could be usefully employed. I was sure that anything I did with and for Hugh Allen was the finest experience and preparation that I could have. I just wondered whether a third or fourth in History could in any way help me to be a better musician.

My father had repeatedly assured me that he was in no hurry for me to begin work. His education had ceased at sixteen, and he wanted mine to be more thorough. The Dean said he could not see that my music could in any way benefit from a longer study of history, so the die was cast, and I was free to take on any number of useful unofficial things such as incidental music to the Oxford University Dramatic Society's productions, a ladies' choir in North Oxford which entered for various local competitions, and other enterprises.

On the outdoor side, the future was vaguer. An Oxford rowing doctor said my heart wasn't fit to row till next year, but strongly advised me to do something regular in the afternoon, as Oxford quickly impaired the health of anyone who did not take exercise. I discovered that the Cavalry branch of the Officers' Training Corps provided a mount for an afternoon 'tactical scheme' for the incredibly modest sum of 3s. 6d. Two or three times a week, I again became the most unwarlike soldier.

I found the tactical schemes were great fun, the officers and sergeant-major friendly, and, at any time of the year, the country round Milton and Stadhampton, Cuddesdon, Garsington and Horspath was every bit as good as those pleasant place-names sound. On other days I was free to walk, and I also hacked (not often, for the O.T.C. rates didn't hold for civilians) occasionally on the other side of Oxford, notably in Wytham Park, much of which is now Oxford's property, thanks to the generosity of Colonel Raymond ffenell, whom I later came to know as a great friend and supporter of Hugh Allen's.

One day I came in at tea-time and saw a visiting card on my table:

Mr. Robert Bridges,
Chilswell,
near Oxford.

Here was a thrill for me. I would return the call instantly. It was almost certain to be a Friday, for he usually walked the four miles down to attend Evening Service in New College Chapel on Fridays. It was unaccompanied and always included a big motet. I believe I dashed up to Chilswell next day; if I had waited till Sunday, I should of course have been certain to find Mr and Mrs Bridges at home, and probably a large crowd of undergraduates there too. I was lucky, they were in, and alone. I repeated that happy experience many times: one of their daughters was both a fine pianist and viola player: she became a friend of my sister's, and sometimes stayed with us. She introduced me to many of the pianoforte concertos of Mozart on two pianos, in days when no one in London knew they existed. As I noted, Pugno had just introduced the A major and D minor to an astonished Queen's Hall, but I had never heard of any others till Margaret Bridges opened their rich store for me. She played the solo parts delightfully. R.B. had the most accurate ear of anyone I had ever met. He disliked what is known as equal temperament on this account, and could get no satisfaction out of the haphazard tuning of an orchestra, and 'anyhow, it made too much noise'. New College on Friday was his satisfaction, and he could give amusing accounts of his schemes to get the organ key at Yattendon lost just before service time, in the days when he ran the music there, and had trained the choir (largely from the village) to sing quite happily (and much more truly) without accompaniment.

There were many other 'open houses' where musical undergraduates were welcomed, and many delightful gatherings took place. Sundays in term time were packed with them, and it was with some regret that I used to hear various neighbours and friends going off about 7 on fine Sunday mornings to catch an early train into the Cotswolds. I was never able to join them, though I longed to do so, if there had been enough Sundays.

One special gathering should be mentioned here, though it has, of course, been heard of before. The beautiful Judges' Lodgings in St Giles were then occupied by the Misses Mabel and Alice Price, both excellent musicians, the one with a fine contralto voice, and the other a violinist, who sat beside Miss Mary Venables at the first desk of the Oxford orchestra for very many years. At the beginning of every vacation they gathered a group of friends, led by Allen and Ernest Walker (with two pianos), and just read music of every kind and age for three whole days.

The backbone of their programmes were the Bach Cantatas, of which they did six (or was it eight?) each meeting, but nothing was excluded, and I owe to them my only introduction, for instance, to Cornelius' *Barber of Bagdad*, with Allen and Walker at the pianos, and Professor Rodgers of Leeds, owner of a fine voice, as the Barber. This custom had gone on for many years, and I believe they actually finished a second complete cycle of the Bach Cantatas. Readers of Dr Cyril Bailey's life of Sir Hugh Allen will remember that it was at one of these meetings that Allen first saw the possibilities of 'Jesu Joy of Man's Desiring'. He asked Bridges to write some English words, and published it with the Church Music Society, with results we all know.

Looking back, I think I ought to have made better use of those wonderfully long vacations. There were some people at that time who went abroad every vac., and Charles Gladstone, the G.O.M.'s grandson, who later became a great figure at Eton, told me he always went abroad by a different route. The choice became more and more difficult, until he had to go to a place like Plymouth, and beg a tramp steamer to take him across to Brest.

At home we were a small family, and there was always plenty to do; somehow one just could not bear to make other plans. My mother loved going abroad, but she hated leaving my father, who tied himself perhaps over-conscientiously to his business. I hated the idea of going abroad when she couldn't go, so the impasse was complete and we all stayed at home, which was what my father and sister far preferred, anyway. The summer flit to Scotland lasted six weeks or more. We all loved that too, for various reasons, except my poor mother who, however, as mothers do, entered into everything with us, and never let us see how much she was hankering after Spain or Italy instead.

The actual music-making in Oxford was phenomenal. Allen organized most of the public concerts and actually conducted many of them. He tried to ensure that anyone who stayed in Oxford for the usual three years could get a good cross-section of the greatest things in music. The first thing that happened after the Reading 'Mass' that I have already mentioned, was a choral and orchestral concert devoted to the works of Hubert Parry, who had just ceased to be Professor of Music. This too was a revelation. I had been brought up to think of English music as rather small beer, and as the magnificent choruses of *Job* and the beautiful little 'Glories of our Blood and State' were rehearsed again and again, getting finer and finer with repetition, I rubbed my eyes, for I could hardly believe that it really was great music, and wondered somehow whether Allen's dynamic rehearsing was filling the music with a power it didn't really possess. Allen's rehearsing was certainly terrific, but twenty years later when the

Oxford Bach Choir came to the Maida Vale Studio to sing *Job* with the BBC Orchestra, their equally convincing performance put *Job* for me, once again, on the map as a work with a future.

The second year in Oxford saw me established in rooms in Tom Quad, where I could indulge my passion for two-piano music, and also a 'thirder', a comparatively rare third room with a window seat looking across to the Cathedral and Staircase Tower. I became Secretary of the Oxford University Musical Club, not an arduous post as, by custom, the President did all the correspondence with artists, as he was responsible for the programmes for the term. In those days the OUMC was quite independent of the OUMU over in 'the oldest music room in Europe'. We had a room in the High, now, I believe, occupied by the Society of Friends, and our eight concerts were almost entirely professional chamber-concerts: mostly quartets, or solo recitals. The fees were preposterously low even for those days, but the artists enjoyed coming: they didn't have to bother with evening dress, and they were entertained in the Colleges by any one of a group of dons whose support of the Club greatly helped matters, and also any undergraduates who had access to College guest rooms. As Secretary I naturally took a fair share of this pleasant work, and a year later I took my term as President, a most enjoyable office, though rather hectic until the term's programmes were settled and the artists engaged.

One very great help to all Presidents at that time was the presence of Dr Ernest Walker, the organist of Balliol, who was always there, and always ready to play anything classical including masterly realization of figured basses, at a moment's notice, and without fee. He appeared at least two or three times a term, for all visiting quartets enjoyed joining him in a quintet, and soloists and singers were more than happy with his accompaniments, but he was equally helpful at short notice, and in every way an invaluable ally to a Club.

One day I went into the Town Hall to hear a rehearsal of the Allen orchestra and found them doing the Joachim Hungarian Violin Concerto with the composer's great-niece, Jelly d'Aranyi, playing the solo. The rehearsal was going badly—the soloist was at her most Hungarian, and nearly every bar was either faster or slower than its predecessor to the considerable discomfiture of the excellent but mainly amateur orchestra. An elderly don, whose grandfather was Felix Mendelssohn, was sitting near, and presently he leant over to me and said: 'I once accompanied Joachim himself in this concerto and I played in strict time practically throughout the work'.

I have no doubt that one performance sounded just as Hungarian as the other. Joachim was said to have a wonderful gift of rubato inside the bar, so that the bar lines themselves were always equidistant. Jelly's borrowings were on a broader scale, and therefore far more difficult to accompany.

There were a great many first-class musicians of all kinds in Oxford who never refused an opportunity of joining in any form of music-making. My sister spent most of 1911–1912 with me. My father had taken a few rooms in the Old Bishop's Palace just below Pembroke where we could live (as I was a B.A.) and she often accepted invitations to tea and to bring her viola. After tea the party amused themselves playing through works like the Brahms sextets. A German lady present at one of these gatherings was amazed, and said she had never heard of such a thing happening in her 'musical' country.

The name Heyford is now known all over the English-speaking world, as the two secluded villages of Upper and Lower Heyford, on the Upper Cherwell between Oxford and Banbury, gave their name later to a busy airfield. But in 1908 the name was unknown and soon after I came to Oxford I found myself invited to sing in a concert in this remote village. I accepted eagerly and thereafter was always happy to take part in these amazing concerts. The proceedings never varied; we assembled about 3 p.m. at Oxford Station, took a slow train to Heyford and walked up to the vicarage. There a sumptuous tea was provided by the rector and his lady, interspersed with frantic rehearsing, backed up by their son, Reginald Lennard, who has other claims to fame as he became Sub-Warden of Wadham, and an eminent historian. He organized the concerts and fixed the programmes with the performers.

Most of the concerts took place in the neighbouring village hall of Steeple Aston, and the charge for admission, I believe, was always one penny. The end of the concert often ran pretty close to the returning Oxford train, and a horse wagonette was provided by the thoughtful management. It was often escorted to the station by half the audience.

I remember once when an eminent Greek scholar was expatiating in a loud voice on all his sins of commission and omission in the cello part of a Beethoven quartet, we suddenly discovered that the back window of the wagonette was wide open, with the escort enjoying every word.

A summary of Heyford programmes gives a remarkable list both of the performers who later became professonals, and still more perhaps of the amateurs who distinguished themselves in other fields. Here are some of the second category:

Singers: Lord Normanbrook
             Professor Cecil Day-Lewis
             The late Professor R. M. Y. Glendowe
Violinists: The late Air Chief-Marshal Sir Guy Garrod
             Professor C. R. Cheney, of Cambridge
             Sir Geoffrey Lawrence, Q.C.
Viola: Edward R. Morgan, late Bishop of Truro

Cello: The late J. D. Denniston, a very distinguished Greek
             scholar
Flute: Sir Kenneth Anderson, of the Post Office
Clarinet: Lord Bridges

The future professionals included George Butterworth, Henry Ley,
Reginald Thatcher, Thomas Armstrong, William McKie, Jack Westrup,
Sydney Newman, Sydney Watson, Walter Stanton, Douglas Fox. Senior
musicians who also took part were Dr Ernest Walker, Mr Campbell
McInnes, Sir William Harris and Sir Hugh Allen.

The doctor I consulted in 1908 had, a year later, given me permission
to start rowing, and I began the laborious processes of fixed seat training
(with the usual saddle-soreness) and Freshman's Fours (the annual joke
of the Isis), while my contemporary friends (a year ahead of me in experience) had great fun at my expense. But it was all worth it: blisters,
icy splashings with a vile north-easter in winter, and merciless heat
in summer. I remember one February, being sent a 'long journey'
just before the Torpids. This was a fearful undertaking, even in decent
weather, its purpose being to banish any remaining stiffness.

We went about 8 miles down, through two locks, to the railway bridge
below Nuneham Courtenay. I always look out of the train when passing
this point, to see if there are any miserable crews turning round there.
Then worse still, back upstream with very long stretches of paddling.
Sandford Lock is one of the deepest in the whole river and so the slowest
to fill. On a wet and windy day it can be imagined that the climate at the
bottom of this cavernous empty lock is not improved by a costume of
damp shorts and vest. The final straw, when one is champing to get circulation going again after the long wait, is to receive the lock receipt, labelled
'pleasure vessel'. I found it all well worth while, and to compete at Henley
is a wholly delightful experience.

We all lived together in a little inn called the 'Traveller's Rest', which
stood exactly at the top of the Fair Mile where the road turns up the hill
to Nettlebed. It has disappeared, and I believe it was burnt down. The
upper bedroom windows commanded a view right down the straight, and
possessors of stopwatches used to spend hours timing fast cars and motor-
cycles up and down the mile. Christ Church put on two fours that year,
I stroked the second which fluked its way into the final. In the presence of
Their Majesties King George V and Queen Mary, we were left almost
standing by our own first crew, which bore the Visitors' Cup back in
triumph.

Several of us bicycled back to Oxford next day, and took our last farewell as inhabitants. I have been particularly lucky that so many friendships
and engagements of all kinds have drawn me back. In particular the Honor-

ary Studentship of Christ Church given me in the 1940s is something I prize very greatly, and I only wish I could make fuller use of its privileges.

Three days after leaving Henley in 1912, I was off with my mother to Munich where we were at once captivated by that lovely city with its great broad avenues, always culminating in some handsome building, and its magnificent river Isar. Post-war Munich I have also seen, but the change is so devastating that the mind cannot accept it as the same place at all.

We wallowed in pictures by day, and at night we heard the first three performances conducted by Bruno Walter on assuming the direction of the Munich opera houses. They were *Don Giovanni*, *Cosi*, and *Figaro* in the exquisite little Residenztheater, unaltered since Mozart had conducted *Idomeneo* in it in 1788. The new Director had certainly got into his stride; I didn't suppose I should ever hear Mozart performances of such all-round perfection, and certainly I never have again.

Bayreuth next day offered a sorry contrast: by 1912 the efforts to keep everything 'as the Master had left it' were wearing themselves out; the theatre was dusty (curtains included), props shoddy, mise-en-scène prehistoric. The chorus also sang woefully out of tune, but the orchestra, and many soloists, were magnificent.

Coming down from the theatre arm-in-arm with my mother, I suddenly realized that we were dashing along at a great pace, when we had a comfortable hour to spare before taking our train back to Nüremberg where we were sleeping. I suggested slowing down, but she pushed on, gasping as we dodged in and out of the crowd: 'I—hate—walking—behind—fat—people'. Each person or couple seemed fatter than the one we had just overtaken.

On our way to Munich we had an amusing interlude. There were I think three days between the day of our departure and our bookings in the Munich hotel. In those days European railway tickets were booklets of considerable size, comprising, I should think in this case, something like sixteen separate sheets which were torn out by the guards as we went along. As soon as we got into the (English) train we searched through our books (which gave many tempting alternatives) and hunted for places to look at during our two spare days. We pounced on Heidelberg, which was well off our main route, but included in the all-embracing through ticket.

We got there comfortably but found the place packed tight. However, rooms were finally found after a considerable search, and we discovered that the town was so full because the Castle was to be lit up and there would be fireworks. In those days when illuminations in England usually meant the most tawdry gas affairs with coloured glass all over them, we feared the worst, but crossed the bridge after dinner, and sat on a grassy bank with a good view across to the Castle, and prepared ourselves for a good laugh. We were in for a surprise; the thing was most charmingly done, with (I think) gas, but so cleverly screened that the effect was quite fairylike, and we were thankful that we had chosen Heidelberg on such an occasion. It was nearly forty years before I was to see the place again. The London Philharmonic finished its German tour there in January 1951.

More events of 1912–13 will be mentioned later, but it would I think be convenient here to go on with the English part of it—as continental contacts were cut off abruptly when I returned home in the summer of 1913 with a heart that needed watching, though it gave little trouble if I did things in moderation.

If anyone sees these pages before he is too old for any sort of 'training' may I urge him to watch his step when going *out* of training? I believe that my trouble was mainly if not wholly due to my going off to an easy life of sight-seeing and stodgy food two days after leaving Henley. Doctors always seem to forget that part of it: the heart has enlarged considerably, and should be allowed to go back gently.

'Doing things in moderation' seemed to provide a good opportunity to get on with work for the D. Mus. exams: I could take the papers even though I was not allowed to take the degree until five years after becoming a Bachelor. I hovered between Oxford and Cheshire, and helped with rehearsals of the Parry music to the *Acharnians*, the OUDS play for 1913. I also became an extra member of the musical staff at Covent Garden for the winter season and this consisted mainly of the first London performance of *Parsifal*. This was a remarkable example of incompetent management.

The first Act of *Parsifal* finishes with the full company on stage for the last forty minutes. In the third Act, the full company is required for the last twenty minutes. Until then there are only a few soloists. The chorus scene in the second Act is short, and independent of the solo scenes on both sides of it. Surely the chorus scenes should have been all rehearsed first? They were not.

We began with the overture (at 7 I think), and arrived at the transformation about 10.30, and by this time it was necessary to put on an extra rehearsal next morning. When we got to the Grail Scene, the chorus found it impossible to keep their pitch. They had been hanging about for three hours, and anyhow they weren't good enough. The importation of a chorus master from Yorkshire and a few voices with him, would have been simple at an earlier stage, and would have solved the problem easily, but now the only thing anyone could think of was to put a viola behind one of the pillars. One wasn't enough; a chorus of violas behind a chorus of pillars finally made a bigger contribution to the ensemble than the chorus of knights.

In 1914 I had been keen to join the Liverpool Scottish, as I knew many of them, but my father persuaded me to wait until my heart was better.

Probably he was right, but it was uncomfortable because I looked and felt fit enough. In October I went back to Oxford and worked with Walker, Tovey and others for the second D.Mus. exam which I passed in December. I have had good cause to thank my father's judgement on all this. In fact I doubt if I could have brought myself back to doing eight-part counterpoint (very strict in those days) after four years of war.

After the exam I came back to Cheshire, put on my old Oxford uniform, and went into the village every day to do recruit drill with a battalion of Lancashire miners—the rawest recruits, who were billeted in the same public hall where, just before the war, I had tried my hand for the first time with a professional orchestra. This amateur soldiering went on for two years, half of it at St Asaph in Denbighshire whither the battalion had been moved, and finishing in the Reserve Centre office as a sort of orderly-secretary to the DAQMG, who ran the office for the General. Colonel Mitchell and his wife were kindness itself and we became great friends, having some quite hilarious evenings at the boarding house in the village where we all lived.

Before we were moved to St Asaph I was able to organize a few more concerts in Liverpool with an orchestra of about thirty drawn from the Philharmonic, who were very glad of opportunities to play, as people had largely stopped taking lessons. This Mozart-Haydn orchestra covered a good deal of ground, both classical and modern, and I was surprised and delighted that the concerts resulted in an invitation from the very conservative Committee of the Philharmonic Society to conduct a concert for them in January 1916. The programme included Bach's Third Brandenburg Concerto, a Haydn symphony, Parry's Symphonic Variations and a suite by Arthur de Greef, the well-known pianist, based on Flemish folksongs. Solomon, aged fourteen, was the pianist in Liszt's Hungarian Fantasia and this was the first of a long series of occasions when I have been privileged to collaborate with this magnificent artist. A refugee from the Antwerp Opera sang, and the Belgian National Anthem opened the proceedings—the fate of Belgium seemed much nearer to us in 1914 than it did in 1939.

The Royal Liverpool Philharmonic Society, as it now is, has remembered me almost continuously since, and I have many happy memories of their concerts. The next occasion was in December 1919 when I had to travel overnight both ways in order to interrupt my nightly work with the Diaghilev Ballet as little as possible. In 1921 I had the thrill of accompanying Pablo Casals in the Schumann Concerto, an indelible memory, never fading although followed by other wonderful experiences with him, including the recording and several other performances of the Elgar.

Another privilege which I greatly valued in Liverpool was attendance at rehearsals. Whenever I was at home I used to go in and learn a great deal from many of the great conductors who visited us. In particular I remember Gabriel Pierné who came several times during the 1914 war, and as he did not speak English I was asked to sit with him on the platform at rehearsal and translate for him to the orchestra.

At that time he was the leading conductor in Paris and I was able to gather a really authoritative view of the Debussy 'Nocturnes', a charming Basque Suite by Pierné himself called 'Ramuntcho', and, above all, the César Franck Symphony, which was in those days in London often tinged with a strong Russian flavouring. Pierné's straightforward rendering seemed just right for the simple and direct music, and I think that my efforts to simplify and smooth out the performance of the B.B.C. Orchestra when we first rehearsed it ten years later caused me actually to spend a longer time than I had planned for rehearsal. It was always the rule in those happy days that we found my time schedule was too generous and the rehearsal could finish early, but here was an exception—the only one I can remember.

Another foreigner whose English was inadequate for rehearsal was Vaclav Talich, conductor of the Czech Philharmonic all through the 1914 war. I had been immensely happy with his orchestra when I conducted it in 1922, and it was a great pleasure to help him on his subsequent visit to England, both in Liverpool and London. He gave us a memorable performance of the Dvorak G major Symphony (No. 8 nowadays— formerly No. 4).

There was another useful thing I managed to fit into the Oxford vacations. I got to know a very able musician, named Gordon Stutely, who was first violin in the Liverpool Philharmonic Orchestra and also musical director and conductor of the Liverpool City Police Band. He was expert on every instrument of the band, and naturally had access to them all, and he gave me lessons on every one in turn. Of course it took me several weeks to master some of the embouchures and fingerings, but we never went on from one instrument to the next until I had a good know-ledge of the fingering and could blow a few notes both loud and soft. That was a long time ago, and I fear I couldn't do much about it now.

When the Reserve Centre office broke up in 1916, I was offered a job in the War Office, concerned with the German Press. Hardly had I begun, when I ran into Fred Marquis (later Lord Woolton) who had, earlier in the war, lent me his theatre and his administrative resources at the Liver-pool University Settlement to house some concerts at low prices, which I have already mentioned.

Marquis insisted on my transferring to the War Office branch in Tothill Street where he was gradually assuming control of the country's leather resources. Work as his personal assistant took me almost to the end of the war, and also, with Marquis' permission, enabled me to organize four concerts with the London Symphony Orchestra in the spring of 1918, where we gave the second and third London performances of Vaughan Williams' London Symphony, the audience for the first being rather spoilt by a Zeppelin raid.

The score of the symphony had been put together from the separate parts by a number of friends, as the original score was in Leipzig (for engraving) when war broke out. The composer gave it to me later, bound in such a way that one can see the processes of revision very clearly. It has now gone to the British Museum.

I had put the work into the 1918 programme because I felt it was due for a second performance in London, although I had neither heard nor seen it. When I got possession of the score, I was just beginning a tour of the West Country to boost Marquis' most ingenious scheme for a war-time standard boot to suit all pockets. Touring with eighteen sample boots and the Vaughan Williams symphony I first met Arthur Bliss staying with friends in Bath (he was in the Guards) and he was thrilled to see the score, but not the boots. We met again, surprisingly, a week or two later in the courtyard of Buckingham Palace where I was on duty as a special constable and he, as a Guards officer, was marshalling a gigantic parade of women car workers.

Just before the Armistice, Gustav Holst burst into my office: 'Adrian, the YMCA are sending me to Salonika quite soon and Balfour Gardiner, bless his heart, has given me a parting present consisting of Queen's Hall, full of the Queen's Hall Orchestra for the whole of a Sunday morning. So we're going to do "The Planets" and you've got to conduct.' Then followed feverish activity: I think the whole of St Paul's Girls School helped to copy the parts. Somebody trained the choir. Scores were sent me as they were released from the copyists, and the great day came. Most of the school and all his friends were there, and we had a happy party. When the score was engraved he wrote in my copy: 'This score is the property of Adrian Boult who first caused The Planets to shine in public and so earned the gratitude of Gustav Holst'.

Our office usually absorbed one or two invalided officers for a few months' duty before their return to active service when convalescence had been slow. A shy youngster was with us at Armistice time, and next morning it was natural that we should be comparing experiences of the night before. Our youngster was silent until I asked him what he had been doing. 'Well,' he said, 'I realized my life's ambition.' For two minutes he had conducted the band at the old Frascati's Restaurant in Oxford Street.

Chapter Four

'ARTHUR NIKISCH CONQUERS APATHETIC LONDON'

ANYONE WHO cares to dig into the files of the old *Morning Leader* and turns to the issue of 1 May 1902, will find the above headline in surprisingly large print, for those unmusical days. The notice was by *Sforzando*, a critic of great understanding whose real name I never learnt.

There is no doubt that the entry of Arthur Nikisch into the London scene suddenly aroused and stimulated public interest in conducting as such. The great work that Wood had been doing at Queen's Hall, Hans Richter in Manchester, August Manns at the Crystal Palace, Dan Godfrey in Bournemouth, and others too, was steadily quickening the taste for orchestral music, but the conductor was looked on as a part of the orchestra, and people weren't much interested in how he got his results, or indeed whether he or the players, or both, were responsible.

I can remember that when Hans Richter came to the Hallé Orchestra in Manchester in 1900 and the Liverpool Philharmonic Society decided that they would prefer to keep Sir Frederic Cowen as their conductor, my mother was thought to be a most curious person when she expressed her annoyance over Liverpool's stupidity at missing this chance. Now suddenly in 1903, in the middle of a week's festival, this man appeared and, in a perfectly familiar programme, extracted an utterly different sound from the orchestra, and threw an utterly different light on the music.

Some years later, Richter and Nikisch both conducted the *Dutchman* Overture in Queen's Hall with the same orchestra within a few days of each other. *Sforzando* said: 'With Nikisch we felt that Fate was pursuing us wherever we went, with Richter Fate faced us wherever we turned'.

It is not often that the underlying force of a musical interpretation can be put into words so simply, but that sentence might perhaps give even to the unmusical some inkling of what audiences now get from conductors. In these seventy years the cult of the conductor has gone too far: discussions of 'X's Beethoven' and 'Y's Brahms' have thrown the whole thing out of perspective. Toscanini was an example to us all in his attitude of humble service to the composer and his music, and surely the finest praise a conductor can wish to hear is: 'I have always loved that work, but thought tonight that it seemed more splendid than ever, and I *heard new beauties in it*'.

Nikisch was a most subjective conductor, and often, under his spell, I have felt: 'Yes, this is wonderful, but it isn't Beethoven'. I remember thinking, when I was hearing him several times a week in Leipzig, that if I were asked to write down all the music I would rather hear conducted by Nikisch than by anyone else, it would be only a short list. Beethoven's and Brahms' monumental designs and romantic power could better be realized by Richter, Weingartner and Steinbach; Tchaikovsky in Sefonoff's hand became a strong man, no longer neurotic or effeminate.

The Wagner of the *Meistersinger* belonged of necessity to Richter's irresistible rhythmic impulse and powerful grasp of architecture. There sometimes seemed, as the last scene developed, a kind of spiritual identification of Hans Sachs with 'the Old Man' whose guidance of the performance, so powerful and yet so sensitive, seemed to coincide with Hans Sachs' management of the stormy affairs of his temperamental neighbours. Perhaps the fact that Richter had stayed at Triebschen and copied Wagner's full score sheet by sheet as he worked on the orchestration, contributed also to his deep understanding. *Tristan* on the other hand fitted Nikisch like a glove. His impetuous irregularities of tempo (particularly if the singers were not very good musicians!), and the glowing warmth of tone he drew from the orchestra must surely have realized Wagner's deepest desires. His first appearance in opera in London was in January 1907 when a season of German opera included in the first week *Tristan* (twice), *Holländer* and *Der Freischütz*, all conducted by Nikisch. I heard them all from the Gallery, which nearly went mad each night.

These reservations about Nikisch as an interpreter could not affect one's judgment about him as a director of the orchestra. It is impossible to believe that anyone could ever (or will ever) hold orchestras in the hollow of his hand, or produce the essence of the music with the point of his stick, with such power, and with such economy and beauty of gesture. And so, when I learnt that he directed the conductors' class at the Leipzig Konservatorium, I determined to go there, if I could, instead of, or directly after, the years at Oxford.

A happy personal link helped this scheme. Amongst the first friends I remember at home were Mr and Mrs E. C. Hedmondt and their two daughters. He will still be remembered by older opera-goers, for he was principal tenor of the Carl Rosa Opera Company for many years. A Canadian, he took this name and joined the Leipzig opera house where he married a beautiful young Czech soprano. Through some misunderstanding, he broke one of the sacred laws which used to tie up German opera houses, one violation of which spelt the end of a German career. So he had to move to England, joined the 'Rosa' and came to live in Liverpool.

After some years Mrs Hedmondt, who was an excellent musician, accepted an offer to join the staff of the Leipzig Konservatorium, where one of her first pupils was Elena Gerhardt. One summer, when I was about sixteen, she came to stay in London at the time when both Gerhardt and Nikisch were fulfilling a large number of engagements here. I was thrilled to be invited to lunch at the Savoy with them. Mr Robin Legge of the *Daily Telegraph*, who had been a fellow-student with Nikisch at Leipzig, was also there with Mrs Legge. Nikisch told me then that he was about to give up the conducting school, but if I still wished to come to Leipzig, he would do all he could to help me with rehearsal passes and in other ways.

In the meantime there were always his summer visits to London, where he was doing more and more work with the London Symphony Orchestra, and it must not be forgotten that when an American enthusiast offered to finance a month's tour of the USA, and left the choice of orchestra to Nikisch, who was then permanent conductor of the Berlin Philharmonic and Leipzig Gewandhaus orchestras, Nikisch chose the LSO.

In September 1912 I left the Scottish family holiday before its due end, and being a bit of an adventurer (though a shocking sailor) I chose the route from Grimsby to Hamburg, and on by sleeper to Leipzig. There Mrs Hedmondt and the girls gave me a very kind reception. I was always welcome at their flat, and they took immense trouble in finding an excellent lodging for me, and introducing me right and left. A few weeks after this we were all most happy at the announcement that the King of Saxony had conferred on her the title of Royal Professor in her own right (and not shared by her husband). I believe there were only two others in the German Empire.

As she was the leading teacher at the Konservatorium she had naturally a large number of advanced pupils. In order to help them she engaged, for two hours a week, the concert hall of the Hochschule as it is now called, where she sat well back and could judge (and later comment on) the aptitude of the girls to handle a large space. She always engaged a student to accompany these special lessons and on many other occasions, notably at her flat on Sunday afternoons when she often had parties. As her previous accompanist had left at Christmas, she asked me to take his place for the two terms of 1913. I was delighted, and learnt a great deal from her; on one occasion we were sent for to sing to an architectural conference which was inspecting the Gewandhaus, and I realized the extraordinary properties of that wonderful hall, because although the singers were standing at the front of the platform and directing their voices away from me, I seemed to be able to judge the total effect as if I had been sitting well down the hall. Because of this the accompanist's permanent problem: 'Am I too loud?', ceased to exist. It is always cropping up even with an artist as admirable as Gerald Moore, who chose it as the title of one of his delightful books.

Mrs Hedmondt's method had one remarkable feature which is of importance to all teachers. About the time her husband left Leipzig, her career as a singer was ruined by a careless operation on her throat: in some way her control of it became imperfect and she could not trust it. She therefore decided, when she began to teach, that she would never risk 'patterning' anything, except of course the shades of vowel sounds, patterned always on her speaking voice.

Accordingly she made use of very telling and stimulating verbal descriptions, having a fine command of German, Czech, English, French and Italian, and left the girls (she never taught men, by the way) to interpret these descriptions for themselves. This method developed their styles independently, as they had no one whose mannerisms they could ape. So differently in style did the various pupils sing, that at her parties when several of them would perform, people often said they could hardly believe that they had all come from the same mould.

I am endlessly grateful for that year's vision of the Germany of Goethe and Schiller, particularly from the viewpoint of peaceful, easy-going Saxony, in a Konservatorium where the pupils included Poles, Czechs and Hungarians as well as young people from all over Germany. I packed my days pretty full, beginning with lessons at 8 a.m. sometimes in the summer term, and finishing with a concert, opera or play. At this time the Leipzig theatre was enjoying one of its greatest periods, and the performances of Shakespeare, Schiller, Goethe and Hebbel were unequalled in Germany.

I think still that Jakob Feldhammer's *Hamlet* was the finest I have ever seen, and the teamwork was far more closely studied and rehearsed than anything in England in those days, though our development since has been phenomenal. I managed to fit in an occasional dash to Dresden, Prague or Berlin for some special performance and on my way home for the holidays I was able to hear festivals at Meiningen under Reger, and Cologne under Steinbach, who gave monumental performances of Beethoven's Ninth Symphony and of Mahler's VIII. In the summer term, with no work on Saturdays and fewer Sunday parties at Mrs Hedmondt's I was able to escape to worship Bach at Eisenach, and explore the Hörselberg and the Wartburg. After a night in a hostel near the Wartburg, I followed the ancient track (called the Rennsteig) along which Tannhäuser toiled to Rome. Then, after twenty miles or so right along the crest of the Thuringian Forest, I was able to drop down to Friedrichroda and take the train. This kind of trip was possible in many directions as several trains left Leipzig about 7 a.m. Saxon Switzerland round the Elbe above Dresden was another happy hunting ground.

One day in a ravine up there I found an invitation to walk for ten minutes and visit the 'Famous and Original Wolf's Glen of Weber's *Freischütz*'. This could not be resisted, and I hurried up the gorge which presently opened out into the inevitable beer garden complete with postcard-and-souvenir stall.

At the far end of the garden was a rather watery cave, and around it children were playing. There was also a good clientèle at the tables. Before sitting down I wandered round and spotted a notice close to the cave: 'Beware! When the bell rings, the waterfall will burst into activity, and the cave must be instantly cleared, otherwise a thorough wetting will result. Parents are responsible for their children'. I enquired of the postcard lady when the next performance was expected. She indicated that it might happen any moment, if someone would pay. 'How much?' 'It doesn't matter.' 'Would a penny do?' 'Oh yes.' On receiving my penny she leant out of the stall, and reaching upwards grasped a most suggestive-looking handle on a long chain, and pulled firmly. The bell rang fiercely, the trickle over the cave mouth became a torrent, and after about two minutes stopped abruptly, leaving its trickle behind. After I got away from the spell of all these excitements, I looked round—the beer garden was nearly empty. The frugal Saxons had all been waiting for someone else to pay for the deluge.

Living was incredibly cheap in those days: my midday meal was usually taken at one of three or four restaurants and at each of them one could buy books of meal tickets. They cost 10s. or 12s. 6d. a book and covered ten good meals, and one might reckon 3d. or 4d. extra for beer and a tip. The whole of life was on that scale, in that passportless, happy Europe, and I seem to remember that third-class travel in pre-1914 Germany cost less than a halfpenny a mile.

The difference between Nikisch in London and in Leipzig was brought home to me with a bang soon after the season started. After his week-end with the Berlin Philharmonic, Nikisch rehearsed the Gewandhaus Choir on Monday night, and the orchestra on Tuesday morning, privately, with a few privileged students in attendance. Wednesday morning saw the public rehearsal, at which the programme was usually played straight through before a full house, with Thursday evening for the concert. At this event Leipzig musicians turned up their noses on the ground that it was purely for 'society' (they were the only concerts in Germany where dinner-jackets were worn), and 'that the really musical audience came to the [cheaper] rehearsal, which the dear Professor himself always enjoyed more'. The rehearsal audience was admittedly more demonstrative, but I'm not sure that the dear Professor hadn't some of his tongue in his cheek, as the following story may prove. I attended the first public rehearsal, and while enjoying it, rather vaguely felt that Nikisch got better results in London. Then, a week later, came the second rehearsal with the

'Jupiter' on the programme: it was definitely untidy in the first movement, with many exaggerations of nuance. When the second movement
began with the first violins *in canon* (a quaver apart) until Nikisch collected
matters over the crash in the second bar, I lost my temper, and all further
interest in the proceedings.

In this mood I went across to the Kon., met Mrs Hedmondt in the hall,
and she immediately offered me her subscription seat for the concert next
day! I just checked an indignant refusal, feeling that I was still a new boy,
and that anyhow it would be fun to see the Gewendhaus in full panoply.
I dressed up and strolled round half-heartedly, but sat up at the first note
and remained entranced by the beauty of the performance, even if I had
some reservations about interpretation. It was clear that here was a performance, and yesterday had been a rehearsal, whatever its audience had
been thinking about it. Later that week I secured my pass for the private
rehearsals, and I learnt still more about his rehearsal method which accepts
the rehearsal as a preparation for the performance, and in no way as a
performance itself.

No one who hears me rehearsing nowadays could possibly suspect it,
but at that time my voice was good enough to get me into the Gewandhaus
Choir. This was a fashionable but efficient gathering of Leipzig society,
strengthened by the choir from Bach's Church of St Thomas, and also
one of the University Guilds which made a powerful addition to the tenors
and basses. We always sang the Ninth Symphony at the closing concert
and that year there was also a beautiful work by Reger ('The Nuns', poem
by Boelitz); and a large slice of *Parsifal*, which incidentally Nikisch
repeated at Leeds Festival the following October. Rehearsals, as I said,
took place on Monday evening in the Chambermusic Hall.

This was set as for a pianoforte recital, Nikisch at the piano, with the
men sitting round him on the platform, and the ladies and boys in the
body of the hall. Our conductor never conducted: he guided our singing
from the keyboard, playing always from the full score, and often playing
wrong notes when new and unknown works were in rehearsal.

It was noticed that he never took scores home, and in a work like Reger's
'Die Nonnen' he sometimes played the orchestral interludes to himself
while the Choir was 'resting' (or rather chattering hard). I maliciously
followed his playing in my vocal score, and found he was continually
playing wrong accidentals.

There would usually be two orchestral rehearsals, and at these, when
we knew the music pretty well, we could of course follow the beat properly.
There is not much point in a conductor's powerful antics if the choir have
their noses in their copies frantically reading new music; it is only the
experienced orchestral player who can sight-read and follow the beat at the
same time.

Another of the works we sang that year besides the Ninth Symphony and the Reger work, was the Brahms 'Requiem', and we had the co-operation of the great Karl Straube at the organ. I was astonished that at the final rehearsal Professor Straube played a dominant seventh with a very strong F for the penultimate chord of the great C major fugue at the end of the sixth movement. Nikisch, apparently, didn't notice, and we had a repetition of this embellishment at the performance. I wondered whether Brahms was turning in his grave!

I have recently read a book written by that splendid conductor Nikolai Malko, published posthumously and called *A Certain Art*.[1] In a generous tribute to Felix Mottl, he quotes his opinion of Nikisch, and it would not have been shared by many of his contemporaries:

> It is difficult in a few words to sum up the musical image of Felix Mottl. He was the brilliant representative of those who combined great erudition with high personal endowment, characteristic of the best among the followers of Wagner and Liszt. Just as each of them possessed his own individual personality, so the unique characteristic of Felix Mottl might be termed his sincere abandonment of himself to his deep love of music. I once mentioned Nikisch in one of our conversations, and the maestro immediately said, 'Well, his technique is immense, but here', and he indicated his heart, 'nothing'.[1]

In my opinion he was dead right about Nikisch's technique but I think few people would have denied him that wonderful warmth of tone the strings gave him whenever he lifted the stick.

I cannot resist another quotation from Malko. On the vexed subject of technique:

> He should rely on gestures more than words. It often happens that a conductor begins to talk when gestures fail him, and then becomes accustomed to his own chatter.

Nikisch never used an unnecessary word and there were no thrills at his rehearsals. He always believed in saving up for the concert, and remembering that a rehearsal is a preparation and not itself a concert, he never stretched himself or anyone else unduly, until the audience were in the hall. He would never have countenanced the modern American habit of 100 per cent rehearsals, with everything screwed up to concert pitch all the time.

Nikisch had a rather unusual plan with his Leipzig programmes. Each season featured one of the great masters, and devoted a number of programmes to him. In 1912–13 it was Beethoven, and we had all the symphonies and most of the concertos and overtures spread over six of the

[1] William Morrow and Co. Inc. New York, 1966.

twenty-three programmes. The last time I saw him in Amsterdam in 1920, he told me that it was Bruckner that year, and that he had done all the symphonies. He was a great admirer of Bruckner, and at the Savoy lunch when I first met him years before he had said he felt the slow movement of the 7th to be one of the loveliest slow movements in the whole symphonic literature, and also told a story of how Richter, rehearsing one of the symphonies in Vienna (the first occasion, I believe, on which Bruckner ever heard any of his own orchestral work), suddenly spotted a discrepancy between an accidental he saw in the score, and the note played by the orchestra. He turned round to Bruckner, sitting in the stalls, and asked which it was. 'Whichever you prefer', answered the poor old man, thrilled beyond the power of thought.

Though I sometimes felt very far away from home, I was sad when the Leipzig year came to an end, and toyed with the idea of embarking on a career in the German opera house, as had another Englishman ten years before me: Albert Coates, who by that time had achieved the Direction of the Imperial Opera at what was then called Petrograd. My heart had given me some trouble during the later months at Leipzig, and my father wanted me to come home, so I got an engagement at Covent Garden for the winter season of 1914 which included the first London performance of *Parsifal*, and the summer season following at which Nikisch conducted two cycles of the *Ring*.

I last saw—and heard—Nikisch in 1920. Scott Goddard, then a student at the Royal College of Music, heard from friends in Holland that he was to go there about Easter time, so we organized a party from the Royal College, and included the Palm Sunday 'Matthew Passion' which in those days was always conducted by Mengelberg. It was a cheery party, Scott Goddard (whose fluent Dutch was a great asset), Boris Ord, Leslie Heward, Arthur Bliss, Armstrong Gibbs and Hugh Ross (now in America). We were actually present at Nikisch's first rehearsal (he had not been in Amsterdam for twenty-four years) and were all amazed at the way he conducted the music (and not the beats) from the very first moment. It will be remembered that the first bar of Schumann's fourth symphony is a long way from the kind of time-beating that an orchestra might expect of its conductor: nothing happens at the beginning of the first full bar, therefore Nikisch gave no beat and the stick was quite still until he turned to the second violins (placed on his right, as always in those days), and brought them in in the middle of the bar. The rehearsal went on gently, almost lazily, until the coda of the last movement. Suddenly we saw a new nervous energy coming from the point of that long stick, the orchestra responded instantly, and the work finished in a blaze. That was enough: Nikisch now knew he could get what he wanted when he wanted it, which was of course only at the concert. So for three more days he rehearsed in ample detail, but never at more than half the emotional pressure, and so the concert was all the more exciting.

I am satisfied that this is the right treatment for Anglo-Saxon and Nordic musicians. They are a self-reliant crowd, and can be trusted when adequately led, even if the more Southern and Oriental types only fully respond when driven, as indeed all the American orchestras are now driven by their conductors who treat every rehearsal as itself a concert at 100 per cent pressure. Personally I look on a group of rehearsals as a cumulative series, and only rarely do I ask for full concert pressure. I like to feel that each rehearsal is a step forward, with a further step still to be made from the last rehearsal to the concert itself. We are a sporting people and I cannot see why our artistic processes should not be managed in a way similar to the main rules of sports training.

In another respect Nikisch's rehearsal methods were opposed to most modern practice. We have seen that at Leipzig (and presumably also Berlin) he did not regard the public rehearsal as a concert, but as a preparation for the concert next day. Accordingly, at the preliminary (private, except for a few students) rehearsal, any work (including all concertos) which might reasonably be expected to go well at the public rehearsal was left till then, and the whole time was devoted to examination of new or, at any rate, non-repertoire works (often in great detail) or difficult passages chosen out of the more familiar things. At other places, in London for instance, where there were no public rehearsals, he would reverse the process, and play straight through a work, and only after that go back on any passages that needed special attention. He would carry in his head a list of 10 or 12 such passages, and it can easily be seen how much less of a strain this is to the player, than the usual practice of stopping the moment the conductor hears anything he wishes to change. An orchestral leader once whispered to me just before a very important guest conductor's concert: 'Do you know, I don't think we have ever been allowed to play more than ten bars on end, even at the final rehearsal, without being stopped'. I wonder if the sweep, continuity, and build-up of a symphonic work can safely be all left to the final moment like that. This particular conductor often achieved magnificent results—but for masterly management of the psychology of rehearsing, Arthur Nikisch knew no equal.

I often tell my long-suffering pupils that there is no use trying to control other people until you have learnt to control yourself, and I remember a good example of this from Nikisch in Leeds when he came to conduct the Festival of 1913. A kind Oxford friend had invited me to stay with him for the Festival and also the two or three days of public rehearsal beforehand. Nikisch had conducted the morning rehearsal and had said that he was very tired. I think he had come straight from Russia. He went down to the Queen's Hotel and instead of lunching, sat down in the first armchair inside the lounge, close to the door through which everyone passed into the hotel. In two or three minutes he was fast asleep and exactly twenty minutes before the afternoon session he woke up and went straight back to the hall.

In the programme there was a slice from the *Parsifal* Grail Scene which he had given in Leipzig during the previous winter, when I was singing in the choir. The beauty of the Leeds singing was evidently impressing him and finally when after the long soprano high A flat the Yorkshire ladies unanimously dropped to the octave below instead of yielding to the temptation to resolve it on D flat (a temptation that some of the Leipzig ladies had found it impossible to resist until the very last rehearsals), Nikisch put his fingers to his lips and blew a kiss up to the sopranos. This sudden sign of humanity coming from this sphinx-like, slow-moving, grave figure who had as yet hardly spoken to them produced a sudden roar of applause from the chorus men, equally suddenly stopped when their imperturbable conductor proceeded solemnly with the orchestral close, his eyes on the score.

Chapter Five

OPERA

I HAVE SAID that when my year at Leipzig was finished, I had had several kind offers of introductions from various friends which would probably have given me a choice of opera houses to which I might have attached myself for some years. A life of that kind is a very important part of a young conductor's training, consisting, as it does, mainly of teaching the singers their roles, but also of learning the operas, and of course hoping that some conductor will obligingly default so that the understudy gets a chance. Several circumstances, including health and the 1914 war, prevented this, to my great disappointment, and my contacts with grand opera have, since that time, been intermittent. In 1914, I served on the staff of Covent Garden, playing some of the bells in the first performance of *Parsifal*, and doing various odd jobs with lighting cues, and so on. We had a rather terrible experience one night in the last act of *Siegfried*; I had to start a shaft of moonlight from the prompt flies, and then hurry round through the paint room to the O.P. side where three successive gauzes (clouds) had to descend slowly and atmospherically just before the elaborate change to the Valkyrie's rock for the last scene. I did my moon all right, but when I got round to the other side with about twenty bars still to go, I was horrified to find not a single stage hand there to start the gauzes. I had to wait, and when they gradually drifted in, our clouds had to descend with unseemly speed, and I fear the atmosphere was crudely shattered. Two reasons were produced at the inevitable post mortem; it was Saturday night and they were being paid; but they maintained that Nikisch (it was his first Covent Garden performance) had taken 20 minutes off Richter's timing for the spear scene. I wonder!

Another incident in the 1914 season comes back to me as so fantastic that I sometimes wonder if I dreamt it all.

It is essential that the singers who take the parts of the three Norns in the *Götterdämmerung* Prologue convey in their singing a deep knowledge of the whole legend.

It is often found convenient that these three singers should duplicate the parts of the three Rhinemaidens, though here none of the wisdom

46

and knowledge of the Norns is necessary. In 1914 it certainly wasn't there for this is what I heard when they were waiting for their final (silent) appearance as Rhinemaidens:

First Norn: 'Oh, look, who's that they're carrying along there?'
Second Norn: 'Why, that's Mr Cornelius, that's Siegfried.'
Third Norn: 'Cor, does he die in this piece?'

At the Royal College, opera sometimes came my way, and I have happy memories of *Hänsel and Gretel*, and a number of other separate acts, and most of all of several performances of *Parsifal* with Trefor Jones, who had just come as a scholar (but later made his name in lighter parts), as a dedicated and moving exponent of the title role. It was said that the Director, Sir Hugh Allen, one day told him he would have to sing *Parsifal* in ten months' time, and that he thought of nothing else for the whole period. One of our audiences included Frederic Austin (whose son Richard is now Opera Director at the R.C.M.). He asked me to take charge of the *Parsifal* performances of the British National Opera Company, which he then directed, throughout the subsequent winter. It meant a good deal of night travelling, for the company was often in Edinburgh or Newcastle, but it was a great experience, and I particularly remember Percy Heming's very moving performance of Amfortas. The company came to Birmingham every winter for two or three weeks, and usually invited me to join them for one performance. I remember a thrilling *Otello* with Licette, Mullings and Heming, *Walküre*, and other things.

That able composer and charming man, Napier Miles, who lived in a beautiful Vanbrugh house just outside Bristol, used to summon me there for occasional weeks of opera. Stanford's *Travelling Companion*, Falla's *Maese Pedro*, and several of Napier's own works figured in the bills, and as most of the company stayed with Mr and Mrs Miles at King's Weston, a delightful week was certain. The Bristol companies played in London occasionally at that time—at the Royal Court and also the Kingsway, at Sir Barry Jackson's invitation. Walter Johnstone-Douglas produced those seasons.

Barry Jackson's long management of the Birmingham Repertory Theatre did not give him much opportunity to indulge his love for music, but he opened his 1924 season with an opera by Granville Bantock, called *The Seal Woman*, the text having been written by Mrs Marjorie Kennedy Fraser, who based it on a Hebridean legend which she had collected with her tunes. Nearly twenty of the tunes in Mrs Fraser's collection were used in the opera, which was admirably suited to Barry's beautiful little theatre, as the orchestra was only nine strong; five strings, four wind. The lovely Hebridean tunes were beautifully set for this tiny combination, but in between, the music did not always seem quite appropriate. It was written at the time of Bantock's passion for Richard Strauss, and so we had a strong flavour of 'Zarathustra' and 'Heldenleben' in between the folksongs, which didn't quite blend with the island scenes, but astonished us all by their effectiveness when arranged for an orchestra of nine!

Vladimir Rosing, a refugee tenor from Russia, made an instant reputation with his recitals in London and the wonderful intensity of his performances; later he moved to America where he added teaching and operatic production to his attainments. He once organized a week of 'Opéra Intime' at Aeolian Hall, and secured as producer none other than Theodor Komisarjevsky, who had also arrived in London, after many adventures, from the famous Moscow Art Theatre. He asked me to look after the music, and we decided that the intimacy of the whole production would be nicely caught by an orchestra of seven: five strings, a pianoforte played by Leslie Heward, and a chamber organ played by Arnold Goldsbrough. Both of these young men were then students at the Royal College, and took great pains to adapt the scores of Tchaikovsky's *Pique Dame*, *I Pagliacci*, and *Bastien and Bastienne* with surprisingly fine results.

Chapter Six

LONDON AGAIN, BIRMINGHAM AND EGYPT—1919–1930

SIR HUBERT PARRY DIED in the autumn of 1918, and I think that Dr Hugh Percy Allen was offered the Directorship of the Royal College of Music very soon afterwards. Anyhow, he in all secrecy told me that *if* it were offered him (I don't think he would have said that if it hadn't already happened!) he wanted me to go there and start a class for conductors, and act as Sir Charles Stanford's assistant as conductor of the orchestra. I eagerly accepted, and was able to join at half-term, in February 1919. The returning warriors were beginning to stream back, and though Allen hadn't known them before, no one could have been more fitted to welcome them and help them find their way into civilian life—the place simply buzzed with optimism and energy, and Allen seemed the hub of it all, himself taking charge of the choral class, in which everyone, pianists, violinists, conductors or whatever, joined, including Clive Carey, myself and other members of the teaching staff.

The class for conductors gave me very great pleasure. Amongst the first students were Leslie Heward, surely one of the finest conductors of his time, sadly taken from us when barely forty; Boris Ord who became organist of King's, Cambridge, and kept up the tremendous tradition there; Armstrong Gibbs, one of the happiest lyric composers of his time; Scott Goddard, long critic of the *Daily News*; Constant Lambert, composer, conductor and writer—equally successful in each province; Richard Austin, still ably steering the operatic activities of the Royal College; Hugh Ross, conductor of the Schola Cantorum of New York; Herbert Sumsion, organist of Gloucester and conductor of the Three Choirs Festival; Patrick Hadley, Professor of Music at Cambridge, and many others. The future Master of the Queen's Musick, Sir Arthur Bliss, was often with us, and took over the class whenever I had to be away.

Lunch at the R.C.M. was always most enjoyable, for near Allen at one end of the table there were, on different days of the week, a number of distinguished musicians, many of whose names are still well known. Sir Walter Parrott, Sir Charles Stanford, Sir Walter Alcock, were always there at least once a week, and many others. Dr Herbert Howells has been faithful to the R.C.M. ever since those days, and his composition students value their hour with him as much as did those in the twenties.

Frederic Cliffe, a popular pianoforte teacher, gave lessons there more than once a week, and was getting news of a brilliant son at Eton. That son was the late Cedric Cliffe whose outstanding memory often surprised those who heard him on B.B.C. quiz programmes.

Another distinguished pianoforte professor at the Royal College of Music at that time was Miss Fanny Davies. The last of Clara Schumann's pupils to have an international reputation, she was still greatly in demand as a soloist in Europe and at home, and had a number of excellent pupils. One night Allen asked me to go round and see her about some student, and after we had settled the matter I asked her how far she felt that orchestral performance of romantic music might go in the direction of the freedom to which, for instance, the pianoforte recitalist naturally went. I was specially thinking of the beginning of the last movement of the Schumann C major Symphony, which, if played with a literal obedience to the absence of expression marks, can be made to sound dreadfully monotonous and solid. Her answer was to take down her volume of the Symphonies for four hands, and taking of course the treble part, she gave me a marvellous lesson in the interpretation of that movement. That done, we played the rest of the symphony, and then all the others. By the time she finally brought out Suk's Asrael Symphony, it was well after midnight and I am afraid I felt bound to go off to bed! But I had had a wonderful lesson.

The Patron's Fund of the Royal College of Music was the generous foundation of Lord Palmer of Reading. It was to be administered by the College, but for the benefit of all British musicians. It had, of course, lapsed during the war, and Allen was therefore closely concerned with its revival. Hitherto the fund had financed concerts of British music by British artists which were expensive and drew poor audiences. Allen wisely thought that the money would go much further if composers could hear their work under less formal conditions, and so he engaged the London Symphony Orchestra for ordinary morning rehearsals in the R.C.M. Concert Hall. The programme consisted of an hour's British music, which was rehearsed from 10 till 11.45 and performed at 12, so that critics and anyone interested could come in (there was no admission charge) and hear everything in that last hour; but the composers (who could conduct if they wished) had the benefit of hearing the rehearsal as well. I was in attendance to help the composer, or to conduct if he wished to listen.

The war had piled up an accumulation of scores, which were chosen by the College authorities with some outside judges. I believe Bantock helped a good deal. Many well-known musicians made use of this excellent chance, and Holst's *Perfect Fool* ballet was played at one of the earliest rehearsals. He was doubtful about several points of scoring and notation (I remember how cumbersome the Spirits of Earth looked in their original 7/4 guise; 7/8 seems to suit them much better). With his right-arm neuritis he got rather tangled up with the uneven rhythm, and soon handed the stick over to me, and I conducted the performance. When the score was engraved later he sent me a copy inscribed 'To its first Conductor from his Inefficient but Grateful Pupil. G.H. 9th July 1923'.

Another branch of music to which Allen introduced me at this time was the musical festival. This term covers a wide range, as everyone knows. There is the international Edinburgh type at one end, and at the other the kind where there are very many classes from vocal and pianoforte solos for children, to choral competitions. I did some judging at these, but I soon gave it up, and concentrated on a type which naturally appealed to me more—the purely choral. This often begins with a meeting in the early autumn where eight or ten village conductors meet the chief festival conductor—sometimes they each bring some singers from their choirs. The chief conductor goes right through the festival programme, giving all his ideas on performance, perhaps a few notes on the history of the works, and prepares the separate conductors as completely as possible for the winter's work which is usually a weekly practice in each separate town or village. Before Easter there may be some group rehearsals, but the festival itself takes place before farms and gardens claim a very long day's work from their occupants, and it usually consists of morning competitions, where the separate choirs 'pace each other on the road to excellence' as Sir Walford Davies once said; then a long afternoon rehearsal of all competitors massed into one choir, and finally an evening concert.

I have many impressive memories of those Festival days. The standard of choral singing is always marvellously high, and I can think of the complete 'Matthew Passion', Brahms' 'Requiem', and works like Parry's *Job* and Vaughan Williams' 'Sea Symphony' at places like Petersfield, Winchester, Andover, Newbury, Newtown, Truro and Tunbridge Wells, and also at the Mary Wakefield Festival at Kendal, which was the foundation of the movement and from which radiated many others, notably Leith Hill, which was directed by Dr Vaughan Williams for very many years. I had the privilege of conducting at Petersfield for twenty years, and looked forward to these annual events with great keenness.

I think I must tell the story which, although it has gone the rounds, did really refer to me, and was told me within a few hours of its occurrence. There were often friends who came to sing in the chorus at Petersfield, and one of these, who was immensely impressed by the quick reaction of the choirs ('So much more alive than the Bach Choir', she used to say), had just responded to my request at the start of the rehearsal for the choirs to

stand up. As she was in the first row and pretty tall, she turned to the
soprano just behind her and said 'Is it all right, can you see the conductor?'
'Oh yes, miss, thank you; you see I saw him last year.'

The Petersfield mood was always very free and easy and on one occasion
in the early days we were being visited by a young conductor who came
down for a day or two. We asked him to take over 'The Revenge' by
Stanford, which he obviously knew very well. He gave us a brilliant
performance and we all enjoyed it immensely—perhaps you won't wonder;
his name was Malcolm Sargent.

When Allen took over the Royal College he did his best to spread a
sense of responsibility and opportunity as widely as possible, where the
activities of students had previously been considerably restricted. There
were soon three orchestras instead of one, the number of students'
concerts was greatly increased, a new series of informal concerts started
for the third-raters. It was all most stimulating, and I found myself
drifting there almost every day of the week, although my official calls were
never for more than three.

I wish I had kept some hour-to-hour record for a few weeks at this time
—for life soon became almost unbearably full, and I wonder now why I
often had no time to get back to Chelsea to change in the evening as
evening dress was usually worn in those days. I certainly went to a great
many concerts, and took students to hear all the rehearsals we could get
into, notably those of Albert Coates, who, when he arrived here after the
war, did a great deal to pull up the rather wrinkled socks of London
orchestral performance. I remember hearing him spend fifty minutes on
the *Meistersinger* Overture, every moment badly needed. This was the
first rehearsal after his return, and we are now apt to forget what great
things he did for our music in the early twenties, when, except for Sir
Henry's sterling work, our standards were pretty low.

Amongst my varied activities was a governorship of the Old Vic, which
I reluctantly gave up when I went to Birmingham. Lilian Baylis was then
at the height of her power, and obviously revelling in her daily task of
making bricks with one wisp of straw each. Another member of the board
whom I was very happy to meet again was my old friend the Rev. Edward
Gordon of St John's, Waterloo Road, the Vic's parish church, whom,
with his delightful family, I have described earlier.

It so happened that several of my school friends were on the staff of
Lancing College, and they jointly asked me to spend a very pleasant
weekend with them there: they were W. B. Harris, who later took over
his brother's famous preparatory school, St Ronan's, at Worthing;
G. L. Troutbeck who later returned to Westminster; also a Carthusian
who lived close to my home in Cheshire, J. F. Roxburgh who later
became first Headmaster of Stowe. I knew the Music Master, Alexander

Brent Smith, who had just won a noble battle for Vaughan Williams' 'For All the Saints'. There was a strong party who objected to his supplanting the old Barnby tune, and so for (I think) a half-term they sang the hymn week after week to alternate tunes. Needless to say repetitions sent Vaughan Williams upwards, and Brent won his battle.

We went for a good walk along the downs on Sunday afternoon, but were caught in an unexpected shower near Chanctonbury Ring. We were soaked, and as I had nothing else but my dinner jacket to change into, I had to appear at school tea looking much too festive. Amongst the boys I was introduced to were two Trevelyan brothers, whose sister Mary was a pupil of mine at the Royal College, and was then going to an organist's post in Oxford. All three have distinguished themselves in public service.

About this time, when so many warriors were returning to civil life, there were a number of orchestral players who had to find new jobs, and decided to form themselves into a symphony orchestra for which they took the title British—it will be remembered that the only other symphony orchestra at that time was the London Symphony Orchestra. They chose as their conductor Raymond Roze, who had had a good deal of theatrical experience, and whose mother, Marie Roze, was one of the most famous 'Carmens' of her time. They had only given a few successful concerts when Roze died, and I became his fortunate successor. The honorary secretary of the orchestra was the young Eugene Cruft, who led the double basses, and became a life-long friend and colleague, as leader in the B.B.C. Symphony Orchestra, on the staff of the Royal College of Music, and with other pleasant contacts. He has always found time for useful jobs outside, or more accurately, beside music, for a few years ago, on his eightieth birthday he was given a worthily generous testimonial by the Royal Society of Musicians after he had served it as Honorary Treasurer for more than twenty years. The son of a respected viola player in the London Symphony Orchestra, he has himself two sons, John, now Musical Director of the Arts Council, and Adrian, my godson, who is well known as a composer, and like his father, has recently found extra time to act as an energetic President of the Composers' League. The fourth generation of this distinguished family is now coming into prominence: Benedict, the son of John, has recently given a striking performance of the Sibelius Violin Concerto with the British Youth Symphony Orchestra at a concert in Birmingham organized by the Schools Music Association.

The British Symphony Orchestra, as an ex-service institution, caught the eye of a go-ahead manager who had had considerable experience of operatic tours, but not so much in the symphonic field. He organized a series of what he decided to call super-concerts in the Kingsway Hall (I believe this was the first introduction to orchestral music of what is now the most sought-after recording studio in London) with some very distinguished soloists with whom he was already in contact on account of his many tours. Unfortunately, after half-a-dozen concerts or so the gentleman's sudden bankruptcy put an abrupt end to the series, but later we were able to give a series of Sunday afternoon concerts at the old building of the People's Palace in Mile End Road. Greatly daring, I used to preface the performance with a few words of introduction until I found that most of the audience had come from the West End and knew as much as I did about the music. I think this experience cured me of any further desire to talk to my audiences. One other pleasant thing about the place was the swimming pool next door, to which several of us would repair after the concert. The Governors of the People's Palace were very kind to the project, and I believe we were allowed to use the hall rent free. I have a recollection of one interview with the Chairman, Sir William Macartney, in the handsome board-room at Lord's, where he was also a Governor.

It has not been my good fortune to see inside many of the great London homes of the early days, but a few have been opened at times, and it is fun to think about them. Soon after the first war an energetic Yorkshireman named Eaglefield Hull, who had written several not very scholarly textbooks, had the idea of founding a British Music Society, which with a large number of branches in the North particularly, gave a helpful fillip to music-making in the country, and particularly to the composers who had nothing like the opportunities that they get nowadays. I still have the B.M.S. list of current British music, and its usefulness is by no means over. Dr Hull managed to collect an influential committee, including Lord Howard de Walden, who very kindly offered to give a party at Seaford House, Belgrave Square, for the first of the B.M.S. conferences. I vividly remember the scene as the guests trooped up the splendid staircase to be received by Lord and Lady Howard (who were more than delighted when one of their guests responded to their welcome with a 'Nicely, thanks'). In those days staircases were staircases! Often occupying the centre of the block, they were usually lit by a very large skylight (and of course a wonderful chandelier) and after rising from the hall they split to the left and right, and twin flights led you to the upper floor. Another feature of many of the town houses was that they stood in the corner of a square, and looked across diagonally to the far corner giving the impression of looking through an enormous garden. Neither Grosvenor House nor Dorchester House, which have given way to the hotels of the same name, enjoyed this corner effect, but both looked across to Hyde Park. Devonshire House in Piccadilly not only enjoyed a frontage on the Green Park, but had a fine garden behind. It is hard to believe that the whole block bordered now by Piccadilly, Berkeley Street, Berkeley Square and Stratton Street was occupied by one house in a garden. During the last

The author at a meeting of the ISCM jury at E. J. Dent's house at Cambridge, 1931: (*l. to r.*) Koechlin, Casella, Boult, Berg (holding score of Webern's op. 21 symphony), Dent, Fitelberg and Defauw

With Dame Ethel Smyth and Sir Henry J. Wood, about 1928

Yehudi Menuhin with the composer
at Abbey Road Studios at the time
of the recording of Sir Edward
Elgar's Violin Concerto, 1932

Yehudi Menuhin with
the author, 1965

months of the 1914 war I lived in the Bath Club, and the building at 34 Dover Street ran right through to Berkeley Street, where the ladies had their entrance, and their rooms looked over the Duke of Devonshire's beautiful grounds.

Another house which intrigued some of us in our school days was the town house of the Duke of Portland, in the centre of the west side of Cavendish Square. The house was on the Square, but the garden ran right back to Wimpole Street, and on top of its wall was a very high screen of opaque glass which must have made the garden completely private. There were queer stories about various members of the family in the 1890s—it was said that one of them owned and managed Druce's in Baker Street, and had a secret passage from his garden to the shop. I only know that when the house was demolished some time about 1906 to make way for Harcourt House in Cavendish Square, and the Post Office in Wimpole Street was built at the garden end, a very strict guard was kept on the entrances, and one inquisitive youngster in a top hat, who tried to get into the garden through the workmen's gate in Wimpole Street, was firmly sent about his business.

I often went home to Cheshire for weekends. My father's health had been getting worse, as war restrictions made his diet more difficult to follow, and we all felt that something drastic must be done, as his weight had gone down alarmingly. So young Dr John Weir came up for a weekend—with the ultimate result that Father lived for thirty-one more years—he was ninety-six when he died. But as soon as the war finished he decided to give up his business and move: my mother had always wanted to live in the South, and after a good deal of house-hunting they came to the edge of the New Forest, naturally a much simpler proposition for my weekends. I had also hoped they would come to London a good deal: the Chelsea flat was big enough, and my mother loved it. I suggested that father should join the Savile Club and two of my friends there kindly put him up—I just signed the supporting column 'to show there was no ill feeling', and was rather surprised to get the usual circular asking what I knew of the candidate. Being more fortunate (or more of a prig) than Sir Osbert Sitwell, I replied as follows: 'You have asked me what I know of Mr Cedric Boult in regard to his candidature for membership. I have known him for thirty-one years during which he has performed the duties of a father to my complete satisfaction'. But he was a countryman, and his release from business made him realize this more than ever. He resigned after a few years, having hardly spent any time in London, but a great deal on his farm.

Looking back I find it hard to see how I can have been so busy. I had to have a secretary for a few hours in the morning, and as I said before, I often didn't get back to change in the evening. After three years it was becoming increasingly clear that if I wanted to become a conductor, I must do something decisive about it. I had the College, where Stanford was doing less and leaving more to me, and occasional guest dates in London, in the provinces, and abroad, but it wasn't a career. I finally decided that if nothing appeared by the summer of 1924 I should go off to Canada and/or U.S.A., where, as I have mentioned, I had already had an exciting trip with Robin Barrington-Ward. I hadn't much idea what I should do, but I wanted to conduct. Thanks to Sir Henry Wood a glimmer of light appeared on the horizon. In the summer of 1923 he resigned from the Birmingham Festival Choral Society, a magnificent choir with a splendid body of tenors (Wales wasn't far off), and proposed me as his successor. I was delighted. Sir Henry told me he only resigned because orchestral conditions were so hopeless: one hectic rehearsal with soloists on the morning of the concert, and no opportunity for the choir to hear the orchestra or get balanced with them, until the concert itself. He had just tried to do Beethoven's 'Mass' under those conditions, and he couldn't go on. I was in no mood to pick or choose and cheerfully accepted the difficulties, also Sir Henry's plans for 1923/4 which included the Verdi 'Requiem' and Ethel Smyth's 'Mass' which had never been performed since Barnby produced it at the Albert Hall in 1893. I soon found that I could still concentrate mostly on the choir even at the concert, for a young man named Paul Beard, who in his early twenties had just been promoted to the leadership, could be trusted to lead the orchestra and control it perfectly. He and I were to work together for twenty-seven years (there was a six-year gap after I left Birmingham), and from the conductor's point of view, it was a perfect partnership. Toscanini was alleged to have said that he had never known a finer leader.

Sir Henry was always most kind to younger musicians and I was no exception. He came with me one night to the Diaghilev Ballet as he was anxious to hear and see the Falla *Three-cornered Hat*, then quite new to London. I remember an amusing story he told me about his anti-union activities, which gave a fine insight into his judgment of human nature. After the bankruptcy of Mr Robert Newman, when the Queen's Hall Orchestra was formed into a limited company with Sir Edgar Speyer as chairman, it was arranged at Sir Henry's request to have a rehearsal every Friday morning throughout the season, which could be used for the Sunday concerts, hitherto unrehearsed, or as an extra for the Saturday Symphony Concerts, in fact, anything Sir Henry wanted. Just before he left for his early pre-Promenade holiday, he heard a report that the union might try to confine these rehearsals to music for the very familiar Sunday programmes, which of course didn't suit him at all. So he sent telegrams to the whole orchestra to come to Queen's Hall at 9 on the morning on which he was leaving for his holiday. When he got to the hall, this is all he said: 'Ladies and gentlemen, I have just heard that there is a move on foot to restrict our new Friday rehearsals to music for the following Sunday. If you wish, I will agree to this suggestion, but I would remind you that it isn't much fun rehearsing the *Tannhäuser* Overture desk by desk'. He heard no more of the idea.

It was during this winter season in Birmingham that it became clear that all was not well there, and I very soon sensed that the direction of the orchestra might be offered to me. I didn't need to think it over: about fifty concerts in the six winter months with nothing to do in the summer except prepare for the next season, was a plan which suited me perfectly. The offer was made almost conditionally on my becoming resident there, a very wise provision. As it turned out, I never once slept in London during my first three seasons in Birmingham except on the two nights each term after I had conducted concerts at the Royal College of Music.

I shall never forget a very kind letter of welcome which Granville Bantock, Professor of Music at Birmingham, wrote when my appointment was announced. He was doing great work there both at the University and as Director of Music to the Midland Institute. He was an enthusiastic supporter of my work, and the kindest of hosts.

His opposite number, Alfred Hayes, the Director of the literary side of the Midland Institute, a tireless supporter of the City of Birmingham Orchestra, often came to our Sunday morning rehearsals, as well as to the concerts. His name will be known to lovers of Russian literature as he was amongst the earliest translators of Russian books and poetry into English.

He used to tell delightful stories of Bantock and his eccentricities. One day G.B. put his head into Hayes' office and said: 'Come with me to the market; I want to buy a mongoose'. 'What on earth for?' 'We have rats at home and I want to get rid of them.' Bantock lived in the country a good way out of Birmingham then, but did not realize that a mongoose might well exterminate his six-month-old baby in her cradle as well as the rats. He yielded to persuasion and went home with a cat instead.

Hayes vowed also that G.B. one day came into his office bubbling with excitement: 'My dear fellow, I've just discovered an absolute masterpiece, a most lovely piece of chamber music and you won't believe it, it is by Schubert'. After a good deal more enthusiastic description: 'It's a quintet, my dear chap, with two 'cellos, in C'. The fact that Hayes had played the work as a piano duet since he was sixteen was quite irrelevant; Bantock had discovered a masterpiece—and it may well be that a firmer classical background to his wonderfully skilful and imaginative mind might have given his music greater staying power.

One Sunday in Birmingham I met him in the street and he invited me to supper. I accepted with pleasure and as soon as I arrived, Lady

Bantock welcomed me with a question as to whether I could bear to eat
asparagus. I was delighted by the prospect, and so was she: 'Gran has
bought a large barrel of Californian asparagus and we're all sick to death
of it, so we're specially pleased to see you'.

I found Birmingham in every way a happy place to work in. A cheerful
bracing climate—how I noticed this on returning at 9 p.m. after my weekly
day at the R.C.M.—and a wonderful group of city fathers, who all belonged to the Union Club where I often lunched. Some one said that
Edgbaston was responsible for the good government of Birmingham.
Edgbaston was the closest dormitory: it actually began about a mile from
the Town Hall; but only another half mile from there, one came to the
edge of a valley which included ten or twelve houses with thirty-acre
gardens each, one with 200 acres, and a great allotment field of 100 acres,
all joining each other. Big business men, when they retired, had no wish
to move away (as was the general rule in Liverpool for instance). They
stayed where they were, and interested themselves in public work, and so
the public work was well done.

For the first three years I made a point of attending every concert given
by local artists, in fact I was rarely able to dine at home in peace ('home'
was one of these Edgbaston houses with thirty acres, which was being
most efficiently managed as a very private residential hotel).

I soon saw that, nicely though it suited me (and perhaps the main
audience in Birmingham) to have six months without concerts, it was not
at all good for the orchestra to split up and go off to the four winds during
the summer, and I always dreaded the first few weeks of the season, when
root principles had to be restated and seaside habits unlearned. I had
already secured a few fresh fields for our activity in some of the Midland
public schools, and I now began to try and persuade municipalities like
Cheltenham, which we used to visit now and then, to agree to take us on
bodily for a few weeks each summer. I felt that if my committee could get
themselves into the position of being able to offer the orchestra even a
nine or ten months' contract, it was at any rate a step in the right direction.
But I was 'translated' before I could get very far. However, it was a
great satisfaction to see this come about a few years later by alliance
with the B.B.C.: the right result even though the approach had been
different.

It was my privilege, though in the main we concentrated on British
artists (and local artists for our Sunday concerts), to introduce some great
foreigners to Birmingham, notably Bruno Walter, Ernest von Dohnanyi
(who appeared in his usual triple capacity as pianist, composer and conductor in the same concert) and Ansermet, whose performance of the
Lohengrin Prelude was a revelation. Similarly the great classics were the
background of our repertoire, but once or twice a season we slipped off the

beaten track, Bartók's 'Dance Suite' when it was only a year old; Mahler's IVth and his 'Song of the Earth', and of course, British works like the Vaughan Williams symphonies, 'The Planets', Bax, Bantock, Ireland. Those six seasons were to be the only time in my life that I have been responsible for my own programmes. Looking back I think they covered the ground reasonably well.

I have said that we visited some of the nearer public schools: Rugby, Oundle, Shrewsbury, Repton. But our most exciting excursions were to Cheltenham, which more than once invited us to help them honour their great fellow townsman Gustav Holst in their fine Town Hall. His wonderfully moving work 'Egdon Heath' I think had its first English performance on one of these occasions, and of course, we played many of his other things.

The Birmingham City Orchestra was sometimes engaged for festivals which took place in Wales as a result of the boost to music which Walford Davies had inspired all over the country. It was thus that I was privileged first to go to Gregynog, Montgomeryshire, that wonderful home of the arts, where so many remarkable things took place until the outbreak of war and the Misses Davies' illnesses and death.

There were also festivals at Aberystwyth, and Eisteddfodau at Machynlleth and Mold during these times, and in the summer, I travelled mostly by road. In particular I remember a wonderful mountain road from Aberystwyth to Birmingham. I sometimes made use of the four earliest hours of daylight—starting with a bathe in the sea at 4 a.m., and getting to Birmingham for breakfast.

As I have said, my mother was an inveterate traveller, and had often said she wanted to see Stockholm. In 1926 I noticed a rather attractive Northern Capital cruise in the *Arcadian*, and we jumped at it. We discovered that our friend Sir John Weir was coming too, which added to the pleasure—his presence turned out to be of great support to me as my mother had a bad attack of asthma on the trip. This was unusual as the sea usually suited her. Hamburg, Oslo, Lubeck came first, then we spent one day at Visby (Gothland) the smallest, I suppose, of the Hansa towns. Then came Stockholm, including, of course, the fascinating approach up the harbour, and the voyage by launch to Saltsjöbaden. Back by Helsinki with rocks in its harbour which alarmed our navigators, Danzig with its magnificent rows of warehouses, and Copenhagen last. A pleasant and easy way of getting a glimpse of many things: Danzig was most impressive and unexpected, and one deplored the feverish activity along the coast where Gdynia was beginning to arise. It seemed so outrageous to find Danzig half deserted, while a new port was being built five miles away; surely such nationalism could have been tempered by common sense. I had expected to find at any rate some samples of Russia in Helsinki,

which had gained its independence less than ten years before. One church
and the cabhorses' harness were all I could find.

In the autumn of 1927 a persistent cough refused to yield to treatment,
and early in December I was shipped off to Egypt. I went by way of Milan
and Venice, and thought if I had a night in Milan, I might get a chance of
hearing Toscanini, for the first time. I craned out of the cab to see what
was going on, and presently *Fidelio* unmistakably appeared on a poster.
I rushed off to the Scala to get a ticket, only to find men up ladders pasting
blue slips across the bills to say that Signora Whatnot was ill, therefore
there would be no performance. I could have wept, and after looking at
the Cathedral, I went back to the hotel and an early bed. I was asleep
before the *Fidelio* had been timed to begin—and slept for twelve hours.
Perhaps Fate had intervened to prevent me disgracing myself by falling
asleep in a seat at the Scala!

Next day Venice, and a romantic trip from the hotel to the ship, which,
looked at from the gondola, appeared gigantic. It was indeed said to be
10,000 tons. I soon decided that 9,900 of them must have been above the
water level. Italian ships differ markedly from our own in several respects.
They are beautifully decorated, and both private and public rooms are
charming until one tries to do anything. Perhaps it may be said that
passengers on pleasure trips shouldn't try to do anything. You see a most
comfortable chair and settle down to read, only to discover that the light
is shining directly in your eyes. Any chair that has the light over one's
shoulder is of the ancestral bolt-upright variety. Again in my cabin I never
found anywhere to put a pair of trousers unless I rolled them up tight and
stuffed them into a small drawer. The cabin was delightfully furnished
with little curtains and looking glasses all over the place, but when I
approached any of them, razor in hand, I always found a strong light
focused on the top of my head, which even at that comparatively early
age, *could* not have been shaved. I suppose it was unwise to expect
Italian merchant navy officers to look anything like the British type that
we all admire; anyhow our Italian officers intrigued me: they sat at the
next table and looked, I thought, most like a party of jolly friars in fancy
dress. The hundred tons below the water line did not suffice to keep the
ship anything like steady—we bobbed down the Adriatic to Brindisi, and
there waited for a respite of a few hours. But we arrived at Alexandria on
time and I first encountered the Middle East. I hadn't expected quite that
kind of pandemonium with about a dozen porters screaming and fighting
for each passenger. However, I eventually got to the train and from the
train to the cab at Cairo. I had booked for the Cook Nile vessel which left
the day after I arrived, and discovered that you might go on board the
night before on giving notice. I gave notice in London but it hadn't
reached Cairo, so I found a sleeping ship, but the cabman soon kicked up

some hooded figures which were reclining on the deck, and my cabin was found, also some mineral water and biscuits.

Then began an idyllic trip. The ship steamed up the Nile, and one lazily watched the gentle traffic, and the still gentler drawers of water who were working pumping contrivances that had probably been unaltered for 2,000 years. Almost once a day we stopped, mounted donkeys and rode off to a temple nearby, over which we were conducted in three languages by the dark Dragoman who travelled with us. Away to East and West were always the two red walls of the desert, sometimes near, sometimes far, according to the windings of the Nile. The sunsets were incredible.

We got to Luxor at full moon so a party was made up to go to Karnak that very night. I was to see it thus for the first time. The ship waited two days but I had arranged a longer stay, and transferred to the small hotel, situated just behind the Winter Palace: in the same garden, under the same management, but much cheaper—rather the principle of the Inns in America. I spent Christmas in Luxor—actually I had my Christmas Day in the Valley of the Kings. I went there fairly often, walking the seven miles there and back (to the disgust of the donkey boys) and lunching in Cook's Rest House. One could spend a long time looking at the wall paintings. But I think Karnak was the deepest impression I brought away. I went again by moonlight (walking by myself) and at one moment thought I shouldn't get there as a dog came out of a village on the way and forbade me the road. Luckily a villager soon appeared and one monosyllable from him sent the dog packing.

On to Assuan after a fortnight and another week at the hotel there. This was where the Cook boat turned round, but I had discovered a further trip managed by the Sudan Government Railways, five days in all, I think. We left Assuan on the mail steamer for Wadi Halfa. This was a smaller, but much more businesslike affair than Cook's. She steamed all night, instead of tying up at sunset, but she did make fast in the small hours on arrival at Abu Simbel. At this point the Nile flows close past the rock, out of which the great temple, including the gigantic figures on each side of the entrance are all carved, in such a way that on midsummer day the rising sun shines right through all the temple chambers and onto the inmost altar. Our January sun did not do this, of course, but we could see what happened and the whole magnificence of the place rewarded us for our early rising. At Wadi Halfa the beautiful white desert train was waiting for us and after a night and day across the desert, continually passing mirages of lakes, we got to Khartoum, and felt proud of ourselves as Britons. Where Egypt met us with a yelling chaos, here was order: porters silently waiting to be engaged. Similarly in the bazaars: in Omdurman, instead of being yelled at and bargained over all the time, even the silversmiths would hardly look up from their work if you picked up something, and when you asked for a price they would weigh it and tell you without any sign of haggling.

We went to bed in the train after dining at the hotel, and woke at Wad Medani, a brand new cotton town with a European quarter, and a very tidy native quarter. After a short walk in the town we had breakfast in the train and then got into cars to go through cotton fields to a ginning factory which a young English engineer explained to us, and then on again in our cars; the whole party numbered about twelve. I knew that we were driving away from our train, and wondered what was happening but soon saw it ahead of us: in royal fashion it had come round to meet us. While lunching we were taken on to the Sennar Dam, not long finished, and designed to irrigate an enormous tract for cotton growing in between the Blue and White Niles (which join at Khartoum). Cars again for a drive across the dam (two miles long) and through a forest where monkeys could be seen in the trees. Dinner in the train, and breakfast back in Khartoum, entraining again that night for Halfa and Assuan. Downstream the trip was much quicker, and we hardly stopped at all. I finished with a rather disappointing few days in Cairo, where it actually rained, and the noise, dirt and smells contrasted unpleasantly with the orderliness of Khartoum and Omdurman. The return trip took us up the West coast of Italy: a few hours at Syracuse, an evening view of Etna and an early morning one of Vesuvius' malevolent glow. Naples next day for a few hours also. Having still a few days to spare and having never seen the Riviera, I took the coast train from Genoa where we landed, and stopped two days at Nice to prepare myself for an English February.

Chapter Seven

VICTORIAN FRIENDS IN EDWARDIAN TIMES

ONE OF my first duties on coming home to Lancashire after each term at Westminster was to 'go and see Mrs Wood'. Our house stood alone at the bottom of one of the many roads in Blundell-sands that ran straight down to the shore—a broad expanse of fine hard sand on which one could walk, ride, drive, and even play hockey.

At the bottom of the next parallel road lived Mrs Wood, four or five minutes' walk through the sandhills, but quite a long way round by road. She was a wonderful example of the type which modelled itself on Queen Victoria, to whom the stern rules of convention meant a great deal; we called her 'very proper'. She was the soul of kindness and many grand-children of several families (she had been twice widowed) used to stay with her for long periods. She was horrified one day to go into her drawing-room and find three grand-daughters turning cartwheels across the room. Her protests were met with this excuse: 'Well, Grandmama, we were doing it a lot yesterday at the Boults' and Olive [my sister] is very good at it'. The incident was thereupon summarily closed: 'No, my dears, I'm afraid you must be mistaken; I'm quite sure dear Olive would never dream of doing such a thing'.

She herself gave me a delightful reason for her rather dictatorial nature. Soon after she was first married she had ordered beef from her butcher, and he had sent her mutton instead. When she protested next day he replied that he did not think it could matter much to her, as she had not been very firm about it. 'So that, dear Adrian, is the reason why I have always been very firm about *everything* ever since.'

On one of my visits, having asked how things had gone during the term, she added, 'You know, dear Adrian, my nephew Frank Schuster lives at Westminster quite near the Abbey, and knows a great many actors and musicians. Dr Elgar, the new composer, is a great friend. I will write and tell Frank he must ask you to some of his parties.'

She did so at once, and next term I was invited to go to a concert with Mr Schuster (the only occasion on which I ever heard Hugo Wolf's

'Penthesilea'). I already had a ticket for the concert, but gave mine away and sat with Mr Schuster and we walked together back to Westminster. He didn't seem to mind the prospect of being saddled with the friendship of a lanky fifteen-year-old, because an invitation soon came to an evening party after dinner where I met several musicians who were to influence me greatly.

Frank Schuster himself became a great friend. He spent his life making other people happy. Both at 22 Old Queen Street, and at a charming riverside house near Bray he entertained tirelessly, and never seemed to mind what his guests said or did, provided they were enjoying themselves. When the great evening came, I was shown straight into the dining room where I found besides our host and Edward Elgar, Generalmusik-direktor Fritz Volbach of Mainz, who had recently conducted 'The Apostles' there in the presence of the composer and Mr Schuster, who had also visited other Rhine towns for performances of Elgar works. Frank afterwards insisted that Volbach had arrived in full evening dress (he was to stay a week) and that he never appeared in anything else. Also dining were Mr (later Sir) Claude Phillips, the leading art critic, who was Keeper of the Wallace Collection and wrote a weekly column on art for the *Daily Telegraph*, and Dr Theo Lierhammer, an Austrian baritone, who became a great friend. He sang 'Anakreons Grab' with Volbach at the piano, my first acquaintance with that lovely song of Hugo Wolf.

Elgar had just received the engraved score of 'The Kingdom', and was delighted with the beautiful work that Novello's experts had put into it. We were sitting together on the long seat which stretched round three sides of the Old Queen Street music room, looking at the score and its accurate alignments, when our host, who had been digging in Miss Edith Clegg's case and discovered a song by Elgar, came over and said: 'Edward, you must come and meet Miss Clegg, who is going to sing "After"'. The great man got up, walked over and shook hands with the remark, 'Well, you have spoiled my evening for me'. A joke, of course, but not calculated to put heart into a nervous young artist, just about to perform to a rather impressive crowd of people. I was curious why a man, who was usually so friendly and helpful, should have this kink about not being interested in his own music, a pose which sometimes caused him to say and do rather absurd things.

When he came to live in London he entertained a good deal in Hampstead, and he and Lady Elgar were very kind to me. I remember at tea one day, when Mr and Mrs Ernest Newman were there too, the conversation turned to books, and they capped each other's knowledge of out-of-the-way ones (mostly novels) to my intense bewilderment and admiration.

One day too when a Royal College student was to play the Violin Concerto at an orchestral concert, we came and played it to Elgar who gave us both most helpful advice. He also came to Queen's Hall in 1918 to hear me rehearse 'In the South' with the London Symphony Orchestra, and wrote charmingly in my score on that occasion.

'In the South' was dedicated to Frank Schuster, and was first played at the Covent Garden Elgar Festival of 1904. An amusing contretemps occurred later over the manuscript full score of the work. During the war Mrs Elgar Blake made a list of her father's manuscripts and their whereabouts and asked me whether I knew where 'In the South' then was. I had had a wonderful legacy, as I shall tell later, from Frank Schuster consisting of all his music, but he had excepted this manuscript and the full scores of the Elgar oratorios.

These had very properly gone to the Royal Academy of Music, of which he had been a governor for many years. Mrs Blake wrote to confirm this with the R.A.M., but their librarians knew nothing of the whereabouts of the score. Somerset House confirmed the legacy, but it was only after a thorough hunt at the R.A.M. that the manuscript was discovered in a brown paper parcel labelled 'Brahms'. I should love to meet the man who did up that parcel, and ask him 'Why Brahms?' Or had Mr Schuster done it up some time without noticing the writing, and the Academy put it away without opening it?

On the occasion of Elgar's seventy-fifth birthday, the B.B.C. devoted three concerts to his music. He conducted parts of these, and at the end of the final rehearsal he made a moving speech of thanks to the orchestra, thinking not only of the present concerts, but reviewing his life's association with British musicians, and the very wonderful experiences they had had together. It was not his farewell; he conducted the orchestra several times later, and I particularly treasure the memory of a magnificently deliberate and dignified performance of 'Cockaigne' in Queen's Hall in 1932.

In the early twenties Elgar used sometimes to give luncheon parties at his club in St James's Street. He would invite a dozen of us young musicians, and excellent food would be mixed with cheerful conversation, for he was a capital raconteur. Once he invited Richard Strauss and his son, who were in London, it was said, to collect the royalties Strauss' performances had accumulated during the war.

The language difficulty made matters rather sticky conversationally (the food was as good as ever), and it boiled down to alternate stories told by Strauss (in German) and Elgar (in English), and then translated by Max Mossel or Victor Beigel, with everyone else quietly listening.

Strauss came to London many times, of course. I heard him conduct the first English performance of 'Heldenleben', and the summer of 1914 was memorable for his performance of the Mozart G minor, which I have described elsewhere. Later again he conducted 'Till Eulenspiegel' in the

Maida Vale B.B.C. Studio, and a day or two after that came again to hear
Menuhin play the Paganini D major concerto. He asked to sit close to the
orchestra, and I was astonished to hear a powerful hissing at the end of the
first movement. I looked round and saw the guest was beckoning to me
most vehemently. I thought he must be ill, so jumped down hastily,
hoping that our soloist would manage to tune a bit to cover up this grave
interruption. When I had bent over the armchair I heard a stentorian
stage whisper: 'It always amuses me to hear that idiotic [pöldsinnig]
music Paganini manages to put into his tuttis'. He then composed himself
for the second movement.

Mention of Yehudi Menuhin makes it quite impossible not to pay a
tribute to this splendid artist and man. I was privileged recently to make a
presentation to him, and thus able to quote my friend Francis Toye, who
writing many years ago of Paderewski's last visit to London said, 'Whatever one feels about Mr Paderewski as a pianist, no one can deny that he is
to us the greatest man who plays the piano'. It is impossible not to feel
that Yehudi Menuhin is now the greatest man in the profession, and more,
he is a pioneer, unconscious perhaps, in the coming art and science of
music therapy. I have a friend who suffers from chronic ill health, and she
has repeatedly found that, after hearing him play, her health improves for
several days.

The Violin Concerto has now dropped into its place in the Elgar
literature, and modern criticism may find it rather long-winded and
cumbersome with all its great beauty, but at the time we found it was
breaking new ground in a striking way on two points of concerto structure,
most notably the way the cadenza grew out of the final movement and
gathered up material from the whole work, incidentally making use of an
absolutely new colour in the string accompaniment. The first entry of the
solo violin, too, in the heart of the texture in the middle of a sequential
passage, unobtrusively yet immensely telling, gave a real thrill when we
first heard it that night.

Elgar's sense of orchestral colour was unmatched and only his friend
Strauss could compete with him in the skilful use of instruments. He was
always listening for new sounds and once in the Queen's Hall balcony
with him, while the orchestra was tuning up before a concert, I suddenly
felt his elbow in my ribs: 'Listen to the trumpet, Adrian. Prodigious, isn't
it? And if I wrote anything like that for him he would say it was unplay-
able!' We all know the kind of fireworks that orchestras delight in when
waiting for a concert to begin.

Chamber music wasn't very much in Elgar's field, but he did write the
Quartet and Quintet close together; very soon after he had finished the
Violin Sonata which Willie Reed first played with Sir Landon Ronald in
the Aeolian Hall.

There were parties both at Old Queen Street and Bray for the two larger works, and I played an uneasy part in the Quintet in which William Murdoch asked me to turn over for him. Elgar's opulent manuscript spread sometimes to the extent of one bar to a page, and so the page turner had few dull moments when the music was moving fast. I don't know why the work hadn't been engraved beforehand. Elgar's sure touch enabled him usually to have this done in advance, and I saw him hand a printed full score at the Leeds Festival in 1913 to Arthur Nikisch who had come down from the platform to hear Elgar take the final rehearsal of the première of 'Falstaff'. It is interesting to see how composers differ in this respect. I have read that Brahms would never allow an orchestral work of his to be engraved until he had heard it at least once. It is known that Mozart had works complete in his head, and delayed writing them down until the last possible minute.

Max Reger told a friend that he had three orchestral works completed and was waiting for time to write them down, while on the other hand Vaughan Williams' publishers always expected to issue sheets of corrections for some time after his first performances. His deafness in later life may have stimulated alterations which played for safety. He would sometimes call out at rehearsal: 'Can you hear the oboe?'—it was usually the oboe—and he was not quite reassured even if one said 'yes'.

I had an early experience with Vaughan Williams over the first performance of the Pastoral Symphony. My work at the Royal College of Music enabled us (with Sir Hugh Allen's ready permission) to have two or three rehearsals of the symphony with the College Orchestra well before the first performance at a Royal Philharmonic concert. I don't remember whether the composer altered it much: I don't think he did. I had forgotten to arrange for a soprano to be on hand for the last movement, and so it was played (as cued in the score and part) by the solo clarinet so charmingly that the composer said it must be played that way at the College concert. The name of the young student responsible was Frederick Thurston, subsequently and until his untimely death, England's leading player.

Throughout this rehearsal Vaughan Williams kept on urging me to 'keep it moving'. My preliminary study of the work had convinced me that its placid and leisurely mood demanded a slow pace. Before we were allowed to see it, he used to say: 'I've written a new tune—it's in four movements, all slow, so no one will like it'. But he made me speed it up and I went on doing so for several years, during which I was working in Birmingham out of touch with London. Much later, in Prague, I think, he came to a rehearsal, and said at the close: 'It's too fast from beginning to end'.

I reminded him of his instructions at the first performance, and his answer was beautifully characteristic. 'Oh yes, but I've heard it a good deal since then, and I've conducted it too, and I see that it isn't as boring as I first thought it was, so it can go slower.'

I have said that another of the guests that night at Old Queen Street was the Austrian singer, Dr Theo Lierhammer. As soon as my voice broke I went to him for lessons, and also accompanied him now and then. He was a great character, and never troubled to improve his ghastly German accent. He had been on the staff of the Royal Academy of Music for some time, but was caught in Austria by the 1914 war, and settled in Vienna after that. I used to see him there, and also in the Salzkammergut where he always went for his holidays.

One day, when I was about eighteen, he interrupted our lesson with this astonishing proposal, 'My old friend Mrs Cornwallis-West has written to say she is having Kaiser William II to lunch on Saturday week, and wants me to go and sing afterwards. She says I am to bring someone with me to accompany and he must be nice because we are to stay on for the weekend. Will you come?' I wondered what the school authorities would say at the unheard-of suggestion that I should take Saturday morning school off (although all the Jews in the school always did), but they were kind, and we set off from Waterloo when the great day came.

The scene was Newlands Manor, near Lymington, and the Kaiser was spending a fortnight convalescing at Highcliffe Castle, near Bournemouth. We arrived while lunch was going on, and were shown to a diminutive room (which was destined to be my bedroom) in which Dr Lierhammer, who was frantically nervous, paced round and round like a caged lion. I can't remember whether we were given lunch, but think we must have had sandwiches in the bedroom. After what seemed an age we were shepherded to the drawing-room and soon afterwards the Royal Party came in. I promptly struck up 'Ombra mai fu', followed by a song by Henschel, and after that we all went into the garden where the Emperor planted a tree, and soon afterwards departed. Mrs Cornwallis-West was the well-known hostess who *Punch* had suggested should be sent to South Africa to catch General de Wet, whose skilfully evasive tactics were prolonging the war there. She had, it was said, successfully caught the two richest noblemen in England and Germany for her two daughters, and she ought to be just as clever with the General.

Colonel and Mrs Cornwallis-West were always in a rather poverty-stricken condition which never prevented them doing whatever they wanted. As soon as the Emperor left, the Colonel announced that if he had only had a little longer notice of his visit, he would have thought about buying a new stair-carpet. 'Stair-carpet, Wallis,' said his lady promptly, 'if you'll get me a new stair-carpet I'll invite the Prince of Wales next week.' Their other house was Ruthin Castle in Denbighshire, quite near our home in Cheshire, and the country resounded with her exploits. It was said that the Prince of Wales (the future King Edward VII) was staying there once for Chester races, and his hostess only discovered at the last minute that the bath he was to use badly needed a coat of enamel. This was given it but too late and His Royal Highness stuck firmly to it. He was not at all amused.

Mrs Cornwallis-West never minded a joke against herself. At tea she told us of a recent experience at Ruthin, where the roof leaked badly. The drips were dangerously near her bed and she put up her umbrella over it, and also wore a scarf to protect her head from the frightful draught in the room. Just before she got into bed she looked in the glass and saw a wrinkle on her forehead and stuck a postage stamp on it. Next morning a new maid came in with her tea, gave her one look, dropped the tray with a scream and was never seen again.

Dr Lierhammer was a remarkable singer; he had a small voice with a compass of little more than an octave, but he was often congratulated on the extent of his range simply because he had such control of tone-quality that it sounded like a voice with a very large compass. He gave a recital, usually at the Aeolian Hall every summer and followed it a few weeks later with an annual pupils' concert. Both events were remarkable for nervous crises. There was a story that once at a pupils' concert in one of those queer silences just before an artist comes on to the platform Lierhammer's frantic voice was heard from backstage saying 'Miss Hoskins, *have you blawn your nawse*?'

He had ample command of English, but could not articulate. This used to show when he sang English songs (he was particularly fond of Arthur Somervell), but his French accent was better. He gave his private lessons in his flat in Hanover Street close to the Royal Academy of Music, at that time in Hanover Square. We were let in by the caretaker, and climbed to the third floor where we rattled the door knocker. A lesson was usually going on and he would dash to the door, open it with 'Haow do you do? Please vill you gom in and take off?' One cold day I came without a coat, and he added, horrorstruck, 'Bott you have no goat? Bott haow you are freevolous!'

He was once engaged to take part in a private performance of a Requiem that had never been performed in public. Everybody was soberly dressed; everybody knew that the Requiem had been the outcome of a personal bereavement. The solitary exception was one of the lady soloists, who scandalized everyone by appearing in gaudy clothes with an enormous hat surmounted by several large feathers. 'All viggly', said the Doctor.

I have remarked that Frank Schuster spent his life making other people happy, and there is no end to the stories of his befriending actors and musicians. I have already mentioned the Elgar Festival of 1904 at Covent

Garden. This grew out of his friendship with the redoubtable Harry
Higgins, Chairman of the Royal Opera Syndicate. Frank once told me how
it began. But I must preface his story with the fact that Lady Elgar was
very tiny indeed, and had a quiet, intimate way of speaking. This caused
her to come close up to anyone to whom she had anything important to
say. As Frank put it, 'You know the way dear Alice used to come up to one
and confide in one's tummy? Well, one day she said to my tummy, "Frank,
dear, we are always going to Gloucester Festivals or Leeds Festivals and
so on. Don't you think we might have an Elgar Festival some time?"
My tummy reported what she had said and I went off to see Harry Higgins
and that's how it all began.'

I once met Mr Higgins at dinner at Old Queen Street, and when I was
Assistant Musical Director at Covent Garden in 1926 I often saw him at
rehearsals. It is impossible to realize how formidable anyone can be without saying a word, provided he stages himself properly. Higgins was very
tall with a big white moustache and imperial, and though faulty surgery
had deprived him of the use of his voice, his whisper could be terrifying.
He had a knack of hissing to attract attention, a sound which could echo
across the opera house and reduce even the orchestra to a tense, expectant
silence. Then would come the comment; usually acid and sarcastic in a
well articulated stage whisper, it would make the poor producer scratch
his head and try again. One day Higgins 'whispered' that the amount of
steam at the (stage) dragon's disposal would disgrace a tea kettle.

I noticed a typical story of Schuster's kindness in the memoirs of Maude
Valérie White, whose many songs were extremely popular when I was a
young man. They are rarely heard now, but there is great beauty, and
sometimes power, in them. She was, I think, living in Rome, and was
looking forward to staying with Frank, who had taken a house in Venice for
some weeks, and had filled it with friends. Miss White became ill and
thought she would have to forgo the visit until she heard that Frank had
extended his tenancy of the house so that she might convalesce there.

Frank was also a master of the art of travelling. Soon after the first war
he said he must go to Bayreuth or Munich at once to see whether the
Wagner spell had lost its power, and I was thrilled to be asked to go too.
The journey to Munich was a wonderful experience, particularly to one
who had had my mother's training: 'Always be the first in any queue,
even if it means going without breakfast or anything else'. Frankie's
amendment to this was: 'If you can't be at the head of the queue, stay
contentedly at the tail end'. I must add that he seemed to have all the luck
as well. He always refused to travel at night, and insisted on sitting in the
middle of every train.

'My dear, we don't want to waste all that money on our journey—let's
go second-class.' Accordingly at Dover we sat ourselves on camp stools

over the stern of the steamer, and waited until she moved outside the harbour. 'Adrian, it is lovely and smooth, shall we go and have lunch?' So we climbed over the barrier in full view of our fellow passengers and proceeded down to the first-class saloon, had our lunches and went back to our camp stools, and *after* that the Purser came for our tickets!

Frank showed no sign of disturbing himself when we reached Calais, where normally I should have been struggling with my luggage in the landing queue. The milling crowd had got itself on to the quay and we were just beginning to think about following when the Purser came past us escorting an impressive lady, who recognized Frank and stopped to exchange a few words with him. It was Queen Amélie of Portugal, and only after Her Majesty had landed did we condescend to follow her on to the quay. We approached the Customs House: 'My dear, the place is swarming with people; we can't possibly go in yet.' So we sat in the sun until the Customs House was practically empty, and the officials thankful to get rid of us, whatever we might have been smuggling. By this time I had given up all hope of getting a decent seat in the train, but we wandered leisurely down the platform until we came to an empty non-smoker, amazingly left in the middle of a full train.

In due time the dining-car waiter came for orders. There were three dinners, at six, seven and eight o'clock. 'Alors,' said Frank placidly, 'nous dinons à neuf heures.' The man looked surprised, but duly booked us, and we enjoyed an excellent quiet meal with only the dining-car staff having theirs at a nearby table. 'My dear, I can't have my food thrown at me like a tennis ball and sit on top of my neighbours while I eat it.'

A small catastrophe overtook us in the Munich hotel. I went to Frank's room the morning after we arrived and found him having his breakfast. This over, he said: 'I will get out the tickets now,' and proceeded to look in his brief-case. After a short hunt he turned to me with a woebegone expression and said: 'I must have forgotten them and they are still in my smallest cupboard at home.' It transpired that the only key to this cupboard was on the chain inseparably attached to him. I knew that he had an elaborate Chubb system with locked cupboards for his butler and his housekeeper each with separate keys, but the one gold key which he always carried opened everything including, apparently, this holy of holies, which I suspected contained many confidential things to which even his devoted butler could not be given access. What then were we to do? We went straight off to the Festival Office and explained our plight. No, they hadn't any record of postal orders for seats, but could issue instructions to the janitors in the theatre that we were to be allowed to sit in any seats which were left empty a few seconds before zero hour. We knew more or less where our seats were, and so this worked quite well. In the autumn after our return Frank gave a party at which the recovered tickets were displayed as a novel form of table decoration.

Frank Schuster had a highly sensitive ear and always insisted on sitting in the middle of Queen's Hall Circle where the orchestral sound was very fine and well balanced. Somewhere about 1910 Sir Henry Wood changed the seating of his strings to the modern system with second violins behind the firsts all on the conductor's left, and all the bass instruments on the right of the platform. Frank promptly took all his tickets back and exchanged them for corner seats on the right, so that the violin tone could come across to him with the bass less prominent; but he still insisted that the new seating was wrong, an opinion which I have also expressed many times. Let me raise the matter again here, since I think it of very great importance.

Few conductors nowadays arrange their orchestras in what I consider is the only right seating plan, with the second violins balancing the firsts at the front of the platform, instead of being tucked in behind them on the conductor's left. If an attentive listener will sit some distance from the platform in a really faithful hall, like the Royal Festival Hall, somewhere near the right-hand wall as you face the platform, he will find that with the modern lay-out of the basses on the extreme right of the platform and the cellos in front of them, their sound will come up to him directly, while that of the violins comes appreciably later; in other words, the tunes of all the orchestral music comes to his ear a little later and therefore much less effectively than the bass. This brings a distorted picture of the music to the ears of nearly half the audience.

I heard a story about Frank Schuster and a former great friend—I believe from schooldays—Kennerley Rumford, the singer, and husband of Clara Butt, one of the most popular ballad singers of the 1890s, who had a voice of remarkable range (somebody once told me he had heard her sing four B flats) but little else except a tall and commanding presence. The story goes that Frank Schuster and Kennerley Rumford, who had seen little of each other since school, went out one day for a bicycle ride. As they went along cheerfully Kennerley said he was going to give his bicycle a name: 'I will call it Santley because it is a Singer.' 'Well,' said Frank, 'I will call mine Clara Butt because it isn't.' He felt the joke had not gone down well, and understood why when a few weeks later the engagement of Miss Butt and Mr Rumford was announced.

One day, after a Crystal Palace concert, we were having tea on the terrace and Frank looked down the hill into the park. 'You see that oak tree down there? I once had a lovely swing on it.' On my exclamation of surprise, he said 'Oh yes, didn't you know we lived here when I was a boy, and my father worked in the City? As a matter of fact my mother refused to clear out when the 1851 Exhibition people wanted to move the Crystal

Palace on to this hill. It was only when Queen Victoria drove down to tea that she gave way and was persuaded to sell it.'

Frank Schuster's friendship with artists took a practical form whenever possible. Gabriel Fauré was also an old friend and for several years running a week in London would be arranged for him. He would stay at Old Queen Street, and there would be a party at which he would play, and any new compositions as well as many old ones would be heard. Our host was never happier than when he could announce something as the first performance in England. Later in the week a Wigmore Hall recital would give the first public performance of the work. A special memory for me was the 'Pavane', exquisitely played by the composer, with Louis Fleury in the important flute solo, and a quartet of singers including Mrs George Swinton, Gervase Elwes and Murray Davey. Naturally, Fauré played the pianoforte part with the full flavour of its delicate humour, in contrast to the melancholy romanticism one sometimes hears attached to it nowadays. I happened to meet Frank Schuster in the street on the morning that Fauré's death was announced. 'I'm driving to Paris this afternoon,' he said. 'Surely I *shall* have some chance of hearing the "Requiem" at last.' He would have been happy to get as many chances of hearing it as we do now.

Dame Nellie Melba, besides being a frequent tenant at Old Queen Street, was also an old friend. I had the good fortune to meet her several times, once when I actually had the honour of conducting for her the little Indian Song of Rimsky-Korsakov. Some musicians who deplored the haphazard way in which the 1919 Armistice Day was celebrated were anxious that music and other arts should be ready with some appropriate organization for moments of national and civic ceremony. I believe that splendid veteran Charles Kennedy Scott, one of the greatest choir conductors I have known, started it off with Frank Thistleton, who has, I suppose, befriended a hundred musicians for every one that most of us have helped. They enlisted the help of Lady Maud Warrender (who gave a number of breakfast parties where the idea was developed), and in order to raise funds, a charity concert took place at the London Coliseum. I can remember nothing of the concert but only the wonderful help that Melba gave us by her appearance, engineered by Lady Maud.

Albert Coates introduced me to Melba. He took me with him to accompany when preparing the opening night of the 1914 Covent Garden season, which was to be *La Bohème*. We went to Melba's club in Dover Street, and after twenty minutes of general talk, Albert said, 'Well, Madame, what about a little rehearsing?' 'Rehearsing?' said the Diva. 'I know my *Bohème* and you do too. Why should we rehearse? I'll tell you this, my dear Coates, that here is my fortissimo' (she sang a single note quite quietly) 'and if you and your something, something orchestra insist on drowning me, my public will decide between us.' So my presence had been unnecessary.

As a matter of fact, it was not quite as easy as that, for the Italian style of performance of Puccini had been modified considerably on the German stage. Coates learnt his Puccini in Dresden, where Schuch was supposed to be the finest Puccini conductor in Germany, but it was not quite the same thing, and it took a little time for things to shake down. The final rehearsal, which usually took about two hours, was still going on at 12.30 when Melba had to go to a lunch engagement, and it finished without her.

She had a generous command of language—no doubt learnt in her early days as an officer's wife—and my mother once heard her slanging an unfortunate maid on a Paris station platform to the surprise and horror of any English-speaking people within earshot.

In the summer of 1926 I had accepted Mrs Courtauld's invitation to act as Percy Pitt's assistant at Covent Garden. He was then holding this post as well as being Director of the B.B.C.'s music. This was Melba's last season, and included the night of her actual farewell, with a moving speech which many people will have heard on record. She often came to other performances and usually arrived with her party at the Stage Door, crossed the stage to the iron door on the O.P. side and went through to her box, the stage box just over the orchestra. She always came in good time, and the stage was empty at the time. Melba had always been a privileged person at Covent Garden (she had her very own dressing-room which was kept empty when she was not singing). Suddenly the mysterious 'Management' decided that this practice must be stopped. No one, of course, had the courage to tell her to bring her friends in by the public entrance; instead the fireman on duty at the iron door was told to lock it and leave his post. I found Melba and her party hammering on the door, stuck on the stage side. I went away to find the fireman, and met one of the 'Management', who told me to go and hide also. I believe she had to go back into the street and walk round, and can imagine she had plenty to say about it.

Schuster had, I believe, served for a year or so in his father's bank in the City and decided that his portion of the family inheritance was all he wanted, and that he could not waste his life making any more money. But he spent unselfishly and entertained a great deal, as I have said, also unobtrusively helping many people. When a crisis loomed in his own affairs, he was prompt and businesslike in dealing with it. I met him one day in St James's Street. 'What do you think has happened? I got a letter yesterday from my bank manager to say that I am overdrawn: the first time in my life. Well, I've let Old Queen Street and we're going to Paris tomorrow where I *have* got a bank balance.' 'We' included his companion and adopted nephew ,a lame New Zealander, one of the many officers he had befriended in the war. 'Anzy' lived with him and married the daughter of a great friend of Frank's to his immense delight.

We didn't ask about the crisis, but six months later we were told that Old Queen Street was to be given up and the Bray cottage enlarged so that it became his only home, and he could go on with all his activities and interests just as before. I wrote a note of sympathy at about the time I thought he would be leaving Westminster, and had a most touching reply: 'The Juggernauts are even now at the door, my dear Adrian, so you couldn't have timed more perfectly your . . . etc.' He said he would never forget that coincidence, and years later after his death, which took place when I was away in Egypt, I was deeply touched when his sister told me that I was to be the possessor of all his music and books on music.

It was a splendid collection—a large number of opera vocal scores, now in Liverpool University Library, and many scores signed by Elgar and Fauré, which I greatly prize. The books included a collection of Wagneriana, including a facsimile of the *Meistersinger* manuscript. I was with him in Munich when he bought it as a present for Elgar. He carried it back himself on the return journey—I think he thought it was too big, heavy and precious to pack, but Elgar had just moved to a tiny flat, where there was no room, and so I am now the lucky possessor.

When I was planning the first post-war trip to Munich with Frank Schuster, Robin Legge, the *Daily Telegraph* music editor, whom I had first met at lunch with Nikisch and who proposed me for membership of the Savile Club, said that I must meet Bruno Walter, and gave me a letter of introduction to him. Walter was most kind and this began a very long and most enjoyable association. He was surprised that I had never met Miss Ethel Smyth (as she then was). This was put right soon after when I gave the second performance of her 'Mass' in Birmingham. We had a great time with the 'Mass'; she was extraordinarily good company, and had delightful friends. She was not the easiest of composers to work for as she enjoyed changing her mind more often than was quite comfortable. Sir Henry Wood very kindly invited us to repeat the performance at one of his Queen's Hall Saturday afternoon concerts, and Dame Ethel's sister, Mrs Charles Hunter, very kindly paid all the expenses for the Choir's visit to London.

A year or two later I ran into Dame Ethel in the street during a Munich Festival: 'You are the man I'm looking for; you've got to come and dine with me at the theatre restaurant to-night during the second act of *Walküre*; all the Walters are coming'.

It happened that I had come a very long way to hear and see the second act of *Walküre*, among other things, but my hesitation was promptly sat on, and I joined a most hilarious and happy party. Muck was conducting, and Bruno having a night off, enjoying himself. We felt particularly

superior when the audience all rushed frantically out for beer and sandwiches in the second interval, while we had dined comfortably and could
go leisurely back for the third act.

Then I learnt a lesson; I thought I knew that act well, but I heard much
in it that I had never heard before, and I decided then and there that to
concentrate on two acts of Wagner was enough for any one evening, and I
have always tried to escape one act, whatever the cost, ever since. It is
worth remembering that in the days when Frederic Austin directed the
British National Opera Company they took the *Ring* on tour once and
spread it over six evenings, with *Walküre* and *Siegfried* taking up three
nights between them and *Götterdämmerung* two.

Bruno Walter has brought the beauty of music to me perhaps more than
anyone else, certainly in later life, and I am grateful to him for a very large
number of lovely experiences. I have described his Munich performances
in 1912. He had collected a fine company, and it already seemed to be the
happy family I found in the twenties when he invited me to a rehearsal
of *Figaro*. He said that he gave *Figaro* at least once every three weeks all
the year round with a single rehearsal.

In effect, the moment one festival was over he began rehearsing for the
next, and *Figaro* was always included. The rehearsal was set for three
hours, with the first half devoted to recitative. Walter always played his
own recitatives, but for rehearsal he stood about, watching the singers,
and sometimes pushing them into new positions. When he did this too
forcibly he would peer into the darkness of the theatre and say courteously:
'Please allow me, Herr Professor'. This was the producer, who gravely
and silently bowed back. He knew his place when the Generalmusik-
direktor was in the theatre.

A short interval at half time was used on the overture, with an orchestra
many of whom had been sitting or standing in their places quite a long
time watching the fun on the stage. As Walter raised his stick to begin,
his perennial joke, 'It's too loud already' shot out, to the amusement of
those who had not heard it before—it was often repeated!

When I was at the B.B.C. he came often and always brought refreshment to us all. I once tackled him on a point which I feel strongly about—
the repeats in the last movements of the three great Mozart symphonies.
I always do both repeats in these finales and have astonished many people
by the effect that it produces; it seems that the movements are not just
played twice through, but they assume a stature far greater, for they become adequate finales to the splendid first and other movements of the
works. I knew that Walter never played symphonic repeats—somehow his
quickness of thought seemed always to push him on to what came next.

When I went into his room after a most exciting performance of the
E flat Symphony on his last visit to the B.B.C. in my time, I said, 'Some

day I will ask you to play that movement with both repeats.' 'Both repeats' he shouted, 'how right you are. It should be done, but it would kill me!'

We saw him for the last time when we lunched with him on a lovely day in Beverly Hills. He had given up public conducting then, but was still issuing fine records and it was heart-warming to see him again.

* * *

I was just leaving the Royal College of Music one Friday evening in October 1919 when I was called to the telephone. It was Edwin Evans, who, as a critic, took the lead at that time in London over all things modern, and was also a close friend of Diaghilev's, acting as a sort of manager for him, particularly where English professional contacts were concerned. Ansermet, who had conducted Diaghilev's long summer season at the Alhambra, had to leave London on Wednesday as his Geneva season began a few days later. Could I take over the whole repertoire on and from that day? I had a few outside engagements and my Royal College of Music work, but rehearsals could be arranged as I wished, and almost all my evenings were free for the performances. I think there were fourteen ballets in the repertoire, none of which I knew better than as a casual member of the audience. I was to go to the theatre next morning at 10, and spend the weekend hearing Ansermet rehearse. Rehearsals continued almost all day as the orchestra was by no means the same as it had been in the summer. Incidentally, another big change occurred two or three weeks later, when the end of the Promenade Season released some important principals for us.

I think it is worth while describing how this emergency arose. Ansermet, who was kindness itself, and took endless trouble to enable me to get the hang of things, had known his opening date at Geneva for months, had told Diaghilev about it early in the summer, and reminded him at frequent intervals. These reminders, he said, were received by the Potentate with complete indifference, until the day before the Friday already mentioned, when the great man fizzed up like a rocket, stormed and raged, taking the line that he was left with no other conductor, and it was absolutely *impossible* that Ansermet could contemplate letting him down in this disgraceful way after all he had done for him. After twenty-four hours of this nonsense, finding Ansermet quietly adamant, he instructed Evans to find someone else.

Another example of this technique, which seems so natural to the Russian mind, was his handling of the rehearsal problem. Owing to the suddenness of my engagement I saw very little of the ballet practice room, but it was obvious that the most intensive rehearsals went on daily with Cechetti, Grigoriev and the young Massine in control, though Diaghilev's eyes were everywhere. But there was not time to keep the older repertoire

pieces always up to scratch, and if any slackness was noted (Diaghilev was
continually wandering round the Promenade during performances) it was
his custom to withdraw from the ensemble a pivotal dancer, and to throw
into his place someone else who knew nothing about it, and had only just
enough warning to dress and make up. He then left him—and them—to it.
This, of course, put the whole crowd on their toes; they had the greatest
fun keeping the new man in his place, and the show as seen from the front
once again assumed the necessary vitality.

M. Ansermet took immense pains to enable me to take on this big
repertoire at such short notice, and I don't think it is unkind to quote a
remark in his fluent and forcible language when a rehearsal had been interrupted by some comic remark. The laughter went on for some time, and when
Ansermet raised his stick to go on with the music there was still some
laughter and people were not ready. Time was short, he wanted to get on:
'Gentlemen, a joke then and now yes very sometimes, but always by God
never!' This immortal remark was written down on the spot by that splendid pianist and teacher Herbert Fryer, who had been specially engaged to
play the important pianoforte part in *Petrouchka*.

When Ansermet came back to London the following summer we were
very happy to meet and exchange reminiscences. 'How did you get on
personally with Diaghilev?' he asked. I said that things went quite well,
if I arranged to have a row with him about once a fortnight. 'Exactly the
period I found necessary', was the answer.

As a matter of fact it took me a good deal longer than the first fortnight
to learn this technique: about four weeks had gone by, and I had seen no
sign of the twenty guineas weekly which was to be my salary. It was dawn-
ing on me that Russian means of communication involved a good deal of
action to support the language, so I went to my room one evening after the
second ballet (there were always three) and sent a message to the great
man to say that I was shortly going home but that if he wanted me to
conduct the third ballet, I must have some money first. Round he came
instantly, his pockets bulging with £20 notes, and asked me what I wanted.
His financial principles were crude in the extreme—I believe he never had
a bank account—but he certainly succeeded in getting first-class work out
of the greatest artists when they interested him. One of his closest friends
offered me a bet at the beginning of the last week. 'Boult, I will bet you a
shilling that you won't get all your money out of Diaghilev next Saturday.'
I won my bet; but he hadn't heard of my earlier success.

It was a great experience, and the simple friendliness of the whole
company, even when we had no language in common, made our work very
pleasant. Many of the greatest artists were still with them: Karsavina,
Lopokova, Tchernicheva; Massine, Woizikowsky, Idzikowsky were
among them. We played a fine repertoire, including *Petrouchka*, *Firebird*,

Scheherazade, Tamar, Three-cornered Hat, Good-humoured Ladies, Boutique Fantasque and the world première of Satie's *Parade*.

In later years M. Ansermet was always a most welcome guest in London, and for many years took over the major part of the B.B.C.'s output of Stravinsky and his school as well as a great deal of French music—there was always a special distinction about his visits and programmes—and it is indeed sad that his splendid career has now come to its close.

There is a difficulty in the art of ballet conducting which I was slow to grasp. Being still mindful of Nikisch and his method I thought I could easily follow the dancers as soon as I knew the scores well enough to watch the stage. This is exactly what one must not do, for dancers cannot initiate a tempo as a singer or concerto soloist can. Dancers can only take the tempo a conductor gives them, and they will kill themselves doing so even if they kill the conductor when he returns on stage after the performance.

Only one dancer in my experience had the initiative power to show me if I had taken a wrong tempo, by stepping ahead of my beat or behind it, and that was Massine himself. All the others had to have their cake and eat it, but I was always told afterwards if anything was wrong.

A ballet conductor must start by spending a considerable time in the pianoforte practice room where he can see the ballets evolving to the right tempo. It was madness to expect a newcomer to gauge all the tempi accurately when they change every few minutes, and there were fourteen ballets, some of them forty minutes long. It is also true that nearly every set tempo managed to develop something of a *stringendo* in itself without any marked change. This dilemma gave rise to an amusing gesture from Diaghilev one night when, I think, *Carnaval* or *Papillons* was being thrown on with a minimum of rehearsal, barely enough to enable me to realize that my remembrance of the original pianoforte music was a very different thing from the ballet version presented by the Russians. In despair, I asked Diaghilev if he could send someone down to sit at my feet and tap my leg at the right tempo whenever there was a change. He readily agreed, and said he would come down himself, and a chair was set at my right, just in front of the first desk of second violins. When called for the ballet I went as usual and stood on the stage by the curtain until sent down by the stage manager. When he gave the signal Diaghilev caught my arm and we walked together across to the stairs: 'Eh bien, mon ami, maintenant nous allons diriger à quatre mains'.

Sir Henry Wood came one night to see the *Three-cornered Hat*, and I well remember his warning me (with perfect truth) that I ought to be spending every afternoon in bed before important performances like this night after night. 'Anyhow you'll have to begin doing it when you're a little older. And remember, no nonsense on sofas or armchairs, take your

clothes off and go to bed, and two hours of it.' Good common sense, as I
have proved ever since.

One of the most distinguished people in London music in my young
days was Victor Beigel, whose greatest claim to fame may have been that
he was Gervase Elwes' teacher. He was a striking figure: very short, very
bald, and rather fat, though there was a most powerful diaphragm under
the façade as all his pupils found out. He was the kind of man who made
an instant impression whenever he went into a roomful of people, and he
was popular everywhere.

I first heard him as accompanist to Gervase Elwes at a Brahms recital
in Wigmore Hall. The tails of his coat, hanging down behind the piano
stool, perfected the egg-like appearance and a much smaller egg, pink and
bald, balanced on top of the large black one, made a perfect ensemble.
Even more perfect was the ensemble between master and pupil. Elwes was
a very great singer, whether as the Evangelist, Gerontius or in many other
parts, and that evening proved unforgettable—I have curiously not forgotten also that it took place on Boat Race night.

I did not meet Beigel until just after the start of the 1914 war, when I
happened to be in Oxford working at my D.Mus. He was spending the
weekend with the Misses Price at the Judges' Lodgings in St Giles, where
they kept open house for musicians. Beigel's German name and accent
made his hostesses anxious about how he would be received, and I suggested that it might be good if I took him to dine in Christ Church Hall
on the Sunday night, so we had a great tête-à-tête and went back to the
Judges' Lodgings after dinner. He had just organized a fund to give concerts in hospitals. It was called the Wounded Soldiers' Concert Fund and
he took enormous trouble over the auditions so that only really promising
artists should perform. The fees were low, of course, but everyone was
paid something, and the Fund did a great deal of good, both to artists and
audiences.

I have mentioned Beigel's dreadful accent. It was most curious that
anyone with his wonderful ear and his fluent command of many languages
should have allowed himself to pronounce one of them so badly. He once
spoke of this to me and explained it as sheer laziness. There was no doubt
that he could have improved enormously if he had given his mind to it.

As a young man in Berlin he began life as accompanist to a great teacher
and singer whose name was Raimond von zür Mühlen. Beigel was always
with his master both at lessons and when he sang. He decided after some
years that he must make a break and left hurriedly for New York. Although young and hard up, he most characteristically decided not to travel
cheaply but took a state cabin in one of the big Hamburg-Amerika liners.
It was luckily a good crossing and Beigel made himself such good company and took part so successfully in the life of the ship, that he already

had many potential friends and pupils before he landed in New York. He spent several years there, and then came on to London.

He lived in that delightful part of London, Little Venice; he enjoyed the name of the road, Howley Place, and it daily re-echoed to the sound of his lessons. His companion was a charming American architect named Dickie Borie, who built a house in Berlin for Fritz Kreisler. It was always a pleasure to dine with them and sit in the garden afterwards, and finally they would bring the dogs for a walk with us to the tube station at Warwick Avenue, with an occasional whiff of what they called 'parfum de Venise' as one passed the canal.

They later took a cottage in the village of Glatton in Northamptonshire. It had a lovely garden which many readers will have known, because Mr Beverley Nichols who bought it after Beigel's death so happily described it in *Down the Garden Path* and his other village books.

Victor also had a fine repertoire of Viennese Fiakerlieder, the songs of the cabmen, which he would sing to his own accompaniment in a superb Viennese dialect.

He died young—Borie's death seemed to break him up completely— and his last months would have been sad indeed without the ministrations of that wonderful man Frank Thistleton. In one way and another Thistleton befriended half the musical profession, mainly as Secretary of the Musicians' Benevolent Fund, where his whole life was devoted to helping lame dogs, and also in many other ways in his spare time. His work as Secretary of the M.B.F. also included supervision of the St Cecilia's Home at Westgate, where countless musicians have been able to rest and to convalesce after illness.

It is interesting to remember that the first house taken by the Musicians' Benevolent Fund as a rest home was Billing Hall on the edge of Northampton. This had been the home of Gervase Elwes and his large family (Beigel often stayed there) and it seemed specially appropriate that the Fund which was originally founded in memory of Elwes should have taken it after his tragic death in Boston. He was caught under a moving train when trying to return an overcoat to its owner. Billing was however found to be unworkable for the M.B.F. and they took the house at Broadstairs instead; later—in 1968—they opened a big house in Herefordshire as a permanent home for retired musicians.

I have mentioned Willie Reed amongst Elgar's friends. He wrote a very good book called *Elgar as I Knew Him*, but it was as a violinist that he helped with the actual process of composition. He described in the book how Elgar gave him a scrap of paper with a few lines of music which he would play while Elgar played the harmonies on the piano. Reed also had a good deal to do with the final form of the solo part of the Violin Concerto. He gave the first performance of the Violin Sonata with Landon

Ronald and played Second Violin (to Albert Sammons) in the Quartet and Quintet premières. He was leader of the London Symphony Orchestra for many years, and also Chairman of its Board of Directors. He had a wonderful collection of stories which he told with such relish (and a slight lisp) that one hesitates to retell them in cold print, but I must try to relay a wonderful scene that I heard him describe more than once.

Klemperer, with the London Symphony Orchestra, had just given a most exciting performance of Beethoven's Ninth Symphony in Queen's Hall at a Courtauld-Sargent Concert. There was always a party at Mrs Courtauld's after her concerts, and Reed found there the great Mengelberg, who had just arrived, ready to start rehearsing with the orchestra next morning. Willie's sense of fun got the better of him and he took Mengelberg into a corner and asked him what he thought of the soloists, of the choir, of the orchestra, and had a detailed discussion on each 'until', he said, 'I thought I would really come to the point.' 'And how did you like the interpretation, the performance as a whole?' 'Ah,' was the reply, '*I make otherwise.*'

Reed's puckishness once led him to the discovery that there were three students at the Royal College of Music who rejoiced in the surnames of Noyes, Rowe and Dinn, and as these fortunately played the appropriate instruments, he of course had to enter them for an informal concert to play a trio together. I did not hear the performance, but was told at the time that it was excellent. One member of the trio is now on the staff of the College.

I wonder how many regular concert-goers can say that they owe their first taste of music to the wonderful foundation of Sir Robert and Lady Mayer's Children's Concerts. Very many thousands of course, but not many will remember its beginnings in the year 1923. I was the conductor for those few experimental concerts, and unfortunately for me, I had to leave for Birmingham after this first series. My mother who was in London insisted on coming to a concert, and she qualified for her intrusion by borrowing the eight-year-old son of the porter of the block of flats where we lived. At a later concert we were happy to welcome as guest Mr Walter Damrosch, the distinguished conductor of the New York Philharmonic Orchestra. He had directed children's concerts for many years, and gave us all a delightful object lesson in just how to do it, and how much, or rather how little, to talk. Sir Robert's ninetieth birthday in June 1969 was celebrated with a splendid concert at the Royal Festival Hall graced by the presence of Her Majesty the Queen. It was very sad for me that, having accepted the conductorship, I had to cry off owing to an operation.

About two years before I came to the end of my time at school, Canon Samuel Barnett was transferred from Bristol to Westminster by Sir Henry Campbell-Bannerman's government. Barnett and his wife, later Dame

Henrietta, were already leaders of many Liberal movements, both being well-off and able to afford almost anything they thought worth while. They began with the foundation of Toynbee Hall in Whitechapel, the first University slum settlement, and many distinguished political figures have spent a few years in residence there as young men. They were closely involved in the government of the Charity Organization Society (now the Family Welfare Society), the Children's Country Holiday Fund, the National Trust, when these things were breaking new ground and were rather despised by Society. Old friends of my parents, they were very kind to me and I met many eminent people at the Cloisters, particularly when the Canon was in residence. Another of their interests was Erskine House, a girls' home situated back to back with the Spaniards Inn at the highest point in Hampstead. Beside it was St Jude's Cottage, their country home, so-called because St Jude's was the parish in Whitechapel in which the Canon, as Vicar, had built Toynbee Hall.

Canon and Mrs Barnett's early days at Westminster were specially devoted to their biggest scheme: the Hampstead Garden Suburb. Their walks over the Heath when staying at St Jude's Cottage gradually stimulated the great project which now seems as if it has been there for centuries, but I remember when there wasn't a house in the whole area, and I saw the early plans on the floor of their drawing-room at the Cloisters. I heard them discussing possibilities with such different people as Emma Cons of the Old Vic, Sir Robert Hunter of the National Trust, Sir Hubert Herkomer, Sir Edwin Lutyens, R.A., and many others.

When Canon Barnett died, a very striking sentence opened his obituary in the *Westminster Gazette*: 'Let's go and talk it over with Barnett! How many Cabinet Ministers have made and acted upon that suggestion?' His memorial in the Abbey shows him as a farmer scattering the seed: 'Fear not to sow, because of the birds'. He scattered lavishly and had no thought for the return, at any rate as far as he personally was concerned.

Albert Coates was very kind to me and I was often asked to his flat after he came to London in 1919. I have said that we seem to have forgotten the tremendous impact he made on London music at that time. He gave performances of the classics with a new (to us) warmth and depth of feeling, and his particular battle-horse, the Scriabin 'Poem of Ecstasy', was played again and again to crowded and cheering houses. Francis Toye's (verbal) comment to the effect that he expected soon to relegate 'Extase' to the category of '1812' was charmingly answered by a simple Norwegian student at the Royal College of Music, who said, 'But I am very fond of "1812".'

I was much touched one day when Albert said he wanted a quiet word with me, just before he was leaving for abroad. So I went to see him off at Victoria, and he told me that he didn't feel I was getting anywhere in my

work, and thought I ought to be doing far more. He gave me an introduction to a Berlin agent which didn't lead to anything more than a very
pleasant week at the Opera House in Cologne (with Arthur Bliss) hearing
the young Klemperer rehearse and conduct some splendid performances.
Coates was right, and a period in a German opera house in the early
twenties would have taught me as much as I had hoped it would do in
1914, but the Birmingham post was already in view, and the problem
was solved in that way.

*   *   *

An amateur of a specially generous turn of mind, Colonel William Johnson
Galloway, whom I first met in the early twenties, had stick fever like so
many of us, and his method of gratifying it was more than usually lavish.
A director of the old Great Eastern Railway and later one of the London
and North Eastern Group, he assembled, across the road from Liverpool
Street station in the Bishopsgate Institute, an organization known as the
Great Eastern Railway Orchestra (later North Eastern Railway Orchestra).
Their weekly practices initiated (as far as I know) the system which has
more recently been followed with such great success by the National
Youth Orchestra.

The practices began in separate rooms (five or six in this case, but more
in the case of the N.Y.O.), with professional coaches for the separate
groups for an hour. Then after a short interval they would all come
together and Colonel Galloway would himself take charge, and enjoy
himself, or if he felt that training should be carried further he would bring
in someone like myself. There was a male voice choir which sometimes
sang with the orchestra and also gave carol concerts and smoking concerts independently. Among the coaches for this department were Stanley
Marchant and Leslie Woodgate at different times.

He gave me a good deal of work in the early days, and I had a thrilling
experience once when he wanted me in Queen's Hall on a Saturday night
and I already had an engagement to rehearse in Liverpool on the Sunday
morning. It was soon after 1918, the full services of sleepers were not yet
in action, and on Saturday nights they were suspended. Nothing daunted,
the Colonel said something must be arranged for me. I turned up at
Marylebone at 11 p.m. and found at the back of the train a sumptuous
director's coach with an attendant and a verandah from which the Chil-
terns looked most impressive under a full moon. We arrived early at
Liverpool Central and before the attendant let me go off to my rehearsal,
he insisted on cooking me a splendid sole.

Willie Galloway always took a house in Surrey or Sussex for the early
summer and had large parties there, before going on to Skaife Hall near

Otley, which with its grouse moor belonged to him. His only heir, a nephew, was killed in the 1914 war, and he left a considerable sum to the Royal Society of Musicians. He was a fine example of the old-fashioned musical amateur.

* * *

I have already mentioned my early experience (when I was thirty-two) of conducting the Schumann Concerto for Pablo Casals. It was my first chance of making music with a supreme musician, and our rehearsal, a long one, with a great deal of stimulating comment, caused one of the business men who formed the Committee at Liverpool in those days, to think that 'young Boult seemed fairly out of his depth in the Concerto, at any rate he let the soloist do most of the talking'.

Casals had told me of his formation of an orchestra in his native Barcelona and I took the opportunity a year later of spending a month there and attending his rehearsals twice a day. I diligently learnt Spanish in order to study his rehearsal methods, but found he always spoke Catalan, a very different proposition. Looking back on it now I think I learnt much. Since then I have always encouraged students at rehearsals, whenever they see a conductor stopping an orchestra, to spot the trouble before they hear him explain his reasons for stopping. In Barcelona I had to be very quick off the mark when I knew that I shouldn't understand what the Maestro said. My musical ear had to do it all.

No visitor in B.B.C. days gave us greater pleasure than Casals, and his wit was a continual joy. One day when we were recording the engineer emerged and said 'Mr Casals, I am afraid we can hear you singing as you play'. 'Ah, then you can charge double for the records' was the shattering reply.

* * *

During the twenties I had many very happy trips to Scotland. In the days when the Scottish Orchestra (consisting of a large percentage of London players) had only a season of thirteen intensive weeks I visited them for a couple of weeks in 1923, and on a number of occasions later I went to Edinburgh at the invitation of that great man Donald Tovey, who, as Professor of Music, had re-formed the Reid Orchestra, and gave many orchestral concerts. When he spoke he had so much to say that his thoughts overran his tongue, and caused considerable confusion where syntax was concerned. His prose style was admirable, and his programme notes had a wide circulation when Hubert Foss of the Oxford University Press reprinted them in six volumes. He began this very difficult art when the

Meiningen Orchestra played in St James's Hall in 1902. My mentor, David Piggott, went to some of the concerts (which I had to miss as they took place on weekdays) and showed me the programmes, which so impressed me that I went to the agents and bought the whole set. Many of them, but not all, were reprinted in the six volumes, and I am also happy to possess nearly twenty other bound volumes of the Edinburgh originals, which Tovey sent me regularly each year as the season ended, sometimes with extra annotations in his spidery but very characteristic writing.

His health was very uncertain and I remember going round to see him on one of my visits and finding him lying on a couch with many of the great volumes of the Bach Society scattered all round—on the floor, on the piano beside him, and on top of him as he lay. I said something about his having a nice time wallowing in J.S.B. 'Oh yes,' he said, 'and it is wonderful to have ample time to read them through *with the repeats*.' I admired his playing immensely though many people did not.

As a young man he organized a series of chamber concerts in Chelsea Town Hall, and his admirers sometimes had to tolerate unexpected occurrences. On one occasion he played the second set of Brahms–Paganini Variations as an encore to the first set in an already long programme. A wonderful evening was spent on the two Brahms clarinet sonatas with Richard Mühlfeld from Meiningen, for whom the works were written. Casals once said to me that Tovey and Enesco were the two greatest musicians he knew. I only met Enesco once or twice, but Tovey's memory was uncanny, and also his power of reading and analysing a composer's mind in his examination of a work. He had a delightful sense of the humorous and the picturesque. The two are often to be found in his essays.

Conductor of the BBC
Symphony Orchestra; with Paul
Beard and Marie Wilson,
April 1942

Last night of the Proms
1942, Royal Albert Hall.
Freddie Grisewood of the
BBC interviewing (*l. to r.*)
Basil Cameron, Sir Henry J.
Wood, and the author

Arrival in Amsterdam, 1947, on the BBC Symphony
Orchestra's first post-war visit to Europe

With Queen Wilhelmina of the Netherlands and (*right*)
Sir Neville Bland, the British Ambassador

Chapter Eight

FRONTIERS

THE LATE Ernest Bevin is said to have expressed the hope that we might soon achieve the happy state of being able to go immediately to the station, buy our tickets and start if we suddenly decided to go to Europe. He did not mention that this was exactly what we were able to do for many years before 1914. In those days one could put down a golden sovereign on the counter of a French shop and receive change in almost any Western European currency. The French, Swiss and Belgian franc, the lira and peseta were all of the same value, and the coinages mixed freely. Only Scandinavia, Holland, Germany and Austria, and of course ourselves, had different currencies.

It was sad indeed that Sir Winston Churchill, who when in opposition made himself so doughty a champion of United Europe, should later have had to drop this policy because so many of his supporters, living on an island and never leaving it, did not realize the ghastly effects that man-made frontiers can have not only on high politics but also on international trade and individual comfort.

In my pre-1914 Leipzig days I travelled home several times for holidays and so on. The stop at the frontier sometimes seemed little longer than at an important junction: sometimes an official came down the train and looked in—but rarely even asked if we had anything to declare. There were no passports in Western Europe. I was told that if I intended to stay out of England more than six months or to go to Russia it would be wise to have one. I had ideas in both these directions, and so I applied for and received a single sheet like, but rather larger than, the old five-pound note, and never showed it to anyone at all.

I had a number of frontier experiences in 1919 when Robin Barrington-Ward, demobilized and joining the *Observer* as Garvin's No. 2, was sent by the great man to visit the *Observer*'s pre-war correspondents and renew contact with them. We planned a clockwise circle through the important capitals. A day in Amsterdam started us off, with a night at Dordrecht with friends. Our journey to Berlin was unusual: I suppose the main lines were still blocked, and so we were sent by the most northerly route

87

possible, crossing the frontier at Nieuwe Schans, and going on through Bremen.

We found Berlin a very different place from before; no uniforms, and drabness everywhere; notices in the hotels to prevent guests risking their boots outside their doors. This was well before the inflation crisis, and we found things in the shops reasonable though dull. A short stop in Dresden was followed by two days' walking in my old haunt Saxon Switzerland, staying on the Elbe at Schandau, near the Czech frontier station, Boden-bach. The elderly Berlin-Vienna express turned us out here and we joined a brand new Czechoslovak train with food that made the Germans' eyes goggle after their own privations. It was a foretaste of Prague, which seemed to have seized all the luxuries we used to expect in Berlin. Here were the uniforms, as one of the Czech Legions had just returned home via Siberia, and to anyone who remembered the Czechs' down-trodden days under the Hapsburg regime, Prague was now a brilliant, independent city. Robin had an interview with President Masaryk which greatly impressed him, and we luxuriously went on in the direction of Vienna.

Our entry into Austria was a shock as we found an almost derelict train awaiting us. Candles were being sold on the platform, but there was no other light anywhere. Many windows were broken, and we were glad that the journey was short, though we found that Vienna could offer little better, either in the hotels or streets. Robin had planned a three-day stop as he had several people to see, but I found it so depressing that I travelled next day to Munich and waited for him there.

This enabled me to hear a performance of *The Flying Dutchman* which was notable for the conducting of Robert Heger 'als Gast auf Engagement'. This distinguished musician's appearance in Munich that night was the beginning of his long and loyal association as second in command to Bruno Walter both in Munich and also in London, where he was for many years a most welcome visitor.

From Munich we went on by way of Lindau and a lake steamer to Merseburg where Kurt Hahn was waiting for us on the pier. An old Oxford friend, he had invited Robin to spend a night at Salem, and had kindly included me. It was most interesting to see that immense building, once a monastery, and now the home of Prince Max of Baden. Built round three quadrangles, it was used by Prince Max for many purposes, particularly the school, which then numbered about twenty girls and boys, including Prince Berchtold, Prince Max's son. They were already enjoying an unusual curriculum, a beginning that spread into a number of schools in Germany, and was transferred (with Kurt Hahn's removal from Hitler's Germany) to Gordonstoun, and has now given birth to the Outward Bound movement. I think Prince Max had started the school and engaged Hahn simply to teach his son, a few children from the village, and a number of children of Russian refugee friends of his, who had escaped the revolution. I believe no one paid any fees.

We were able to listen to a lesson that Hahn himself gave on the causes of the War, and in the afternoon were taken back to the pier at Merseburg. Here we had rather a shock. We were preparing to board a steamer to take us across to Romanshorn and then to go by train to Zurich where our Paris train would pick us up. I read somewhere that a Swiss visa was not necessary for passengers travelling through Switzerland. The note should have read 'straight through Switzerland'; it did not provide for our very crooked journey. Luckily I discovered a copy of the wonderful German 'Reichskursbuch' in the pier master's office, in which every single train in Germany is listed and explained. Ten minutes with the guide and its map enabled me to discover that another steamer (which we could see approaching) would take us to Konstanz, and from there we could get a train to Strasbourg, or rather to Kehl, on the German side of the Rhine. It was nearly dark when we got to Konstanz and our little train pushed its way slowly up through the Black Forest, looking most romantic by moonlight. We got to Kehl about midnight and were delighted to have a meal of sandwiches and beer in our bedroom as we turned in. Next day an early taxi drove us to the great bridge and we had to walk into France carrying our bags. A tram on the other side took us to the station and a war-scarred journey to Paris, and I came straight on, while Robin stayed to finish his *Observer* business.

My first trip across the Atlantic with Robin began in Quebec, and I believe our steamer was the last to reach the American continent before the quota system was brought in in October 1923. Entry to the United States had been entirely free up to that time, and as the frontier between the States and Canada was then virtually non-existent, U.S. immigration officials were sent to Canadian ports to make certain that European immigrants did not reach the States by this route.

Soon after this I went again to Germany and as I returned at a more crowded time of year I have a still more vivid recollection of the treatment of the ordinary traveller in those days. One arrived at the German frontier station. Everyone and everything had to get out and go to the customs, queuing for passport examination, queuing for the customs house, rushing madly back to get any seat one could in the train—of course no one minded who had been sitting where before the exodus. One settled down for the two hours across Holland, but almost immediately the train stopped again, and the same performance was repeated, this time to persuade the Dutch that we were fit to cross their country. Although the two frontier stations were only three or four miles apart, it was not possible for the two authorities to co-operate and save the travellers untold delay and misery.

I was again in Germany in 1923, when, as I have said, Arthur Bliss and

I spent a week following Otto Klemperer's rehearsals and performances in the magnificent opera house in Cologne.

We returned to England on 1 April, which day the authorities had appropriately chosen to change the connection from Cologne to the Hook of Holland, timing it to start one hour earlier. The local train was still running, but no longer connecting with the boat express in Holland. We decided to get in and go as far as possible, hoping we might somehow catch our steamer by hiring a car. Our train took us to Cleve and there we were stranded, except for a tram just about to start for Nijmegen. It brought us first to the roadside customs station and the comparatively perfunctory examination in the tram was going very well, as most of the travellers were commuters going home after their work in Germany. The sight of two Englishmen with large suitcases was too much for the officials —we were obviously doing something irregular—and by the time we had taken ourselves and our possessions to the customs house and been thoroughly well screened, our tram must have been nearly in Nijmegen, and there was not another for an hour. We reached Nijmegen far too late to drive to the Hook. I remember a pleasant hotel, and an easy trip to the following night's boat.

Before the Anschluss, when Hitler was doing all he could to make Austria's existence impossible, he closed the frontier in the summer of 1933, and no Germans could visit Austria without paying a fee of something equivalent to £250. My wife and I had begun our wedding trip in Italy, but I badly wanted to show her the wonderful country north of Innsbruck, where I had often walked, and which I knew pretty well. We were coming up from Mittenwald by one of the hill paths near the Eibsee when we met a bright young S.S. patrol. He asked us where we had come from and where we were going. I told him and offered to get our passports out of my rucksack. He ignored this and finally told me that I must pay this large sum, as I had crossed the frontier. I took my rucksack off and produced my passport, which completely deflated him. In those days my German was adequate with strangers for two or three sentences. Then a grammatical howler would cause the eyebrows to go up, and a tactful 'Are you a foreigner?' would follow. On this occasion my production of the passports preceded the howler.

The horrors caused by the Hitler war had naturally many repercussions on the frontier situation. I first felt this when I was sent by the B.B.C. to visit Amsterdam and Brussels soon after their liberation. After the Amsterdam concert I was taken to The Hague by the kindness of the British Council, and from there I was to fly to Brussels in an English plane which was coming from Hamburg. At 3 p.m. I duly presented myself at the office, and was told to come back at four; there was so far no word of the plane having left Hamburg as it was rather a misty day. I went back to the

British Council office, and was told that if the flight was cancelled I could be sent to the frontier by car, and Brussels Radio could be asked to fetch me from there. At four there was no plane, and so we went off in the representative's car, with a very young chauffeur, who had asked whether his fiancée might come too. Unfortunately the kind representative felt that he couldn't let me be dumped at the frontier, but I must go to Breda, where there had been a Council office, and they could send me on to the nearby frontier. It was a slow trip. The Moerdijk bridge was still in ruins and had been replaced by an antediluvian steam ferry, and it was dark when we got to Breda. The British Council office was said to be in the old Cavalry Barracks, but the young couple in front were getting very nervous of the fog and darkness, and so I let them drop me at the gate.

I found that the Council had closed this office some months before and the Cavalry Barracks were full of Dutch cavalry, who were busy and unable to do anything except tell me that there were some British troops further down the road. Down the road I walked for a mile (it was raining by then), a suitcase in each hand, and found that the troops were not British, but Israeli. Some of them were gramophone addicts; so they gave me a good welcome, and rang up the Town Major, whose job it was to help people in distress. He was kindness itself, took me to the Club and gave me sandwiches, drove me to the frontier, where the Belgian Radio car soon arrived, and landed me in Brussels about midnight.

Soon after this the B.B.C. Orchestra made their first post-war trip. It took us to Paris, Brussels, Amsterdam and The Hague, where the concert was graced by Her Majesty Queen Wilhelmina, who touched us greatly by her kindness, and by the fervent way she joined in singing our National Anthem. By some odd oversight, the B.B.C. Transport Department had forgotten to equip our instrument van either with the appropriate papers or with the G.B. sign. It was driven by Walter Birch, about whose achievements with the van I must digress. On this occasion, after we had embarked at Flushing it was found that the van was too wide for any gangway, and could not be hauled up, as the cranes were not yet in order. There was nothing for it but to lay a couple of planks and hope for the best. The whole orchestra watched from the upper deck while Birch drove with their precious instruments triumphantly along the planks to safety.

One night in Bristol in 1940 we had been playing in a studio with the prospect of a rehearsal somewhere else next morning. This often happened, and gave a great deal of work to the staff whose practice it was to load the van at night, lock it in the garage, and unload in the morning. Birch thought it looked like being a 'dirty night'. Flares were followed by incendiaries, and he thought he would take the van up on the downs a few miles from Bristol, and watch the raid from there. When it was over he drove down to the garage and found only a charred ruin. We tried to get him a special gratuity for this feat, but I never heard of his being given a penny. Bureaucracy is a stubborn thing.

But we must return to my frontiers. Birch's partner on these trips was another splendid Londoner and great character, William Fussell, who for many years had charge of the instruments of the B.B.C. Symphony Orchestra, insured, it was said, for £20,000. He fought in the 1914 war, and this helped him over the next frontier incident. The van, as I have said, had no papers and no G.B. sign. This did not seem to matter much at Calais as we were all there together and our landing qualifications were fairly obvious. But when the van had to cross into Belgium it was not so easy.

We were in the train miles away and Fussell and Birch had to cope alone with some tough Belgian officials. They argued for hours (it was very late at night) and were on the point of giving it up and telephoning frantically to us in Brussels when Fussell suddenly thought of a trump card: 'You are making a fine fuss about this frontier of yours now, but do you know that I have crossed and re-crossed it without a passport or anything else?' 'How did you do that?' 'Wipers, and so on, 1915-1918.' 'Ah, mon vieux, we are comrades,' and after the consumption of some ceremonial beer, the van passed freely to Brussels. After that we succeeded in persuading our London office to send us some official means of recognition.

Things had got a little better by the time the London Philharmonic Orchestra made its German tour in January 1951. I was astonished to see the (to me) unknown name Viersen on the list of concerts, and we found that we were to take part in a subscription series in a pleasant hall in this small town some miles from Düsseldorf. A short time before the concert I went out to get a breath of fresh air and was astonished to see in the car park a large number of cars with the NL sign. Apparently there were not many orchestral concerts in the East of Holland at that time, and many people there subscribed to the Viersen concerts and came over for the evening in their cars.

Since 1945 the Iron Curtain has extended the list of European frontiers and is itself a formidable addition. We first saw it on the way to Moscow in 1956. We were in a through Paris-Warsaw sleeping car. Having had lunch at 11.30 a.m. we found ourselves locked in, our passports removed, and the train stationary for four hours with a man covering it with a tommy-gun from a wooden tower beside the line. This was in the neighbourhood of Cheb (Eger).

We saw no more food (except some boxes of cheese my wife had wisely packed) until Prague at 9 p.m., when we were allowed to buy some garlic sandwiches at a railway servants' buffet, and were delighted to be served by a friendly lady who spoke English. The passengers' refreshment room was already closed. Four hours seemed the regulation time for Iron Curtain frontiers, even those between Czechoslovakia, Poland and Russia. It seemed as if they were making copies of every detail in every passport while we sat in our locked train.

Our return via Berlin provided one more complication; we had obtained our special visas to go through the Russian zone between Berlin and Hanover, and had actually waited an extra day in Berlin to get them, although we had only just come from Russia. They were duly examined first by one set of Russian officials then by some others who were fetched. A great deal of talk ensued but they finally went away and to our intense relief, we were allowed to proceed. We were led to understand that though my permit was right, my wife's for some incredible reason was only valid for transit *by road*!

Chapter Nine

B.B.C.—1930-1939

SOMEWHERE NEAR my fortieth birthday in the spring of 1929 I had an urgent letter from Walford Davies. He and Sir John (later Lord) Reith and Sir Hugh Allen had been having some earnest conversations. Percy Pitt's time as Director of Music of the B.B.C. was to come to an end, under the age rule, on 1 January 1930, and they all felt I might succeed him. Would I go and stay a night with him at Windsor and talk it over? As before with the Birmingham decision, there was no doubt about what was right, though I felt it might well be far less pleasant. In fact, it was made quite clear to me at my first talk with Sir John Reith that I was to *direct* the music. If conducting now and then could be added to direction without impairing it, well and good, but the direction was the principal thing, and Sir John added that he did not like sending for his Director of Music in the afternoon only to be told that he had gone home to rest as he was conducting that evening.

Things were not settled for me until late in 1929. This was far too late to expect Birmingham to find a successor to me, and it was agreed that though I should begin officially with the B.B.C. on 1 January, I should see the Birmingham season through to its finish in March, coming up to Savoy Hill whenever I could during those first three months.

Then a disturbing thing happened. One night during the 1929 Prom season, I had come in late from Birmingham, seized my letters and dashed to Queen's Hall. During the interval I went out into Riding House Street and opened the letters. The first was from the B.B.C. addressed to me as a member of the Music Advisory Committee. I had been a member of it for two years or so. I should no doubt be glad to hear that a series of Popular Concerts had been arranged through the winter and spring, to take place at the People's Palace under the direction of Messrs X and Y. I read it again. It appeared that the Music Advisory Committee were being informed of a new series of concerts but the Music Director elect was still in ignorance of something important that was to go on for several months after his term of office had begun; worst of all, they were popular concerts to be conducted by X and Y, and no Sir Henry Wood at whose feet I and 2,000 others were at this moment sitting (or standing).

Sir Henry was the greatest popular conductor (in the finest sense of that adjective) the world had ever seen. No, I could not be associated with this. I wrote next day asking that the date of my appointment should be announced for some time in May, immediately after the final Popular Concert. I strongly disapproved of a series of this kind excluding Sir Henry Wood, and felt it essential that the public mind must separate me from it entirely.

The Corporation was not amused. I was interviewed by several most important people, but refused to budge. I had made up my mind, and I could not countenance these concerts. Finally, to my alarm and astonishment I was tackled by Reith himself the moment the ladies had left a dinner table in Kensington where I was dining with a future B.B.C. colleague, having been led to expect I was to meet only an outside mutual friend. Reith refused to take the answer no. I already had an appointment to see him in a few days, I must come then, and tell him I had agreed to begin on the first of January. I went away horrified; if this was a sample of life at the B.B.C., I would stay in Birmingham, and I wrote and said so.

The Corporation finally agreed to publish my date, but asked me to work for them privately before that, and generously paid me from 1 January. I believe, too, that Sir Henry was after all given one or two dates in that series.

So I soon started running in and out of Savoy Hill, though I confined myself to contacts inside and didn't go too often, as I was determined not to appear to be Director of Music until May. Kenneth Wright gave me a corner of his office, and his secretary, Mrs Beckett, started at once to work for me too (and bring me the essential cups of tea). I used to say that she and Kenneth Wright did all the work I got the credit for, and it was literally true. Kenneth was for many years the hub of the Music Department, and later transferred to Television, where his industry, tact and genius for friendship all over Europe were, I am sure, invaluable until he joined the publishing firm which he still adorns.

My office in Savoy Hill had a peep of the river and Waterloo Bridge; but a demolition soon began, and revealed the whole west elevation of Somerset House, the Waterloo Bridge end. Before the new building arose on the site and spoilt the view for ever, I rang up Robin Barrington-Ward and he sent a *Times* photographer along. The view was duly printed and I still have a framed copy of the photo which they kindly sent me.

I found out, when I joined the Corporation, how easy it can be in a complex organization to forget someone who is vitally concerned.

When I was dictating to Mrs Beckett, who has managed to survive nearly forty years of keeping me in order, she might gently say 'Would you like me to send a copy of this to Mr So-and-So?' I would then realize that the memorandum I had just dictated to someone else would fling an enormous spanner into *all* the works unless Mr So-and-So, as well, had heard of it, and taken steps to meet it. And this could happen several times a week.

I have said that it was hard enough to find one's way in the official network, but surely a good deal simpler in those days than now. I had seen the inside of the War Office, and now had sterling guidance at my elbow. I found the department already brilliantly staffed. After a long talk with everyone separately I realized that they could be trusted to look after their sections of the work, and when anything happened that seemed out of order, it was far more often 'let's see that that is balanced the other way next time' rather than 'that must be scrapped and done again'. I had realized from outside that relations between the profession and the B.B.C. seemed often to go wrong. Therefore, in addition to the Advisory Committee, chaired in those days by Sir John Reith himself and occupied mainly with major policy, I arranged a monthly informal meeting with a group from the Incorporated Society of Musicians. I think it helped, but I am very much afraid that an organization the size of the B.B.C. cannot, with the best will in the world, always steer clear of errors of tact when dealing with individual artists.

The official is too far removed in feeling, in background and in actual geography, from the artist. Since I retired from the Corporation, I have repeatedly had contracts from the B.B.C. which said they would be invalid if I did not sign and return them by return of post. Unfortunately, the contract was often for a concert I had conducted six weeks before.

In previous years the B.B.C. had planned many notable public concerts, mostly, of course, in Queen's Hall. Recent visits of celebrated foreign orchestras to London had made it clear that the time was ripe for a permanent B.B.C. Orchestra with no deputies allowed. The deputy system had been an institution in London from time immemorial. Players held comfortable posts in theatres (where in those days incidental music was nearly always necessary), but on any night when better jobs turned up in Queen's Hall or elsewhere, there was no difficulty about sending an inferior player to the theatre, to get through, unrehearsed, as best he could. This practice was also rife in the concert world, and in 1904 when Sir Henry Wood first insisted on 'no deputies without a medical certificate', many of his players decided that they could not offer him their whole-time services and sacrifice the many provincial festivals where they were invited to perform, the opera seasons and the other attractive engagements which had always been a part of their lives. Therefore they resigned and formed the London Symphony Orchestra which began its fine history in that year.

It was as early as 1929 that two members of the B.B.C. Music Department, Edward Clark and Julian Herbage, began planning for the possibility of a B.B.C. Symphony Orchestra. This was most cleverly designed to fulfil all broadcasting needs, often two at once, and the arrangements for its splitting up demanded great variety and scope. The total personnel was 110, and this could be divided into two unequal parts, allowing, for instance, the Promenade Concerts to be balanced by a small orchestra of thirty or so who could play lighter music during the Promenade season, or who could undertake Bach cantatas. A complete series of them was planned about that time. At non-Promenade times the divisions were about equal, though the Sunday concert was usually undertaken by the Promenade-sized orchestra (about eighty-five), and the full 110, of course, filled Queen's Hall on Wednesday nights, which were the peak of the week, and still are.

During this time the assistant conductor of the orchestra was Mr Clarence Raybould, a very distinguished musician, who had had great experience also as a chamber music pianist and accompanist. He was with us for a large number of years and did yeoman service as he was very popular with the orchestra.

The recruiting proved interesting. For the principal posts the finest possible players were invited, and when the final list was published it contained almost every player of note in the country. For the rank and file a quite different policy was adopted, and auditions were held (in the provinces also) by well-known string players and so a brilliant group of young and inexperienced players came to sit behind the well-known old stagers.

We had an interesting result of this in our second season. We thought it might be a good thing to play at one of the Queen's Hall concerts an act of Wagner complete with singers. The Third Act of *Siegfried* was chosen and I said at once that we must have an extra string rehearsal in order to get on close terms with the terrible string passages which always frightened players so much. The rehearsal amazed me, for string technique had progressed so far that Wagner had no terrors for these young players. In 1930 the scheduled three hours were quite unnecessary, and we stopped long before time was up.

A sad pendant to this experience occurred a few weeks later when a middle-aged and respected first violin member of London orchestras, who was a familiar figure for years somewhere about the third desk at Queen's Hall and Covent Garden, applied to join the B.B.C. His audition included the last few pages of the *Götterdämmerung* first violin part, and I sat back, prepared to fill in the glorious brass chording in my mind, as Mr X played his arpeggios. Alas, I had no fun; the arpeggios were unrecognizable. I never found out where he was supposed to be playing, and this was a man who had played his *Ring* many, many times, and had got away with it all in the general scramble.

It was natural that the London concert-giving interests at that time should look askance at the prospect of the opulent B.B.C. coming into the concert business with a first-class orchestra and the kind of soloist they could easily afford to engage, and a powerful movement was organized to try and secure a condition that the B.B.C. Symphony Orchestra should be confined to the studio, and other organizations should be employed to undertake public concerts if the B.B.C. wished to give them. Sir John Reith accordingly called a meeting of eminent musicians. I was asked, but was unable to go, but I believe that besides several distinguished academic musicians, Wood, Beecham and Ronald were also there and they all expressed the view that an orchestra which was confined to the studio would deteriorate very fast, and possibly disintegrate also, because first-rate players, however well paid, would not remain members without the stimulus of a live audience.

I was told after the meeting that this was a unanimous view, and I suppose it was the view of these eminent men, not only in regard to their orchestral friends, but also to themselves and their own careers. Perhaps I am a freak but I believe that in my B.B.C. days I was as happy in the studio as at public concerts. I was far more comfortably dressed, and the red light seemed to give me the same stimulus that one gets from an audience. Perhaps I am deceiving myself. I certainly admit that when we went to halls in foreign capitals, the general tension and excitement left with me a more vivid memory than most concerts in the studio. At the same time I am afraid that I dislike intensely the trick the B.B.C. now has of pretending that the studio performance is a full-dress concert. One has to make an entrance; each piece is applauded by a small invited audience of 100 or so trying to sound as if they were a concert-hall full of several thousand. I feel that the impression this creates in the listener's mind is simply one more piece of B.B.C. make-believe. In my time studio concerts took place in comfortable silence where the listener was concerned. If the studio audience wished to applaud they did so after the red light had gone out and the studio was off the air.

I remember that Edward Clark and Julian Herbage took a trip to Birmingham in order to travel back with me and have two hours' real peace discussing programmes. I had myself previously adopted this technique, and when in possession of a season ticket between London and Birmingham, if I had some important work to do, would make the journey up and come straight back again.

In July 1930 the Central Hall at Westminster had been taken for the first week of the orchestra's existence. We rehearsed, I think, for the whole week, concentrating on the music for our first concert on 22 October. Sir John Reith very kindly accepted my invitation to come and welcome them to the Corporation, which he did with his fine sense of the appropriate, and we then played him the *Flying Dutchman* Overture at

sight. This first reading was so impressive that I wondered whatever I
was going to find to rehearse in it, but somehow when I got down to it,
a certain amount emerged. We spent many hours on the Brahms E minor
Symphony, and Laurence Turner said it was like rehearsing chamber
music, and I could feel that they were interested. After our week together
we dispersed, eighty-five of them to the Promenades where they had the
wonderful experience of two months' intensive work with Sir Henry, and
the other thirty to the studio where they did a great deal of happy work
with my old friend Joseph Lewis, who had recently come to London from
the Midland Region of the B.B.C. in Birmingham.

Our first concert at Queen's Hall on 22 October 1930 was a milestone
in my life. The programme read:

NATIONAL ANTHEM

WAGNER	Overture, *The Flying Dutchman*
BRAHMS	Symphony No. 4 in E minor
SAINT-SAENS	Violoncello Concerto—GUILHERMINA SUGGIA
RAVEL	Closing Scene, 'Daphnis et Chloe'

A copy of a coloured picture postcard of Augustus John's wonderful portrait of Suggia and her cello was given with every programme, and I
believe that this was the first occasion on which an English orchestra wore
white ties and white waistcoats.

We had a good press. During the first season there were twenty-three
concerts; Sir Henry Wood did six; Sir Landon Ronald one; I did nine;
and foreign visitors the others. The visitors would stay for three weeks
including the three Wednesday Queen's Hall concerts, as well as two or
three Sunday concerts with the eighty-five section of the orchestra. It was
a much better arrangement than a single guest concert, which I personally
always find unsatisfactory. It needs more than one performance and one
group of rehearsals to get on to proper terms with a strange orchestra.

At the end of the season the Director-General sent for me. He had been
to several concerts, and one of the B.B.C.'s Governors, Ethel, Lady
Snowden, was a most regular attendant. D.-G. said: 'I don't pretend to
know about these things, but everyone tells me that the orchestra plays
better for you than for anyone else, and they also say it is time we had a
permanent conductor. Would you like that post? If so, will you cease being
Music Director or would you like to do the two? I must warn you that if
you opt for conducting only, you must, of course, be on the staff of the
Director and not in any way independent of him'. I decided to try and do
both jobs. It now seems an outrageous proposition, and I was immersed
often in a seven-day week, and administrative decisions had to go down
the telephone in the short intervals of long rehearsals, but I was almost

always able to keep the B.B.C. rule that if one was involved in an evening session, one must have the afternoon off. The thing would have been impossible without the most efficient and loyal staff I found at Savoy Hill when I came, in particular the two musicians I have mentioned already in connection with the orchestra, with Kenneth Wright, Owen Mase, Victor Hely-Hutchinson and many others. Everybody had his or her work to do, and I tried to make them all feel that they could do the job well needing little support from me, unless they asked for it. But it was not until 1937 when Reginald Thatcher, an old Oxford friend, who was then Director of Music at Harrow, came in as Deputy-Director that I could really feel that the responsibility could be shared, particularly in the upward direction of Administration.

Explaining musical and professional problems to senior officers, who understood little of the point in hand, but had the power of decision, or the power of the purse, is a taxing task, and Thatcher could do this for me in a way welcome by those above, who liked him, and gave him every consideration, as he so richly deserved. I still had occasional meetings with the Director-General. He would send for me, or I would ask for an appointment and the meeting would always take the same form. We would start by discussing the point at issue, after which he would say: 'Now, let's see, wasn't there a point about X which the Music Advisory Committee discussed but didn't decide about? What has happened?' Or 'I heard that Y was rather disgruntled about such and such a matter. Did you see him about it?'

There might be half-a-dozen of these matters which he would bring up, all apparently straight out of his head, loose ends, in fact, which he would wish to see tied up, and to know how it was done. I imagine that the other dozen Directors of Departments would all have similar interviews every few weeks, and come away from them feeling, as I did, intense satisfaction that their Chief knew so much about their work, and cared so much about it too. I must also mention a remarkable speech he once made to the Worshipful Company of Musicians. He began by saying that on the occasion of one of the General Elections there was an interregnum in the Talks Branch, and so he decided himself to handle the matter of special election broadcasts. He wrote to the main political parties, giving their allocation of time for Election Talks, and asking them to name the speakers to fill the spaces. All but one replied by return, giving their lists, but commenting that they thought their allocation unfairly low. He waited anxiously for the last Party to reply—it was the Party that was then in power, and when they too said they thought their allocation was unfairly low, he knew that he had done the right thing by them all.

From this he went on to apply the point to musical executants and composers. It was natural that they all felt neglected by the B.B.C., and in fact, if he heard an artist or a composer say that he thought the B.B.C. was treating him well, he felt there must be something wrong, that the Corporation must be overdoing it.

Soon after 1920, on a visit to Vienna, I had elicited from Professor Egon Wellesz in reply to some enquiry about a conductor, this sage remark: 'Well, you know, any conductor who doesn't disturb the Vienna Philharmonic gets on well with it'. This was as true as it was amusing, and as I pondered on it, it occurred to me that it also contained the definition of a great orchestra. When I realized that I was now responsible for the playing of this superb body of players, we set to work to confirm in our minds the characteristics of the many different styles that came our way, so that if a French conductor appeared and began to rehearse Debussy, we should not play it to him as if it were Moussorgksy. So far did we go in this way that an observant listener told me he always enjoyed hearing us play the opening tutti of a concerto because it might differ considerably from a previous performance, if the soloist was also playing it differently. He did not know that in those early days I often re-rehearsed the ritornello of a concerto *after* we had been through the first movement, and had heard how the soloist treated it.

This kind of thing impressed both our soloists and our guest conductors, and gradually the very greatest (except Rachmaninov and Kreisler, who had both refused ever to broadcast) began to drop hints as to their willingness to accept invitations. Thus it came about that Serge Koussevitsky visited us in 1933, and again in 1935.

Unfortunately, on this occasion Toscanini also directed some later concerts of the Summer Festival. At rehearsal there was a good deal of innuendo from Koussevitsky about what was to come, particularly in regard to the Maestro's relentlessly high standards. I think we all felt that Toscanini's coming was the culmination and goal of the B.B.C. Orchestra's career, and we felt it to be concentrated in his first rehearsal. I was more nervous than I had ever been—even fetching him from Claridges was a nightmare because he too was always desperately nervous before meeting an orchestra for the first time. I introduced the orchestra to him, and said something about our achieving the desire of every one of us, using the word 'greatest'. At this the Maestro gave me a hearty thump on the shoulders: 'No, no, no, no, no. Not that at all: just an honest musician'. So we all laughed and I left them to it, chose a seat in the circle and waited for the first explosion, wondering what on earth to do when it came. It never came. In fact, the two middle movements of the Brahms E minor went through without interruption. 'Bene, bene, bene,' he said, 'just three things.' He then found three passages, put them right, and went straight on. Toscanini never believed in 'ploughing through' after a thing was once right. But I shall not say more about Toscanini's rehearsing. As

Mr Bernard Shore says in his excellent work on conductors, *The Orchestra Speaks*:[1]

> When will foreign and some English conductors learn that an English Orchestra must have something in reserve for the concert?
>
> Our players will give as much as any conductor need desire. But the night is something different from the morning of the day before. An English orchestra will not look upon rehearsal as being other than a rehearsal. The concert is what matters.

Needless to say, the orchestra worshipped the Maestro from that first rehearsal.

One other aspect of Toscanini's work is worth a moment's consideration. We saw how Nikisch in rehearsing always took an easy-going line, and never demanded 'concert pitch' until the audience was behind him. Toscanini, driven to it, possibly, by the utterly different mentality of his Mediterranean colleagues, would give, and demand, 100 per cent every moment of rehearsal. Some of us attending the final rehearsals on the morning of the concerts felt that they were the finest moments of all. The full hall at the concert perhaps took off some brilliance, but we felt too that our Anglo-Saxons just could not reach a peak twice in one day. Very soon, he sensed this himself, and only asked 95 per cent at the final rehearsal, and got his 100 per cent at the concert.

Toscanini did not come to England in 1936. Plans were going comfortably forward for, I think, eight concerts for a certain fee as in 1935, and as the correspondence went on it seemed that seven concerts would form a better pattern and this was agreed. Soon after this the contract was sent to the Maestro, and an unimaginative accountant, loyal to the B.B.C., filled it in for seven-eighths of the originally agreed fee, as there were now to be seven concerts instead of eight. Toscanini's mind did not work like that. Was it likely that a great artist's would? Correspondence abruptly ceased. We could not understand why, but when we found out the reason for his sudden silence it was too late. Owen Mase, at that time Assistant Director of Music, was dispatched to Stresa later on to try and persuade the Maestro that errors of this kind just could not be avoided in a concern like the B.B.C. His tact triumphed, and the Festivals of '37, '38 and '39 were very high spots in the history of the B.B.C. Orchestra.

Alas, one person was not amused: Koussevitsky. The overwhelming reaction of the London public to Toscanini in 1935 had, of course, faded out the memory of his own fine contribution to that Festival. It was obviously not practical politics to invite them both again, and I wonder whether I was ever forgiven.

I cannot resist telling a story about Toscanini and a soprano who had

[1] Longmans, Green & Co., London, 1938.

been engaged on his recommendation. Her voice was wonderful, but not so her intellectual equipment. On one occasion she stood up to a volley of abusive Italian, at the end of which she said to her neighbour: 'Who is the Maestro talking to?' At a later stage a member of the orchestra who sat very near him vows that he heard him say under his breath: 'De voice it is so 'igh, there is no room for any brain in de 'ead'.

On another occasion I went into the artists' room a few minutes before a rehearsal was due to begin. I found John Barbirolli there with the Maestro who was pouring out a torrent of Italian fury and thumping a table with a folded newspaper. When the Maestro had left to start rehearsing I asked what it was all about. One of the fascist Spanish generals had that morning crashed from his plane and been killed. 'And Mussolini goes on flying and flying; and *nothing* will kill him!' was the comment.

During his 1939 Festival we heard that the King and Queen would come to Queen's Hall on a certain date. Toscanini was duly informed, and asked whether he would join us in receiving Their Majesties before the concert. 'No, no, thank you, I must be on the platform to play the 'ymn.' So the Director-General and I established ourselves by the Royal Entrance to Queen's Hall in Riding House Street, with wives and other members of staff lurking in the Royal Reception Room outside the entrance to Block A. Luckily we were early because very soon a large car drove up, and to our intense astonishment out jumped the Duke of Kent, followed at a dignified interval by Queen Mary. We had had no notification of their coming, and the seats inside the hall had to be hastily re-arranged. Older readers will remember that, when Royalty was expected, Block A, just over the first violins, was cleared of its rows of seats and more suitable chairs, with a table for programmes, were placed on the second row level, with a discreet screen of palms between them and Block B. Queen Mary and the Duke had arrived some eight or ten minutes before time (it seemed like two or three hours) and Mr Ogilvie, then Director-General, engaged the Duke in conversation while I presented the wives and staff to Queen Mary. There was nothing else I could do. She knew none of them, but luckily Lady Bridgeman, wife of our Chairman, was there and they were able to carry on some conversation until Their Majesties arrived.

'Oh Mother, how nice; I had no idea you were coming,' said the Queen as she came in, and confirmed our feeling that Queen Mary's intentions had, for once, not been circulated as far as they should have been.

During the interval, the Queen, who was radiating her enjoyment of every detail, as she somehow always does, said to me that they did want so much to thank the great man. It was, of course, too much to ask him to come up here, but they would come down if he would see them for a moment. I went down, but found him shirtless and breathless, so I returned to find that Paul Beard had gone up to represent the platform, and had been delighted when the King asked whether, when one player stopped to turn over, the other had to play twice as loud. A commonsense question which I had never heard before!

The Beethoven Festival finished with the 'Missa Solemnis', and I was in the artists' room where the Maestro was raging up and down as always before a concert. He came up to me and took hold of the lapels of my coat: 'Please, please, would you go on the platform and tell them we shall 'ave the concert next Tuesday.' Visions of a postponement of a European hook-up flitted across my dazed senses, but the sight of Madame Toscanini, who had obviously heard the remark, scuttling through the door leading up to her seat in the circle, somewhat consoled me. She had obviously heard it all before, but decided I might take charge on this occasion! I began to do what I could, and a moment later Edgar Mays, our splendid platform attendant, poked his head round the door and with a stentorian 'Ready thank you, Maestro' held it open and through it the great man mercifully went, leaving me to go to my own seat.

Another pre-concert story, giving some idea of Toscanini's relentless pursuit of perfection, was told me by one of his New York colleagues. In the interval at Carnegie Hall, there was nothing to come but the Beethoven Fifth, which had already been performed several times that week.

'Maestro,' said a friend, 'why are you in such a state? The Symphony was magnificent yesterday in Brooklyn.' 'Brooklyn?' was the retort. 'Brooklyn? Why, the tempi were *all* wrong in Brooklyn, and I *must* get them right tonight.'

One can still hear countless stories from those who worked with Toscanini, of his uncanny insight into the minds of others, of his prodigious feats of memory, and the amazing acuteness of his ear, but I can cap them all with something rarer still—a story of a mistake—the only one I have ever heard of.

Dame Myra Hess told me that she was rehearsing with him in New York for one of the rare concerts which included a concerto, and she had started the solo at the beginning of the slow movement of Beethoven's C minor Concerto. At the eighth bar, the soloist comes to a half-close in the dominant, but surprisingly moves off again into G major with a phrase not unlike one of the tenor arias in Gounod's *Faust*, and the orchestra comes in only at the twelfth bar. Toscanini at the rehearsal fell into Beethoven's trap, and brought the orchestra in at the eighth bar. Dame Myra, of course, let him go on, but after the rehearsal when they were alone together, said: 'Maestro, you will allow me to play my *Salut, demeure* tonight, won't you?' He enjoyed this joke immensely, and let Dame Myra play her full twelve bars at the concert.

Looking back through the seasonal programme, it may be of interest to pick out some other high spots. Stravinsky came in 1931 to play at **a** concert of his work (including 'The Rite of Spring', brilliantly conducted by Ansermet). A particularly fine list of pianists that first season included also Bartók, Rubinstein, Harold Samuel, Moiseiwitsch, Lamond, Solomon, Backhaus, Dohnanyi, Gieseking, Myra Hess and Cortot.

The 1931–2 season included Strauss, Walter, Weingartner, Malko, Ansermet, Ronald and Wood as conductors, and the first London performances of 'Belshazzar's Feast' and Holst's 'Hammersmith'. A Summer Festival of six concerts included three conducted by Koussevitsky, and three commemorating the Brahms Centenary.

The 1932–3 season dropped to eighteen concerts, and finished in March, in order to make way for the Summer Festival. There were three concerts to celebrate Elgar's seventy-fifth birthday. He himself took part in two and at the last rehearsal he made a most moving speech to the orchestra thanking them for their long and friendly co-operation. Sir Henry Wood conducted the first English performance of Hindemith's 'Das Unaufhörliche'.

The 1933–4 season included visits from Schönberg, Bartok, and Prokoviev. Holst's Choral Symphony and Bax's First Symphony were played, and also the first performance in England of *Wozzeck*, Alban Berg's opera which, in spite of its extreme difficulty, had swept round the opera houses of Europe until Hitler banned it.

We boldly planned it with an all-English cast; except for the name part, which was most powerfully sung by Hermann Biterauf of Stuttgart. The English singers covered themselves with glory. The B.B.C. engaged for three months a young coach who had recently left Berlin. Kurt Prerauer was his name, and he worked all day and every day with these singers, and also gave me most valued help as he knew Berg's mind to the smallest detail, having been recently immersed in the Berlin production. The orchestra too had a generous rehearsal allowance. I think it was eighteen three-hour rehearsals, spread over the previous three weeks. A few days before they began I happened to be lunching with an old friend from the Vienna Opera House, who was in London, and I pulled the rehearsal plan out of my pocket, and asked him what he thought. He pondered over it for some time, and then said: 'My friend, I know your orchestra, I know you, I know *Wozzeck*. You will have to postpone your performance. It cannot be done.'

I was horrified, but we went ahead, and I still treasure a long letter from the composer, who heard it by wireless, and his only criticism was that, after so much hard preparatory work, there should have been only a single performance. The B.B.C., however, offered to the management of Covent Garden a present of the whole cast and orchestra for three performances on condition they might be broadcast. Plans were going ahead and I actually saw designs for the sets, but at a later stage it was discovered that the B.B.C.'s offer did not also include the cost of scenery. It could not possibly have done so, because the B.B.C. in those days was only concerned with sound broadcasting and could hardly have been expected to provide scenery for the sole benefit of the Covent Garden audience. So the idea fell through.

In January of that season, instead of Winter Proms, six concerts of British music were given. Thirty-one composers were represented.

April 1935 saw the first performance of Vaughan Williams' F minor Symphony; in November Walton's completed Symphony was conducted by Hamilton Harty; and Constant Lambert introduced his 'Summer's Last Will and Testament' in January 1936. In March 1937 we gave a concert performance of Busoni's *Doktor Faust*. This was graced by the presence of Madame Busoni, who gave me a splendid photograph of her husband, and some interesting programmes written in his handwriting.

In 1937–8 Toscanini conducted the Ninth Symphony and the Brahms 'Requiem'; Wood, the Eighth Mahler. I did Tovey's Cello Concerto with Casals as soloist, and Schumann's lately-discovered Violin Concerto was played by Jelly d'Aranyi. New works by Prokoviev and Malipiero were heard; and Her Majesty the Queen (now Queen Elizabeth the Queen Mother) honoured with her presence a special Walton-Ireland programme.

Sir Henry Wood's jubilee was celebrated by two concerts in the autumn of 1938; and Bruno Walter gave us the Mozart 'Requiem' and Beethoven's Ninth soon afterwards.

Our last pre-war memory is Toscanini's Beethoven Cycle, including the Ninth and the Mass. It was the last time we were to hear him until he conducted the four Brahms Symphonies in the Festival Hall in 1953.

The first seven years of the B.B.C. Orchestra also included a great deal of importance in the studio concerts. As a general rule these had no publicity beyond the advance notice in the *Radio Times*, and occasional radio critics' comments. An appendix will enumerate the first perfor- mances given by the orchestra before the outbreak of war—some first renderings in England, but most of them world premières.

My first invitation to go abroad as B.B.C. Director came from Vienna, and in March 1933 I had two thrilling concerts with the famous Philhar- monic, led by Arnold Rosé, with Julius Buxbaum leading the cellos—in fact the whole Rosé Quartet played the solos in the Elgar Introduction and Allegro. I remember seeing Buxbaum hold up his part by the corner to gain his neighbours' sympathy that, though a solo, it was such a small part. We tempered British music with the great classics, rather to my trepidation, but the fourth Brahms and the Mozart G minor were both suggested by our hosts, and we had an amusing incident when rehearsing the Mozart.

At the beginning of the second movement I was astonished to hear the violas, followed by the seconds and firsts, slur their first two notes. This is printed in the parts, but there is no sign of it in the full score and I always supposed that it was just put in by the nineteenth-century editor when the parts were engraved. I stopped at once when the firsts followed the others, and asked Professor Rosé whether that was how they usually played it. He gave me a delightful Viennese shrug and said they did whatever the conductor directed. I said with some heat that I didn't think it mattered much what the conductor directed; we wanted to know what Mozart wrote. I added: 'We have the autograph manuscript of the symphony upstairs in this very building—we can find out at once.' We sent up, found no sign of a slur in the autograph, and duly separated the two notes.

The orchestra was most intrigued that a foreigner should have questioned a point of this kind and remembered where the autograph manuscript was, and a few weeks later I was charmed to get a nicely bound folio with all their signatures as a memento of the concert. Let into the outside cover was a photograph of a page of the autograph, the first page of the minuet. There seemed very little point in the choice of this page until it occurred to me that they had meant to photograph the page I had disputed and examined, but with Vienna's famous irresponsibility they had photographed the first page of the wrong movement. I showed the document to Bruno Walter later and he was thrilled to see the signatures of so many of his old friends.

The years 1931 to 1939 saw a meteoric development in broadcasting. The move from Savoy Hill to Broadcasting House (already too small for a full orchestra on the first day of its occupation) took place gradually in 1933 and I had a lovely room in the middle of the fifth floor. The whole floor had been reserved for the Music Department, with the Music Library in the Studio Tower on the same level. This luxury was not ours for long, as the whole department was fired out into Great Portland Street before four years had passed.

The housing of the orchestra had caused some headaches. The Concert Hall in Broadcasting House was designed for the pre-1930 studio orchestra of thirty-five, and of course, Savoy Hill could provide nothing adequate. We began in a huge disused wine warehouse immediately east of Waterloo Bridge. To begin with, the traffic rumble seemed to rule it out, but experts soon discovered that the frequency of this was far too low ever to trouble a microphone, so we went ahead, and became quite attached to this place, which soon held memories of many great visitors and great occasions.

Richard Strauss and Bruno Walter both conducted there. Gustav Holst often came as a listener whenever important works were being played. He formed in this connection the BMB (= Bother Mrs Beckett) Club. Since his time the Club has had an enormous membership, as Mrs

Beckett made herself personally responsible for the issue of studio passes often to several hundred visitors a night. We had an inner warehouse of like size which was never used; at the far end of this there was a sinister iron gate which must have given on to Thames mud. Fortunately we had no murderers in the B.B.C. Symphony Orchestra.

I am reminded of two rather amusing things that happened in that old studio under Waterloo Bridge. The first incident was on my return from my wedding trip in 1933. I called for the Rimsky-Korsakov 'Capriccio Espagnol' at the beginning of the first rehearsal—I think I just said: 'We'll start with the Rimsky, please.' Of course, the Mendelssohn Wedding March began with my down beat. Now the first bar of the March might well be something Russian, and I remember thinking to myself: 'What on earth have they got hold of? Is it something else of Rimsky's?' before the second bar made things clear. A few hours later a very handsome silver tray was given us by the orchestra.

On another occasion one of the older players, whose taste in drink was on the strong side, was seized with a coughing fit. Somebody got him some water, and this was passed over as I went on with the rehearsal. Gradually I became more and more conscious of disturbance, so I stopped and shouted: 'What *is* the matter? Haven't you ever seen a man drink a glass of water before?' '*Not that man!*' came the response in perfect unison.

A year or two later the big block on Delaware Road in Maida Vale, built as a roller-skating rink, was taken over. To this the orchestra soon moved, and we returned there after the war. I can say from experience that other orchestras in London envy the B.B.C. the comfort, warmth, and permanence of their studio with its restaurant and rest rooms.

A delightful incident soon after our move to Broadcasting House occurred when a very houseproud new house manager discovered that Cedric Sharpe, the well-known cellist, who was taking part at that time in a good many ensembles, delighted, like so many cellists (I wonder why?), to come in at the last moment, throw his hat and coat anywhere, and strike up in record time. The new studios were *not* to be spoilt with odd clothes strewn about. The cloakroom *must* be used, and Arthur Wynn, our amusing artists' manager, was instructed to re-state this firmly to 'a certain Mr C. Sharp who has repeatedly broken the rules about cloakrooms'. Arthur Wynn replied a few days later to the house manager, 'I have seen Mr C. Sharp as you wished, and he is now D flat.'

It was some time before we began to think that the B.B.C. Orchestra belonged not only to London listeners, but the whole country, and the idea of provincial visits began to take shape. We went first to Manchester in December 1934, giving the Strauss 'Hero's Life' with Manchester's own Arthur Catterall in the solo part. Although we had kept in close touch with the Hallé management about our visit, and were most courteously treated by them, some Manchester musicians who knew better than the Hallé committee organized a boycott of the concert: the only time this has happened. It is worth adding that Dr W. G. Whittaker when a member of the Music Advisory Committee expressed the opinion that a visit to Glasgow from the orchestra would damage 'the Scottish'. This postponed our first visit to Glasgow for three or four years.

A quick trip, for a single concert, to Brussels took place in March 1935, and the following year something much more adventurous was planned: Paris, Zurich, Vienna, Budapest, all inside six days. The programmes too were full of interest, each containing a classic, a work, a compliment to the country we were in, and a show piece. This was very cleverly carried out by Edward Clark and Julian Herbage as follows:

Monday, April 20th 1936

Paris, Salle Pleyel

ROUSSEL	Pour une Fête de Printemps
LAMBERT	The Rio Grande, for Pianoforte, Chorus & Orchestra: CLIFFORD CURZON; LES CHOEURS RUSSES VLASSOV
BEETHOVEN	Symphony No. 8
STRAVINSKY	Le Sacre du Printemps

WAGNER	The Ride of the Valkyrie (encore)
WAGNER	Overture, Die Meistersinger (encore)

Tuesday, April 21st 1936

Zurich, Tonhalle

WAGNER	Prelude, Die Meistersinger
BUSONI	Two Studies for 'Doktor Faust', Sarabande: Cortège
WALTON	Viola Concerto: LIONEL TERTIS
HONEGGER	Chant de Joie
BRAHMS	Symphony No. 4

WAGNER	The Ride of the Valkyrie (encore)

Thursday, April 23rd 1936

Vienna, Konzerthaus

BRAHMS	Tragic Overture
SCHÖNBERG	Variations for Orchestra

VAUGHAN WILLIAMS	Symphony in F minor
RAVEL	Daphnis and Chloe (2nd series)

WAGNER	The Ride of the Valkyrie (encore)
WAGNER	Overture, Die Meistersinger (encore)

Friday, April 24th 1936
Budapest, Municipal Theatre

ELGAR	Introduction and Allegro, for String Quartet and String Orchestra
BARTOK	Four Orchestral Pieces
BAX	Tintagel
BEETHOVEN	Symphony No. 5

WAGNER	The Ride of the Valkyrie (encore)
WAGNER	Overture, Die Meistersinger (encore)

We had some adventures naturally, and some are perhaps worth recording. On the journey from Paris to Zurich my large suitcase fell out of the rack on to my head; luckily it only grazed the skin and slipped past, and I was none the worse. Admiral Sir Charles Carpendale, who was in administrative charge of the tour, was taking no chances, and on arrival in Zurich he insisted on my seeing a doctor (who charmingly refused a fee for the examination, but asked for tickets for the concert) and our Admiral being a resourceful sailor, rigged up a protecting rail behind me as I stood, for the Zurich Tonhalle has a rather high platform with no rail at its edge.

Next day saw us on the long trip from Zurich to Vienna, over the Arlberg Pass, where the snow was still lying. This was too much for the more adventurous spirits (including our Admiral), who began pelting each other until the train authorities ordered us back to go on with our journey. The wonderful country round Innsbruck and Salzburg appealed to many of our musicians, and holidays in that region were much in favour that summer. The Vienna concert was, of course, unforgettable, and the enthusiasm most heart-warming. The first public performance of Schönberg's Variations caused something of a sensation, and in the interval the Federal President of Austria, deeply shocked, asked me the naïve question: 'Who is this Schönberg, anyhow?' In 1936 Vienna was still a very conservative place.

The concert had been preceded by a notable tea-party given by the Vienna Philharmonic Orchestra to our orchestra with Bruno Walter and several other eminent musicians there to welcome us. It was a splendid occasion.

Our departure from Vienna also was something of a sensation. As my taxi drew up at the station I noticed a lorry carrying a load of music stands and so on, and these were taken off and brought on to our platform. In a few minutes a large contingent of the Vienna Symphony Orchestra had assembled and were playing their lovely waltzes and marches to bid us farewell. This gesture was more than our Admiral could bear, and he climbed up one of the ladders which were to be found at the end of every Austrian railway coach, and, from the roof, took over the musical direction of the proceedings. The train only started ten minutes late.

I had an unnerving experience in Budapest. The orchestra were in an hotel close to the theatre where we were to play, and a few of us were taken to a Palace on the banks of the Danube, to see a wonderful view across the river. After an early meal I decided I would walk to the theatre, as I had noted the way, and had plenty of time. However, I soon decided that it was a stupid idea. It was a very important concert, and I should not have set myself to walk so far.

I hailed a taxi, but—could I remember the name of the theatre? I made a gesture of fiddle playing which the Jehu cheerfully accepted, and started off in the opposite direction. I had a good deal of trouble to stop him, and the prospect of a European hook-up (several other countries were to relay the concert) now made the time factor a matter of anxiety, but mercifully I soon saw some of my orchestral friends walking to the concert, so I thankfully paid off the taxi, and walked on with them. The theatre was packed and many extra chairs were put into the gangways in a way which would have shocked our British fire authorities. When I reached my place on the platform I discovered an old friend, Joseph Szigeti, sitting in the middle of the front row; I could easily have kicked him in the face. I was told next day that a great many of my colleagues had spent the night at one (or more) of the many night-clubs, and it was said that the B.B.C. might have spared itself the expense of hotel beds; but everyone was present at the station next morning and they spent a long and sleepy travelling day before catching the evening boat from Ostend.

On 1 July 1933 I gave the very finest performance of my life. At noon, at the Old Meeting House at Ditchling, under the Downs, there took the name of Ann Boult one who had been born Ann Bowles. Only our three parents and two sisters were present, with three or four friends including Walford Davies, who played the harmonium for us to sing the Bunyan 'He who would valiant be', and Lady Davies. Scott Goddard, another old friend, lived at Ditchling, so I rang him up just before the service. He arrived with an enormous armful of delphiniums, which greatly brightened the Old Meeting House.

Afterwards we all drove up on to the Downs and had a picnic lunch, to which my parents-in-law coming from Kent contributed an enormous half-sieve of cherries, and then we drove away to Dover. Ann, who began the day with a bathe at Brighton, finished it with another at Calais, and from there I selfishly insisted on revisiting many old haunts, among them the Portofino promontory, a visit to Mrs Hedmondt, now retired at Ragaz, and several days walking in the hills north of Innsbruck.

We were anxious to keep the ceremony secret and so it was impossible to collect Ann's four children from their various schools.

We returned just as their holidays were beginning, and I had much to learn about being a paterfamilias. I have gone on learning this art, as well as the art of music, ever since. We have now been enriched by two sons-in-law and eleven grandchildren but we suffered one terrible loss through the war in the carnage of 1944.

Holidays abroad were fairly frequent in these years and Salzburg Festival, before it became too fashionable, was always memorable, even when that valley was showing that it could produce rain of tropical intensity. One year my wife and I took our two daughters, and the four of us enjoyed many country walks together. An English friend told me one evening that he had lunched at a restaurant in one of the villages and was informed by the landlord that the day before he had given lunch to Sir Beecham, the English musician, and his three beautiful daughters—a mistake which one could easily make at that time. I may add that Beecham was not then in Austria and he had no daughters.

Towards the end of 1936 Walford Davies, as Master of the King's Music, asked me whether I should be willing to help with the Coronation of King George VI. Of course I agreed, and Sir Ernest Bullock and Sir Walford and I had many talks together, but the main lines were at once clear. Bullock took charge of the Service proper and all the choral work in it. I was to look after the framework, the orchestral music which preceded the Service and again while the congregation dispersed, and this of course took a good deal of time. The orchestra was collected from the leaders of all the London orchestras, and we were a tight fit in that rather narrow gallery. It was a great occasion, indeed, and there was no hitch, except at the very beginning when Sir Walter Alcock had to improvise for a long time before the Royal Party arrived; but he never seemed at a loss. As I had become a New Year Knight in 1937 I was particularly happy to be taking part in this great and moving ceremony on 12 May.

In 1953, another invitation of the same kind came from Sir William McKie (whose knighthood was happily announced on the day of the Coronation). It was for the Coronation of Queen Elizabeth II. My share

was again the framework of the Service and included the first performance
of another fine Walton March, 'Orb and Sceptre'—he had written 'Crown
Imperial' in 1937—also a splendid Processional with an important organ
part by Sir Arthur Bliss, written for Her Majesty the Queen Mother's
Procession into the Abbey. We played it to her again some years later at
a Royal College of Music concert, when other Coronation works were
included in the programme, notably Parry's noble 'I was glad'.

Chapter Ten

WAR—1939-1945

MUNICH IN 1938 gave the whole European world a horrid jolt. The outcome was a tremendous relief, of course, but from then on people were preparing themselves, and an example of this was a hideous hour I spent with the orchestral manager of the B.B.C. 'They have decided,' he said (we never discussed who 'they' might be in the B.B.C.), 'that in the event of war the orchestra is to be reduced to ninety and they ask us to list the thirty who can most suitably be sent to war work, leaving a balanced orchestra behind.' It was a dreadful task—we felt as if those young men were dead already. As it turned out the orchestra suffered few casualties. Three who went into the Fire Service, Terence MacDonagh, William de Mont and Edmund Chesterman, gained British Empire Medals for a very brave rescue in a London raid. One other, 'Flatiron' Southworth, was long a prisoner, but our only fatal casualty was a bass player, Albert Cockerill, who, with his wife, was killed in their flat in Bristol. He had been with me in Birmingham, and was an old friend.

The reaction to war in 1939 seemed to me to be far more intense than it was in 1914, but perhaps this was merely the difference of circumstances. In 1914 I was staying with friends in the Lake District (which in 1939 too was said to be wonderfully aloof from war) and even when Territorials came to guard Thirlmere (we never discovered what against) we could hardly have been quite as impressed as friends living near the railway at Winchester in 1914, who heard trains going through every few minutes all night for nearly a week, according to the detailed plans drawn up by Lord Haldane many years before.

Surrey in 1939 was to be an evacuation area, and we spent a good deal of time doing odd jobs like filling mattresses, and preparing the village hall for reception, and so on. We had been told that as soon as we heard 'This is the B.B.C. Home Service' coming from our loudspeakers we must take this as an order to get ourselves to Bristol as soon as possible. It came on Friday night, and we set out at 8 o'clock on Saturday morning, joining a procession which was, of course, the centre of interest in every village we passed. Rows of people watched us as we went through, and somehow we felt rather ashamed of ourselves. Those who travelled by train had very different experiences.

Blackout, mercifully, began late at this time of year, but it was startlingly complete everywhere, and we heard that even Queen Mary had to sit in the dark on her way to Badminton. Apparently nothing could be done about the signal boxes, which cheered the travellers all the way with their brilliant lighting. Bristol Station at 3 a.m. was not exactly a haven of refuge, but even here people did their best to direct travellers, and some hotels near the station (one couldn't walk far in the blackout) kept their lounges open even when their bedrooms were full. The Bristol B.B.C. also was in every way ready to help us all, and the billeting officers did prodigious feats of putting gallons into pint pots. By Monday the whole orchestra was in Bristol as well as the entire Drama, Variety, Religious and Children's Hour Departments.

We gathered at the office. We hung about. We waited. No orders. All our friends were saying 'Can't you at any rate play us a Beethoven Symphony between the News Bulletins?' But no! It transpired that Whitehall, some months earlier, had decided that only the lightest fare would be wanted by this frivolous nation while it was coping with evacuation and the early problems of war, so my friend Sandy Macpherson, the organist, who did a grand job, had a sixteen-hour day. The Variety Department ran out of jokes, while the Symphony Orchestra went for long walks exploring the lovely country round Bristol. My wife and I were lucky to find a furnished house, and the owners were kind enough to turn out immediately. In time Authority began to let us do some of the work that many people were clamouring for. Looking back, it seems extraordinary how slowly everything moved. It was several months before we were allowed to give public concerts in Bristol. When we did begin there was a big demand.

It had been decided that though the orchestra, and other departments I have mentioned, came to Bristol, the rest of the Music Department should go to Evesham, where they had billeting problems that were even more difficult than ours. Dr R. S. Thatcher, my Deputy Director of Music, took charge at Evesham of a somewhat smaller department, for here too, as in the orchestra, reductions had been planned. The Evesham office had been prepared for some time as the B.B.C.'s No. 1 Evacuation Post. The house, Wood Norton, stands on a steep hill and commands a fine view of the Avon Valley. As a boy I had often heard of it because at that time the Duke of Orleans, pretender to the throne of France, held his court there and his movements were closely watched by the English papers. The B.B.C. had done much to prepare it for broadcasting, presumably via Droitwich and Daventry, in the event of London failing. I knew that such a place was being prepared, but had no idea where it was. This secret was guarded by three or four of the highest officials.

However, during the 1939 summer at some international conference it was reported that a German official asked one of our people how Wood Norton was getting on. How characteristic, or at any rate how very un-English of him, to give away the fact that he knew its name. I wonder if international affairs would go better if people studied these traits more. I think we all can think of stories which show a lamentable ignorance of the point of view of the foreigner. The delicate perception shown, for instance, in a book like *A Passage to India* could surely have saved countless misunderstanding or 'incidents' in the history of the British Raj.

The curious way in which Germans work in blinkers was seen by some of us one night when we were on Home Guard duty at the B.B.C. head-quarters in Bristol. At the time the Germans were bombing Birmingham and by ill-luck Wood Norton, which was full of panelling with the Duke's fleur-de-lys on it, caught fire. Communication between Evesham and London happened to be going via Bristol, and we could overhear it on a loudspeaker, as the details of the fire were reported from time to time. Now and then London repeated the question: 'Has Jerry spotted you yet?' Always the same answer: 'Not yet.' Evesham is not more than twenty-five miles from Birmingham as the crow flies, and a flaming Wood Norton must have been a tempting target. Apparently not—I suppose they were flying up and down a beam, and could not leave it.

It used to be at about tea-time when we would hear that the beam was on Bristol, though as the same beam also served some tempting targets in South Wales, it was not until the flares began coming down that we knew we were actually for it.

There was a good deal of talk about Fifth Columnists, and no doubt, Bristol, particularly after the fall of France, might have been a happy hunting-ground for them. The nearest thing to Fifth Column activity that came my way happened one summer evening when everyone was away and I was alone in the house. I had gone to bed early and was asleep when the sirens went off about 11.30. Drowsily I was about to get up when a stick of bombs fell nearby. Outside I found that some troops billeted in two neighbouring big houses were out in the road in some excitement. They had been chatting at the gate where their sentry was posted when a car entered the avenue of Sneyd Park, switched its head-lights full on straight down the avenue for a moment, and the bombs fell immediately. One smashed a big staircase window in the house of a member of the orchestra, and smothered his daughter in glass, cutting her badly.

There were many other stories of air raid adventures during our time in Bristol. Paul Beard, Leader of the B.B.C. Symphony Orchestra for over twenty years, was flung off his motor cycle on one occasion, and on another took over the musical part of the Sunday night Epilogue with Stuart Hibberd, both lying under a table for protection.

By 1 November, after repeated requests, we had been allowed to give a public concert in the Colston Hall, and after that things improved. I recently found in my score of the Franck Symphony a postcard signed by H. C. Colles (the chief critic of *The Times*) saying 'Thank you very much for the Franck last night. These things help.' The public concerts were an immediate success with the Bristol audiences. I remember when Sir Henry Wood gave his rousing performance of Tchaikovsky's Fourth Symphony, and I sat at the back of the hall, and was very happy to see how the audience revelled in it.

We were in Bristol almost two years, and, apart from the raid nights, there was much to make it a pleasant life. Mrs Napier Miles was the widow of the composer whose opera seasons in pre-war Bristol had attracted a good deal of attention. She now lived in the house she had built in the walled garden of the magnificent Vanbrugh house Kings Weston, which had been their home. One day Mrs Miles asked me whether the orchestra would like to come and help eat her strawberries. I accepted with alacrity, and in spite of bad news from Italy one or two days before the date we had fixed, we had a most enjoyable afternoon with the war almost banished from our thoughts.

On 30 August 1940 I was in London to conduct a concert with the London Philharmonic Orchestra at the Central Hall, Westminster. It was an invitation concert. The London County Council had gathered the Mayors and Corporations of all the Boroughs of Greater London as a gesture to the London Philharmonic Orchestra at a moment of crisis, in the hope that some of the suburban municipalities would themselves be inclined to promote something orchestral.

I should think that at least two-thirds of those who had accepted invitations must have come to the concert, and many distinguished Londoners were there.

All went well until, when Mr J. B. Priestley was speaking during the interval, we gradually became conscious of a distant wailing background to his speech. Yorkshireman that he is, he carried on to the finish. We adjourned for refreshments, and then went on with the second part of the concert without visiting the fine shelters in the basement of the Central Hall.

Most of us left the hall at once at the end of the concert, and I walked up Whitehall with two or three members of the orchestra, watching the brilliant flashing of searchlights and hearing the distant drone of engines. My way home took me past Queen's Hall, where I had heard that Keith Douglas and Owen Mase, the organizers of this year's Proms, had been keeping their audience indoors until the 'All Clear' was sounded by

ingenious impromptu concerts which were called 'Siren Sessions'. I
reached the hall about eleven, and found the fun in full swing. With
Mase at the piano and Basil Cameron conducting, the audience was heart-
ily singing away at such old favourites as 'Shenandoah' and 'Rio Grande'.
I was glad to see that the firm regulations of the London County Council
had begun to relax and by this time most of the Promenaders were sitting
on the floor instead of standing. The hall had been sold right out, and
two-thirds of the audience were still there.

After a pianoforte solo from an anonymous member of the audience,
I was asked to 'go and talk to them'. I managed to re-tell a story which
I had just heard Priestley tell his Central Hall audience, but without his
delightful Yorkshireness. A Vivaldi Double Sonata played by two members of the orchestra came next, and then Keith Douglas conducted quite
superbly a sort of inverted Farewell Symphony, showing what might
happen if anyone really did bomb London or interfere with the orchestra's
punctual arrival. It was unthinkable that our beloved Prom conductor, Sir
Henry Wood, should ever be late, and so the conductor had to begin
alone, and was gradually joined by members of the orchestra (in which I
had the great privilege of playing the triangle) until we found ourselves
in the full flood of the *Faust* ballet music.

Songs followed from a young Australian student, who was acting as
general assistant and librarian to Sir Henry. Once again the orchestra
assembled—the London Symphony Orchestra were doing the Proms that
year—that is, the thirty members who were still in the hall—and the
librarian gave out material for the *Figaro* Overture. A hush spread through
the hall: who was going to conduct? To our astonishment, a brisk,
bearded figure mounted the rostrum, and what appeared to be one of our
most famous conductors galvanized the band into its 'fastest ever'. Sir
Thomas Beecham's impersonator, I might add, characteristically found it
necessary to make speeches both before and after his performance, and
also to shout 'stop talking' in the middle.

A member of the audience then mounted the platform and said that she
felt everyone would agree that they were getting so much more than their
original money's worth that they ought to contribute to the Musicians'
Pension Fund, in which Sir Henry was known to have a keen interest.
Basil Cameron seized his hat, and I (having come without one) was given
a large wastepaper basket (lined with newspaper to keep the coins in),
and we circulated, Basil round the Grand Circle (still quite full), and I
threading my way through the Promenade, which had now been filled
with seats, all occupied.

Cello solos from another orchestral artist, some capital Dickens
sketches, and several more contributions from members of the audience,
including Mimi's Song from *Bohème* sung in German by a refugee, led

With Pablo Casals, 1937

With H.M. The Queen Mother, 1954, and
(*left*) Friedrich Gulda

The grasp of the stick: two views

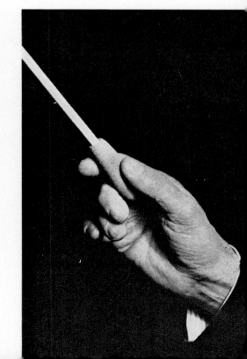

up to another group of community songs, after which, at 3.55 a.m. the 'All Clear' was heard, and we went out into the blackout.

We were glad to find buses and tube trains running and got to our beds quickly for what was left of the night. It had been a noisy raid, we were told, but we had heard none of it, and we owe a real debt to Keith Douglas and Owen Mase for keeping the ball rolling in a way which seemed effort-less and easy, but must actually have involved much quick decision and anxious spade work behind the scenes. They certainly infused a new kind of liveliness into the dear old Queen's Hall.

This touching note, which was signed, but with no date or address, has just turned up in a textbook which I very rarely open. It refers, of course, to the occasion I have just described:

Sir Adrian Boult

As this is the only opportunity I shall probably ever have, I would like to thank you for making an unpleasant air-raid a memorable occasion. You may remember the time in Queen's Hall when you played the triangle as an extra to keep the audience entertained until we could venture out. It was the only time I was not petrified during a raid.

Towards the end of 1940 the raid situation at Bristol had become so tiresome that it was decided we should record our concerts in the afternoon and then disperse to our homes, leaving a few brave engineers to play it. Unfortunately, the quality of war-time recording was very variable, and we had to listen—from our shelters—to stuff which made us sometimes rather ashamed, and this, as well as the actual raids, began to suggest a move to a quieter spot.

Variety had already gone to North Wales, and Drama to Manchester which, however, was not very quiet! By March the Corporation had agreed that somewhere else should be found for us. In August, when we moved, Bristol had seen its last raid, bar one. The Corporation emissaries had a difficult time in their search. They went to eight or ten Mayors with the same question: 'Can you produce two hundred and fifty beds, forty offices under one roof, ten studios of varying sizes, including two really big ones for orchestras?' Finally Bedford, already crammed with refugees, gallantly said 'Yes', and set about the preparations. The adaptation of the studios presented problems but worst of all was the question of the forty offices. Two small residential hotels, filled mostly by old people, were requisitioned by the Mayor, and I felt awful when I inspected them and wondered how the poor residents would find accommodation else-where.

We were very sad to leave Bristol. We had all made many good friends; it was in every way a delightful city, and we had splendid audiences there. It was deplorable that the fine Colston Hall should have been burnt down one night from unknown causes when it had safely escaped the raids, largely owing to the vigilance of the caretaker.

The orchestra and the Music Department travelled to Bedford by special train over a devious route avoiding London. It was the last luxury journey before dining cars disappeared for the duration. I missed the fun as I made the journey on a push-bike. I remember running into Mr Eshelby of Steinways outside the British Restaurant in Aylesbury where I had been having lunch.

Bedford, already overcrowded, welcomed us in a very friendly way even though some people wondered whether we should attract air raids. I gather that our principal defences were: the climate and the local geography. The place was so thickly covered with trees and mists that no invader would be able to find it. We lived in Clapham, a village two miles to the north of Bedford, and I was told that by river it was fifteen miles. One was unable to walk far in any direction without finding the river bank.

The authorities let us alter the platform of the Corn Exchange, and it made a reasonably good studio, but a rather overpowering concert hall, and when it was used as a Corn Exchange, we moved to the Great Hall of Bedford School. This place with its wooden galleries made a fine soundbox, and the school authorities were most co-operative, only asking that the boys might have access to the galleries, while we often had several hundred troops, American and our own, on the floor.

Bedford Corn Exchange is right in the centre of the town, and at the mid-morning break, or the tea interval, it was easy to get sustenance quite near. I used to go across to Woolworths where a friendly Welsh lady would always have a beaker of Ovaltine ready for me. One day we were rehearsing incidental music for a play in which Laurence Olivier was taking part. He had some difficult synchronization with us and very kindly came down early in order to do his special pieces before the main rehearsal.

At the beginning of the break he was telling me how, in his young days at the Birmingham Repertory Theatre, he used to come to the City of Birmingham orchestral concerts and always found music a great stimulus in helping him to learn a part quickly. As we talked I realized he might like some coffee, and discovered that he shared my preference. Off we went to Woolworths: I was terrified he would be mobbed, but, although he looked strikingly handsome in his Naval Air Force uniform, mercifully no one spotted him, and we got him back intact to the Corn Exchange.

Another Bedford guest, whose visit none of us will forget, was Yehudi Menuhin. He flew over simply to play to American troops, but the B.B.C. asked him to give two performances of the Bartók Concerto (the first in England), and we had several memorable rehearsals. The night of his arrival, W. W. Thompson, our concert manager, asked me to come with him and dine at the hotel in order that Mr Menuhin should not be left by himself. We had the usual rationed dinner, and it could not have satisfied our guest, who, having flown in from Timbuctoo or somewhere, had had no lunch. We all decided that the savoury would be more filling than the sweet, and were regaled with a mushroom, on a large piece of toast. 'Tommy' and I gobbled our toast, but Menuhin left his. When the waitress took our plates he said to her: 'Now, please, I would like a nice beef steak'. We all laughed and the waitress said: 'But look, Sir, you haven't eaten your toast.' 'I'm sorry,' said our guest, 'but I have VERY strong views on the subject of soggy toast.'

After the performance he flew off again and was back in about ten days for the second performance. We had a refresher rehearsal, and I arranged for lunch and transport so that we could get back in good time. 'No thanks, I think I must just stay right here and sleep.' We were at Bedford School where there was nowhere to sleep and nothing to sleep on. However, a little Red Cross room was open just by the hall (most rooms were locked) and I suggested putting two or three chairs together for him. 'No thanks, this will do nicely—please wake me at 2.' He curled up on a quite small table, and was asleep almost before I had left the room. He had not moved when I went in to wake him. Had he done so, he would have been on the floor.

Ordinary touring was, of course, suspended for us during the war, but we did get about a little. We went off by bus to Oxford one day and played to a Sheldonian packed with khaki. We gave a good many concerts in Cambridge, only an hour away by train, also Leicester and Nottingham.

The biggest occasions for us were when we visited the Services. We had, at different times, one week with the Navy, one with the Army, one with the United States Army and two with our Air Force. A section of the orchestra spent a week in Aberdare where we played every night with a different choral society from one of the valleys. They came over by coach with numerous supporters. These were exciting nights, and the singing was, of course, memorable.

When we visited Portsmouth, the gymnasium of the Naval Barracks had been converted, by means of acres of bunting, into a delightful hall. At rehearsals we had a big unofficial audience whose attention was extraordinary. One old seaman was spotted, always in the same place, standing, enthralled. Walter Legge asked him if he had always enjoyed music. 'Music, Sir? I didn't know what it was until this week, but it's fair got me, it has, Sir. It's worse than the drink.'

The Aldershot Week was very exciting, too, with the Garrison Theatre packed each night. We were told that we had beaten the record for takings, hitherto held by Miss Gracie Fields, by one and ninepence.

We went twice to the enormous Air Force Station at St Athan near

Cardiff, and also for a few days to a big camp in Shropshire. There is a fine theatre at both of these, and at St Athan our entrance was just beside that to the swimming bath. I hadn't realized how important swimming was from the Air Force point of view, and how vigorously encouraged, with rubber dinghies in the pool always available for rescue practice. 'Go and have a look in there, sir' was my first introduction to it from the driver of our instrument van, 'those boys they're just made of india-rubber' The horseplay going on at the top of the twelve-foot board certainly made one hold one's breath, until we realized that what he said was just about true.

There were six or seven concerts here, and we invited Albert Coates to conduct one night, and I sat at the back, and had a lesson in concentration. The audience was so still that it was a shock to see anyone move a pipe or cigarette to keep it alight. By the time the interval came the air was quite clear, to become thick with smoke a moment later when everyone had lit up. It became perfectly clear again during the second half of the concert.

Our American tour centred round Bristol as we were always comfortably accessible to the other big American area in Bedfordshire; I got a shock when, after a sumptuous high tea, I approached the officer in charge, and thanked him for everything. 'That's all right, sir, a great pleasure. Would you mind answering a question for me, sir ? My wife says she is the daughter of a guy called Nikisch who was in your line, I believe. Was he any good?' He was greatly reassured to hear that his father-in-law had held down Koussevitsky's post in Boston for five years and had been supreme in Europe for many years.

It will be remembered that all places of entertainment were closed on the outbreak of war. This, of course, included the Proms which could hardly have been kept going with the orchestra on a war basis. The following year, as we have seen, Keith Douglas and Owen Mase re-organized them and carried on with Sir Henry Wood, booking the Albert Hall promptly when Queen's Hall was bombed.

The B.B.C. was ready to relieve the plucky exponents of private enterprise by the summer of 1942, but the advantage of using the other London orchestras was not dropped. Sir Henry felt it wise to invite Basil Cameron to be associate conductor with him, and with the return of the B.B.C. Orchestra I was privileged to join as second associate. It was a great thrill to play to that wonderful audience, and I greatly regretted that administrative difficulties made it impossible to adopt permanently an arrangement tried in that year when three orchestras were engaged, and alternated in such a way that no one played more than two nights in succession. There was nearly always a free day between concerts when it was possible to rehearse or rest, as seemed most advisable. This is, of course, now the

rule. I feel so strongly that the nightly concert, particularly with programmes of such great length, does not allow the music to be played as
finely as those splendid audiences deserve. Indeed it has always been a
marvel to me that Sir Henry achieved and maintained so high a standard
in the face of such a long season, and the same instrumentalists playing
night after night though with varied programmes.

In 1942 and 1943 Basil Cameron and I were associates; in 1944, the
fiftieth year, Sir Henry began the season with the London Philarmonic
Orchestra. However, Hitler was again at work, and flying bombs were
coming over in large numbers. 'Never mind,' said the Promenaders,
'we don't care whether we're killed at home or in the Albert Hall.' To
those in authority it was not as simple as that. A V.2 on Clapham or
Brixton might kill a dozen people; one on the Albert Hall might kill
6,000. The season ended in the middle of the second week.

Nothing daunted, Sir Henry came along to Bedford where our orchestra
had already reassembled after the holiday, and each night we played and
broadcast, not the whole Prom concert, but that portion of it which it had
been planned to broadcast.

On Friday, 28 July we had a brilliant performance of the Seventh
Beethoven from Sir Henry. We all felt him to be in specially fine form that
evening. Next day we heard he had been taken ill in the night, and soon
realized it had been his swan song. He died a few weeks later, after more
than fifty years of superb service. Basil Cameron and I felt most uneasy
about facing the 1945 season without him, but of course it had to be done,
and the support we had from orchestra and audience was magnificent.

The orchestra were then in particularly good form because we had left
Bedford in July, just before the season opened. There had been some
unrest during those last months because the B.B.C. showed no sign of
bringing us back to London when peace came, and we were all anxious to
return. Many had houses which had been deserted or requisitioned for five
years, and nearly everybody wanted to leave Bedford, splendid wartime
base through it had been. As it was, the B.B.C. had had great difficulty
in finding London studios, and for many months the People's Palace in
Mile End Road was our principal home, with occasional public concerts
in the Royal Albert Hall.

In one of the wartime seasons, before the space was railed off between
the platform and the front of the Promenade, I was conducting on the
Last Night and there was a mass attack on the platform immediately the
orchestra walked out at the end of the concert. Souvenirs were taken, and
I believe some sheets were torn out of the music and taken away, as well
as two of my precious conducting sticks (I often had a spare there in case
of accidents). This was immediately reported to us in the artists' room
where I was changing, and my wife went straight out to the artists'

entrance, and harangued the crowd there, explaining that the sticks were not being made in wartime, and I hadn't many left. They were both returned immediately—they are a good-natured crowd.

My younger stepdaughter did me a great service during several of the war seasons. We lived out at Oxshott, and she insisted on keeping goats to make up for our milk shortage. Every day she would milk the goats in the late afternoon, and come straight up to the Albert Hall, carrying a most welcome bottle for me to drink in the interval.

Keith Douglas, besides his promptness in taking the Albert Hall for the Promenade Concerts the moment Queen's Hall was destroyed, also took advice from Hope Bagenal on its acoustic properties. This expert designed a movable shell of screens which made a very great difference to the projection of the sound, while also enhancing the lovely quality which the Albert Hall gives to all sound that leaves that platform.

The difficulty and expense of erection, and the fact that the screens masked a good many of the chorus seats which are usually sold at orchestral concerts, caused, as time went on, a gradual reduction in the number of screens used. Concert promoters disliked losing revenue, and the hall authorities often found it difficult to spare staff and time to put them up. They had been used less and less; I made myself unpopular by insisting on having them after everyone else had stopped, but now I, too, have given up the struggle.

In the autumn of 1944 I was greatly honoured by the award of the much-coveted Medal of the Royal Philharmonic Society. It was, of course, a tribute just as much to those who had been working with me, and I accepted it in a speech telling something of the war adventures of the members of the B.B.C. Symphony Orchestra, who all shared the honour, I felt.

Before the war was over Moura Lympany and I were invited to one of the Paris Conservatoire concerts. It was a great thrill to see Paris so soon after its liberation, though there was, of course, a great deal of sadness and difficulty everywhere. The members of the orchestra said they had seen no butter for weeks, and the hot water systems were not working in even the most expensive hotels. That splendid musician and wonderful colleague, Charles Munch, who was responsible for the original invitation, absolutely refused to allow me to stay in any of these hotels, and I was entertained in princely style by Monsieur and Madame Margot-Noble-maire who had a lovely flat near the Eiffel Tower. They had converted their dining-room into a storehouse for firewood, and as they possessed farms both in Normandy and the South, had continual supplies of almost any food one could desire.

In the interval of the concert I was asked to go down to meet the committee of the orchestra with Monsieur Munch, and I was greatly touched when given a splendidly bound copy of the Requiem of Berlioz with an embossed monogram C.S-S. It had been signed by all the Committee and Munch himself, with an inscription to the effect that the score had been Camille Saint-Saëns' property and it was thought that I would like to possess it as I had mentioned at the beginning of our first rehearsal that I had as a boy heard a great deal about the Conservatoire Orchestra because my mother was translating Berlioz' letters and memoirs for the Everyman Edition. I have little doubt that Munch had pulled the copy off his own shelves and devoted it to this charming gesture.

In November of that year another invitation came from abroad—Amsterdam and Brussels. I was the first foreigner to conduct the Concertgebouw after the war. Holland was recovering from its Occupation as quickly as possible, but things were still *very* difficult. A small airfield near Leyden was all that civilian traffic could use, and I was fetched from there by a member of the Concertgebouw staff in a car which he had taken to pieces and dispersed in a dozen different friends' houses during the war. He had only just assembled it, and it was still one of the very few private cars in Amsterdam. As the railway had not been repaired, I should, without him, probably have been unable to reach Amsterdam till next day. The orchestra had suffered serious losses, and the wartime replacements were naturally of a different calibre from their older colleagues, though Edvard van Beinum was quickly effecting amazing improvement.

I had flown over in 1940, and had two or three wonderful days in a neutral city with amazing food and no black-out. That concert took place on 29 February 1940, and had, of course, been a pre-war engagement from which they offered to release me, but I saw no reason why I should not keep my promise, though there was every chance that Hitler's superstitious mind might choose 29 February as a good day to invade Holland. However, he waited a little longer, and it was the poor Sadler's Wells Ballet who had to fly for their lives a few weeks later.

Two years later, the big Choral Society in Amsterdam called Toonkunst, which always sings the Annual Matthew Passion performance and took part in the Mahler Choral Works which Mengelberg had in his programmes so often, decided to make a thanksgiving gesture to this country for our help in the war. They gave a pair of performances of 'The Dream of Gerontius' in English (I believe that they sing in six or seven languages) and engaged me to conduct.

The chairman and chorus-master came over in the early autumn to talk things over, and just as we had finished lunch the chairman said: 'But we have forgotten a very important thing, we want to settle the soloists.' I said, of course, that I was in their hands; they knew the available singers, and I could not possibly choose. 'But we want English singers; this is all agesture to your country!'

At once we went off in a taxi to see Mrs Tillett, whose wonderful diary system enabled us to book Mary Jarred, Parry Jones and Harold Williams on the spot; the whole thing was arranged in twenty minutes. Early in January 1947 we went over, and were given a wonderful reception. I particularly remembered Edvard van Beinum's comment in the interval: 'But this is a masterpiece!' I was able to remind him that fifty years before, fifty miles away Richard Strauss had said exactly the same thing after a performance in the Lower Rhenish Festival at Düsseldorf.

During the next dozen years or so I went abroad a good deal; Holland seven times, Paris and Vienna five times each, as well as a quick Paris-Brussels-Scheveningen dash with the B.B.C. Symphony Orchestra, and German and Russian tours with the London Philharmonic Orchestra. I think I managed to get at least one British work into almost every concert.

Chapter Eleven

UNITED STATES OF AMERICA

I HAVE MADE in all eleven trips to that most hospitable of countries the U.S.A., always by sea in varied conditions. Robin Barrington-Ward was responsible for the first, in 1923, just after his brother Lancelot (later Sir Lancelot) had removed my appendix. He had a sheaf of letters of introduction, and used to come round to the nursing home in the evenings to discuss itineraries with the aid of the marvellous complete guide to the Railways of the United States. We crossed in the Canadian Pacific cabin steamer *Montlaurier*.

On arrival at the Château Frontenac Hotel at Quebec we were startled to see a number of our co-guests strutting about in eighteenth-century uniforms. We thought that a film was being made, but it turned out that the Honourable Artillery Company of Massachusetts was enjoying its annual 'conference', and had chosen Quebec as the nearest place that could enable its members to snap their fingers at the Prohibition Law which at that time had the United States in its grip. If you had had a grandparent in the H.A.C. it was considered right to wear his uniform. Quebec was a very pleasant sight on its great river, with the maples beginning to show their wonderful autumn colour.

After a single day in Montreal we went on to Toronto to spend a week with Alice and Vincent Massey. Vincent and Robin had become close friends at Balliol, and Alice and he had kindly included me in Robin's invitation and gave us a wonderful time, including a drive to Niagara.

After a weekend at their beautiful country house near Port Hope, I was taken to a rehearsal of the Toronto Symphony Orchestra (before the time of Ernest Macmillan, who made it one of the great orchestras of North America) in the days when, as there was only one bassoon in Toronto, the second bassoon parts were played by a curate on a bass clarinet. Vincent Massey's patronage of Canadian artists had already begun, and we saw some striking examples of their work and met a number of them.

Two days in Chicago enabled me to hear a fine performance of the Beethoven Fifth Symphony under the direction of Frederick Stock, and we then took a long plunge southward, changing stations at Cincinnati,

and running down the Kentucky River to Charlottesville, Virginia, near
Nancy Lady Astor's first home, where she had given Robin an introduction to her relatives. I spent the day at Charlottesville charmed with the
quietness and beauty of the University and its buildings. A short visit to
Richmond, and a few days in Washington led us inevitably to New York,
where we were to be the guests of Whitney and Eleanor Shepherdson,
who also kindly included me in Robin's invitation. Their friendship with
a member of Stokowski's board of directors enabled me to take an afternoon trip to Philadelphia to hear this world-famous organization with the
already legendary figure at its head. We heard a lovely performance of a
Haydn symphony, followed by Stravinsky's 'Nightingale', then terrify-
ingly new. I was most impressed that Stokowski, who always conducted his
whole repertoire from memory, had the courage on this occasion to have
the score in front of him, although he naturally did not look much at it.
I left New York by an earlier steamer than Robin, as I had to get back to
the Royal College.

In 1927, after three seasons in Birmingham, I was feeling rather stale
and anxious to get away from things. I had always been attracted by a
large colour photograph of the Grand Canyon in Arizona. An uncle had
given it to my mother when I was a small boy, and I longed to see the
place. Here was my chance. I remember a fine crossing in the old *Carmania*,
followed by a few days in Washington, where Vincent Massey was
Canadian Minister, and then I set off to Chicago to board 'the Chief'.

In those days one had to cross Chicago by taxi. It was curious that in
the most advanced country in the world it was not possible to travel from
New York to San Francisco without a change. Also in Canada, the trans-
continental trains start from Montreal, and one must change if bound for
Quebec. The Santa Fé route had excellent food, and it was a thrill to
think that we were to stay undisturbed for three days. The Grand Canyon
was reached in time for breakfast in the hotel. This like most holiday
hotels worked on the 'American Plan'. All meals were included (except tea,
at which in those days Americans turned up their noses), but were served
at most stated times, and if you had a bath on your arrival you had to be
quick about it, or you would find the breakfast room doors firmly locked
at 9 a.m. I only then discovered that these big American-Canadian holiday
hotels are almost always linked with an Inn situated in the background
somewhere. Here you could get a bed for a much more modest price, and
the cafeteria is open all day. 'American Plan' hotels, while strict about the
time of meals, will usually give you a packed lunch. 'European Plan' is, of
course, more often the rule in the cities.

I had wisely kept three days for the Canyon—I could have done with
more, but I think that the twelve-hour stopover which is an easy and popular thing to do on the way across the continent is almost valueless. You

see the Canyon, it is true, from several points along the rim, but you come away with no idea what you have been looking at, for the air is so clear that ninety miles look like ten. From the top I noticed something moving on the plateau two-thirds of the way down; they looked like insects. I put up a strong pair of glasses, which I had hired, and found they were horses, but even then I could not see if they were mounted. On the first evening, anxious to watch the sun set, and how it changed the colours of the Canyon, I walked along the rim about half a mile from the hotel, and leant against the wall and watched as the colours darkened gradually into an all-pervading blue and finally black. I was reconciling myself to the end of it, and to return to the electric light of the hotel, when I became conscious of a movement down in front of me on the edge of the five-thousand-foot drop to the bottom of the Canyon. To my astonishment, up came two muleboys, vaulted over the parapet beside me and went back to the hotel. I imagine they were college boys who had come for the season. They had probably not been there long, but I think one would have to work in the Canyon for some time before its spell could wear off. A great many holiday hotels in U.S.A. and Canada are entirely staffed by college boys and girls who earn their year's fees in this way.

Next day I started to walk down the mule path. It was five thousand feet to the bottom of the Canyon. It was a brilliant day; I intended to sleep at Phantom Ranch that night, across the suspension bridge on the north side of the Colorado River. The ranch is ideally placed at the bottom of a tributary valley and the stream comes southwards from Utah. Just above the camp the stream splits up so that a small trickle flows beside every hut in the Camp—a beautifully cooling feature. I had run for part of the way down, and thought I might be in time for lunch at the ranch. There was nothing. The 'American Plan' in force down there included an obligatory packed lunch.

About eight or ten people were staying there and riding all day. There were not many trails, but riders could enjoy four or five days of it. I wished I had two more days in hand to enable me to climb up to the rim on the Utah (north) side and down again for another night at Phantom Ranch, and next day I could have walked to what was then the only other camp on the floor of the Canyon, twenty-seven miles away, and after another night there, climbed back to the hotel. Unfortunately reservations had been made all the way for me by the American Express in New York, and so next morning at 4 a.m. I set off up to the south rim. They had packed my breakfast, as I intended to get an hour's climb done before the sun came up, and it was already hot, although early in May. As soon as I had climbed into the sun I sat down and ate my breakfast, getting to the rim exactly at 9 o'clock; too late for another breakfast in the hotel; but by that time I had discovered the cafeteria. I spent a day rubbernecking

in Los Angeles, where I saw the famous Hollywood Bowl by daylight, and
one at San Francisco, and then on through the great forest of Oregon to
Tacoma where I had been advised to go and see the wild flowers in
Mount Rainier National Park. I was to travel by coach to the Inn at the
Gate of the Park, sleep there, and then continue next day up a trail to
Paradise Inn. This stands on a plateau looking up to the summit of Mount
Rainier, and is the base for those who make the three-day climb to the
summit.

More and more snow appeared in the path, and I began to wonder
where I was going. There was no doubt about the occasional signpost, and
when I reached the plateau I found the snow was twelve feet deep. The
hotel was being thawed out, but the Inn was open and victualled by sleighs
drawn by a magnificent team of huskies. The celebrated wild flowers were
not on view. Next morning we were met with an apology at breakfast.
There was nothing to eat but eggs, as a bear had devoured all the bacon.
Apparently larders were not used in the winter: the staff open a ground-
floor window and push the food into the snow. They had not realized how
fast it was thawing. The snow had fallen back from the wall of the Inn
leaving a narrow space, and through it the bear crawled for his bacon.

I remember starting the walk down in some light tennis shoes which
I exchanged for dry shoes and socks when we got below snow level. This
made some young Americans envious. Their unexpectedly light footgear
had been completely soaked. American ideas about boots and shoes are
changing nowadays, but I remember how London marvelled at the first
march of the U.S.A. troops in 1917, and pitied the wearers of those light
boots and canvas leggings when they got into the trenches.

Northwards again to Vancouver where there were still a few Boults,
children of a first cousin of my father's who had taken his family there
somewhere about 1880. A day with them and a wonderful drive to Capi-
lano Canyon, and then began the most original part of my trip. I had
discovered in the Canadian Pacific Time Table a humble railway line
(called Kettle Valley) which ran eastwards parallel to the main line and
close to the United States border. It seemed to traverse a country full of
lakes and hills and I thought I would try it, as far as Nelson, B.C. There
I could take a lake steamer and join the main line at Revelstoke.

I woke at a place called Penticton and found the train standing on a little
jetty with a lake steamer moored beside it. Train and steamer left almost
together, but were not to part for some time. I think it took four hours
for us to climb away from the lake: we could look down and see the steamer
crossing and re-crossing the glassy water, leaving its herring-bone wake
behind it. At last we reached a station which reminded me of a friend at
home, who was to make a great reputation one day in that far country.
Its name was Myra. Then we came through a short tunnel, and began the

downward journey to the next valley. Two nights and a good walk at Nelson were followed by a twenty-hour journey by lake steamer up the Arrow Lake.

Like the steamer at Penticton, she crossed and re-crossed the lake, stopping here to pick up an old lady, there to land a pig or a crate of merchandise, and we finished our journey in the evening at Arrowhead, near Revelstoke, where the trans-continental train picked me up.

Short stops at Lake Louise and Banff, and the memory of a fine sunset over the Rockies as we approached Calgary, and a day or two again with kind friends in Toronto, end my impressions of this second trip.

In 1929 I made two trips to the American continent. The first was very short. I attended a conference of the National Federation of Music Clubs, an organization which, like our own here, helps Music Societies to plan their seasons and share the services of artists. On a previous trip I had learned that in those days Canadians always hoped English people would not restrict their American trips to the United States, but would include Canada, and indeed it is always a pleasure to go there.

On this occasion Vincent and Alice Massey, who were by now a most impressive and valuable element in diplomatic and social Washington, picked me up in New York, and we drove first to New Haven. Here Vincent received an Honorary Degree at Yale University. A dinner party was given the night before, and I was most kindly included. In due course two resplendent champagne bottles were produced and those who were suffering from the Prohibition laws looked at them with eager anticipation. The uncorking seemed to lack its usual vigour, and our poor host then poured a rather dull-looking red liquid into his glass. Amid the general disappointment Vincent, as usual, rose to the occasion and pronounced it to be a most excellent red Burgundy!

The degree ceremony had been very impressive, and I was pleased to find that Miss Willa Cather, the novelist, some of whose work I had greatly enjoyed, was also honoured. We had a night in Boston and then drove right up through much lovely New England country, crossing the frontier at Sherbrooke, Quebec, and arriving finally at Montreal on the evening of the second day.

In December of that year my friend Keith Falkner also travelled to the States. We sailed in the *Olympic*, which had given such splendid service in the War. Keith had a number of professional engagements, but we began our trip in Washington where Alice Massey had arranged a wonderful party in their beautiful Legation house, attended by diplomatic Washington at its most impressive. Keith undertook the whole programme; I did what I could with his accompaniments.

This was only a few weeks before I joined the B.B.C., which naturally excluded any globe-trotting for some time. It was not until I had been five years in the Corporation's service that I was able to accept an invitation from Dr Serge Koussevitsky, who had visited us once or twice, to undertake two pairs of concerts with his famous orchestra in Boston.

My wife and I sailed in the United States liner *Washington* and spent a very rough week in a thoroughly unfriendly January. Our return in the *Berengaria* (a German leviathan taken over by Cunard after the war) was less objectionable, but in between we had a wonderful time with the superb orchestra and an old friend, Dr Archibald T. Davison, who with Mrs Davison opened their house to us and undertook the rather onerous job of 'manager'.

Archie always answered the telephone himself, and said that I was lying down and could not be disturbed. We finally decided that I was the most horizontal conductor who had ever visited Boston. He was the recognized leader of the impressive Faculty of Music at Harvard. As a young man he had taken over the Harvard Glee Club. At that time it existed in order to give its members a good 'sing'. They did not worry much about the audience. In a few years he had trained them to a staggering height of artistry in every aspect of their work, tone, ensemble, diction, spirit, and above all, a profound understanding of everything they touched. 'Doc', as he was called by generations of Harvard men, not only took all the responsibility for their performance, but he began to arrange every kind of choral music for male voice choir. There are now several volumes of his collected arrangements. A further evidence of the artistic transformation he effected was their association with the choir of Radcliffe Ladies' College to sing the greatest masterpieces of choral music at the Boston Symphony Orchestra's Concerts. Doc, by his example, transformed all the university glee clubs throughout the United States, and the extended tours that many of them now make all over the world, and the tremendously high standard of their work, come fundamentally from his courageous handling of the Harvard Glee Club. They have even struck a beautiful medal, which is given on rare occasions to musicians who have had the good fortune to be associated with them. When they came to England in 1956, I was greatly honoured to receive it with Ralph Vaughan Williams at the hands of 'Woody', Doc's most able successor, the late Professor Wallace Woodworth.

While we were at Boston we heard of the wonderful gift made to the Boston Symphony Orchestra by two ladies. This was the estate of Tanglewood, where Nathaniel Hawthorne wrote the *Tanglewood Tales*, two hundred acres of it, about a hundred miles from Boston in lovely New England country. Dr Koussevitsky was said to be full of plans to found a permanent Summer School there, and Doc suggested a trip to the estate on a free day. Mr Judd, the manager of the Boston Symphony Orchestra, came too, and though it was a wintry day, we were able to see the splendid layout of the land, and the great Shed holding six thousand people under cover, but open on three sides so that six thousand more could enjoy the music sitting on the grass or deck chairs. One could visualize how lovely the summer scene could be. It was like Gloucestershire country with hills more thickly wooded and three or four times the height and depth of the smaller English landscape. Koussevitsky's creation has now become a great tradition, as I saw for myself later.

I have already spoken of the wonderful American hospitality, which can often make us ashamed of our poor efforts. Symphony Hall's attention to its guests must be experienced if it is to be understood. Dr Koussevitsky's office was put at my disposal as it was close to the platform and so also formed his 'artists' room'. Round the walls hung or stood a remarkable collection of paintings, sketches and busts of Koussevitsky himself. I think there were thirteen or fourteen—a striking array as one entered the room. We were admiring them when Mr Brennan, who had just retired from the position of manager of the Boston Symphony Orchestra which he had held for many distinguished years, caught my wife by the elbow: 'My dear, if you ask me, I think there is just *one* too many.'

The concerts with that superb orchestra were for me naturally a great experience. The first included Elgar's Second Symphony, Haydn 88 in G, and the rarely heard Mendelssohn Scherzo in G minor (from the Octet) and a Gabrieli brass sonata. It is impossible to say that any one of the great orchestras of the world is better than any other—as corporate instruments they all have their own qualities—as individuals some may be more sensitive as musicians, and others greater players as soloists. There is no 'better' and 'worse', only a difference. We had three rehearsals before the first programme was performed, first in Cambridge (the Harvard suburb of Boston), then twice in Boston, and once each in Concord and Providence. The second programme, including the Schubert C major, Holst's Fugal Concerto, Bliss's Introduction and Allegro and Bax's 'Garden of Fand', we only played three times, and on the morning after, before leaving Boston, we had the great experience of hearing Dr Koussevitsky rehearse 'Zarathustra' for a recording a day or two later. It was not well known to the orchestra, and at one point when something unexpected occurred the great man put down his stick and looked across at the trombones: 'Eef you think that is goot, you are *wrrrong*.' With that immortal comment (and some splendid playing) ringing in our ears, we went off to our train.

Although, as I have said, we sailed from New York on our return, I was mindful of what I have said above about the pleasure of a visit to Canada whenever one is on the other side. Accordingly, when the Boston trip was finished, I had arranged a quick dash to Toronto where my friend Ernest Macmillan had a concert with his splendid orchestra. We could only reach Toronto late in the afternoon of the concert day. It was arranged that I should begin the programme with the *Meistersinger* Overture. I had sent a letter to Ernest making a few suggestions about the performance, all of them happily taken up by the players, but even so I felt a rather exceptional pressure of 'butterflies' as I went on to the platform. The orchestra did not know me from Adam; suppose my down beat were received in stony silence? I need not have worried: my advance suggestions had been well digested by the players and they were superb. It was a great pleasure to play to that brilliant audience, and bring them, as it were, greetings from home.

On our way back from Toronto we stopped to see Niagara in its winter dress, at night. We did not stay very long, as our ears began to freeze.

On 30 April 1938 I set out alone on my sixth trip. Its object was mainly due to inter-broadcasting courtesies for I had been invited to conduct two concerts with the orchestra which the National Broadcasting Company had formed for Arturo Toscanini, and my invitation was in the nature of a return for the wonderful visits which Toscanini had paid us since 1935. This time I crossed in the *Britannic*. As I had discovered that there was only one rehearsal each day, I asked the N.B.C. whether they could suggest somewhere outside New York where I could live and go into New York each morning. They suggested a delightful country club called Seawane on Long Island near the sea, less than an hour from the city, set in the middle of a golf course in a very exclusive suburb, with a good walk from the station. Mr Joinreau Williams, the secretary of the club, often joined me for meals and took me some delightful drives about Long Island.

My two concerts with the famous N.B.C. Orchestra were most enjoyable. I was able to include one or two works new to the series, such as Busoni's Comedy Overture, and the first New York performance of Copland's 'El Salon Mexico'.

I unwisely chose also to include Beethoven's Seventh Symphony. This was one of the misjudgements of youth (though I was old enough to know better) to try and do that kind of work on Toscanini's home ground. Everyone was polite, but I realized (after the event) that no one could possibly stand up to Toscanini in such a work.

At a lunch kindly arranged by Mr John Royal, President of the N.B.C., I was given a beautiful gold watch by the veteran Walter Damrosch, to whom New York owed so much both for his long tenure of the direction of the Philharmonic Orchestra, and for his splendid pioneering work with children's concerts. The occasion enabled Mr Royal to tell us a delightful story of Toscanini. At one of his less harmonious rehearsals he appears to have taken his watch from his pocket, flung it down and ground it under his heel. After the rehearsal the fragments were faithfully collected by the orchestral manager, and Mr Royal had it 'fixed'. When it was ready it was duly returned to the Maestro, but with it were two very cheap watches, on which was engraved the inscription 'FOR REHEARSAL PURPOSES'. The great man was delighted, and when I got back to London, I showed him my watch and said: 'They gave you a watch, too, didn't they, Maestro?' He roared, and dug his elbow into my ribs: 'Yes, for re'earsal purpose.'

We landed in Glasgow on the very morning of Toscanini's Queen's Hall concert, the last, I think, of that series, so I did what I could to get to London in time. The railway companies had recently begun to experiment with special light-weight expresses which took several hours off the normal schedules from Edinburgh and Glasgow. I was able to catch one of these (called, I think, 'The Coronation'). It left Glasgow at 2 and got me to Queen's Hall in time for the concert; and afterwards we had a talk, about watches and other things.

But to return to New York. After my second N.B.C. concert I took the night train to Boston, and a short visit to the ever-hospitable Davisons at Brant Rock. That night Archie and Dorothy had invited six or seven of the other members of the Harvard Music Faculty to spend the evening with us and we discussed many aspects of music, and a few other things as well. Musicians do not always talk shop although they usually do, and I formed the impression that Archie had collected a most impressive group of experts round him. A few months later came a wonderful invitation to accept a six-months' Fellowship at Harvard. I was to lecture a little on subjects of my own choice. I was to be accessible to music students at times to suit myself. In fact I was to have what would have been a splendid holiday with pleasant contacts thrown in, but there were already far too many engagements awaiting me at home.

Three more peaceful days at Brant Rock ended with the usual journey North, this time to Ottawa, where my former B.B.C. colleague and friend, William Ewart Gladstone Murray, was now in command of Canadian broadcasting. He gave a large and pleasant lunch party for me, and afterwards suggested that we should go across and see his office. He turned on the wireless as we went into the room, and the first thing I heard was Purcell's 'Fairest Isle'. It seemed to be coming from a large number of voices, and I suddenly remembered that it must be a Royal Albert Hall broadcast of a concert which Walford Davies had arranged for King George VI as it was Empire Day. I had helped him with the programme, and was sad that my long-planned journey prevented me from taking part. Four hours separated Ottawa time from London, and so the concert had just begun at 3.30 in the afternoon—I remember Murray saying with pride that that programme was going out from over fifty transmitters. Canada had already organized a long series of relays across the continent as the population of the country is so closely spaced along the South border.

I travelled to Toronto later that day and on arrival at the hotel found a charming note from Dr Graham, the chairman of the Promenade Concerts, as he wished to show me some Canadian hospitality if I could dine at his home the following day. I was not to write a reply, but simply to tell the manager of the concerts, who would pass on the message while I was rehearsing. I rather wondered what to wear, and the manager advised a white tie, rather to my surprise. It was as well that I had asked him, for the Canadian hospitality involved a balanced party of twelve with superb food and flowers, and some of the leading figures in Toronto City and University, all presumably collected by telephone. At this distance I have a stronger memory of the dinner party than of the concert next day or my overnight trip to Montreal to catch the *Duchess of Atholl*.

A year later, on 27 May 1939, I experienced a perfect Atlantic crossing —blazing sun and a blue calm sea for eight days. An official mission sent me on this occasion, as the British Council had commissioned from Vaughan Williams, Arnold Bax, Arthur Bliss and William Walton, works to be dedicated to the people of the United States as part of the British contribution to the World's Fair. The scores and a performance of them by the New York Philharmonic Symphony Orchestra were offered, and I was sent over to present the scores, and conduct the performances.

My first full day was spent at the Fair, and I specially remember the British Pavilion, where Magna Carta, some of the Crown Jewels, and other very special national possessions had been allowed out of the country on this very special occasion, and had been most effectively displayed. Many other countries had fine exhibits, and I was most impressed by a wonderful show of leather goods in the Polish Pavilion, and my first experience of conditioned air seems to link itself with that day.

A reasonable temperature was maintained in all the Pavilions, but as one went from one to the other the open air seemed more than tropical. I saw the concert hall, a great disappointment, inadequately insulated, and badly sited. I had already been told that our concerts could not take place there. Carnegie Hall took us over, but without air conditioning, and the temperature each night was over 90°F, with the whole audience fanning itself with programmes and the somewhat corpulent 'concertmaster' having the greatest difficulty in keeping his violin under his chin.

The programmes were:

June 9th 1939

SMETANA	Overture, the Bartered Bride
BAX	Symphony No. 7
EUGENE GOOSSENS	Concerto for Oboe and Orchestra
	LEON GOOSSENS

| DEBUSSY | Prélude à l'Après-midi d'un Faune |
| BACH, arr. Elgar | Fantasia and Fugue in C minor |

June 16th 1939

WEBER	Overture, Der Freischütz
BLISS	Concerto for Piano and Orchestra
	SOLOMON
WALTER PISTON	Prelude and Fugue
VAUGHAN WILLIAMS	Five Variants on Dives and Lazarus
RAVEL	Daphnis and Chloe (2nd series)

Walton's name was not there. It was sad that the Violin Concerto was not ready in time and had to have its first performance at Chicago later on.

My second day in New York included the ceremony of presenting the three scores at the New York Public Library on 42nd Street. They were received by the Chief Librarian and a Senator, who took them back with him to the Library of Congress in Washington.

I had heard that Toscanini was rehearsing one day in the N.B.C. Studio, so I went across to greet him and hear some of his rehearsal. I got there early and was chatting with some of the players who remembered me from the previous season when we were joined by another, who, obviously a Frenchman, said: 'I want to tell you that Pierre Monteux is a great friend of mine and always stays with me when he comes to New York. One evening we were talking of old times and I asked him what he remembered as the most enjoyable experience of his whole life. He answered without hesitation: "The fortnight I recently spent with the B.B.C. Orchestra in London".'

My next engagement was with the hospitable Davisons at Brant Rock, and as there were several days to spare I chose an unusual route. I took the Long Island Railroad then wallowing in steam from the softest, dirtiest coal in the country, as far as Greenport, and after two days' walking and bathing a short journey to the northern tip of the island, and a ferry steamer from Montauk Point over to New London, which had recently experienced a cyclone. As we approached the mainland it was terrible to see the houses all falling forward towards the sea; bowing, as it were, to great Neptune who had apparently removed all the fronts from the houses downstairs.

Professor Davison's lovely house and garden were perched on a sandhill overlooking the Atlantic, not far from Plymouth Rock, Mass., where the Pilgrim Fathers first set foot on the coast of America. After some lazy and very happy days there I moved on to Lenox and Stockbridge in the Berkshire Hills of Massachusetts, where I stayed a few days with Mr and Mrs Hofmann, an uncle of Lady Bliss, at their 'Garden Centre' only a few miles from Tanglewood. The Berkshires, besides showing lovely wooded hills and lakes for a large area, have many other attractions. Mr Hofmann took us to tea at a Bird Sanctuary on one of the hilltops, and near to it was also an amusing dam made by beavers over a large stream. Also one afternoon at the Garden Centre we attended a gathering where we ate large quantities of strawberry shortcake, a gloriously rich confection peculiar to the neighbourhood. The Festival was just starting, and we were able to hear a beautiful Mozart programme by Koussevitsky and the Boston Orchestra.

Work soon called me to Chicago, where the orchestra has a summer home, Ravinia Park, about twenty miles from the city, close to Lake Michigan. In fact the hotel where artists usually stay stands right over the Lake in a splendid position. There were eight concerts spread over a fortnight, and we covered a good deal of ground, both classical and modern. Vaughan Williams' *Job* made a deep impression, helped perhaps by my idea of putting up some large cards with numbers, which showed the nine scenes, so that the audience could follow dramatically as well as musically.

The Ravinia Park management, like all other concert organizations in the United States, believes in very full documentation for their audiences. The large programme books are given to every seat-holder. Two of the Blake engravings were reproduced, and everything was done to make the audience's understanding of *Job* as full as possible. Amongst other soloists we had the privilege of hearing two concertos played by Josef Hofmann; and Arthur Bliss, two of whose works were included, came to several concerts. The evening after Mr Hofmann's second appearance the secretary of the concerts, Mrs Hazel Moore, kindly asked me to come with her and her husband to see Mr Hofmann off at the Chicago airport. This was my first experience of hearing the bewildering announcements of airport loudspeakers; 'Mexico City' one moment, then 'Montreal' followed by 'San Francisco'; one seemed to belong to a crazy new world.

From Chicago it was an easy trip to Toronto, where we had a promenade concert. The concert had to be followed by a night journey to Montreal to catch the *Alaunia* for the homeward journey.

Except for the trip to Holland in 1940, I was fortunate to avoid the discomforts of war foreign travel which some of my B.B.C. colleagues had to endure. There was an invitation from Boston for the winter of 1944, but it was postponed at my request until the end of the war. It was a most attractive invitation for a long period, including a tour in New England and three pairs of Boston concerts. I was to sail in the *Queen Mary* on 29 December 1945, and I had been asked by the Cunard Company to sign a declaration that I would be willing to put up with only two meals a day, and various other discomforts, as the *Queen Mary* was still a troopship, and twelve thousand returning U.S. troops were with us.

We left Waterloo forty minutes late, with no heating, and were not sorry to find a warm ship and a hot meal on arrival. I had been given a V.I.P. cabin to myself with a good-sized table to write on. The meal times were 9 a.m. and 7 p.m., but a noble plate of sandwiches was brought in at 1, and tea and cakes at 4, so we did not do badly. The officers were most hospitable, and there were a number of parties in their cabins.

My accountants had warned me not to take a fee for my services as it would be taxed by both countries and nothing would be left of it. So the Boston authorities paid all expenses and provided very handsome pocket money which was more than adequate to meet the lengthy clothing list I had brought with me in hopes that I might help replenish my family's war-scarred wardrobes. Our old friend, Mrs Hamlin Hunt, entered fully into this exercise, and we spent many hours in wonderful shops stocking up for my return.

Ten days in New York were full of interest and wonderful hospitality. Besides Mrs Hunt's continual invitations, I had the pleasure of seeing Elisabeth Schumann, Toscanini, Bruno Walter, Carl and Annie Friedberg, and several B.B.C. friends. I also heard a wonderful performance of the Mahler IVth by Bruno Walter, and a fine concert with Koussevitsky and Piatigorsky, and I saw *Life with Father* and *Oklahoma*, which were beginning their long careers. The temperature too was over 60°F one day, and New York was generally kinder than one might expect in January.

Work began in earnest in Boston on 14 January, as we had to rehearse not only the first programme for the 18th, but Vaughan Williams' *Job*, which had been specially asked for at some of the New England concerts early the next week.

The first programme was:

PURCELL/WOODGATE	Trumpet Tune and Air
IRELAND	A Forgotten Rite
ELGAR	Enigma Variations
HEMING/COLLINS	Threnody for a Soldier
BRAHMS	Symphony No. 1

The second:

WALTON	Scapino
HAYDN	Symphony No. 86 in D
VAUGHAN WILLIAMS	*Job*

The third:

BAX	Tintagel
MOZART	'Prague' Symphony
HOLST	The Planets

The concerts took place on Friday afternoons and Saturday evenings each week. In the second week we had our New England tour with concerts on

Monday, Tuesday and Wednesday, and after that the remaining ten days
were as full of meetings and entertainments as was consistent with proper
preparation for the concerts. I remember particularly lunch with the
Boston Saturday Lunch Club as the guest of W. G. Constable, the English
director of the Art Gallery. There were about sixteen men sitting at a
round table, and no speeches, but after lunch, Dr Conant, the President
of Harvard, told us of a recent trip to Moscow with Mr Averell Harriman
to undertake some negotiations about the atom bomb.

I also remember a small dinner party at which another guest, a Harvard
professor, had just heard a wonderful explanation of the Mona Lisa theft
from the Louvre. According to his story the picture, which disappeared
one day in broad daylight and was returned by parcel post a year or two
later, was taken to America, and a dozen very good copies of it were made
either by the thief, or an accomplice. Each copy was then offered as the
original picture in great secrecy to one of the less reputable American
millionaires, who bought it for a large sum and hid it in his cellar, display-
ing it occasionally to his intimates. Having safely disposed of all the copies,
the thief then returned the original to the Louvre.

Back to New York after the last concert, there was no need to hurry
because the 'Mary' was held up by a strike and other post-war troubles,
and I enjoyed another fortnight, daily wondering whether to embark or not.

There was a great deal going on in New York, and with Mrs Hunt
helping with more shopping, time filled up completely. I spent a delightful
evening with Dr and Mrs Löwenbach, who had entertained me with many
other foreigners years before in Prague at the time of the Contemporary
Music Festivals, which were often held there. I also met two very famous
Czechs, George Szell and Bohuslav Martinü, and also Olin Downes, the
redoubtable critic of the *New York Times*.

In my report to the B.B.C. about the trip and the orchestras I had heard,
I said:

On landing, and before departure, I spent altogether nearly three weeks in
New York. This enabled me to hear four other orchestras, and to compare
them with Boston and our own.

I heard two performances at the Metropolitan Opera: *Magic Flute* and
Fidelio, both in English, and both conducted by Bruno Walter. I gather that
the Metropolitan now play a good deal in English, but not Wagner nor,
apparently, Puccini. The performances were both fine, but the mixture of
soloists and their accents produces an incongruity that takes some getting used
to. The 'Pamina' of Nadine Connor and the 'Leonora' of Regina Reznik and
also, I think, the 'Florestan' of Arthur Carron were perhaps the most notable
performances. The orchestra is adequate, but not of the quality of the old
Covent Garden Orchestra.

The Philadelphia Orchestra came to New York with Bruno Walter and gave the Brahms Tragic Overture, Haydn's 'Oxford' Symphony and Mahler's Fourth with Desi Halban. This concert was throughout memorable for many qualities, and it seems to me Ormandy has trained a remarkable instrument, which contains a very high percentage of first-class artists. Walter tells me also that they have an excellent spirit and are always eager for work. I have never enjoyed a concert more.

The National Broadcasting Corporation's Orchestra I heard twice with Toscanini, at a rehearsal of the Prokofieff Classical Symphony and the performance of Acts III and IV of *Bohème*, which commemorated Toscanini's conducting of the première in Turin just fifty years before—a wonderful occasion. I think they are better than the Metropolitan, but not what they promised to be. There was an extraordinarily flabby Brass attack near the end. There is a curious hardness and coarseness in the playing which showed particularly in the Prokofieff. The orchestra was often too loud (from the studio point of view) for an excellent group of soloists in *Bohème* (including Albanese and Peerce).

The Philharmonic-Symphony played the First Brahms, the Copland 'Lincoln Portrait' (Kenneth Spencer, a coloured actor with a full bass voice often dangerously near being covered by the orchestra), the First Enesco Rhapsody and the Szymanowski Violin Concerto (Corigliano, concert-master of the orchestra). The Enesco, however impossible musically, showed off finely the virtuosity of the orchestra, and the Szymanowski was most effectively displayed, but sounded pathetically dated, in my opinion. I am afraid I was most disappointed with the Brahms which was uneventfully hustled on its way—giving no time even to play the repeat in the Third Movement—although I must add that Mr Olin Downes called it spacious and finely-proportioned. It is a splendid orchestra.

I heard the Boston Orchestra three times in New York with Koussevitsky. The symphonies were Brahms IV and Sibelius V, the latter flawless in technique and magnificent in conception; the Brahms fine in its main lines, but curiously sloppy in ensemble and detail. Dukelsky's Cello Concerto was splendidly played by Piatigorsky. It seemed a thankless work and was over-scored and over-played by the orchestra. Prokofieff's Fifth Symphony also had a fine performance. It is obviously a work of major importance, but I was rather alarmed to find how easy and agreeable it seemed to me at a first hearing.

The Boston Orchestra is a superb instrument. I have had great enjoyment from my three weeks' work with it. It has, however, several traits which are most disconcerting. Koussevitsky evidently treats them like children and insists on hearing everything in its final form at rehearsal, never trusting his players to act on a verbal hint. Even the concert-master is unable to remember a thing he is told unless it is rehearsed, and although we played the Brahms Symphony six times he never began his solo quietly enough, although I asked him four or five times. There is a general aversion to playing really quietly, unless the thing has been long prepared and/or long rehearsed, and a diminuendo needs a great deal of rehearsing always. To compare them with our own orchestra, I think we may claim greater reading ability, greater range of tone, far greater musical perception and apprehension of conductors' wishes, mastery of an enormously greater repertoire, and a much greater sensitivity to the sound that is being produced by the orchestra as a whole. Individually there are only two principals in the Boston Orchestra who could in any way be considered superior to their opposite numbers in London, though I venture to think that the promotion of two sub-principals might bring this number up to four.

May I quote an outside view to support my claims? I saw Mr Menuhin after the Toscanini broadcast and said I was sorry I had missed his recent performances of the Bartók Concerto with Ormandy in New York and Burgin in Boston. He promptly said: 'They were nothing like as good as yours in London.'

The ninth trip began on 18 June 1949. The *Caronia*, whose Captain Sorrell became a very kind friend, and wrote a delightful book about his life, *The Sea my Steed*, had brought everything back to pre-war standards, though our few hours' stay at Le Havre showed a port still terribly war-damaged. The luxury of the trip was rudely dispelled by a 6.30 a.m. breakfast on the final day and then the bedlam of the New York dock. Miss Annie Friedberg, whose management is always efficient, was waiting for me at the hotel, and I soon had a telephone call from Mrs Guggenheimer, the lady who organizes the concerts in the Lewisohn Stadium, inviting me to her country home in New Jersey for lunch on Sunday, preceded by a bathe in some formidable Atlantic breakers.

Miss Friedberg had fitted twelve concerts into the six weeks, six in New York, four in Chicago and two in Toronto at the Varsity Arena. They were called 'Promenades' although there were seats for everyone. In between I spent some time with Archie Davison at Brant Rock, and with Elisabeth Hunt at Stockbridge in the Berkshires whence we visited the now mature Tanglewood estate on the opening day of its summer season, very different from the embryo we had seen in 1936.

The New York Stadium is a remarkable place for music. It holds about eighteen thousand people, and the amplification of the sound seems to work very well. Mrs Guggenheimer runs a long series of concerts, and seems able to persuade the very greatest artists to perform there, though I found that two objections, neither of them insuperable, made the whole thing far less pleasant than it might have been. The floor is largely covered by gravel and it scrunches horribly as late-comers walk in, and no one seems to mind that the young people in the neighbouring streets play noisy games of baseball during the concerts. In contrast all the paths between the grass stretched round the Esplanade Orchestral Shell in Boston are asphalt, and the police control the traffic most strictly, certain roads being closed while the concerts are in progress. We were lucky that rain stopped only one of our concerts.

The Toronto Promenades take place in the vast Varsity Arena which is excellent for sound. As at Chicago and New York, the full Toronto Symphony Orchestra plays, and the concerts are well attended. I was surprised to find that the audience at Ravinia Park was now covered with a fine roof with open sides. I commented on this improvement and was told that I was responsible for it. When I was there in 1939 we had been treated to a terrific thunderstorm. The management thereupon decided that they must find money for a roof, and in due course this was built. The Ravinia Concerts take place in a beautiful park far from traffic noises or any interruption, except that once each evening a Chicago-Minneapolis train called the '400', because it does 400 miles in 400 minutes, washed out about thirty or forty bars of whatever was going on as it passed. No doubt things are different now.

Back in New York I had an invitation to a rehearsal of the Philadelphia summer concerts in what they call The Dell. Iturbi was rehearsing the Grieg, playing and conducting at the same time. This plan is delightful when Bruno Walter has a few Vienna Philharmonic people sitting round the piano, but it does not suit the Grieg. It was marvellous to hear the unaminity with which the orchestra brought in their crashes just after Mr Iturbi had finished the famous scales in the last movement.

Homewards by *Caronia* again, and Captain Sorrell, as before, a most kind host. He invited me to go up Southampton Water in the little perch that is just over the navigating bridge. I found it a bracing experience to be up there.

In 1954 a two-month trip to the States was planned. It began with the Hollywood Bowl which had sent an invitation for several concerts, opening the season with an operatic programme with Metropolitan artists, and ending with a performance of 'The Messiah', a comparative rarity in the United States. To this the indefatigable Miss Friedberg in due course added some Lewisohn Stadium Concerts, and Archie Davison asked us to Brant Rock whenever there was time to spare. The *Queen Elizabeth*'s dates fitted both crossings, but on the outward trip I slipped a disc and fainted on deck. A clever homoeopath and a skilful Finnish masseur, however, soon made me fit again and I had the pleasure of working with Mr Firkušny, Mr Elman, Mr Rabin, and other great artists, though two concerts were spoilt by rain.

Mrs Hunt was at Lenox—she always liked to take her holiday near Tanglewood, and we went to the Lenox Inn for a few days and included a visit to Tanglewood and Dr Koussevitsky in his wonderful home looking down on the whole estate.

One more Stadium Concert, and we took the long trip across the continent by the same train that had taken me twenty-seven years before, though it had now become the 'Super-Chief'. 'Chief' had been its title in those early days. We spent several hours in Chicago's wonderful Art Gallery where there was so much to see besides the pictures. One remembers especially a wonderful room of snuff boxes, and a fine Wedgwood collection. This specially interested us as only two weeks before we had been at Leith Hill Place and Lady Wedgwood had shown us a vase which she said was unique except for its pair in the Chicago Museum—and there indeed it was. Before we boarded our 'Super-Chief' we were delighted to meet Mr Lionel Sayers, librarian and percussionist of the Chicago Orchestra on my Ravinia visits—a faithful friend of long standing.

I had suggested that it might be a good idea to stay somewhere outside Los Angeles, possibly on the Pacific Coast, where we could bathe and have some quiet between the concerts. Mr Barnett, the Musical Director of the Bowl, accordingly fixed us up at the Huntington-Hartford Foundation. This was an estate of several hundred acres in a lovely canyon some sixteen miles from the Bowl. It consisted of a central 'community house' where we took breakfast and dinner, and where Dr and Mrs John Vincent, directors of the Foundation, lived. Dr Vincent is one of the leading American composers, and is also professor of music at the University of California. His works have been played in this country from time to time, but I am afraid he shares the apathetic neglect that England maintains towards all American composers.

The Foundation, now closed, gave a delightful opportunity for artists of all kinds to immerse themselves in special tasks. They were invited to stay up to six months, and the cabins, more than twenty of them, scattered about the Canyon (with the pianos well separated) had been fitted up as studios for painters, sculptors, musicians, writers or researchers. Lunch was brought round in baskets in a jeep so that the Fellows could work undisturbed all day. We were captivated by the peace of the place, and the pleasant company in the evenings.

The cabins were all near the bottom of the Canyon, and higher up the landscape was wild, with thick scrub and some trees. We were told on arrival that we should be given three dollars for each dead rattle-snake we brought in or twenty dollars for a 'mount'n lion'. We did not compete—in fact I am still not certain what a 'mount'n lion' looks like.

The Hollywood Bowl was sixteen miles away. It so happened that a large new car park had just been opened there. The concert had been widely advertised, and the 'whole of California' invited to come to the Bowl. John Vincent kindly drove us in and allowed ample time for the drive. It was as well, for it soon appeared that large numbers had accepted the invitation, and there were considerable traffic jams. Finally, about a mile from the Bowl we stuck completely. I told John to tell us when we were to get out and walk, and this moment came, about twenty minutes to zero hour with the thermometer somewhere about 120°F, and the concert due on the air then. Both wives nobly decided to walk too, while John stayed with the car, and the trio, dripping, and purple in the face, arrived at the Bowl to meet a battery of photographers with about four minutes to spare. It was bad enough to have to conduct, but poor Eleanor Steber arrived in the same way, and only had a few minutes' Overture to get her breath before she sang her first aria. Jan Peerce was luckier as he came later in the programme. Various members of the orchestra were held up too, but I think we were complete by the end of the Overture.

Our Los Angeles stay was punctuated by other delightful meetings. Arthur Bliss' mother-in-law, Mrs Gertrude Hoffman, who was still doing important film work, welcomed us on a very hot morning with cool drinks. We lunched with Bruno Walter, where we renewed acquaintance with Mahler's daughter as well as Bruno's daughter and son-in-law. Tea with Mr and Mrs Jascha Heifetz in their seaside home gave us a chance of wading in the Pacific, and meeting Gregor Piatigorsky again. It was also a great pleasure to meet and conduct for William Primrose, who played the Rubbra Concerto. I had not seen him for a long time.

The 'Messiah' night was most impressive. The Roger Wagner Chorale is world famous, and they sang splendidly, with soloists to match, all revelling in the music with a fresh approach which we find hard to achieve at home where everyone knows the oratorio by heart.

We stopped at the Grand Canyon on the way back and its wonder and colouring seemed as striking as before, even though I missed this time the amazing experience of sleeping in the valley.

The eleventh crossing—the last no doubt—took place in 1966. The invitation had this time come from Tanglewood and the Boston Symphony Orchestra. I was asked to come for a fortnight in early July, and besides conducting a Mozart programme with the Boston Symphony Orchestra, to take the first concert of the Students' Orchestra with seven rehearsals, to include the Vaughan Williams 'London' Symphony, and also to take a 'seminar' of a dozen conducting students. These people were tremendously keen, with the result that almost every afternoon they gathered (with an appreciable number of hangers-on) for a couple of hours or more. I did most of the talking, but we had some healthy arguments, and a certain amount of conducting to the piano.

My wife decided that she shouldn't come, as we were about to move to a Hampstead flat, and she must face the frustrations and dilemmas concerned. I had the very pleasant company of Jasper Parrott, who was lent to me by Mrs Tillett, and did a great deal to help me in the strenuous, tropical, but delightful fortnight. We had crossed in the luxury of the *France*, and returned in the *Queen Mary*.

Chapter Twelve

POST-WAR—1945–1950

NOW BACK to England. In 1945 the B.B.C. Orchestra and I settled down to life mainly at the People's Palace, which made a good studio, though it was a long way from most of our homes. The girls in the Orchestra, and those who did their own house-keeping, liked it for one reason. The Whitechapel shops were less expensive, and had often a wider selection than the post-war shops in the places where most of us lived. I have no special record of important novelties at this time. We did *Wozzeck* in the Albert Hall in March 1946. It seemed just as exciting and fresh as at its first performance in Queen's Hall twelve years before, but I am afraid it did little to help me towards an understanding of the power of twelve-tone music. I still feel that the last act, where it becomes tonal, is the most powerful of all.

I have always maintained that I as an executant am not, and have no right to be, a critic of any kind, even to the extent of having preferences and favourites. I consider it is my job to make the best of whatever is put before me once I have agreed to conduct the work. I am often asked which is my favourite Beethoven or Brahms symphony, and I can only answer that my favourite is the one I am at the moment performing, or studying, the one that is uppermost in my mind. It is therefore no business of mine to say that an artificial treatment of twelve notes as if they were equidistant (which they cannot be) and of equal importance, would seem to be such a violation of the harmonic series (surely the basis of all music) that it cannot last for long, but I can relate something which at any rate shows that I am not fitted to have much to do with this music.

Very early in the B.B.C. Orchestra's career, 1931 I think, we performed the Schönberg Variations. I could not enjoy them, but I did admire their craft, and myself found a craftsman's pleasure in seeing that his H.S. and N.S. Directions (Hauptstimme and Nebenstimme, chief subject and subsidiary strand) were faithfully observed, serving as they did as a check on the dynamic signs in the score, which he placed so wisely that they almost always tallied perfectly. Schönberg did not hear the performances, but some of his admirers expressed their approval, and I may perhaps add that I still have a very happy and cordial letter from Berg after he heard the broadcast of *Wozzeck*.

Three years later the Variations again came into rehearsal for a performance in Vienna (the first ever heard in public there) and when I opened the score I found nothing in it to remind me of the previous performance, and actually said to myself that if someone had told me it was an entirely new set of variations on a different theme, I could have believed him. I heard recently of a much younger colleague who had said that he always had to re-study twelve-tone music afresh as if he had never seen it before even after many performances.

Looking back on these years 1945–50, little more seems to emerge of special note. I have mentioned a number of journeys abroad, and I seem to have been working very hard for these last B.B.C. years. I knew that the B.B.C. had a dismissal rule on reaching sixty-one, and that I should come under it in April 1950. A casual remark made by one whose position was much senior to mine gave me hope of extension, and this was not uncommon at that time. However, I was given due notice to go exactly on the official date. As soon as this news became public property I was greatly honoured by an approach from Mr Thomas Russell, then Manager of the London Philharmonic Orchestra, and as it turned out, I was only unemployed for two or three days.

I think I should set down an extra-musical activity which came mainly into these five years, after we had returned to London. I felt somehow that I should take some other work and perhaps even, given time, devote myself to a deserving cause which needed support. Therefore I asked the advice of Lady Snowden, Philip Snowden's widow. Ever since she had been a Governor of the B.B.C. Lady Snowden had kept a close interest in the work of the orchestra, and helped me a great deal. We discussed various possibilities and she took me to a table in her room, loaded with pamphlets and tracts of all kinds, on many subjects. 'Now take your choice', she said, but evidently had long come to the conclusion I gradually reached, that a supra-national authority of some kind was essential for this world if the risk of war could be kept at a distance. So I joined Federal Union, and was in due course elected to the executive committee. The brilliance of the thinking in that assembly staggered me. I listened but could not contribute a word, because I felt completely out of my depth. After a discreet interval I was offered a vice-presidency, and made room on the executive for a nimbler brain. I was, however, very glad to attend the Congress of Europe at The Hague in 1948, graced on a number of occasions by Queen Juliana, and splendidly addressed by Sir Winston Churchill before United Europe slipped from the front of his platform. Leonard Cheshire, the V.C. airman, who has done such wonderful work for elderly invalids, spoke most movingly on one occasion.

Amongst other highlights at this time were some recording sessions, both in London and Vienna, with Madame Kirsten Flagstad. She had by this time retired from grand opera, but was still a very great singer, and a delightful artist to accompany.

We began to have visits from foreign orchestras again, and I specially enjoyed that by the Cadets du Conservatoire with their splendid Director, Claude Delvincourt. This brave man kept this students' orchestra together in Paris for nearly the whole of the occupation. The German authorities were naturally keen to make all possible use of seventy or eighty able-bodied young Frenchmen, and Delvincourt kept on promising that they would soon be ready to undertake a concert tour of staggering virtuosity, and they must be spared for this great propaganda effort, until one day he had a hint that the authorities' patience (like Hitler's on many occasions) was exhausted. He sent hasty messages round, with the result that the whole orchestra disappeared in a night, and not one was heard of till the liberation of Paris. Their playing had the kind of spirit and verve that one would expect.

It was a great pleasure too to welcome to London Georges Enesco, who though crippled with arthritis, managed to conduct some beautiful performances in the studio. In 1922 when I was in Barcelona hearing Casals rehearse his orchestra there, I remember his saying that Tovey and Enesco were the two greatest musicians in Europe. I was always sorry not to see more of Enesco on his visits. Nadia Boulanger was also a frequent and welcome visitor, and still is.

During these years the National Youth Orchestra started its meteoric career. I believe I was one of the first musicians visited by Dame Ruth Railton when she inaugurated the project, and I thought it a fine idea, but I gathered that some of my colleagues did not. I was honoured with the Presidency, and later on I had the pleasure of conducting courses and concerts for them in Manchester, Bournemouth and Edinburgh. I hope Dame Ruth will write a book of her early adventures—some of them unbelievably frustrating. The National Youth Orchestra has had much well-deserved publicity, and the performances are often excellent, but I feel that the fundamental asset has been Dame Ruth's genius at auditions. She made no mistakes to my knowledge, and with her it has always been a matter of saying 'No', 'Yes', or 'I will take you in one or two years', not an easy thing to decide after a few minutes' hearing. Again, the presence of a number of greatly experienced professionals who coach the separate instruments for several hours a day has ensured the technical efficiency of every one of the young players.

There is another point which I feel should be made in regard to my 'retirement' from the B.B.C. It is easily forgotten that we were still living in something like war conditions. Food rationing still existed, and life in many ways was very uncomfortable—in fact, some of our homes were still requisitioned.

For this reason I never rehearsed the orchestra for one minute longer than I thought necessary, often stopping well before the scheduled close. When this was reported to the senior B.B.C. officials responsible for finance, they were displeased.

Nobody ever complained openly of unrehearsed performances (I don't think there were any), and I doubt whether it can be said that I was responsible for the undoubted fact that the B.B.C. Symphony Orchestra of 1951 was not quite the superb instrument it had been in 1939. After all it was smaller by twenty players, and many of the leaders had changed.

After twenty years' service the B.B.C.'s farewell arrangements were generous. At a small luncheon party in Broadcasting House, Sir William Haley spoke in such kind terms that I began to wonder whether I had really been asked to go or had insisted on going, to their great regret. At a much larger dinner at the Connaught Rooms I was given a beautiful silver inkstand, 'A Mozart of inkstands' as Sir William said. 'Which your wife will have to clean', remarked Mrs Mary Agnes Hamilton, one of the Governors.

On my sixtieth birthday the orchestra, many of whom had worked with me for twenty years, including the war, gave my wife and myself a wonderful dinner at the Savoy. This was a family affair with no one else beside my own family and secretary, Mrs Beckett, and Ralph Vaughan Williams and his wife. Ernest Hall took the chair, and the organization was in the very capable hands of Sidonie Goossens.

This was mentioned on the B.B.C. News, and to our astonishment, Gillie Potter, who had been listening, took the trouble to come down during the speeches and contributed some of his inimitable fun to grace the occasion. I am sure no man ever had a more delightful sixtieth birthday evening.

Chapter Thirteen

LONDON PHILHARMONIC—1950–1956

IT WILL be remembered that Sir Thomas Beecham founded the London Philharmonic Orchestra two years after the B.B.C. Symphony Orchestra began its work, and until the war broke out they had a most eventful and exciting life, playing at the Covent Garden season, touring frequently, and giving a brilliant series of concerts in Queen's Hall as the backbone of their activities.

Their founder went abroad in 1939, and observers feared the orchestra would have to disappear as well, as the authorities were very slow to realize that the first year of war saw little change in conditions at home. No concerts in London? If so, the L.P.O. would find somewhere else to play, and they invaded many concert halls (some a long way off) which had never heard an orchestra before, and had hardly room for one anyhow. They planned their trips only a few days ahead, when even in wartime the B.B.C. Orchestra was working eight weeks ahead, and so we were unable to give the L.P.O. any support by offering them broadcasts, though we greatly wished to help in this fine effort.

Someone hit on the idea of occasionally lending them my services as conductor; and I much enjoyed working with them, though I saw comparatively little of their frustrations and discomforts, and the almost endless difficulties faced by their courageous management. I met them one day in the Town Hall at Abingdon, near Oxford, where the only possible artists' room was a not very long passage under the stage. Here we all got into our boiled shirts when the time came. On another occasion in midwinter we met at Blackburn in Lancashire. Knowing this was near Preston where there was then an excellent Railway Hotel, I slept there and took an early train to Blackburn for the 10 o'clock rehearsal. The L.P.O. were there to a man, and it was only later that I found out that most of them had spent the night in the station waiting-rooms. They had come on from a Manchester concert, and arrived about eleven to find a very heavy blackout with snow, not worth penetrating to search for lodgings at that hour.

At Cheltenham one day the programmes had not turned up in time for the concert, so I had to be a walking programme, and also supply

With Ralph Vaughan Williams, August 1949

Welcoming H.M. The Queen to the Royal College
of Music, London, 20th February, 1968: (*l. to r.*)
the author, Lady Bliss, Sir Arthur Bliss, Lady
Redcliffe-Maud, H.M. The Queen and Sir Keith Falkner

(albeit in short measure) the analytical notes. Cheltenham was, I think, their favourite hall for the corridor round it has a large number of excellent sofas. These made it unnecessary for quite half the orchestra to bother with lodgings; and they could hardly wait for the audience to leave the hall after the concert!

I already had a very pleasant association with the orchestra when Mr Thomas Russell, who had been the moving spirit in all this wartime activity, invited me to become their conductor. They had had the privilege of Edvard van Beinum's help as conductor for some years after the war, but his time was coming to an end, and as he was also directing the Amsterdam Concertgebouw, it was better that a whole-time conductor should take over. We shared, however, a Belgian-Dutch tour in May 1950, and soon after that I became permanently associated with the L.P.O. Sometimes for several weeks I did everything that the orchestra did, travelling with them in the coaches and getting back to London very late night after night. However we soon saw that they could not go on like this indefinitely, and my ration of concerts had to be reduced. For a short and very pleasant period George Hurst acted as associate conductor, but more important work called him away all too soon.

Thomas Russell rightly believed in frequent tours abroad. It is a great incentive to finer playing, and the freshness of approach intrigues foreign audiences, just as foreign orchestras intrigue us here. Tiring though they are, these tours stimulate morale, and there is always better playing not only on the tour, but afterwards. Accordingly we set off on 15 January 1951 for a strenuous German tour. I was able to start early that day crossing by the Dutch day steamer, and sleeping on board, while the orchestra arrived next morning by the night boat. We went straight through to Essen, where the first concert took place, and I was glad to have had a quiet night in harbour before the ordeal, as there followed on successive nights concerts in Hanover, Berlin, Hamburg, Münster, Dortmund, Viersen, Düsseldorf, Nüremberg, Munich, Stuttgart and Heidelberg. This was on a Friday. We travelled all Saturday and crossed at night to Harwich, and took Ipswich in our stride for a Sunday afternoon concert on our way back to London. Among the works played were the Elgar Introduction and Allegro, the Holst 'Perfect Fool' Ballet, with symphonies by Haydn, Brahms, Beethoven, Schumann and Schubert, as well as Strauss's 'Don Juan'.

Three times we had to spend the night in sleepers, and of course, we had various contretemps and adventures. The press was uniformly enthusiastic. We had one very bad house—in Düsseldorf, where there was a large British colony as it was in the British zone. We were told that some welfare officer with the task of exchanging British currency for marks in order that the British in the district could pay for their tickets and come to the concert, had forgotten to do his stuff, and this mistake cost our poor German manager a pretty packet.

An odd thing happened in Munich. I was sitting in the artists' room a few minutes before the concert started, when the door opened. I looked up, and a blinding flash from a press camera followed. I felt certain that the photographer had tipped the man who was supposed to be guarding the dressing-rooms, and was furious. I went straight out and reported him to the manager.

We greatly admired the opera house in Nüremberg, and I was glad to meet again an old friend, Robert Heger, who had been a regular visitor to Covent Garden, and was Bruno Walter's second-in-command there and at Munich for many years.

We made a pleasant excursion to Cambridge in August to give an open-air concert in Neville's Court in Trinity. We played the Vaughan Williams 'London' Symphony and had a very hot and sunny rehearsal. Patrick Hadley, Professor of Music, had had much to do with organizing the concert, and just before the rehearsal I said that I thought I had better get my hat and keep the sun off my defenceless head while rehearsing. 'I'll get you one,' he said, and dashed off. I began the rehearsal and in a short while noticed that he had duly put the hat down at my feet. When a convenient pause came, I bent down and picked it up. Before I put it on, however, I discovered that some of the orchestral wags had put a few coppers in it.

In February 1952 we caught an early train for a concert in Wolverhampton. On arrival we found that some of the orchestra had been listening on a portable wireless during the journey and had heard of the sudden death of King George VI. We went to the hall, uncertain whether to cancel the concert or improvise a memorial. The concert was postponed, and I remember being greatly impressed with the memorial edition of the Wolverhampton evening paper. The provincial papers often show they have nothing to learn from London.

Later in the year we had the great pleasure of accompanying Kathleen Ferrier in what was destined to be her last recording sessions—four Bach arias and four by Handel. She was particularly happy as she had just had a very satisfactory medical test, but these things can be most deceptive and we little thought that she was so close to the end of her all-too-short career.

The following year, 1953, had many unusual events. I have said that I was privileged to help Sir William McKie at Queen Elizabeth II's Coronation, exactly as I had done sixteen years before, taking charge of the framing music. Here the Duke of Norfolk took much firmer charge than he had as a very young man in 1937. With his historic Earl Marshal's baton in one hand and in the other the latest model of a microphone, his voice was easily heard all over the Abbey. I remember one of the papers asking whether the Hollywood authorities were not half asleep as they had failed to sign him on as one of the greatest producers in the world.

At one moment of rehearsal the Peers' pages were all to bring their coronets to their Peers and there was some confusion and a long silence. Then someone, I think the Archbishop, gently suggested that a little organ music might be appropriate. 'I think not, sir', said the Duke, 'this operation has just taken five minutes and forty seconds. It has to be done in one minute and a quarter. Will all the pages please come to my office at four this afternoon.' 'The Headmaster's study in fact', said one of the orchestra quietly to me.

My wife was sitting with Lady Bullock in the nave and had a fine view of the entrances and exits. She particularly noticed the demeanour of some of the Communist representatives. They came in with a jaunty air, but they came out looking very solemn, having obviously been through an experience that they were not going to forget. They had been just as moved as the rest of us, whatever part we had to play.

My first experience of being presented to Royalty is something I shall never forget. It was at the Royal Albert Hall and there were a good many performers lined up a long distance from King George V and Queen Mary, who were standing at the far corner of the supper room. I nervously hurried across the space towards the Queen—ladies first was on my mind and she was standing considerably nearer. As I approached her, I sensed a rather forbidding attitude. The royal right hand did not move at all, and just at this critical moment a very slight inclination of the head towards His Majesty reminded me that where the King and Queen were concerned, ladies were *not* first. I was touched by the delicacy of the hint.

The honour of presentation to Her Majesty Queen Elizabeth II has been mine on a number of pleasant occasions. The Royal College of Music was, I believe, the first of the many institutions which she as Princess Elizabeth honoured with her Presidency several years before she finished her teens. She used to come annually to hear some music, give some prizes, and attend a tea-party, meeting a number of students. When she became Queen the office of President was taken by Her Majesty Queen Elizabeth the Queen Mother, whose annual visits are always a very special date in the College year.

My wife and I had an unexpected encounter with her present Majesty in a Suffolk by-road. We were going to Hintlesham Festival, and had put on our evening dress to drive across from the country hotel where we were staying. It was a very hot night and I did not put a coat over my dinner jacket. As we passed through the villages we noticed many little groups of people standing waiting expectantly and I remembered that the Queen had been visiting several places in Suffolk and was to be driving back to the Royal yacht at Harwich. So we backed our car into a side road and waited for the Royal car which soon came past with headlights blazing and the Queen and her lady-in-waiting looked with astonishment and amusement at the over-dressed pair of villagers bowing and curtseying.

A few months before my eightieth birthday I was most gratified to be offered the Order of Companion of Honour, which is limited to sixty-five holders. This is bestowed in private audience and Her Majesty read me the quotation from a poem by Alexander Pope which is on the Order: 'In action faithful and in honour clear'. It is a humbling thought.

Years earlier on the day after the Coronation my diary reports a wet drive to Cambridge and dinner with our good friend Patrick Hadley, Professor of Music, who had recommended me for the honorary degree of Doctor of Music. At the ceremony next morning I was in splendid company—Mr Nehru, Thomas Mann, G. M. Young, the writer, amongst others.

We drove straight away from the ceremony to Gloucester where in the evening I had the excitement of conducting Elgar's Second Symphony with the L.P.O. in the ideal setting of the Cathedral.

Autumn saw a good deal of work of different kinds of importance; an Edinburgh Festival Concert with the Philharmonia Orchestra, including the Mozart Concertante played by Stern and Primrose, with the first performance of the Fricker Viola Concerto, a Walton March and the 'Enigma'. And another concert at the same Festival with the National Youth Orchestra, who were in a large educational camp at Abington, the point where the road from the South splits into its Glasgow and Edinburgh branches. A camp is an agreeable enough place in a fine summer and we were lucky with cricket matches and so on in between rehearsals and classes, but the story of Dame Ruth's introduction to the camp deserves telling. In the comparatively early days of the N.Y.O. an invitation from the Edinburgh Festival was a great prize, even more so when it was coupled with a promise to provide lodging in one of the many available schools in the Edinburgh area. Later in the proceedings Dame Ruth asked whether she might see the accommodation, and it turned out that the matter had 'slipped the memory' of the Festival authorities, who by then had nothing available. Extremely worried, she began to search the whole of the South of Scotland and eventually came upon this, which had many advantages and was equally well placed from both Glasgow and Edinburgh, though forty miles away.

The following winter we spent much time recording. This included a complete 'Messiah', the beginning of the complete Vaughan Williams Symphony series, all in the presence of the composer, with the strange omission of No. 9. This did not come about until 1958, on 26

August, the very day on which that great man died. We had been looking forward to his attending the session, but just before breakfast Mrs Vaughan Williams rang up to say that he had died in the night. It was a poignant moment when I told the L.P.O. that he would not be with us. I was upset also on artistic grounds. I had never performed No. 9, and had not had the score very long for study.

About a week before the session I went to see him, heard a rather poor recording of a performance, and was able to discuss points with him. As I have said before I do not think it my business to comment on or criticize music from the artistic point of view, though I do sometimes butt in on matters of craftsmanship. However, as this recording came to a close I could not resist saying: 'Ralph, forgive me, but I do feel that ending is rather too abrupt. Couldn't you add about twenty more bars?' To my surprise he said 'I'll think about it, but meanwhile you could play the ending a good deal slower if you like', and I availed myself of this permission.

During the next months I accompanied the L.P.O. to many places. The orchestra was still to be heard in a number of halls to which other orchestras did not go at all, and our programmes were always introducing fresh material. Going to Cork in January I was able to start early and take the coward's route—a U.S.A. liner from Southampton to Cobh. I was delighted to find Yehudi Menuhin and his family on the boat train, to be invited to their table at meals, and spend a good deal of time with that wonderful man who is such good company in many other fields besides music. There was a Welsh tour when we had the collaboration of Emlyn Williams, a delightful companion on a number of long car trips. There were journeys abroad to Basel (where I made the acquaintance of the 'Carmina Burana' of Carl Orff, and enjoyed its overwhelming iteration), Montreux, The Hague, Hilversum, and an amazing experiment by the Decca Company, who curiously decided to send an elderly Englishman to Paris to conduct Russian music with a French orchestra. We recorded the 'Lieutenant Kije' Suite of Prokofiev and Tchaikovsky's splendid Third Suite, which, besides the well-known variations, has three other movements which to my mind place it beside the greatest of his symphonies.

Our Russian trip must have a chapter to itself, but the autumn of 1956 seems to have been very full of home events besides. It was a great pleasure to welcome Ernst von Dohnanyi again. We had collaborated in Birmingham in the twenties; he had been several times to the B.B.C., and now here he was, as brisk as ever, playing the charming 'Variations' with us at the E.M.I. Studios. I believe it was the last time he left the United States as he died soon after.

This too was a time of recording activity with Dr Kurt List of the

Westminster Company. We did all the Berlioz Overtures, all the Schumann Symphonies, the Elgar Second and 'Falstaff', as well as the Walton Symphony, and other things.

In December of this year Ralph Vaughan Williams paid a fine tribute to his friend Holst by planning a concert devoted to 'rarely heard works by Gustav Holst'. The programme included the Choral Fantasia, Fugal Concerto and Fugal Overture, and the beautiful 'Ode to Death'. It was a most impressive occasion, and there was a very good audience, including a large number of young people who, we hoped, found a new delight in this fine music.

You will see how it came about that the Russian expedition was suddenly forced on us when we were expecting a nice holiday, simply because I held the title of Conductor of the London Philharmonic Orchestra. In order to avoid this kind of thing in future, I reluctantly told the orchestra that I must officially resign at the end of 1956, though I was ready and willing to do whatever work the new conductor did not want, and could, of course, carry on until they found him. John Pritchard, then in Liverpool, was appointed and steered the orchestra through a most successful period, at the end of which Bernard Haitink came, and combined it with the Concertgebouw, as had his predecessor, Edvard van Beinum, years before.

The Cancer Research Fund asked me to go with the London Philharmonic Orchestra to Woburn Abbey to give a Summer Concert in the courtyard offered by the Duke of Bedford. When we got there we found a splendid covered stage had been put up and everything had been carefully planned for us. We were most interested to see parts of the house and the fine pictures. A very large bedroom was given me to change in. After the concert I dashed up to change again, and was in the middle of this exercise when the Duke came in to ask us to stay to supper. My appearance surprised him. 'Oh, poor chap,' he exclaimed, 'he's in his pants.'

On 14 April 1955 we spent a very happy evening. I have already spoken of my B.B.C. secretary, Mrs Gwen Beckett. Now twenty-five years of devoted care and wise counsel and wonderful service cried out for some special kind of celebration. Living in Whitehall Court at that time, it naturally occurred to us that the reception suite in that building would be a very pleasant place to meet. Thirty of us sat down to dinner. All were friends of Mrs Beckett's choosing, and hardly any introductions were necessary at all. There were, of course, many professional musicians, but also many non-musicians, and I hope they all enjoyed the charming performance of folk songs from many countries which Mr and Mrs Kitching gave us after dinner. We had heard a great deal of Mr and Mrs Kitching, whose work for music is well-known in the Abingdon and Oxford area where several of our grandchildren have taken part in musical events under their direction. Another pleasant link was that their son Colin had been my pupil at the Royal College of Music, and I often run into him at orchestral concerts where he is an eager viola player.

A very pleasant addition to L.P.O. work was planned about this time— concerts in churches. Many of the great East Anglia churches were used, among them, Boston, Beccles, Great Yarmouth, Blakeney, Bury St Edmunds, Lowestoft, and some splendid cathedrals too. Peterborough, Lincoln and Ely were visited. We usually had short programmes; though we generally sang a hymn in order that the audience might have a change of position once in the programme. Soloists were rarely engaged, and I suppose their fees were probably outside the range of the cheap admission charge of five shillings. But I remember with pleasure meeting Mr Tortelier at Great Yarmouth. He arrived in a rather disturbed state. It seems he had a suitcase identical with that of a fellow traveller on the 'plane. The two had somehow exchanged owners and he had arrived with an exciting collection of lingerie. He was wearing grey flannel trousers, sports jacket and a pair of bright yellow shoes.

Early in 1957 I heard from an old friend in America, E. Power Biggs, one of their most brilliant organists, who had, as a young man, played in 'The Planets' with me in Boston. He said that he and his wife had been scouring Europe to find the most suitable organ on which to record all the Handel Organ Concertos. They had decided that Great Packington Church, Warwickshire, had the best of all, and asked whether I could collect an orchestra for a week during the summer, and conduct the recordings. This delightful idea was welcomed not only by myself but by the London Philharmonic Orchestra, who provided the necessary strings, oboe, flutes and horns. My wife and I decided to stay at Leamington for the week, but some of the orchestra took tents, and Lord Aylesford and his son Lord Guernsey, who took great interest in it all, gave permission for camping, even also for a cable to be laid across the Park in order that electric blowing might be installed by Mr Biggs.

On Monday we began our series. Mr Biggs had discovered that the organ was exactly a semitone away from concert pitch, and there would be no difficulty in transposing. Unfortunately, it turned out to be a few vibrations under the semitone, and we spent a difficult afternoon trying to get our oboes into line. Americans are nothing if not thorough, and when the afternoon session had finished I found that Mrs Biggs had already rung up Mr Mander the organ builder in London. Mr Mander was by now in his car coming to dismantle the organ and take it to London bodily, to be returned in time for our session on Wednesday morning. His factory was prepared to work all night.

We had hardly begun our work on Wednesday before Mrs Biggs, who was acting as Recording Manager, drank a glass of milk which unfortunately contained a piece of tinfoil which caught in her throat, and she had to be rushed to Coventry Hospital for immediate examination. Meanwhile some slight fluctuations in pitch had made us suspicious about the power being brought to us over the new cable. It turned out that an electric stone crusher was stealing some of our juice, and so we had to readjust our sessions to late afternoons, 5 to 8 p.m., and then 9 to midnight, and Lord Aylesford summed it up to my wife: 'My dear, it seems that old Handel is disapproving of this exercise.' However, Handel relented after that and we were able to finish our work on Sunday afternoon just in time, most of us having other engagements on Monday. We had expected to finish on Saturday at the very latest. Mrs Biggs proved a tower of strength throughout the sessions, and the success of the records shows how accurate was her ear and discerning her taste. Mr Biggs' performances were all masterly. We were most hospitably entertained at Great Packington Hall, and on one occasion after lunch when I had suggested that it was time to go back to work, our host said: 'Oh, yes, you must get your organ grinder back on time.' 'Him?' said his loving wife. 'Him? Why he's only the monkey.' Our Leamington beds seemed far away when the sessions ended at midnight, so we were very kindly taken in by Mr and Mrs Goldberg, friends who lived in Packington Old Hall, also in the Park, where we stayed for the three late nights and were shown every consideration and kindness.

Chapter Fourteen

RUSSIA—1956

WHEN, EARLY in 1956, I heard rumours of a possible Russian trip by the London Philharmonic Orchestra, I at once blessed it, but was afraid I could not go with the orchestra. Ears that made me dislike flying, coupled with a back that was troublesome on long journeys, kept me well out of it.

The Administrator of the L.P.O. took a trip to Moscow about Easter time and all details were fixed up and my absence was understood. A list of conductors was discussed, and soon afterwards, settled. It may be added that after a short holiday in June I had arranged for a busy summer with recordings and concerts, hoping for a good rest while the orchestra was abroad. The Russian trip was to be followed by several weeks in Germany, and a few concerts in Paris.

Two or three weeks before zero hour, which was for the orchestra Sunday 16 September 1956, a strange young man from the Soviet Cultural Attaché's department in Kensington Palace Gardens called at Welbeck Street and asked numerous questions. The answer seemed usually to have been 'It was settled in Moscow six months ago that . . .'. Finally he asked to see the programmes, and noting the absence of my name, asked why was not I going. Again the answer had to be that 'Moscow knew six months ago . . .' His reply was true to Soviet technique, 'Oh, but if Boult does not go I think I shall have to cancel the whole trip.' No one had any idea how far this gentleman was bluffing, but an alarmed meeting of British Council, Arts Council and General Administrator waylaid me immediately afterwards. This was followed by a summons to the Foreign Office and the exercise of all Lord Reading's persuasive powers. I did not see how I could risk being the cause of this cancellation. It would almost certainly spell the bankruptcy of the L.P.O., and so my wife and I began to plan how to go to Moscow by train.

A through Paris-Warsaw sleeper seemed to have much to commend it. It ran only three times a week, so we chose Thursday, 13 September, as the next would reach Moscow only just in time. As we had several hours between arrival in Paris and departure from the Gare de l'Est in the next

street, we hired a porter with a barrow and dined at the Écu de France
before finding our sleeper at 9 p.m. All went well (as well as it could in the
old-fashioned wagon-lit we had) and breakfast and lunch were given us in
a German restaurant car, with the promise that we should lunch at 11 a.m.
This over, we found ourselves facing the iron curtain. Our passports
removed, we were locked into the coach, a soldier with a tommy-gun
covering the train from a watch tower, and a dreary vista of trenches and
barbed wire to cheer us up and introduce us to contemporary civilizations.
This four-hour delay seemed to be the practice at every frontier behind
the curtain—apparently they copied every word that was in our passports,
and going into Poland I found that the series number of every one of our
travellers' cheques had to be duly copied out.

The last half-hour of our wait was spent at an outlying station of Cheb
(Eger) where there was no food. A new wagon-lit attendant appeared and
told us that a wheel had come off our restaurant car, but that we could eat
at the buffet at Pilsen or wait to dine in Prague. At Pilsen there was a howl-
ing mob trying to board the train. We had no idea how long it would wait,
and could see no buffet, so we gave up and let ourselves be swept back
by the mob into the train. Prague was due at 8.30 and by that time we
were in urgent need of food (after our 11 a.m. lunch) and we knew we had
a three-hour wait there. However, we found the station restaurant closed,
and only a little buffet for railway servants available. Discussing the not
very appetizing foods displayed on the counter, we were surprised to hear
an English voice, and one of the ladies behind the counter informed us
that she had lived in the Finchley Road! We took some very garlicky
sausage and sat in the dark on the platform until our sleeper (which as
usual was being shunted miles away) returned, and we went to bed to wake
up in Poland with yet another sleeper attendant. Yes, he said, breakfast
was along in that direction and we began to move through three coach
loads of sleepers, sleepers in the compartments, and sleepers in the corri-
dors. The recent 'thaw' had permitted holidays over the frontier, and here
was a mass of Poles who had been to Czechoslovakia for the first time
since the war, returning home after suitable celebrations. After we had
climbed over dozens of them we achieved the dining-car. My wife caught
her foot in one of the slotted mats over the coupling and twisted her
ankle. She bound it up with her scarf, and we went on to breakfast. This
consisted of sausages which foamed when cut. What was inside them we
still have no idea. As we had no Polish money the kind O.C. let us eat
free, on our assurance that the British Embassy would meet us at Warsaw
Station—in the person of a nephew of Miss Carey-Foster (who until her
recent death had been a great helper with all students' activities at the
Royal College of Music). His kindness to us knew no bounds. Driving
away with him, I asked whether all would be well for our journey to

Moscow next day, to be met with a blank expression. His instructions were to meet us and look after us as we had not been well. Not a word about our further journey. Luckily we had these two days in hand. An interregnum between Ambassadors gave us the clear run of the Residence and besides lunches with members of the Embassy, we were taken for a drive to Chopin's birthplace. We attended an English service on Battle of Britain Sunday morning. After endless preliminaries, we were given our tickets and passports, and put into a morning train for the thirty-hour journey to Moscow, and Mr Carey-Foster gave us a grand nosebag, which was most welcome.

Our four-berth sleeper compartment was to be shared with a young Pole, who was travelling with an enormous amount of luggage. He asked us to post a letter to his wife, who was in Paris but could not return to Warsaw. We did, and there was no answer. We reached Brest about eleven next day, and I was expecting to change into the wonderful broad gauge Russian coaches one had heard so much about, when to our astonishment we found ourselves shunted into a siding where the coach was jacked up by its four corners, and sixteen stalwart Russian matrons hauled the bogey out from under us, pushed another in its place, and clamped us down to continue our journey. While this was going on what should we see in the next siding but the L.P.O. eating as if their lives depended on it. They had arrived from Berlin (where they had flown) an hour earlier, and we were now to go on together. I was not sorry to see the inside of that dining-car. It was very well managed, in fact after one great meal at three, we were offered another at eight and this many of us refused. It was interesting to discover that this was not a special dining-car put on for us. It was the usual service on this train, but because we were there no ordinary passengers were allowed to use it. The Russian public is certainly long-suffering. Several interpreters had appeared by this time, and one asked how I came there. I replied with a few remarks about the red carpet we were told we should find waiting for us at Warsaw. 'Oh dear,' he said, 'but we all understood that you were going to flo'.'

Moscow received us with great bunches of the largest chrysanthemums we had ever seen, half an orchestra, its conductor, Mr Gauk, and many photographers and also, luckily, some people from the Embassy who spirited us away after we had done our share of interviews. The entrance hall of the Moscow Hotel is the size of a large railway terminus. We had to walk a considerable distance before we could sit down to wait until an interpreter found our rooms.

The dining-room would easily seat a thousand, and the orchestra was lost in one corner of it. We all sat near them at a large table, soloists, interpreters, managers and conductors.

The musicians, who came repeatedly to the artists' rooms with congratulations and comments, were friendly throughout. Several well-known composers came to all our concerts.

In Moscow we gave nine concerts, and four in Leningrad. George Hurst and Anatole Fistoulari were the other conductors, and the soloists were Campoli and Moura Lympany. The programmes were terrifying. Overall, I should say they consisted of about sixty per cent British music, and that was what they (i.e. the Ministry of Culture—I'm not so sure of the public!) wanted, and insisted on.

The concerts were said to have been sold out within a few days of announcement, and no further advertising was necessary.

In Moscow I gave four concerts as follows:

BERLIOZ	Carnaval Romain	
VAUGHAN WILLIAMS	5th Symphony	} twice
HOLST	Planets	

BRAHMS	Tragic Overture	
WALTON	Violin Concerto	
	CAMPOLI	
SCHUBERT	C major Symphony	

BLISS	Blow Meditation	
RACHMANINOFF	Paganini Variations	
	MOURA LYMPANY	
VAUGHAN WILLIAMS	Fourth Symphony	

and in Leningrad the Schubert Campoli programme.

As always with visitors, many events were laid on for us. We saw part of *Ivan Sussanin* at the Bolshoi—the magnificent Court Scene with all the resources of the ballet—and it was interesting to watch the audience very much excited to see a real Palace and a King and his Court. Part of *Coppelia* at the Second Bolshoi Theatre was beautifully done. We all went to Shostakovitch's fiftieth birthday celebration. The Moscow Philharmonic Orchestra played for Part I with a cantata and violin concerto. The Moscow Radio Orchestra took over Part II. I did not hear it because I was conducting next day, but many of our players said they were nothing like as good, and after this the platform was cleared, Shostakovitch was placed on it in an armchair to receive greetings, floral, verbal and osculatory from the sixteen republics.

One of our interpreters, discussing this beforehand, remarked that Shostakovitch was shy and modest and would hate it all, but would have to go through with it, if necessary till 2 a.m. My wife replied that when our leading composer had his eightieth birthday he was *asked* what he would like. The answer was 'a conjurer', and that is what he had for his birthday party.

The orchestra was also taken to the Agricultural Exhibition at the Kremlin. Mrs Parrott took us alone to the Kremlin and its museum, also to a monastery (now a museum) where several Tsars retired, and to another in the country called Kolomemskoye, which has links with Catherine the Great and Peter the Great. Here the caretakers pressed illustrated catalogues on us, refusing payment as we were their guests.

The Kremlin museums are staggering; the jewellery on the bridles of imperial harness must be seen to be believed; and so must the gigantic coaches and a covered sledge big enough to have a table and armchairs in it. In this huge vehicle Catherine the Great travelled from St Petersburg to Moscow for her coronation. She did the three hundred miles in three days (resting at night) and used a thousand horses in relays of twenty-five at a time. There were many other superb exhibits including fine pictures and a lovely collection of the Fabergé gifts Nicholas II gave to the Tsaritsa.

As in Warsaw, our Embassy could not have been more helpful: the Ambassador, Sir William Hayter, was away, but the Minister (Parrott, whom I had met in Prague years before) and his Norwegian wife were kindness itself, and invited us several times to their flat, and Mrs Parrott was entirely responsible for the four wonderful mornings we spent, twice on the outskirts and twice in Moscow.

The British Minister kindly gave a party to enable us to meet Moscow musicians. On the night after our last concert (the night before we left for Leningrad) we were all bidden to an enormous supper. The Cultural Minister, Mr Mikailov, was host, Mr Gromyko also was there talking with the orchestra and practising his English. It was all set like a great banquet, a cross high table, and so on, but *no* chairs. Mr Mikailov's high spot was at the end of his speech. For his toast he dispensed with his interpreter. We all expected he would raise his glass to Universal Peace or something brotherly. He went close to the microphone, held his glass up to it, and 'VIVE VIMMEN' was the unexpected dénouement.

A number of the Ballet people attended this party and went next day to the British Embassy to get their visas for their Covent Garden tour.

I had said to Mr Mikailov that I was very sorry that they had no day trains between Moscow and Leningrad, as we should have liked to see the country. There is, I believe, one in the summer, but it did not run in the winter. The reply I got was 'Well, you can get up at 6 a.m. and see quite a lot of it.' I looked out occasionally and only saw what we had seen between Brest and Moscow. There were endless plains, with scrub and birches. However the night trains are good, and there seem to be two or three in each direction. We had a two-berth compartment to ourselves, and both were lower berths.

The passion for propaganda in the U.S.S.R. is considerable. From the train, even after midnight, the moment it stopped at any station, we could hear loudspeakers blaring until we moved out of hearing. There were also loudspeakers in every compartment of the train, often on, night and day.

On arrival in Leningrad we had a pleasant surprise. As we stepped down from the train two girls on the platform were laughing, really laughing, a sound we had not heard for a fortnight. The hotel, just opposite the concert hall, was a very comfortable Victorian building with luxurious appointments. We had a suite with a dining-room and small study, and even our bedside lights were enormous, made of bronze, and too heavy to lift.

Almost immediately on arrival we were taken off to Peterhof in coaches. We were very glad to see it. The Germans used it as headquarters when besieging Leningrad and destroyed it as completely as they could when they retreated. They did the same thing at Tsarskoye Selo. The Peterhof gardens and façade have been reconstructed but the Palace, behind its front walls, is said to be in ruins still. The fountains are magnificent, and the position on the Baltic looking across to Finland most lovely. Peter the Great had a small house where he could live and work right on the sea, while the Palace lies about half a mile back on a hill with canals and rides and gardens in between. On our drive through Leningrad we passed a very large and splendid church, and were informed that it is now an anti-religious museum.

A lovely concert hall with artists' rooms spacious and comfortable—and in the hall six chandeliers each with a hundred and twenty lights, originally, of course, seven hundred and twenty candles. We had very little time for sight-seeing, but spent half-an-hour in the Hermitage, which is now entered from the Winter Palace up the Ambassadors' Staircase, a fabulous thing in white and gold, and then over the upstairs bridge the Tsars used to visit their pictures when the gallery was closed. Our interpreters jumped every queue on our behalf.

The situation of the gallery and the Winter Palace on the river looking across to the Bourse and the Fortress of Peter and Paul is magnificent, and the whole plan of the city, with canals and gardens, make it seem like a great capital instead of the overgrown village which is Moscow. The atmosphere of Leningrad is much more friendly and cheerful too.

The audiences were kind everywhere, but in Leningrad they *looked* happier too, and the beauty of the hall naturally helped. We had only a short time to catch our train back to Moscow after the concert, for we had decided to have one more quiet night there before spending two nights between Moscow and Berlin, and we had difficulty in extricating ourselves from the hall. Madame Mravinski's volubility in regard to the Schubert C major Symphony (in German) was almost embarrassing, even though gratifying and flattering to hear such things from a distinguished conductor's wife.

Our final departure from the Moscow Hotel was characteristic. Three coaches for the orchestra were laid on, and they filled only two of them. We were in a car, but our luggage was put into the third, and otherwise empty, coach. I suspected this, and watched anxiously for the arrival of the third coach outside the station. After ten minutes there was no sign of it so I complained, and some of the interpreters got busy.

The coach (and our luggage) had been sitting by themselves at a side entrance of the station. It was, in fact, the exit that we had used on arrival to get away quickly! They might easily have stayed there all day.

Chapter Fifteen

'RETIREMENT'—1957–1968

AFTER THE Russian Tour I had said that though I must no longer be called the Musical Director of the London Philharmonic Orchestra, I was ready to work with them as much as possible, at any rate until the successor was found and free to take over. As it turned out, it was some time before John Pritchard was able to leave Liverpool. He was already deeply involved in Glyndebourne and a number of foreign commitments, and so life changed very little for me. Perhaps the high spot of the year were two performances of Elgar's 'Kingdom', with the Croydon Philharmonic Society, who, under Alan Kirby's penetrating and inspiring direction, had a command of all Elgar's choral work which was unmatched anywhere.

The first took place in Croydon, unfortunately just before the fine Fairfield Hall was opened, and on 29 May we repeated it in the Royal Festival Hall with the B.B.C. Symphony Orchestra. A friend of mine, Wulstan Atkins, took an excellent tape of this performance. The son of one of Elgar's close friends, Sir Ivor Atkins, he has wisely kept his music for his spare time, but has made very good use of it. The quality of that tape is such that, when played to representatives of one of the great recording companies, they seriously considered the possibility of its transfer to wax, and of putting it on the market. The advice of their American contacts, however, finally dissuaded them.

The year of my seventieth birthday (April 1959) had a special interest for me. In succession to Vaughan Williams I was offered and accepted the Presidency of the Royal Scottish Academy of Music by my friend Henry Havergal. Coupled with my Honorary Doctorate of Edinburgh University it makes a very pleasant link with that lovely country where at least thirty summer holidays have been spent, where I have many good friends, and whence came one of my grandparents. Soon after my appointment my wife and I had the pleasure of giving the prizes to the successful students, and soon after this it was my great privilege to congratulate our ex-student Alexander Gibson on his appointment as first British conductor of the Scottish National Orchestra. Since his appointment he and the orchestra have developed year by year, and are now world-famous. His leader, Samuel Bor, is also an old friend as he was a founder-member of the B.B.C. Symphony Orchestra.

Two recordings of special interest were 'Acis and Galatea' in June, with the young Joan Sutherland and Peter Pears in the cast, for the enterprising Oiseau Lyre Company, founded by Mrs Louise Dyer (who had already done a great deal for Australian and British music before she began work in publishing and recording), and 'The Planets' for Dr List of the Westminster Company in Vienna.

Before this I had another invitation to Edinburgh Festival for a Vaughan Williams commemoration concert, which gave me an introduction to the splendid Vronsky-Babin partnership. They played the two-pianoforte version of the concerto, and I shall never forget their magnificent summing up of the whole work in the great final cadenza. The programme also included the 'Sea Symphony' with the fine choral union.

In the autumn I took part in two concert performances of unusual operas, Busoni's *Faust*, which we did in the Royal Festival Hall in November, and Vaughan Williams' *Pilgrim's Progress* for the B.B.C., with a brilliant cast and chorus in their studio at Camden Town. A week's rehearsal gave us the chance of soaking ourselves in its quiet beauty, and John Noble repeated his very fine performance of the Pilgrim.

The year 1961 opened with a very charming tribute from the London Philharmonic Orchestra to the man who had begun to be their permanent conductor ten years before. It was a delightful idea to commemorate our ten years' work together, and to persuade Yehudi Menuhin to play the Elgar Violin Concerto at the concert. When the time came he was unable to play, but was well enough to come to the Hall and present to me a beautifully bound copy of the Bliss 'Colour Symphony' (probably the first work that had honoured me with its dedication), signed by the composer and everyone in the L.P.O. Campoli played the Elgar very finely in Menuhin's place, and we also played a Dance Concerto 'Phalaphala' by Priaulx Rainier which had been specially written for the concert.

Another very pleasant compliment was paid me that year by Malcolm Williamson, who had been commissioned by the B.B.C. to write a work for the Henry Wood Promenades. It took the form of an organ concerto, played by the composer, each movement of which was built on one of my initials A. C. B. We repeated the work some months later in Vienna, where it scored an even greater success, increased, I could not help feeling, by the hitherto unknown and very boyish figure of the composer, who had given a prodigious musical and technical display in the solo part.

About this time came another invitation from the Dutch Radio. They wished to give some performances of Walton's 'Belshazzar's Feast'. Hervey Alan came too, and we had a number of performances in Hilversum,

Amsterdam and Scheveningen, with the Radio Symphony Orchestra and Chorus, splendidly trained, and singing faultless English. It is a great convenience in Holland that distances are so short: everyone can drive home after each concert. I think I was the only performer who slept each night close to the hall we had played in.

It is well known that the Gold Medal of the Royal Philharmonic Society is much prized among musicians all over the world. I was greatly honoured to receive this decoration from the chairman of that time, Mr Theodore Holland, a composer who worked for the Society for many years. The war was nearly over, and I was proud to receive it at a time when it was, I think, generally felt that the B.B.C. Orchestra had done a great deal to help the morale of the country. In a way, perhaps, I may claim to have been even more deeply honoured by the Society, as they have, no less than four times, invited me to make this presentation to colleagues.

The first was to Felix Weingartner, whose work as an interpreter of Beethoven gave him an honoured place among musicians for something like fifty years. I first heard him at the only orchestral concert I ever attended in the old St James's Hall in Regent Street. This must have been somewhere about 1902. I can still vividly remember the Seventh Symphony, and the Egmont Overture. The Medal presentation took place in Queen's Hall, but next day we were asked to visit the very early television studio in Alexandra Palace and display the Medal to viewers, with Mrs Weingartner ('Formerly my pupil, now my vife') in the picture with us. He was one of the first conductors of international fame to visit the B.B.C. Symphony Orchestra, and was kind enough to give his very cordial impressions to a press meeting afterwards

The Fairfield Halls in Croydon were opened on 2 November 1962. As far as I remember, I had been asked to conduct the opening concert, but circumstances (not unusual with modern building!) caused the postponement of the date, and so our concert had to be transferred elsewhere, and somebody else opened the hall. However, for the first year I was honoured to be asked to be President of the Corps of Honorary Stewards, which was founded on the model of the Royal Albert Hall Corps, and does splendid work at the functions in the hall. They have a very nice Corps tie, and I am pleased to be able to wear the one they gave me.

My first concert there was on one of the foggiest days I had ever known, and I found the hall because I had the luck to run into an orchestral player in the train who piloted me across the (then) big parking space, and took me in. My wife, coming later, was at one moment hopelessly lost until someone came by and told her she was standing on the doorstep.

On another occasion I had to miss an engagement at the last moment. This happens very seldom and disappoints me very much. I had had some very busy weeks and had let myself get more tired than was sensible. One day I sent for the doctor after a very bad night, which is rare with me, and I take it as a firm warning. There was a very important Festival Hall concert three days ahead, and I was told that I could do this only if I kept perfectly still for the next thirty-six hours. A breakdown was the cheerful prospect otherwise. It seemed appalling to give up the Croydon concert yet go to the Festival Hall, but I have been taught to give way to illness at once. It may appear cowardly at the time but it usually means that one is able to resume work soon.

The second Medal recipient at my hands was Bruno Walter. Almost all through this century he had made great contributions to British music-making, not only in London, including several notable opera seasons at Covent Garden, and I can also remember a thrilling concert with the Birmingham Orchestra during my time there in the late twenties. Unfortunately, illness prevented him coming from America to receive the Medal, and it was decided that Dame Myra Hess, herself a holder of the Medal, should receive it on his behalf and take it to him when she crossed the Atlantic a little later.

The other two presentations were more recent. In the late autumns of 1962 and 1963 Yehudi Menuhin and Pierre Monteux were two artists who equally conferred lustre on the Medal which was to honour them. I have worked many times with Mr Menuhin, and find every time I meet him there are new things in his mind and fresh thoughts and ideas as he approaches his work.

Mr Monteux at this time had accepted a short contract as permanent conductor of the London Symphony Orchestra, and we were delighted to have him as a regular contributor to our London music, particularly when, at the age of something like eighty-four, he signed a renewal of this contract—this time for twenty-five years.

That evening we had an alarming moment as we left the platform after the presentation. Mr Monteux gave two little groans as we walked down the passage, and I suddenly found my arms full of violins and bows. The orchestra had recognized the signs. Their beloved chief was fainting. Some of them supported him to the couch in the conductor's room, and then took their fiddles again and left him to Mrs Monteux. I was afraid I had spoken too long with my presentation; he had refused the chair I offered him and had insisted on standing throughout. My wife hurried to the hotel next morning to see Mrs Monteux, who said that he fainted on the slightest provocation. A day or two earlier in Berlin she had fainted, and on seeing this he followed suit and there was a fainting duet on the bedroom floor. No indeed, he was now quite well, sitting up in bed eating a hearty breakfast and playing with his Medal.

The year 1965 began with a risky, but pleasant trip to Vienna. We had already decided that travelling in January and February, even in Great Britain, was to be avoided if possible, but somehow this invitation got itself accepted without my realizing what a dangerous time of year I had let us in for. However, we had fine weather and a splendid guardian and 'manager', our old friend Richard Rickett, to arrange everything for us. The homeward journey had to begin with a motor trip from Graz to Vienna as the trains were inconvenient. The roads were clear though the snow was thick on the hills each side of us. The Graz concert included the Second Sibelius Symphony, curiously inserted, I feel sure, because the management had suddenly discovered that it was the composer's centenary year and they had done nothing about it. English conductors were rash enough for anything, and they decided to saddle me with it. The result surprised them and it was a great success. I have already told how the Vienna audience rose to the sight and sound of Malcolm Williamson's mercurial performance of his organ concerto in the same programme.

This year also included my first professional visit to the Three Choirs Festival. My friend Herbert Sumsion extended to me a charming invitation to conduct an Elgar Symphony at Gloucester, and the famous Three Choirs weather did its usual wonderful best.

Other interesting events were the re-opening of the Royal Festival Hall after its closure for alterations. These have considerably improved it, and have added much greater comfort to the performers' accommodation. We began very happily with an eloquent performance of the Elgar Concerto by Menuhin, a performance we have since recorded, nearly fifty years after his famous performance on record with the composer.

I was also asked by an enterprising recording company called Lyrita, in association with the John Ireland Society, to undertake the complete works of John Ireland. Two full records were made that autumn, and we hope for completion soon.

As a tribute to Sir Henry Wood his birthday anniversaries have been celebrated by concerts when orchestras and choirs from the four London Music Colleges combine to give music of some special importance. Each year a different conductor is appointed, and my turn had come round two or three times and works like 'The Hymn of Jesus' and Walton's Second Symphony were given. This year, however, it was decided to perform Mahler's Eighth Symphony with a large string group, but otherwise as directed by the composer, rather than with heavy doublings (or more) as was usually the custom at these concerts where four orchestras were combining. We also decided to audition and engage sixteen soloists, so that the colleges might be well represented, the cast being entirely changed for the second movement. The Mahler scholar and expert Deryck Cooke kindly helped me with this, and I thought the soloists filled the places well. The orchestra, who had, I think, fourteen or fifteen rehearsals, also did splendidly, and many of the orchestral soloists achieved notable performances. Unfortunately, the chorus did not come up to this high standard. I have an idea that singing students are inclined to think they can sing anything at sight. The result was that at the final rehearsal in the Albert Hall I sent the orchestra home more than an hour before the end, and kept the chorus and, with the organist's help, tried to get the music into their heads. Music students nowadays are very busy people; many of them have to do the domestic chores that mothers and landladies did in my own time, and their choice of activities naturally puts choral work low on the list. I think too that the attitudes to this concert vary very much in the different colleges, many of them having such crowded schedules that there is no time for extras.

Another gigantic work came my way at that time. This was Havergal Brian's 'Gothic' Symphony, planned on a scale like the Mahler; I believe that Sir Henry Wood had suggested to the composer that he should write a work exploiting the sonorities of all possible instruments, including many like basset horns outside the ordinary run of orchestral work. It has much in it of great beauty, and finishes with an extended setting of the 'Te Deum'. This work was revived (it has been once performed by Bryan Fairfax) on the initiative of Dr Robert Simpson, who though himself a most impressive composer, seems to spend his time at the B.B.C. further- ing the works of other people, and writing books about them. It was an impressive moment when the ninety-year-old composer appeared on the platform at the end, and the big audience rose to acclaim him.

As a one-time town boy of Westminster School I was very happy to get several invitations from Westminster Abbey during 1966, their 900th anniversary year. Douglas Guest planned a wonderful twelve months of music in that marvellous setting, and I much enjoyed taking part in programmes with the London Philharmonic Orchestra, the Royal College Orchestra, and hearing some lovely chamber music and poetry reading, as well as an evening tour in the charge of my old school friend Lawrence Tanner. One of the most impressive ceremonies I took part in with the B.B.C. Orchestra during the year, was the memorial service to the dis- tinguished broadcaster Richard Dimbleby, attended by a vast congrega- tion (Lawrence Tanner said it was the largest, except for the Coronations, in his memory, and that goes back beyond the turn of the century) of every sort of person who had been moved by Dimbleby's wonderful broadcast descriptions of every sort of important occurrence for many years.

The year 1966 also began a pleasant association with the young people comprising the B.B.C. New Orchestra, now called the Academy, in the organization based in Bristol, and working daily in the Colston Hall, to provide a bridge between the colleges and the profession. They contribute an hour a week to broadcast programmes; they had the privilege at that time of intensive training with Leonard Hirsch and others, and outside conductors visit them often. I have happy memories of the Schubert C major in Bristol, the 'Siegfried Idyll' in Gloucester Cathedral, and the first performance of a set of variations on a Welsh folksong, three of them by English and three by Welsh composers, played by us in Swansea some weeks after the opening of the Severn Bridge, and commissioned by the B.B.C. for this orchestra.

We usually try to combine our holidays with visits to 'stately homes' wherever we are. In fact we often make plans to include some homes, as when we endured an unpleasant little cottage in Tideswell in order to visit Chatsworth, Kedleston, Haddon, Lyme, Bramall, and Hardwick, which so thrilled us that we went to see it twice.

Another holiday we tacked on to a Glasgow engagement, and at one point, north of Oban, I was sorely tempted to drive through a most inviting entrance gate and see what was at the end. My law-abiding wife held back my desire to trespass, but we both regretted it, when a later look at the map showed it to be Lochnell Castle. Only two weeks later in an hotel in the south we were talking to a lady and told her of our temptation. We mentioned Lochnell, and she said, 'Good gracious, I live there, I do wish you had come in.'

I suppose it is natural for what our children used to call a 'Public Body' to be spoken to sometimes by strangers in buses and tubes. It usually takes the form of a pleasant word of thanks, and no more, but sometimes matters are pressed further. I was recently accosted with a knowing wink by a bus neighbour: 'I know you quite well, don't I? I see you often at Lord's.' So I answered that I went very seldom to Lord's—cricket isn't much in my line. 'Oh, yes, I know, you are one of the policemen there.'

A more gratifying occasion was on a rush-hour bus where I was standing on the platform while the conductor was upstairs. When he came down, I started to go inside where I hate standing as I always bump my head. 'Stay outside with me, sir, it's all right; you're too tall to go inside; besides I know you're a member of the Conductors' Union.'

For some years there was a rather lean period where recordings were concerned, and it was refreshing, during 1966, to have a renewal of invitations from several companies. It began, I think, with the suggestion that I should conduct for Yehudi Menuhin, with whom I always enjoy collaboration, a recording of the Elgar Violin Concerto which he had first made with the composer many years before. For the sleeve we were asked to ape the well-known picture of the boy and the composer standing on the steps of No. 3 Abbey Road, the recording headquarters of E.M.I. The light was quite different, and I'm afraid I made a very poor substitute for the great composer. Since then I have much enjoyed sessions of Elgar's 'Kingdom', 'Music Makers' and many of the shorter orchestral works, Parry's 'Blest Pair', several Vaughan Williams symphonies, Holst's 'Planets', a day of sprightly Marches including four of Sousa's finest, and other things.

There is a great satisfaction for me in recording, though it is hard work, and the recording managers and engineers are splendidly co-operative, so much so that I am coming more and more to trust their judgement as to what is suitable for recording. It is, I know, my business to produce in the studio the finest sound I can and it is theirs to adapt it to wax. I feel that no one can do this better than men like Christopher Bishop of E.M.I., and several of his colleagues.

A very exciting pendant to my recording activities came with the B.B.C. invitation to conduct 'Gerontius' for colour television in Worcester Cathedral. It was then a new technique to broadcast a large-scale work with a certain number of shots of the performers in the old way, but also a good showing of pictures connected not so much with that actual performance as themselves an expression of the meaning behind the work itself. During the early stages of planning it was decided that even with all Elgar's links with Worcester, Canterbury would be a more suitable place for the setting. Elgar had also conducted there; it was nearer London (the chorus, for instance, could make their contribution without having to sleep out of town), and had, inside the building, an amazing variety of wonderful material.

The plan was to spend two days recording the music. First there was a day with soloists, chorus and orchestra, and the second day with soloists and orchestra, rehearsing from 11 to 1 p.m. and 'taking' from 3 to 7 p.m. The cameras were hard at work when I looked into the Cathedral on the evening before the first day, and I know they spent a whole third day photographing other parts of the Cathedral. The Cathedral authorities were kindness itself. It must have been a difficult decision to agree to a three-day closure with the minimum obligatory services in the crypt, and to have the peaceful precincts invaded by a dozen great B.B.C. Outside Broadcast vans, and five enormous red generators, which together could produce enough power to supply Canterbury for two days. They gave a menacing hum all day and well into the night. This resulted in throwing a revealing light on many details of the building, not evident before.

We all met in good time to begin at 11 a.m. on 27 February 1968. The soloists were Janet Baker, Peter Pears and John Shirley-Quirk, the London Philharmonic Orchestra, led by Rodney Friend, and the London Philharmonic Choir with its conductor, Frederick Jackson. Vernon Handley acted as deputy conductor, and saved my energy a great deal during the rehearsal periods. Besides this I think we must put it on record that as the Canterbury Cathedral organ was completely disabled, Allan Wicks the organist felt that the electronic instrument temporarily replacing it was quite unequal to taking part in a performance of this importance and so a church organ nearly two miles away was pressed into service. Charles Spinks, the B.B.C. organist, with a loudspeaker and a closed circuit television screen, could see and hear everything that we were doing, and could play Elgar's organ part with his tone blending perfectly with ours. Such are the achievements of modern science.

Television cameras are temperamental machines and there were a number of stoppages owing to 'technical troubles'. Dr Brian Large, an understanding musician as well as a brilliant producer, had prepared a schedule which allowed us to make full use of the presence of the choir, and leave everything else for the next day. At lunch time we had rehearsed the more important parts, playing sections several times, and when we re-assembled at three o'clock we were hoping to work very quickly in order to get more than halfway by tea-time. However, we had hardly begun when we were stopped and told that the most important central camera was out of action for some reason and we must wait to see what was wrong, and whether the camera must be replaced. This did not sound too pleasant a prospect, as I had been told that there were only nine colour T.V. cameras in the country, and eight of them were already in Canterbury. We waited as patiently as we could. I often wonder why it is that orchestras can only relax when they are playing ridiculous little passages which the less musical among us call 'twiddly bits'. This went on happily for just over half-an-hour, before the word came for us to begin again. After that things progressed until very near the end of our last 'take' when another camera struck work, and the whole long passage had to be replayed. Luckily arrangements had already been made for overtime and we were able to disperse at 7.10 p.m.

Next day we had a schedule which was musically shorter, but had some difficult problems for the cameras. These entailed many repetitions, and our soloists were most patient in repeating passages of considerable strain. We were all greatly relieved when everything was finished just before 7 p.m., though Dr Large told me that he would have another day's work with the cameras.

On Easter Sunday 1968 we were invited to see the result at the B.B.C. Television Centre. There were many splendid sequences and Dr Large's study of the Canterbury windows gave those who had colour T.V. sets a number of wonderful moments. Even in black and white I think that those who have far more television experience than I would agree the production is a milestone whence television technique can move in a fresh direction.

Chapter Sixteen

THE TORCH—1969

THE CONTACTS and contrasts of young and old are full of interest even when near to friction, and I am sure that problems amongst artists can be as thought-provoking as anywhere else. I often say after listening to a wireless performance by a younger man: 'That would have been splendid if only he had . . .' and I can remember, in my young days, older men offering advice I did not like, even though I politely gave it some attention. I have a note in my score of Beethoven's Ninth Symphony to the effect that Sir George Henschel, of all people, was good enough to call at the B.B.C. and suggest to me (amongst other things) that the scherzo of that monumental work must never be taken so fast that the second and third notes of the initial figure cannot be clearly heard and separated by the ear: in other words that the quaver should be a quaver, and not a slipshod grace note.

Music is full of points of this kind, and when they occur to us they clarify and if put into practice ennoble the performance, and many of them could be passed on to others, if only the passer were less diffident and the potential recipient free of that closed mind which prevents so much wisdom from being shared. The gramophone can perpetuate much of this to those who can spot things as they go along. I have always felt that the privilege of listening to other conductors' rehearsals enables one to learn to a wonderful extent. This was particularly true in B.B.C. days when the visitor's corrections and suggestions could expose the gaps and shortcomings in my own methods of training.

The art of performance inevitably progresses, and I can remember much that would have passed at the beginning of the century, but would never do nowadays. In the audience, too, during the genteel patronage of 1900, it was considered quite in order for people to begin putting on their overcoats forty bars from the end of the last piece, or to make a quick remark to one's neighbour in the middle of the music. Such conduct would fare badly amid the almost visible concentration of the audience at to-day's Henry Wood Proms.

I have been lucky enough in my time to hear a great many superb performances, and to me these memories seem to take to themselves an architectural quality. They are no longer a stream of wonderful sound; one can almost see them; they are solid, permanent and splendidly balanced, and I should like to hand on all I can remember of them to my many gifted friends of the younger generation. Unfortunately there are no records of Richter's Beethoven, Steinbach's Brahms, Safonoff's Tchaikovsky, Nikisch's Liszt and Weber, and one can only talk about them.

Conductors can be split into two classes and Bruno Walter put it charmingly when he divided us into those who enjoy the even-numbered (and more thoughtful) symphonies of Beethoven, and those who favour the odd (and more glamorous) ones. Another distinction might well contrast those who like hearing the sound of their voices at rehearsals, and those who prefer to talk with the points of their sticks.

Of these Nikisch was far the greatest practitioner in my experience. I have already described how he managed to trust his players; his rehearsals were short, and when there was a public rehearsal (as at Leipzig) he rehearsed blatantly, in front of the audience, entirely by gesture, noticed by very few beyond those who were meant to see.

It is in this respect that I can perhaps help younger people to recognize that choirs and orchestras like to sing and play and not to listen to dissertations largely on subjects to which they also have given much thought. It is not generally realized how much can be expressed by gestures (even to inexperienced amateurs), and how great is the power a conductor can have over people who are themselves only vaguely conscious of his influence over them, and probably quite unconscious that this power flows in both directions, and the conducted are urgently looking to the conductor for guidance without realizing this at all. It is not necessary for the conductor who feels he is not getting the response he wants to break out into bigger and fiercer gestures—the opposite will be more effective—attention will be attracted to him, even when players are inexperienced and immature.

What then is the method by which this expressive stick will save us all this talking? The answer, naturally, sounds simpler than it really is, and it is not easy to put it into a few words, any more than is the technique of singing or violin playing. However, we can say this: that the point of the stick can only move with real power of expression if it is actuated simply by fingers for the smaller indications, with wrist and elbow static (but not stiff) standing by to join in with movements when wanted. They can come into action gradually and rarely as needed when broader beats and greater power are indicated. It is possible for this manipulation to come from the thumb and two fingers, provided that the fingers are separated by about a finger's width, and the thumb touches the stick at the point opposite this space, so that the slightest pressure from either finger moves the stick by levering it against the thumb. It is also worth remembering that a few rubber bands wound round the handle of the stick will help one to hold the stick quite lightly and so avoid stiffness, and get greater flexibility.

These principles have been elaborated twice in print. The first in a small handbook, originally written for the students of the first conductors' class at the Royal College of Music.[1] Sir Hugh Allen asked me to start this class in February 1919. This handbook was originally printed for private R.C.M. use, but was later published. I thought then that it was a concise and useful book for students. Re-reading it later, I realized that it was simply a description of Nikisch's practice, which I was trying to hand on. This has been recently re-published by Messrs Paterson of Glasgow.

In 1963 a larger book was published. This grew out of some wireless talks I had given. Somewhat discursive, it elaborates much that was in the little handbook, without necessarily repeating the principles laid down there.

My urge towards handing on the torch has found several other outlets. During two summers before 1939 I collected a number of B.B.C. conductors for a week at Peaslake, where we then had a country bolt-hole. It was done in B.B.C. time, and it combined a good deal of talk from the victims as well as from me (they were all experienced conductors), the examination of some scores, and each evening we listened to Sir Henry Wood at his Promenade Concert. Ralph Vaughan Williams, who lived a few miles away, came over, I think, every year, and my old friend Marie Wilson, then sub-leader of the B.B.C. Orchestra, always came and gave us the benefit of her ringside experience.

A similar scheme was arranged many years later by the kindness of my old friends the late Misses Marjorie and Dorothy Whyte at Bromley. Themselves fine string players (they had originally founded a string quartet with two other sisters) they had for many years been responsible for much splendid music-making, choral and orchestral, in the Bromley area, and lived in a beautiful house with a big music room. It was originally my wife's idea that we should ask the generous Whytes for their help and support and to our joy they jumped at the thought of a course at Ripley in the summer, and we had five or six weeks through the years after 1958. I know that over a hundred conductors came altogether, and it was really wonderful to realize how much trouble was taken to make it easy and pleasant for us all. Miss Whyte turned her drawing-room into a snack bar, and many kind friends came to help with these arrangements (including even a secretary for hospitality, as many students came from a distance),

[1] *A Handbook on the Technique of Conducting.* Patersons Publications, Glasgow 1920; revised 1968.

but the greatest privilege of all was the loan of the string orchestra of some sixteen players which Miss Whyte gathered and led, with Miss Dorothy either leading the violas or supporting us at the pianoforte. They nobly came every morning, while we spent the afternoon discussing the morning's work. Ripley and its garden have been such a wonderful home for music that efforts are being made to keep it permanently as a music and art centre, and I wish the project every success.

When Sir Hugh Allen decided, on taking over the directorship of the Royal College of Music in 1919, that conducting was something that ought to be taught, he asked me to start a Conductors' Class. I was again very happy when Sir Keith Falkner, soon after his appointment as director, asked me to put the clock back to 1930, when the B.B.C. appointment had stopped my work in South Kensington. I had four very happy years there with some of the embryo conductors, and one of the orchestras. For this I sacrificed practically all my Thursday conducting engagements, until it became clear after four years that it was almost impossible to miss visits to Scotland, Birmingham and Manchester, etc., any longer. The blow was somewhat softened by a very kind invitation to rejoin the Council and Executive Committees on which I had served for some years before I rejoined the staff.

My three- and four-day courses have been useful, I think, to a large number of people. That enterprising body, the Schools' Music Association, has organized others for me at what is now the Newham School of Music (a most progressive and active institution), and other schools near London. I have helped with another, held at Reigate by the Surrey County Authorities, and also at Stockport.

The Gulbenkian Foundation has helped musical education in many most useful fields, and has offered to pay the salary of an apprentice conductor, who is to stay for three years with a provincial orchestra, first as observer, but gradually to reach the goal of public concerts with the full local orchestra. It has been most interesting to join the judges on these occasions. Glasgow and Bournemouth have, we hope, greatly profited by this scheme, and it is felt that others will follow.

I am often asked where I get my sticks, and whether I always use the same kind. Conductors are not like string players, whose bows are almost identical in shape and balance. Conducting sticks vary greatly and have developed considerably since the heavy clubs used a century ago, sometimes audibly, to keep body and soul together. I have myself heard a noisy clapper used in a Royal Opera House in Europe whenever the chorus were singing. The poor conductor was well out of it on that occasion.

I am unhappy unless I can use my own stick. My fingers get damp, and unless I can have well-roughened cork to hold, or, better still, several rubber bands wound round the handle, this dampness will cause the stick to slip, with the result that the grip will tighten and stiffen most uncomfortably. It is vital that everything should be as easy and relaxed as possible, and rubber bands secure this better than anything else. I use a very long stick, 21 inches, because I am lazy and I like to work on a high gear; a very little work with the fingers will project the point of the stick a long distance, and I do most of my work with the fingers, and wrist and elbow do very little. The stick must be coated with white enamel, to be easily seen from a distance, and its point of balance must be as near the hand as possible.

The story of my final choice of stick might be of interest. Soon after I joined the B.B.C. I was asked for an appointment by a Colonel Porteous, who came to Savoy Hill with several samples which I at once welcomed as the most comfortable I had ever used. My friend and colleague, Joseph Lewis, came into my room a few minutes later and said the same. Colonel Porteous confessed that he had moved the natural point of balance nearer the hand by means of a little lead inserted in the cork handles, and he soon marketed them, and they are very popular. Several years later, when he died, his obituary notice in *The Times* ran to a considerable length, and I found that my stick-designer had been an eminent irrigation engineer, who had done notable work in Asia Minor.

I often feel it is a pity that there is a tradition of the greatest secrecy where orchestral rehearsals are concerned. In fact many of my colleagues refuse to rehearse at all if they can see a single figure concealed in the furthest corner of a hall. Perhaps I am sometimes too easy about it, for on one occasion my wife was told by an exasperated usher 'Really, madam, you are the third lady who has said that Sir Adrian is her husband, I must ask you to leave at once.' I was told by a friend that when he was studying in Vienna, it was the practice for students to get into the hall with the connivance of a kind janitor and lie on the floor in the balcony. He said he had actually heard me rehearse from this position when I was there in 1933.

There are in rehearsal, many matters of commonsense and common consideration which should, I think, be always in the conductor's mind. For instance, in what order does one rehearse a Brahms symphony?

I think it is true that the first movements of all Brahms symphonies bring us problems which often need a good deal more time to unravel than those in the others. For this reason I always begin the symphonies with their last movements. They are not so hard to play or to interpret. Then, having established contact, one can turn to the first, and to serious work with its major problems. The second and third can then take up the remaining time available.

A slight variation might be made with the Fourth Symphony, which I usually take in the order III, IV, I, II. The Third is the easiest movement of the four, and the only one which makes use of the triangle, piccolo and double bassoon who can then leave the rehearsal. This consideration carries, I believe, no weight at all with some of my colleagues, who take the line that as everybody is paid his fee for the three-hour rehearsal there is no point in letting him go any sooner. Musicians are human and naturally are always happy to be released before the scheduled time. Two of the Brahms symphonies only use trombones in their last movements. Why ever should not one rehearse them and let the players go? To me it is always unpleasant to think that people are hanging about aimlessly.

To repeat—somewhere in the middle 1920s, I had the privilege once of hearing Leopold Stokowski in Philadelphia, when he enjoyed a world-wide reputation. I found it hard to believe that with an orchestra of this calibre he could possibly make full use of the four rehearsals which were the practice in America in those days when, as often, the programme consisted mainly of well-known music. I later had the chance of asking one of his principals about it, and he told me that Stokowski's usual practice at that time followed this plan: Monday, straight through the programme, spending perhaps a little time on special passages; Tuesday, hard work on the programme (usually a short rehearsal); Wednesday, the widest exploration of any new works that might be of interest—a great deal of ground was covered in many fields of music; Thursday, straight run through of the programme. This was at the time when the Philadelphia records (78s of course) were the world standard of orchestral virtuosity.

Going back to Toscanini, his annual visits before 1939 were wonder-fully stimulating to us all—though we felt exhausted when he had gone. It was interesting to note how differently our guest conductors affected the orchestra in the long term. One very distinguished visitor produced a record of four nervous breakdowns during his fortnight, whereas Bruno Walter would leave the orchestra refreshed and eager for more.

Of all the conductors I have known this great man had the power to extract the best out of anyone he met. His opera company in the wonderful days at Munich was just a happy family giving superb performances, having also the choice of three opera houses. They were the little Residenz, untouched (as I have said) since Mozart conducted *Idomeneo* there in 1788: the Prinzregenten, a copy of Bayreuth but much more solidly built: and the Nationaltheater, of the old-fashioned type. Plays and operas could all be ideally staged.

I noticed a remarkable occurrence when Walter was conducting in the Prinzregentheater with the concealed orchestra on the Bayreuth plan. After a number of warning bells the house lights went very gradually down and finally nothing could be seen but the faint glow coming up from the very deep orchestral pit. By this time, with Walter at the helm a tense silence enfolded the house well before the music began. With any other conductor (and I heard a good many) there was always a perceptible rustle

in the audience until the music had begun. I do not think this had anything to do with the audience's knowing who it was: it was something to
do with his own power of concentration. Possibly in addition he called his
orchestra to a state of tension earlier than the other conductors, but I do
not know that he did.

*   *   *

I am often asked who were the greatest conductors in my experience, and
it might perhaps be of interest to try and name those who stand out in
memory.

For BACH	Fritz Steinbach, Hugh Allen
MOZART and HAYDN	Richard Strauss, Bruno Walter
BEETHOVEN	Hans Richter, Wassily Safonoff, Furt-wängler, Weingartner
BRAHMS	Steinbach
WAGNER	(*Ring*, *Mastersingers*) Richter, Walter
„	(*Tristan*) Nikisch
TCHAIKOVSKY	Safonoff, Wood.

*   *   *

I have now entered my eighty-fifth year, and it seems a fitting moment
to finish these stories, but this cannot be done without a very full recognition of the enormous debt anyone in the public eye owes to those around
him. The conductor, of course, has the inherent debt to the choirs and
orchestras who work with him, and loyally go through performance after
performance, often doing violence to their own musical perception. It will
only be realized by those who attend orchestral concerts directed by
different conductors, how widely their interpretations of works can vary,
and change. I hope that most orchestral players acquire the habit of seeing
the point of the most widely differing interpretations, and adapting to
their disagreements, just as I do myself where concertos are concerned;
the soloist of the moment is the artist whose interpretative mind is in
control, and we all conform as closely as is within our power.

It is a charming thought that Edward Elgar dedicated his 'Cockaigne
Overture' 'to my many friends, the members of British Orchestras'. He
rightly had a sense of deep affection and recognition of the debt he owed
them all.

In my B.B.C. days I used to say that the whole department did the
work for which I got the credit. It was true, and, in particular, it was
true of the second in command, and the secretary. Here I have been

extraordinarily fortunate. It is, I think, true to say that anyone who knows me knows Mrs Beckett, who after more than forty years still looks after my office, which includes the many young conductors who come for talks (I will not call them lessons when the instrument isn't there), and also invitations to rehearsals. These are the results of a monthly list which is sent to students and other friends. This kind of thing can swell to un-wieldly proportions when there is a distinguished soloist, and in War days in Bedford, Mrs Beckett often sent out several hundred studio passes to troops, American and British, stationed near by.

Finally, what can adequately be said of the sacrifices made by the wives of musicians? The man's work takes him out at night very often indeed, and whether she comes or not it means that evenings at home, which I was brought up to look forward to and enjoy, are practically non-existent. Compared with the regular life of the business man who is out of the house for most of the day, and always out to lunch, whose movements, for five days a week, can be predicted and planned for, the musician is the twenty-four-hour servant of his muse. His wife must sacrifice all her own musician-ship, her interests in sport and all activities which do not coincide with those of the one-idea'd and over-absorbed creature she has chosen to marry. In my own case this wonderful renunciation is carried right through to splendid support at rehearsals and concerts (with numerous picnic meals) and on almost every journey at home or abroad.

And what happens in the musician's house? In my young days the Victorian 'gracious living' held sway with a vengeance. My mother did a great deal of elaborate sewing and ribbon work; she made needlework pictures which are still worth showing. She wrote some books and she translated others. Yet she still had time to care for a very large stamp collection, and read a great deal. Nowadays—well, we all know about nowadays!

Now my wife and I try to restrict our journeys during the winter months. How well we did this in 1967 is shown in the following diary extract:

JANUARY 1967

8	Travel to Bristol
9	Two rehearsals with B.B.C. New Orchestra
10	Two rehearsals with B.B.C. New Orchestra
11	Swansea; travel, rehearsal and concert
12	Return to London
13	Recording session
16	Travel to Bournemouth
17	Rehearsals with Bournemouth Orchestra
18	Travel to Plymouth; rehearsal and concert with Bourne-mouth Orchestra

The author, from the drawing by Joy Finzi, 1968

With Mrs G. Beckett after she had
been awarded the MBE, February 1973

19	Return to Bournemouth; concert
20	Return to London; rehearsal with London Philharmonic Orchestra
22	Royal Festival Hall, rehearsal and concert with L.P.O.
23	Hastings, rehearsal and concert with L.P.O.
24	Return to London
25	Travel to Glasgow
26	Two rehearsals with Scottish National Orchestra
27	Rehearsal and concert in Edinburgh
28	Concert in Glasgow
29	Travel to Manchester
31	Two rehearsals with Hallé Orchestra

FEBRUARY

1	Rehearsal and concert in Manchester
2	Concert in Manchester
3	Concert in Sheffield
4	Return to London

Between 5 January and 12 February it totals twenty rehearsals, twelve performances, three recording sessions and fourteen long journeys.

There was plenty of work in London before and after this little stretch, but it will not happen again.

*   *   *

As we near the end of this odd collection of reminiscences, I must give some account of my eightieth birthday.

As 1969 approached many kind invitations seemed to be in the air, but we had harboured a notion that we would like to give our own concert on the day itself. So we set about booking the Royal Albert Hall and the London Philharmonic Orchestra (many of whom very kindly returned their fees) and going forward with plans. I asked all those who were interested whether they would give their support to our venture, which was to be in aid of Oxfam, so that we could concentrate their generosity to this end. We were most loyally aided and everyone proved to be kindness itself.

The programme, all British, originally consisted of three works, the Parry Symphonic Variations, the Elgar Violin Concerto played by Mr Menuhin, and the Vaughan Williams London Symphony. Soon we had messages from many friends who had sung with me in choirs to say they wanted to take part. Therefore we substituted Parry's setting of the John of Gaunt speech in *Henry V*, 'England', followed by 'Blest Pair of Sirens', a work which always seems to grow greater whenever one looks at it. A

very large number of friends came together to form the choir, and represented no less than six of the leading choral societies in and around
London. We suddenly felt the close of the Vaughan Williams with its
lovely mystic atmosphere and the Westminster Chimes would be rather
sombre at the end of this particular evening and we added Eric Coates's
rousing 'Dam-busters' March' for obvious reasons.

I was immensely touched that the audience included many of the
greatest musicians in the land, and I only hope that they all enjoyed it as
much as I did.

As I put it in a note, printed in the programme:

> This concert is a gesture of thanks to the very many people who have
> supported a career lasting fifty-one years. Friends in audiences, colleagues on
> platforms, backroom boys and girls have all, under Providence, made heavy
> contributions to a life of almost unclouded happiness, domestic, social and
> professional. Thank you.

*   *   *

Since then four years have passed, years of consistent work, both with
pupils, at concerts, at recording sessions, and with one educational film
called *The Point of the Stick* which is being sold here and in America to
demonstrate to conductors, professional and amateur, how the simplest
gestures can be effective. The first showing of the film was graced by the
presence of Her Majesty the Queen Mother, on the invitation of the
Schools Music Association, of which she is Patroness. The Secretary of
the Association, Mr Stephen Moore, is an old friend who was a pupil and
can therefore understand the importance of this (Nikisch's) method of
conducting.

One other special occasion must be mentioned: Mrs Beckett, already
well known to readers of this book, recently received the M.B.E. from the
Queen and, after our forty-four years together, could anything have been
more fitting?

APPENDIX I

First Performances from 1931 to 1971
All with B.B.C. Symphony Orchestra except Boston and Salzburg

ALEXANDER MOSSOLOV	Factory—The Music of Machines	25.2.31	1st perf. in England
RICHARD STRAUSS	Kampf und Sieg	27.3.31	1st perf. in England
ARTHUR BLISS	Colour Symphony	27.4.32	1st perf. (revised version)
RALPH VAUGHAN WILLIAMS	Pianoforte Concerto Harriet Cohen	1.2.33	1st perf.
R. O. MORRIS	Symphony in D	1.1.34	1st perf.
ARTHUR BENJAMIN	Violin Concerto Brosa	5.1.34	1st broadcast perf.
FREDERICK DELIUS	Fantastic Dance	12.1.34	1st perf.
JOHN IRELAND	Legend for Piano and Orchestra	12.1.34	1st perf.
ALBAN BERG	Wozzeck	16.3.34	1st perf. in England
GUSTAV HOLST	Lyric Movement Lionel Tertis	18.3.34	1st perf.
GIOVANNI GABRIELI	Sonata Pian e Forte	10.1.35	1st perf. in Boston
FELIX MENDELSSOHN	Scherzo in E minor Orchestrated from the Octet	10.1.35	1st perf. in Boston
ARTHUR BLISS	Introduction and Allegro	18.1.35	1st perf. in Boston
GUSTAV HOLST	Fugal Concerto	18.1.35	1st perf. in Boston
GUSTAV HOLST	Scherzo	6.2.35	1st perf.
FREDERICK DELIUS (arr. Tertis)	Double Concerto for Violin, Viola and Orchestra May Harrison, Lionel Tertis	3.3.35	1st perf.

GIRALAMO FRESCOBALDI	Toccata, transcribed for String Orchestra by Malipiero	20.3.35	1st perf. in England
GIAN FRANCESCO MALIPIERO	Sinfolia No. 1	20.3.35	1st perf. in England
RALPH VAUGHAN WILLIAMS	Symphony No. 4 in F Minor	10.4.35	1st perf.
ARTHUR BLISS	Music for Strings	11.8.35	1st perf. (Salzburg Festival)
PAUL HINDEMITH	Trauermusik (King George V)	22.1.36	1st perf.
GRANVILLE BANTOCK	A Pagan Symphony	8.3.36	1st perf.
ELIZABETH MACONCHY	Piano Concerto Harriet Cohen	20.3.36	1st broadcast perf.
BÉLA BARTÓK	Cantata Profana	25.3.36	1st perf. in England
FREDERIC d'ERLANGER	Ballet, Les Cent Baisers	24.5.36	1st broadcast perf.
MARY CALLANDER	Suite	5.6.36	1st perf.
VLADIMIR VOGEL	Ritmica Ostinata	5.6.36	1st perf. in England
RALPH VAUGHAN WILLIAMS	Five Tudor Portraits	27.1.37	1st perf. in London
FERRUCIO BUSONI	Dr Faust	17.3.37	1st perf. in England
YORK BOWEN	Piano Concerto No. 4 York Bowen	19.3.37	1st perf.
LEIGHTON LUCAS	Sinfonia Brevis for Horn and Orchestra Aubrey Brain	30.4.37	1st perf.
WILLIAM WALTON	March—'Crown Imperial'	9.5.37	1st perf. (Coronation)
JOHN IRELAND	'These Things Shall Be'	13.5.37	1st perf.
HOWARD FERGUSON	Partita	29.6.37	1st perf.
YORK BOWEN	Rhapsody for Cello Florence Hooton	7.9.37	1st broadcast perf.
ROBERT SCHUMANN	Violin Concerto in D minor Jelly d'Aranyi	16.2.38	1st perf. in England
GIAN FRANCESCO MALIPIERO	Symphony No. 2	23.2.38	1st perf. in England

JEAN RIVIER	Symphony No. 2	8.4.38	1st perf. in England
ERNST KŘENEK	Piano Concerto Ernst Krenek	8.4.38	1st perf. in England
ALBAN BERG	Three Orchestral Pieces	8.4.38	1st perf. in England
HERBERT HOWELLS	Concerto for String Orchestra	16.12.38	1st perf.
EDMUND RUBBRA	Symphony No. 2	16.12.38	1st perf.
CYRIL ROOTHAM	Symphony No. 2	17.3.39	1st perf.
RALPH VAUGHAN WILLIAMS	Five Variants of Dives and Lazarus	1.11.39	1st perf. in England
HUBERT CLIFFORD	Five English Nursery Dances	17.5.41	1st broadcast perf.
WILLIAM ALWYN	Pastoral Fantasia for Viola and String Orchestra Watson Forbes	3.11.41	1st perf.
DARIUS MILHAUD	Fantaisie Pastorale Irene Kohler	12.1.42	1st broadcast perf.
GEORGE DYSON	Violin Concerto	16.2.42	1st perf.
ALEC ROWLEY	Suite in A	6.4.42	1st broadcast perf.
ERIK CHISHOLM	The Adventures of Babar	13.4.42	1st perf.
ROY HARRIS	Symphony No. 3	28.5.42	1st perf. in England
ALEC ROWLEY	Three Idylls for Pianoforte and Orchestra Alec Rowley	7.8.42	1st perf.
THOMAS DUNHILL	Triptych—Three Impressions for Viola and Orchestra Lionel Tertis	19.8.42	1st perf.
ARMSTRONG GIBBS	Dance Suite	26.8.42	1st perf.
FREDERICK MAY	Suite of Irish Airs	22.10.42	1st broadcast perf.
ARAM KHACHATURIAN	Ode to Stalin	21.12.42	1st perf. in England
ARMSTRONG GIBBS	Concertino for Piano and Strings Yvonne Arnaud	22.12.42	1st broadcast perf.
WILLIAM SCHUMAN	Symphony No. 3	29.7.43	1st perf. in England

EDMUND RUBBRA	Sinfonia Concertante for Piano and Orchestra Edmund Rubbra	10.8.43	1st perf.
WILLIAM BUSCH	Concerto for Cello and Orchestra Florence Hooton	13.8.43	1st perf.
ARNOLD VAN WYK	Serenade for Violin and Orchestra	14.8.43	1st perf. in England
DMITRI KABALEVSKY	Suite from 'Colas Breugnon'	17.8.43	1st perf. in England
E. J. MOERAN	Rhapsody No. 3 for Pianoforte and Orchestra Harriet Cohen	19.8.43	1st perf.
HERBERT MURRILL	Set of Country Dances	21.9.43	1st broadcast perf.
MICHAEL TIPPETT	Fantasia on a Theme of Handel for Piano and Orchestra Phyllis Sellick	22.10.43	1st perf.
IGOR STRAVINSKY	Symphony in C major	17.11.43	1st perf. in England
PHYLLIS TATE	Elegiac March	13.12.43	1st perf.
D. MOULE-EVANS	Divertimento for Strings	14.2.44	1st broadcast perf.
ROY HARRIS	Chorale	22.7.44	1st perf.
BÉLA BARTÓK	Violin Concerto Menuhin	20.9.44	1st perf. in England
EUGENE GOOSSENS	Phantasy Concerto for Piano and Orchestra	1.11.44	1st perf. in England
SERGEY PROKOFIEV	A Toast to Stalin B.B.C. Chorus	21.12.44	1st perf. in England
WILLIAM WALTON	Memorial Fanfare	4.3.45	1st perf.
BÉLA BARTÓK	Violin Concerto Menuhin	28.11.45	1st perf. in London
BOHUSLAV MARTINU	Symphony No. 2	9.12.45	1st perf. in England
BÉLA BARTÓK	Concerto for Orchestra	6.3.46	1st perf. in England
E. J. MOERAN	Concerto for Cello and Orchestra Peers Coetmore	10.4.46	1st broadcast perf.
SAMUEL BARBER	Second Essay for Orchestra	13.4.46	1st perf. in England

GORDON JACOB	Symphony No. 2	1.5.46	1st perf.
HUMPHREY SEARLE	Piano Concerto in D minor Colin Horsley	17.5.46	1st perf.
BENJAMIN BRITTEN	Festival Overture	29.9.46	1st perf.
PATRICK HADLEY	'The Hills' Elsie Suddaby, Heddle Nash, Harold Williams, B.B.C.Choral Society	17.1.47	1st perf.
JOSEPH HAYDN	Concerto per l'Organo Susi Jeans	23.7.47	1st perf. in England
VICTOR HELY– HUTCHINSON	Symphony for Small Orchestra	25.7.47	1st perf. in London
GORDON JACOB	Concerto for Bassoon, Strings and Percussion Archie Camden	20.8.47	1st perf.
WALTER PISTON	Symphony No. 2	22.8.47	1st perf. in England
ELISABETH LUTYENS	Petite Suite	26.8.47	1st concert perf. in London
VÍTĚZSLAV NOVÁK	Triptych	5.9.47	1st perf. in England
GERALD FINZI	An Ode for St Cecilia's Day René Soames, Luton Choral Society	22.11.47	1st perf.
EDMUND RUBBRA	Symphony No. 5	21.6.49	1st perf.
LÁSZLÓ LAJTHA	In Memoriam	5.2.49	1st perf. in England
ARNOLD COOKE	Symphony	26.2.49	1st perf.
AARON COPLAND	Symphony No. 3	4.6.49	1st broadcast perf.
ANDRÉ CAPLET	Epiphanie for Cello and Orchestra	10.6.49	1st perf. in England
PAUL LADMIRAULT	Prelude, Tristan et Iseult	24.9.49	1st perf. in England
HENRY BARRAUD	Pianoforte Concerto Yvonne Lefebure	19.11.49	1st perf. in England
GÖSTA NYSTROEM	Sinfonia Espressiva	3.12.49	1st broadcast perf.
ELIZABETH MACONCHY	Symphony	27.4.50	1st perf.
ILDEBRANDO PIZZETTI	Symphony in A	6.5.50	1st perf. in England

RANDALL THOMPSON	Symphony No. 3 in A minor	9.6.50	1st perf. in England
MALCOLM ARNOLD	English Dances (Set 1)	14.4.51	1st perf.
THOMAS WOOD	The Rainbow Jan Van Der Gucht, Maurice Bevan, The London Songmen, Massed Bands and Choirs	12.5.51	1st perf.
WILLIAM WORDSWORTH	Symphony No. 2	19.8.51	1st perf.
FRANCIS CHAGRIN	Overture 'Helter-Skelter'	16.1.52	1st perf. in England
MARTIN PENNY	Deus Misereatur Max Worthley, London Philharmonic Choir	4.2.52	1st broadcast perf.
ANTHONY MILNER	Improperia London Philharmonic Choir, Charles Spinks	4.2.52	1st broadcast perf.
HOWARD FERGUSON	Pianoforte Concerto Myra Hess	29.5.52	1st London perf.
HOWARD FERGUSON	Pianoforte Concerto Myra Hess	31.5.52	1st broadcast perf.
FRANZ REIZENSTEIN	Voices of Night Elsie Morison, Arnold Matters, London Philharmonic Choir	20.6.52	1st perf.
WILLIAM WORDSWORTH	Symphony No. 2	6.11.52	1st broadcast perf.
GEOFFREY BUSH	Nottingham Symphony	11.12.52	1st London perf.
FRANK MARTIN	Violin Concerto Hans-Heinz Schneeberger	10.1.53	1st broadscat perf. in England
ERIK CHISHOLM	Piano Concerto No. 2 Agnes Walker	6.3.53	1st London perf.
NORMAL FULTON	Sinfonia Pastorale	21.3.53	1st broadcast perf.
IAIN HAMILTON	Symphony No. 2	10.6.53	1st perf.
PETER RACINE FRICKER	Concerto for Viola and Orchestra William Primrose	3.9.53	1st perf.
IAIN HAMILTON	Symphony No. 2	7.9.53	1st London perf.

MALCOLM ARNOLD	Flourish for a 21st Birthday	7.10.53	1st perf.
FRANZ REIZENSTEIN	Concert Overture, 'Cyrano de Bergerac'	1.2.54	1st perf.
HAVERGAL BRIAN	Symphony No. 8	1.2.54	1st perf.
PETER RACINE FRICKER	Piano Concerto Harriet Cohen	21.3.54	1st perf.
HUMPHREY SEARLE	Symphony (1953)	1.6.54	1st perf. in England
ROBERT SIMPSON	Symphony No. 1 (1951)	24.9.54	1st perf. in England
FRANK MARTIN	Harpsichord Concerto George Malcolm	29.9.54	1st perf. in England
CEDRIC THORPE DAVIE	Diversions on a Tune by Dr Arne	27.8.55	1st perf.
STANLEY BATE	Symphony No. 4	20.11.55	1st perf.
DANIEL JONES	Symphony No. 3	9.7.56	1st public perf.
ROBERTO GERHARD	Symphony	31.5.57	1st perf. in England
MICHAEL TIPPETT	Symphony No. 2	5.2.58	1st perf.
ROBERT SIMPSON	Violin Concerto Ernest Element	25.2.60	1st perf.
MÁTYÁS SEIBER	Renaissance Dance Suite	7.5.60	1st perf.
PRIAULX RAINER	Dance Concerto, Phalaphala	17.1.61	1st perf.
JOHN MAYER	Chamber Symphony	8.5.61	1st perf.
MALCOLM WILLIAMSON	Organ Concerto Malcolm Williamson	8.9.61	1st perf.
JOHN VINCENT	Symphony in D	10.3.62	1st perf. in England
JOSEPH HOROWITZ	Fantasia on a Theme of Couperin	29.7.62	1st perf.
BRAHMS (orch. SCHÖNBERG)	Piano Quartet in G minor	21.8.62	1st perf.
WILLIAM WORDSWORTH	Symphony No. 5	5.10.62	1st perf.
DIMITRY SHOSTAKOVICH	Symphony No. 12	28.11.62	1st London perf.
DEREK BOURGEOIS	Symphony No. 1	19.6.64	1st London perf.
ARTHUR BUTTERWORTH	Symphony No. 2	30.10.64	1st perf.
MALCOLM WILLIAMSON	Sinfonietta	16.3.65	1st perf.

DON BANKS	Divisions for Orchestra	12.7.65	1st perf.
MALCOLM WILLIAMSON	Piano Concerto No. 3 Malcolm Williamson	16.2.66	1st British perf.
ALUN HODDINOTT and others	Severn Bridge Variations	11.1.67	1st perf.
HAVERGAL BRIAN	Violoncello Concerto Thomas Igloi	5.2.71	1st perf.

APPENDIX II

B.B.C. Symphony Orchestra Visits, 1934–1950

1934	December	5	MANCHESTER	Free Trade Hall
1935	February	13	BRISTOL	Colston Hall
		27	BIRMINGHAM	Town Hall
	March	12	BRUSSELS	Palais des Beaux Arts
	April	3	DUNDEE	Caird Hall
	June	18	CANTERBURY	Cloisters
	October	31	SWANSEA	Brangwyn Hall
1936	March	11	LEICESTER	de Montfort Hall
	April	1	GLASGOW	St Andrews Hall
		20	PARIS	Salle Playel
		21	ZURICH	Tonhalle
		23	VIENNA	Kuzerthaus
		24	BUDAPEST	Municipal Theatre
	June	24, 25	CANTERBURY	Cloisters
	October	14	HANLEY	Victoria Hall
1937	March	10	SOUTHAMPTON	Guildhall
		31	EDINBURGH	Usher Hall
	April	14	LEEDS	Town Hall
1938	January	12	NEWCASTLE	Town Hall
	March	9	NOTTINGHAM	Albert Hall
		23	ABERDEEN	Music Hall
	April	20	PLYMOUTH	Guildhall
	June	8	NORWICH	Cathedral
		13	GLASGOW	Empire Exhibition
1939	March	29	PRESTON	Public Hall
	April	15	BRISTOL	Colston Hall
		19	WOLVERHAMPTON	Civic Hall
1940	January	11	CHELTENHAM	Town Hall
		17	NEWPORT	Central Hall
		24	BATH	Pavilion
	September	29	TAUNTON	Grand Palace

1940	November	3	CARDIFF	Empire Theatre
1941	March	2	BRIDGWATER	Odeon Cinema
	October	22	CAMBRIDGE	Arts Theatre
	November	15	CAMBRIDGE	
1942	January	3	NOTTINGHAM	Albert Hall
	February	7	OXFORD	Sheldonian
		15	KETTERING	Savoy Cinema
	March	11	CAMBRIDGE	Arts Theatre
		21	RUGBY SCHOOL	
	March	28	ROYAL ALBERT HALL	
	June	18	NEWPORT	Central Hall
		19	ABERDARE	Coliseum
		20	SWANSEA	Brangwyn Hall
		21	CARDIFF	Empire
		22	TREORCHY	Park Dare
	July 25, 27, 28, 29, 30, 31		ROYAL ALBERT HALL PROMS	
	August 3, 4, 5, 6, 7, 8, 10, 11, 12, 13, 14, 15, 17, 18, 19, 20, 21, 22		ROYAL ALBERT HALL PROMS	
	September	20	ROYAL ALBERT HALL	Holt
	October	31	CAMBRIDGE	Guildhall
1943	January	1	NATIONAL GALLERY	(Lunch Concert)
	February	13	CAMBRIDGE	Guildhall
		26, 27	ABERDARE	Coliséum
	March	1, 2, 3	ABERDARE	
		13	CAMBRIDGE	Guildhall
	April	5	MAIDA VALE I	
		7	LEICESTER	De Montfort Hall
	May	19	ROYAL ALBERT HALL	
		24	ALDERSHOT	Garrison Theatre
		26	ROYAL ALBERT HALL	
		27, 28	ALDERSHOT	Garrison Theatre
		31	PORTSMOUTH	R.N. Barracks
	June	2	ROYAL ALBERT HALL	
		5	SOUTHAMPTON	Guildhall Matinee
		5	PORTSMOUTH	R.N. Barracks
	July 17, 19, 20 21, 22, 23, 24, 26, 27, 28, 29, 30, 31		ROYAL ALBERT HALL PROMS	

1943	August 2, 3, 4, 5, 6, 7, 9, 10, 11, 12, 13, 14, 16, 17, 18, 19, 20, 21		ROYAL ALBERT HALL PROMS	
	September 13, 15, 18, 19		ST ATHAN, Glam.	R.A.F. Station
	October	2	NORTHAMPTON	St Matthew's
	November	10	MAIDA VALE I	
1944	February	12	CAMBRIDGE	Guildhall
	March	12	CARDIFF	Empire Theatre
		16	ASHCHURCH	U.S. Army
		16	NEWPORT	Central Hall
		17	BRISTOL	Colston Hall
		25	ROYAL ALBERT HALL	
	May	12, 15	ROYAL ALBERT HALL	
		18	MAIDA VALE I	
		19	ROYAL ALBERT HALL	
	August	23	LUTON	Vauxhall Works
		28, 29	GOSFORD, Salop.	R.A.F. Station
	September			
		1, 2, 3	DONNINGTON	R.A.F.
		5, 6, 9, 10	ST ATHAN, Glam.	R.A.F.
	October	28	CAMBRIDGE	Guildhall
1945	January	28	LUTON	Odeon Cinema
	February	3	CAMBRIDGE	Guildhall
	April	19	CANTERBURY	Catterel
		27	NORWICH	St Andrew's Hall
1947	June	18, 19	PARIS	Champs-Elysées
		22	BRUSSELS	R.N.B. Studio
		23		Palais des Beaux Arts
		25	AMSTERDAM	Concertgebouw
		26	SCHEVENINGEN	Kurhaus
1948	February			
		26, 28	CAMBRIDGE	Guildhall
	April	3, 4	NEWCASTLE	City Hall
		24	NEWPORT	Central Hall
		25	BATH	Pavilion
	May	11	OXFORD	Sheldonian
	June	12	WOLVERHAMPTON	Civic Hall
		13	HANLEY	Victoria Hall
	September	3, 4	EDINBURGH	Usher Hall
1949	May	10	NOTTINGHAM	Albert Hall
		11	LEICESTER	de Montfort Hall

1949	May	14	TRURO	Cathedral
		15	PLYMOUTH	Royal Cinema
		18, 19	BOURNEMOUTH	Winter Gardens
	November	19	CAMBRIDGE	Guildhall
		20	CAMBRIDGE	Royal Cinema
1950	May	13	LEEDS	Town Hall
		14	HARROGATE	Royal Hall
		15	BRADFORD	Eastbrook
		16	LIVERPOOL	Philharmonic
		17, 18	BELFAST	Ulster Hall

APPENDIX III

Orchestral Work out of England, 1912–1966
Nearly every programme included at least one British work

1912/13　LEIPZIG
Royal Konservatorium (now Hochschule) Winter 1912/13. Among the works conducted were the fourth Beethoven and fourth Schumann symphonies, and Festklänge by Liszt (which I have never conducted since). At the end of the year Professor Hans Sitt wrote on my certificate 'Herr Boult besuchte meine Klasse rogelmässing und zeichte namentlich bei der Dirigierübung sehr viel Begabung'. 'Mr Boult came regularly to my class and showed, specially in conducting, very great ability'.

1922　PRAGUE (Czech Philharmonic Orchestra)
5 January. Elgar II Butterworth, Two English Idylls.
VIENNA (Symphony Orchestra)
6 April. Elgar II Holst, Four Planets (1, 3, 5, 4).
BARCELONA
May. I spent a month listening to Casals' rehearsals. He invited me to conduct 'The Perfect Fool' Ballet and Butterworth's Two English Idylls on 26 May.
MUNICH (Konzertvereinsorchester)
18 November and 8 December 1922. Wasps Overture and 'Perfect Fool' Ballet. Symphonies: Schumann IV and Brahms II. Soloists: Katharine Arkandy, a British-born coloratura soprano at the Munich Opera, and Mitja Nikisch, the conductor's younger son, whose brilliant career was cut short when he was about 40. I remember that snow held up his journey and the Brahms D minor concerto had to be rehearsed by our combined singing in his hotel bedroom.
It is an echo of German post-war finances to think that each of these concerts was completely paid for with one English five-pound note.

1925　PRAGUE (Czech Philharmonic Orchestra)
17 May. Vaughan Williams, Pastoral Symphony.
AMSTERDAM
21 June. Vaughan Williams, Wasps Overture; Holst, 'Perfect Fool' Ballet; Elgar, Violin Concerto (Alexander Schmöller); Parry, Symphonic Variations.

1930 NEW YORK
National Broadcasting Company. Holst Double Concerto.

1933 VIENNA (Philharmonic Orchestra)
2 March. Holst, 'Perfect Fool' Ballet; Elgar, Introduction and Allegro; Symphonies: Brahms IV and Mozart G minor, No. 40. The Rose Quartet played the solos in the Elgar, and before rehearsing Buxbaum held up his part to show his disappointment at having so little to play. It was at this rehearsal that I queried the slurring (in one bow) of the two first notes of the Slow Movement of Mozart No. 40. We referred to the Autograph score, which was upstairs in the same building, and the Orchestra were so astonished that a foreigner should remember this that they all signed a portfolio with the programme of the Concert, and sent it to me afterwards.

1935 BOSTON
(Cambridge) 10 January, (Boston) 11/12. (Providence) 15 January. Elgar II. 16, 18, 19, 21 January. Bliss, Introduction and Allegro; Bax, Fand; Holst, Fugal Concerto.
BRUSSELS (B.B.C. Symphony Orchestra)
12 March. Vaughan Williams, Tallis Fantasia (Arthur Catterall, Barry Square, Bernard Shore, Lauri Kennedy).
SALZBURG Festival (Vienna Philharmonic Orchestra)
11 August. Bliss, Music for Strings (First performance); Bax, Tintagel; Holst, 'Perfect Fool' Ballet; Vaughan Williams, Job.

1936 GENEVA (Orchestre de la Suisse Romande)
4 March. Elgar, Cockaigne Overture; Vaughan Williams, Job.
PARIS, ZURICH, VIENNA, BUDAPEST (B.B.C. Symphony Orchestra)
20–24 April. These programmes were planned to include a British work, a compliment to the city we were visiting, and a show piece for the orchestra, as well as a great classic. The programmes were:
PARIS: Roussel, Pour une Fête de Printemps; Lambert, Rio Grande; Beethoven, Symphony No. 8; Stravinsky, Le Sacre du Printemps; (Wagner, Ride of the Valkyrie; Wagner, Overture, Die Meistersinger, encores).
ZURICH: Wagner, Prelude, Die Meistersinger; Busoni, Sarabande, Cortège; Walton, Viola Concerto (Lionel Tertis); Honegger, Chant de Joie; Brahms, Symphony No. 4.
VIENNA: Brahms, Tragic Overture; Schönberg, Variations for Orchestra; Vaughan Williams, Symphony No. 4; Ravel, Daphnis and Chloe (2nd series).
BUDAPEST: Elgar, Introduction and Allegro; Bartók, Four Orchestral Pieces; Bax, Tintagel; Beethoven, Symphony No. 5.

1937 BRUSSELS (I.N.R.)
29 September. Bax, Tintagel; Vaughan Williams, Job.

1938 NEW YORK (N.B.C.)
14 May. Walton, Viola Concerto (William Primrose).

21 May. Holst, Fugal Concerto; Vaughan Williams, Symphony No. 4; Butterworth, Shropshire Lad; Elgar, Enigma.

TORONTO

26 May. Holst, Somerset Rhapsody; Vaughan Williams, Wasps Overture.

1939   OSLO

12, 13 January. Vaughan Williams, Symphony No. 4; Bliss, Things to Come.

STOCKHOLM

18 January. Bax, Tintagel; Bliss, Music for Strings.

19 January. Vaughan Williams, Sea Symphony.

MONTE CARLO

22 February. Bliss, Things to Come.

24 February. Vaughan Williams, Job; Bax, Tintagel; Holst, Fugal Concerto.

NEW YORK (Carnegie Hall (World's Fair) (N.Y. Philharmonic Orchestra)

9 June. Bax, Symphony No. 7; Goossens, Oboe Concerto (Leon Goossens); Bach/Elgar, Fantasia and Fugue in C minor.

16 June. Bliss, Piano Concerto (Solomon); Vaughan Williams, Two Variants on Dives and Lazarus.

RAVINIA PARK (Chicago Symphony Orchestra)

29 June. Holst, Fugal Concerto; Bach/Elgar, Fantasia and Fugue in C minor.

30 June. Elgar, Enigma.

2 July. Vaughan Williams, Tallis.

6 July. Ireland, London Overture; Ethel Smyth, Two Interlinked French Melodies; Bliss, Things to Come (first time in Chicago).

7 July. Vaughan Williams, Job (first time in Chicago); Bliss, Introduction and Allegro (first time in Chicago).

9 July. Holst, Beni Mora.

TORONTO University Arena (Toronto Symphony Orchestra)

13 July. Bliss, Introduction and Allegro; Holst, Beni Mora.

LUCERNE Festival

7 August. Vaughan Williams, Tallis.

1940   AMSTERDAM

29 February. Bliss, Music for Strings; Elgar, Enigma.

1945   PARIS (Orchestre du Conservatoire)

25 February. Walton, Scapino; Rawsthorne, Piano Concerto (Moura Lympany).

1 March. (Radio Paris) Elgar, Introduction and Allegro; Bliss, Miracle in the Gorbals.

THE HAGUE (Concertgebouw Orchestra)

3 November. Ireland, London Overture; Elgar, Enigma.

AMSTERDAM (Concertgebouw Orchestra)
4 November, afternoon and evening. Ireland, London Overture;
Elgar, Enigma; Bliss (evening only), Dances from Checkmate.
BRUSSELS (N.I.R.)
7 November. Vaughan Williams, Wasps; Britten, Scottish Ballad.
8 November. Rawsthorne, Cortèges; Vaughan Williams, Dawn
Scene from Music to a Flemish Town.

1946   CAMBRIDGE, MASS. (Boston Symphony Orchestra)
16 January to 2 February. Three weeks spent with the Boston
Symphony Orchestra, including a tour of the New England towns
which they visit four or five times each Season. There were 12
concerts (7 in Boston Symphony Hall) and the British works
included:
    Purcell/Woodgate, Trumpet Tune and Air (8 times)
    Bax, Tintagel (twice)
    Elgar, Enigma (8 times)
    Michael Heming, Trenody for a Soldier killed in action (twice)
    Ireland, A Forgotten Rite (8 times)
    Holst, Planets (twice)
    Walton, Scapino (twice)
    Vaughan Williams, Job (3 times)
PRAGUE
23 May. Britten, Peter Grimes Interludes; Ireland, Piano Concerto
(Moura Lympany); Elgar, Introduction and Allegro; Vaughan
Williams, Pastoral Symphony.
24 May. Britten, Peter Grimes Interludes; Goossens, Oboe
Concerto (Leon Goossens); Vaughan Williams, Serenade to Music
(B.B.C. Singers); Elgar, Introduction and Allegro; Vaughan
Williams, Pastoral Symphony.
THE HAGUE
3 July. Elgar, Introduction and Allegro.
5 July. Vaughan Williams, Wasps; Vaughan Williams, Symphony
No. 5.

1947   PARIS Théâtre des Champs Elysées (B.B.C. Symphony Orchestra)
18 June. National Anthems
    Berlioz   Overture, Carnaval Romain
    Beethoven   Symphony No. 7 in A
    Rawsthorne   Piano Concerto (Louis Kentner)
    Debussy   3 Nocturnes
19 June
    Bax   Overture to a Picaresque Comedy
    Ravel   Schéhérazade (Janine Michaud)
    Roussel   Symphony No. 4 in A
    Bartók   Concerto for Orchestra

BRUSSELS R.N.B. Studio
22 June
Bliss	Music for Strings
Mozart	Violin Concerto from Serenade No. 7 in D (Paul Beard)
Franck	Symphony in D

Palais des Beaux Arts
23 June
Poot	Overture Joyeuse
Walton	Violin Concerto (Arthur Grumiaux)
Ravel	Alborado del Gracioso
Beethoven	Eroica

AMSTERDAM Concertgebouw
25 June
Wagenaar	Overture, Taming of the Shrew
Vaughan Williams	Concerto for two pianos (Cyril Smith and Phyllis Sellick)
Stravinsky	Scherzo Fantastique
Schubert	Symphony No. 9 in C

SCHEVENINGEN Kurhaus
26 June
Van Anrooy	Rhapsody, Piet Hein
Britten	Violin Concerto (Theo Olof)
Rimsky-Korsakov	Capriccio Espagnole
Delius	Song before Sunrise
Elgar	Enigma

1948   AMSTERDAM
29, 30 January. Vaughan Williams, Job.
1, 2 February. Elgar, Gerontius (Mary Jarred, Parry Jones, Harold Williams).
VIENNA
25, 26 March. Walton, Scapino; Britten, Peter Grimes Interludes.
VIENNA
23, 24 June. Britten, Sinfonia da Requiem.
GRAZ
2 July. Elgar, 'Cello Concerto.

1949   AMSTERDAM
9 January. Elgar, Enigma.
MILAN (Orchestra Sinfonica Stabile da Camera)
15, 16 January. Purcell, Comus Suite; Holst, Fugal Concerto; Bliss, Music for Strings; Elgar, Introduction and Allegro; Vaughan Williams, Greensleeves; Berkeley, Divertimento.
ROME (Accademia Nazionale)
19 January. Holst, Fugal Overture; Vaughan Williams, Symphony No. 6.

TORONTO Varsity Arena (Toronto Philharmonic Orchestra)
7 July. Vaughan Williams, Wasps Overture; Holst, Beni Mora.
NEW YORK Stadium (Philharmonic Symphony Orchestra)
13 July. Ireland, London Overture.
RAVINIA PARK (Chicago Symphony Orchestra)
26 July. Elgar, Enigma.
28 July. Holst, Beni Mora.
30 July. Walton, Portsmouth Point.
31 July. Vaughan Williams, Job.

1950   PARIS (Concerts Colonne)
8 January. Elgar, Enigma.
(Radio Paris, Orchestre Nationale)
9 January. Vaughan Williams, Symphony No. 6.

1951   GERMAN TOUR (London Philharmonic Orchestra)
ESSEN
16 January. Elgar, Introduction and Allegro.
HANOVER
17 January. Elgar, Introduction and Allegro.
BERLIN
18 January. Holst, 'Perfect Fool', Elgar, Introduction and Allegro.
HAMBURG
19 January. Elgar, Introduction and Allegro.
MÜNSTER
20 January. Elgar, Introduction and Allegro.
DORTMUND
21 January. Elgar, Introduction and Allegro.
VIERSEN
21 January. Elgar, Introduction and Allegro.
DÜSSELDORF
22 January. Holst, 'Perfect Fool'.
NÜREMBERG
23 January. Elgar, Introduction and Allegro.
MÜNCHEN
24 January. Elgar, Introduction and Allegro.
STUTTGART
25 January. Elgar, Introduction and Allegro.
HEIDELBERG
26 January. Holst, 'Perfect Fool'.

1953   PARIS (Lamoureux)
22 February. Rawsthorne, Street Corner.
FRANKFURT a/M
21 September. Vaughan Williams, Symphony No. 6.

1954   BASEL
15, 16 March. Vaughan Williams, Symphony No. 5. Bliss, Music for Strings.

HILVERSUM
3 April. Vaughan Williams, Tallis; Elgar, In the South; Vaughan Williams, Wasps.
6 April. Holst, The Planets.
NEW YORK (Philharmonic-Symphony Orchestra) Stadium
22 June. Walton, Portsmouth Point.
24 June. Vaughan Williams, London Symphony.
8 July. Vaughan Williams, London Symphony.
HOLLYWOOD BOWL
20 July. Holst, The Planets (4); Elgar, Enigma.
22 July. Fricker, Viola Concerto (Primrose).
27 July. Handel, Messiah.

1955   PARIS
6–9 June. The Decca Company chose to send an elderly British conductor to record Russian music with a French orchestra. Tchaikovsky, Suite No. 3; Prokoviev, Lieutenant Kije.
MONTREUX Festival (in the presence of H.M. Queen Victoria Eugènie of Spain.) (Orchestra Nationale de Paris)
18 September. Butterworth, Shropshire Lad.

1956   HILVERSUM
2–10 April. Bliss, Colour Symphony; Elgar, Enigma; Delius, Piano Concerto (Stefan Bergman); Arnold, English Dances; Bliss, Music for Strings; Holst, 'Perfect Fool' Ballet.
MOSCOW
20–23 September. Holst, The Planets; Vaughan Williams, Symphony No. 5.
25 September. Walton, Violin Concerto (Campoli).
27 September. Bliss, Boyce Meditation; Vaughan Williams, Symphony No. 4.
LENINGRAD
30 September. Walton, Violin Concerto (Campoli).

1957   VIENNA
17–21 May. Recording with Madame Flagstad (Westminster).

1959   VIENNA
14–30 March. Vaughan Williams, Tallis; Holst, The Planets.

1960   HILVERSUM (Radio Orchestra and Choir)
2 July. Walton, Belshazzar's Feast (Hervey Alan).
AMSTERDAM
4 July. Walton, Belshazzar's Feast (Hervey Alan).
SCHEVENINGEN
5 July. Walton, Belshazzar's Feast (Hervey Alan).
HILVERSUM
7 November. Bliss, Colour Symphony; Walton, Scapino.
13 November. Vaughan Williams, Pastoral Symphony.

1965   VIENNA
        17 January. Vaughan Williams, Job; Malcolm Williamson, Organ
        Concerto played by the composer, Bliss, Music for Strings.
        GRAZ
        24, 25 January. Elgar, Introduction and Allegro.

1966   TANGLEWOOD
        17 June–19 July. Vaughan Williams, London Symphony.

INDEX

Dohnanyi, Ernest von, 58, 105, 155
Donnington, 195
Dordrecht, 87
Dortmund, 151, 202
Douglas, Keith, 117, 118, 119, 122, 124
Downes, Olin, 140, 141
Dresden, 39, 88
Duchess of Atholl, s.s., 136
Dukelsky, Vladimir, 141
Dundee, 193
Düsseldorf, 151, 202
Dvorak, Antonin, 34
Dyer, Mrs Louise, 167

Edgbaston, 58
Edinburgh, 8–9, 85, 148, 183, 193, 195;
 Festival, 154, 167
Edinburgh Bach Society, 8
Edinburgh University, 166
Edward VII, King, 7, 69
Egypt, 60, 61–2
Eisenach, 39
Eisteddfodau, 59
Elgar, Sir Edward, 18, 22, 63, 64–7, 75, 105,
 181; 'Cockaigne', 65, 181; 'Dream of
 Gerontius', 125, 173–4; 'Falstaff', 67; 'In
 the South', 65; 'Kingdom', 64, 173;
 Quartet, 67; Quintet, 67; Violin Concerto,
 18, 64, 66, 81, 170, 172; Violin Sonata, 66,
 81
Elgar, Lady, 64, 70
Elizabeth the Queen Mother, Queen, 103,
 106, 113, 153, 184
Elizabeth II, Queen, 82, 112, 152–4
Elman, Mischa, 143
Elwes, Gervase, 73, 80, 81
Ely, 157
E.M.I., 155, 172
Enesco, Georges, 86, 141, 148
Erskine House, 83
Essen, 202
Etna, 62
Evans, Edwin, 77
Evesham, 115–16

Fairfax, Bryan, 171
Fairfield Halls, Croydon, 168
Falkner, Sir Keith, 131, 178
Falla, Manuel de, 47; *Three-cornered Hat*, 56
Family Welfare Society (formerly Charity
 Organization Society), 83
Fauré, Gabriel, 22, 73; *Pavane*, 73
Federal Union, 147
Federation of Music Clubs, 131
Feldhammer, Jakob, 39
Ferrier, Kathleen, 152
ffenell, Colonel Raymond, 26
Fields, Gracie, 121
Firkusny, Rudolf, 143
Fistoulari, Anatole, 162
Flagstad, Kirsten, 148
Fleury, Louis, 73
Foss, Hubert, 85
Fox, Dr Douglas, 30

France, s.s., 145
Franck, César, 21
Frankfurt, 202
Fricker, Pete Racine, 154
Friedberg, Carl and Annie, 139, 142, 143
Friend, Rodney, 173
Fryer, Herbert, 78
Furtwängler, Wilhelm, 181
Fussell, William, 92

Galloway, Colonel William Johnson, 84–5
Gardiner, E. Balfour, 35
Garrod, Air Marshal Sir Guy, 29
Carsington, 25
Gdynia, 59
Geneva, 198
George V, King, 30, 153
George VI, King, 103, 104, 112, 152
Gerhardt, Elena, 38
Germany, 31–2, 37–43, 87–8, 151–2, 202
Gibbs, Armstrong, 43, 49
Gibson, Alexander, 166
Gieseking, Walter, 105
Gladstone, Charles, 27
Glasgow, 109, 135, 178, 183, 193
Glatton, 81
Glendowe, Professor R. M. Y., 29
Glinka, Mikhail, 162
Gloucester, 154, 170, 172
Glyndebourne, 166
Goddard, Scott, 43, 49, 111
Godfrey, Sir Dan, 21, 36
Goldberg, Mr and Mrs, 158
Goldsbrough, Arnold, 48
Goossens, Leon, 136
Goossens, Sidonie, 149
Gordon, Clifton, 13–14
Gordon, Rev. Edward, 13, 14, 52
Gordon, Maxwell, 13–14
Gordon, Mrs, 14
Gordonstoun, 88
Gosford, 195
Goss, John, 18
Gow, R. James, 12
Grand Canyon, 128–30, 145
Graz, 170, 201, 204
Great Eastern Orchestra, 84
Great Yarmouth, 157
Greef, Arthur de, 33
Green (later Boult), Mabel, 6, 10
Greene, H. Plunket, 3, 19
Gregynog, 59
Grieg, Edvard, 143
Grisewood, Frederick, 20
Gromyko, Andrei, 163
Guernsey, Lord, 157
Guest, Douglas, 171
Guggenheimer, Mrs, 142
Gulbenkian Foundation, 178

Haddon Hall, 172
Hadley, Patrick, 49, 152, 154
Hague, The, 90, 91, 147, 155, 199, 200, 203
Hahn, Kurt, 88–9